HARRIS PUBLIC LIBRARY
ACC. No. 68/16606
ALLOC. SP
CLASS F
CAT. MAW
Stamped ✓
Labelled
Checked
VEND. 29/D
RCD. 26.10.68
BD
DATE

X

The Landmark Library
No. 3

MR. PROHACK

The Landmark Library

OLIVER ONIONS

In Accordance with the Evidence

GEORGE MOORE

Celibate Lives

ARNOLD BENNETT

Mr. Prohack

T. F. POWYS

The Left Leg

MARGARET IRWIN

Still She Wished for Company

ANN BRIDGE

The Ginger Griffin

MR. PROHACK

Arnold Bennett

CHATTO & WINDUS
LONDON

Published by
Chatto & Windus Ltd.
London
*
Clarke, Irwin & Co. Ltd.
Toronto

First Published 1922
This edition first published 1968
© *Mrs. Cheston Bennett 1922*

SBN 7011 1382 0

Printed in Great Britain
by William Lewis (Printers) Limited
Cardiff

CONTENTS

MR. PROHACK

MR. PROHACK

CHAPTER I

THE NEW POOR

I

Arthur Charles Prohack came downstairs at eight thirty, as usual, and found breakfast ready in the empty dining-room. This pleased him, because there was nothing in life he hated more than to be hurried. For him, hell was a place of which the inhabitants always had an eye on the clock and the clock was always further advanced than they had hoped.

The dining-room, simply furnished with reproductions of chaste Chippendale, and chilled to the uncomfortable low temperature that hardy Britons pretend to enjoy, formed part of an unassailably correct house of mid-Victorian style and antiquity; and the house formed part of an unassailably correct square just behind Hyde Park Gardens. (Taxi-drivers, when told the name of the square, had to reflect for a fifth of a second before they could recall its exact situation.)

Mr. Prohack was a fairly tall man, with a big head, big features, and a beard. His characteristic expression denoted benevolence based on an ironic realisation of the humanity of human nature. He was forty-six years of age and looked it. He had been for more than twenty years at the Treasury, in which organism he had now attained a certain importance. He was a Companion of the Bath. He exulted in the fact that the Order of the Bath took precedence of those bumptious Orders, Star of India, St. Michael and St. George, Indian Empire, Royal Victorian and British Empire; but he laughed at his wife for so exulting. If the matter happened to be mentioned he would point out that in the table of precedence Companions of the Bath ranked immediately below Masters in Lunacy.

He was proud of the Treasury's war record. Other departments of State had swollen to amazing dimensions during the war. The

Treasury, while its work had been multiplied a hundredfold, had increased its personnel by only a negligible percentage. It was the cheapest of all the departments, the most efficient, and the most powerful. The War Office, the Admiralty, and perhaps one other department presided over by a personality whom the Prime Minister feared, did certainly defy and even ignore the Treasury. But the remaining departments (and especially the "mushroom ministries") might scheme as much as they liked,—they could do nothing until the Treasury had approved their enterprises. Modest Mr. Prohack was among the chief arbiters of destiny for them. He had daily sat in a chair by himself and approved or disapproved according to his conscience and the rules of the Exchequer; and his fiats, in practice, had gone forth as the fiats of the Treasury. Moreover he could not be bullied, for he was full of the sense that the whole constitution and moral force of the British Empire stood waiting to back him. Scarcely known beyond the Treasury, within the Treasury he had acquired a reputation as "the terror of the departments." Several times irritated Ministers or their high subordinates had protested that the Treasury's (Mr. Prohack's) passion for rules, its demands for scientific evidence, and its sceptical disposition were losing the war. Mr. Prohack had, in effect retorted: "Departmentally considered, losing the war is a detail." He had retorted: "Wild cats will not win the war." And he had retorted: "I know nothing but my duty."

In the end the war was not lost, and Mr. Prohack reckoned that he personally, by the exercise of courage in the face of grave danger, had saved to the country five hundred and forty-six millions of the country's money. At any rate he had exercised a real influence over the conduct of the war. On one occasion, a chief being absent, he had had to answer a summons to the Inner Cabinet. Of this occasion he had remarked to his excited wife: "They were far more nervous than I was."

Despite all this, the great public had never heard of him. His portrait had never appeared in the illustrated papers. His wife's portrait, as "War-worker and wife of a great official," had never appeared in the illustrated papers. No character sketch of him had ever been printed. His opinions on any subject had never been telephonically or otherwise demanded by the editors of up-to-date dailies. His news-value indeed was absolutely nil. In *Who's Who* he had only four lines of space.

Mr. Prohack's breakfast consisted of bacon, dry toast, coffee, marmalade, *The Times* and *The Daily Picture*. The latter was full of brides and bridegrooms, football, enigmatic murder trials, young women in their fluffy underclothes, medicines, pugilists, cinema stars, the biggest pumpkin of the season, uplift, and inspired prophecy concerning horses and company shares; together with a few brief unillustrated notes about civil war in Ireland, famine in Central Europe, and the collapse of realms.

II

"Ah! So I've caught you!" said his wife, coming brightly into the room. She was a buxom woman of forty-three. Her black hair was elaborately done for the day, but she wore a roomy peignoir instead of a frock; it was Chinese, in the Imperial yellow, inconceivably embroidered with flora, fauna, and grotesques. She always thus visited her husband at breakfast, picking bits off his plate like a bird, and proving to him that her chief preoccupation was ever his well-being and the satisfaction of his capricious tastes.

"Many years ago," said Mr. Prohack.

"You make a fuss about buying *The Daily Picture* for me. You say it humiliates you to see it in the house, and I don't know what. But I catch you reading it yourself, and before you've opened *The Times!* Dear, dear! That bacon's a cinder and I daren't say anything to her."

"Lady," replied Mr. Prohack, "we all have something base in our natures. Sin springs from opportunity. I cannot resist the damned paper." And he stuck his fork into the fair frock-coat of a fatuous bridegroom coming out of church.

"My fault again!" the wife remarked brightly.

The husband changed the subject:

"I suppose that your son and daughter are still asleep?"

"Well, dearest, you know that they were both at that dance last night."

"They ought not to have been. The popular idea that life is a shimmy is a dangerous illusion." Mr. Prohack felt the epigram to be third-rate, but he carried it off lightly.

"Sissie only went because Charlie wanted to go, and all I can say is that it's a nice thing if Charlie isn't to be allowed to enjoy himself now the war's over—after all he's been through."

"You're mixing up two quite different things. I bet that if Charlie committed murder you'd go into the witness-box and tell the judge he'd been wounded twice and won the Military Cross."

"This is one of your pernickety mornings."

"Seeing that your debauched children woke me up at three fifteen—!"

"They woke me up too."

"That's different. You can go to sleep again. I can't. You rather like being wakened up, because you take a positively sensual pleasure in turning over and going to sleep again."

"You hate me for that."

"I do."

"I make you very unhappy sometimes, don't I?"

"Eve, you are a confounded liar, and you know it. You have never caused me a moment's unhappiness. You may annoy me. You may exasperate me. You are frequently unspeakable. But you have never made me unhappy. And why? Because I am one of the few exponents of romantic passion left in this city. My passion for you transcends my reason. I am a fool, but I am a magnificent fool. And the greatest miracle of modern times is that after twenty-four years of marriage you should be able to give me pleasure by perching your stout body on the arm of my chair as you are doing."

"Arthur, I'm not stout."

"Yes, you are. You're enormous. But hang it, I'm such a morbid fool I like you enormous."

Mrs. Prohack, smiling mysteriously, remarked in a casual tone, as she looked at *The Daily Picture:*

"Why *do* people let their photographs get into the papers? It's awfully vulgar."

"It is. But we're all vulgar to-day. Look at that!" He pointed to the page. "The granddaughter of a duke who refused the hand of a princess sells her name and her face to a firm of ship-owners who keep newspapers like their grandfathers kept pigeons. . . . But perhaps I'm only making a noise like a man of fifty."

"You aren't fifty."

"I'm five hundred. And this coffee is remarkably thin."

"Let me taste it."

"Yes, you'd rob me of my coffee now!" said Mr. Prohack, surrendering his cup. "Is it thin, or isn't it? I pride myself on living the higher life; my stomach is not my inexorable deity; but even on the mountain top which I inhabit there must be a limit to the thinness of the coffee."

Eve (as he called her, after the mother and prototype of all women—her earthly name was Marian) sipped the coffee. She wrinkled her forehead and then glanced at him in trouble.

"Yes, it's thin," she said. "But I've had to ration the cook.

Oh, Arthur, I *am* going to make you unhappy after all. It's impossible for me to manage any longer on the housekeeping allowance."

"Why didn't you tell me before, child?"

"I have told you 'before,'" said she. "If you hadn't happened to mention the coffee, I mightn't have said anything for another fortnight. You started to give me more money in June, and you said that was the utmost limit you could go to, and I believed it was. But it isn't enough. I hate to bother you, and I feel ashamed—"

"That's ridiculous. Why should you feel ashamed?"

"Well, I'm like that."

"You're revelling in your own virtuousness, my girl. Now in last week's *Economist* it said that the Index Number of commodity prices had slightly fallen these last few weeks."

"I don't know anything about indexes and the *Economist,*" Eve retorted. "But I know what coffee is a pound, and I know what the tradesmen's books are—"

At this point she cried without warning.

"No," murmured Mr. Prohack, soothingly, caressingly. "You mustn't baptise me. I couldn't bear it." And he kissed her eyes.

III

"I *know* we can't afford any more for housekeeping," she whispered, sniffing damply. "And I'm ashamed I can't manage, and I knew I should make you unhappy. What with idle and greedy working-men, and all these profiteers . . . ! It's a shame!"

"Yes," said Mr. Prohack. "It's what our Charlie fought for, and got wounded twice for, and won the M. C. for. That's what it is. But you see we're the famous salaried middle-class that you read so much about in the papers, and we're going through the famous process of being crushed between the famous upper and nether millstones. Those millstones have been approaching each other—and us—for some time. Now they've begun to nip. That funny feeling in your inside that's causing you still to baptise me, in spite of my protest—that's the first real nip."

She caught her breath.

"Arthur," she said. "If you go on like that I shall scream."

"Do," Mr. Prohack encouraged her. "But of course not too loud. At the same time don't forget that I'm a humourist. Humourists make jokes when they're happy, and when they're unhappy they make jokes."

"But it's horribly serious."

"Horribly."

Mrs. Prohack slipped off the arm of the chair. Her body seemed to vibrate within the Chinese gown, and she effervesced into an ascending and descending series of sustained laughs.

"That's hysteria," said Mr. Prohack. "And if you don't stop I shall be reluctantly compelled to throw the coffee over you. Water would be better, but there is none."

Then Eve ceased suddenly.

"To think," she remarked with calmness, "that you're called the Terror of the Departments, and you're a great authority on finance, and you've been in the Government service for nearly twenty-five years, and always done your duty—"

"Child," Mr. Prohack interrupted her. "Don't tell me what I know. And try not to be surprised at any earthly phenomena. There are people who are always being astonished by the most familiar things. They live on earth as if they'd just dropped from Mars on to a poor foreign planet. It's not a sign of commonsense. You've lived on earth now for—shall we say?—some twenty-nine or thirty years, and if you don't know the place you ought to. I assure you that there is nothing at all unusual in our case. We are perfectly innocent; we are even praiseworthy; and yet—we shall have to suffer. It's quite a common case. You've read of thousands and millions of such cases; you've heard of lots personally; and you've actually met a few. Well, now, you yourself *are* a case. That's all."

Mrs. Prohack said impatiently:

"I consider the Government's treated you shamefully. Why, we're much worse off than we were before the war."

"The Government has treated me shamefully. But then it's treated hundreds of thousands of men shamefully. All Governments do."

"But we have a position to keep up!"

"True. That's where the honest poor have the advantage of us. You see, we're the dishonest poor. We've been to the same schools and universities and we talk the same idiom and we have the same manners and like the same things as people who spend more in a month or a week than we spend in a year. And we pretend, and they pretend, that they and we are exactly the same. We aren't, you know. We're one vast pretence. Has it occurred to you, lady, that we've never possessed a motor-car and most certainly never shall possess one? Yet look at the hundreds of thousands of cars in London alone! And not a single one of them ours! This detail may have escaped you."

"I wish you wouldn't be silly, Arthur."

"I am not silly. On the contrary, my real opinion is that I'm the wisest man you ever met in your life—not excepting your son. It remains that we're a pretence. A pretence resembles a bladder. It may burst. We probably shall burst. Still, we have one great advantage over the honest poor, who sometimes have no income at all; and also over the rich, who never can tell how big their incomes are going to be. *We know exactly where we are.* We know to the nearest sixpence."

"I don't see that that helps us. I consider the Government has treated you shamefully. I wonder you important men in the Treasury haven't formed a Trade Union before now."

"Oh, Eve! After all you've said about Trade Unions this last year! You shock me! We shall never be properly treated until we do form a Trade Union. But we shall never form a Trade Union, because we're too proud. And we'd sooner see our children starve than yield in our pride. That's a fact."

"There's one thing—we can't move into a cheaper house."

"No," Mr. Prohack concurred. "Because there isn't one."

Years earlier Mr. Prohack had bought the long lease of his house from the old man who, according to the logical London system, had built the house upon somebody else's land on the condition that he paid rent for the land and in addition gave the house to the somebody else at the end of a certain period as a free gift. By a payment of twelve pounds per annum Mr. Prohack was safe for forty years yet and he calculated that in forty years the ownership of the house would be a matter of some indifference both to him and to his wife.

"Well, as you're so desperately wise, perhaps you'll kindly tell me what we *are* to do."

"I might borrow money on my insurance policy—and speculate," said Mr. Prohack gravely.

"Oh! Arthur! Do you really think you—" Marian showed a wild gleam of hope.

"Or I might throw the money into the Serpentine," Mr. Prohack added.

"Oh! Arthur! I could kill you. I never know how to take you."

"No, you never do. That's the worst of a woman like you marrying a man like me."

They discussed devices. One servant fewer. No holiday. Cinemas instead of theatres. No books. No cigarettes. No taxis. No clothes. No meat. No telephone. No friends. They reached no conclusion. Eve referred to Adam's great Treasury mind. Adam said that his great Treasury mind should function on the problem during the day, and further that the problem must be solved that very night.

"I'll tell you one thing I shall do," said Mrs. Prohack in a decided tone as Mr. Prohack left the table. "I shall countermand Sissie's new frock."

"If you do I shall divorce you," was the reply.

"But why?"

Mr. Prohack answered:

"In 1917 I saw that girl in dirty overalls driving a thundering great van down Whitehall. Yesterday I met her in her foolish high heels and her shocking openwork stockings and her negligible dress and her exposed throat and her fur stole, and she was so delicious and so absurd and so futile and so sure of her power that—that—well, you aren't going to countermand any new frock. That chit has the right to ruin me—not because of anything she's done, but because she *is*. I am ready to commit peccadilloes, but not crimes. Good morning, my dove."

And at the door, discreetly hiding her Chinese raiment behind the door, Eve said, as if she had only just thought of it, though she had been thinking of it for quite a quarter of an hour:

"Darling, there's your clubs."

"What about my clubs?"

"Don't they cost you a lot of money?"

"No. Besides I lunch at my clubs—better and cheaper than at any restaurant. And I shouldn't have time to come home for lunch."

"But do you need two clubs?"

"I've always belonged to two clubs. Every one does."

"But why *two*?"

"A fellow must have a club up his sleeve."

"*Couldn't* you give up one?"

"Lady, it's unthinkable. You don't know what you're suggesting. Abandon one of my clubs that my father put me up for when I was a boy! I'd as soon join a Trade Union. No! My innocent but gluttonous children shall starve first."

"I shall give up *my* club!"

"Ah! But that's different."

"How is it different?"

"You scarcely ever speak to a soul in your club. The food's bad in your club. They drink liqueurs before dinner at your club. I've seen 'em. Your club's full every night of the most formidable spinsters each eating at a table alone. Give up your club by all means. Set fire to it and burn it down. But don't count the act as a renunciation. You hate your club. Good morning, my dove."

IV

One advantage of the situation of Mr. Prohack's house was that his path therefrom to the Treasury lay almost entirely through verdant parks—Hyde Park, the Green Park, St. James's Park. Not infrequently he referred to the advantage in terms of bland satisfaction. True, in wet weather the advantage became a disadvantage.

During his walk through verdant parks that morning, the Terror of the Departments who habitually thought in millions was very gloomy. Something resembling death was in his heart. Humiliation also was certainly in his heart, for he felt that, no matter whose the fault, he was failing in the first duty of a man. He raged against the Chancellor of the Exchequer. He sliced off the head of the Chancellor of the Exchequer with his stick. (But it was only an innocent autumn wildflower, perilously blooming.) And the tang in the air foretold the approach of winter and the grip of winter—the hell of the poor.

Near Whitehall he saw the advertisement of a firm of shop-specialists:

"BRING YOUR BUSINESS TROUBLES TO US."

CHAPTER II

FROM THE DEAD

I

"WELL, Milton, had a good holiday?" said Mr. Prohack to the hall-porter on entering his chief club for lunch that day.

"No, sir," said the hall-porter, who was a realist.

"Ah, well," said Mr. Prohack soothingly. "Perhaps not a bad thing. There's nothing like an unsatisfactory holiday for reconciling us all to a life of toil, is there?"

"No, sir," said Milton, impassively, and added: "Mr. Bishop has just called to see you, sir. I told him you'd probably be in shortly. He said he wouldn't wait but he might look in again."

"Thanks," said Mr. Prohack. "If he does, I shall be either in the coffee-room or upstairs."

Mr. Prohack walked into the majestic interior of the Club, which had been closed, rather later than usual, for its annual cleaning. He savoured anew and more sharply the beauty and stateliness of its architecture, the elaboration of its conveniences, the severe splendour of its luxury. And he saw familiar and congenial faces, and on every face was a mild joy similar to the joy which he himself experienced in the reopening of the Club. And he was deliciously aware of the "club feeling," unlike, and more agreeable than, any other atmosphere of an organism in the world.

The Club took no time at all to get into its stride after the closure. It opened its doors and was instantly its full self. For hundreds of grave men in and near London had risen that very morning from their beds uplifted by the radiant thought: "To-day I can go to the Club again." Mr. Prohack had long held that the noblest, the most civilised achievement of the British character was not the British Empire, nor the House of Commons, nor the steam-engine, nor aniline dyes, nor the music-hall, but a good West End club. And somehow at the doors of a good West End club there was an invisible magic sieve, through which the human body could pass but through which human worries could not pass.

This morning, however, Mr. Prohack perceived that one worry could pass through the sieve, namely a worry concerning the Club itself. . . . Give up the Club? Was the sacrifice to be consummated? Impossible! Could he picture himself strolling down St. James's Street without the right to enter the sacred gates—save as a guest? And supposing he entered as a guest, could he bear the hall-porter to say to him: "If you'll take a seat, sir, I'll send and see if Mr. Blank is in the Club. What name, sir?" Impossible! Yet Milton would be capable of saying just that. Milton would never pardon a defection. . . . Well, then, he must give up the other club. But the other—and smaller—Club had great qualities of its own. Indeed it was indispensable. And could he permit the day to dawn on which he would no longer be entitled to refer to "my other club"? Impossible! Nevertheless he had decided to give up his other club. He must give it up, if only to keep even with his wife. The monetary saving would be unimportant, but the act would be spectacular. And Mr. Prohack perfectly comprehended the value of the spectacular in existence.

II

He sat down to lunch among half a dozen cronies at one of the larger tables in a window-embrasure of the vaulted coffee-room with its precious portrait of that historic clubman, Charles James Fox, and he ordered himself the cheapest meal that the menu could offer, and poured himself out a glass of water.

"Same old menu!" remarked savagely Mr. Prohack's great crony, Sir Paul Spinner, the banker, who suffered from carbuncles and who always drove over from the city in the middle of the day.

"Here's old Paul grumbling again!" said Sims of Downing Street. "After all, this is the best club in London."

"It certainly is," said Mr. Prohack, "when it's closed. During the past four weeks this club has been the most perfect institution on the face of the earth."

They all laughed. And they began recounting to each other the unparalleled miseries and indignities which such of them as had remained in London had had to endure in the clubs that had "extended their hospitality" to members of the closed club. The catalogue of ills was terrible. Yes, there was only one club deserving of the name.

"Still," said Sir Paul. "They might give us a rest from prunes and rice."

"This club," said Mr. Prohack, "like all other clubs, is managed by a committee of Methuselahs who can only digest prunes and rice." And after a lot more talk about the idiosyncrasies of clubs he said, with a casual air: "For myself, I belong to too many clubs."

Said Hunter, a fellow official of the Treasury:

"But I thought you only had two clubs, Arthur."

"Only two. But it's one too many. In fact I'm not sure if it isn't two too many."

"Are you getting disgusted with human nature?" Sims suggested.

"No," said Mr. Prohack. "I'm getting hard up. I've committed the greatest crime in the world. I've committed poverty. And I feel guilty."

And the truth was that he did feel guilty. He was entirely innocent; he was a victim; he had left undone nothing that he ought to have done; but he felt guilty, thus proving that poverty is indeed seriously a crime and that those who in sardonic jest describe it as a crime are deeper philosophers than they suppose.

"Never say die," smiled the monocled Mixon, a publisher of scientific works, and began to inveigh against the Government as an ungrateful and unscrupulous employer and exploiter of dutiful men in an inferno of rising prices. But the rest thought Mixon unhappy in his choice of topic. Hunter of the Treasury said nothing. What was there to say that would not tend to destroy the true club atmosphere? Even the beloved Prohack had perhaps failed somewhat in tact. They all understood, they all mildly sympathised, but they could do no more—particularly in a miscellaneous assemblage of eight members. No, they felt a certain constraint; and in a club constraint should be absolutely unknown. Some of them glanced uneasily about the crowded, chattering room.

III

It was then that a remarkable coincidence occurred.

"I saw Bishop at Inverness last week," said Sir Paul Spinner to Mr. Prohack, apropos of nothing whatever. "Seems he's got a big moor this year in Sutherlandshire. So I suppose he's recovered from his overdose of shipping shares."

Bishop (Fred Ferrars) was a financier with a cheerful, negligent attitude towards the insecurities and uncertainties of a speculative existence. He was also a close friend of Prohack, of Sir Paul, and of several others at the table, and a member of Prohack's secondary club, though not of his primary club.

"That's strange," said Mr. Prohack. "I hear he's in London."

"He most positively isn't in London," said Sir Paul. "He's not coming back until November."

"Then that shows how little the evidence of the senses can be relied upon," remarked Mr. Prohack gently. "According to the hall-porter he called here for me a few minutes ago, and he may call again."

The banker grunted. "The deuce he did! Does that mean he's in some fresh trouble, I wonder?"

At the same moment a page-girl, the smart severity of whose uniform was mitigated by a pig-tail and a bow of ribbon, approached Mr. Prohack's chair, and, bending her young head to his ear, delivered to him with the manner of a bearer of formidable secrets:

"Mr. Bishop to see you, sir."

"There he is!" exclaimed Mr. Prohack. "Now he's bound to want lunch. Why on earth can't we bring guests in here? Waitress, have the lunch I've ordered served in the guests' dining-room, please. . . . No doubt Bishop and I'll see you chaps upstairs later."

He went off to greet and welcome Bishop, full of joy at the prospect of tasting anew the rich personality of his old friend. It is true that he had a qualm about the expense of standing Bishop a lunch—a fellow who relished his food and drink and could distinguish between the best and the second best; but on the other hand he could talk very freely to Bishop concerning the crisis in which he found himself; and he knew that Bishop would not allow Bishop's affairs, however troublesome they might be, unduly to bother *him*.

Bishop was not on the bench in the hall where visitors were appointed to wait. Only one man was on the bench, a spectacled, red-faced person. Mr. Prohack glanced about. Then the page-girl pointed to the spectacled person, who jumped up and approached Mr. Prohack somewhat effusively.

"How d'ye do, Prohack?"

"Well, *Bishop!*" Mr. Prohack responded. "It's *you!*"

It was another Bishop, a Bishop whom he had forgotten, a Bishop who had resigned from the club earlier and disappeared. Mr. Prohack did not like him. Mr. Prohack said to himself: "This fellow is after something, and I always knew he was an adventurer."

"Funny feeling it gives you to be asked to wait in the hall of a club that you used to belong to!" said Bishop.

The apparently simple words, heavy with sinister significance, sank like a depth-charge into Mr. Prohack's consciousness.

"Among other things," said Mr. Prohack to himself, "this fellow is very obviously after a free lunch."

Now Mr. Prohack suffered from a strange form of insincerity, which he had often unsuccessfully tried to cure, partly because it advantaged unsympathetic acquaintances at his expense, and partly because his wife produced unanswerable arguments against it with mortal effect. Although an unconceited man (as men go), and a very honest man, he could not help pretending to like people whom he did not like. And he pretended with a histrionic skill that deceived everybody—sometimes even himself. There may have been some good-nature in this moral twist of his; but he well knew that it originated chiefly in three morbid desires,—the desire to please, the desire to do the easiest thing, and the desire to nourish his reputation for amiability.

So that when the unexpected Mr. Bishop (whose Christian name was Softly) said to him: "I won't keep you now. Only I was passing and I want you to be kind enough to make an early appointment with me at some time and place entirely convenient to yourself," Mr. Prohack proceeded to persuade Mr. Bishop to stay to lunch, there being no sort of reason in favour of such a course, and various sound reasons against it. Mr. Prohack deceived Mr. Softly Bishop as follows:

"No time and place like the present. You must stay to lunch. This is your old club and you must stay to lunch."

"But you've begun your lunch," Bishop protested.

"I've not. The fact is, I was half expecting you to look in again. The hall-porter told me. . . ." And Mr. Prohack actually patted Mr. Bishop on the shoulder—a trick he had. "Come now, don't tell me you've got another lunch appointment. It's twenty-five to two." And to himself, leading Mr. Bishop to the strangers' dining-room, he said: "Why should I further my own execution in this way?"

He ordered a lunch as copious and as costly as he would have ordered for the other, the real Bishop. Powerful and vigorous in some directions, Mr. Prohack's mentality was deplorably weak in at least one other.

Mr. Softly Bishop was delighted with his reception, and Mr. Prohack began to admit that Mr. Bishop had some personal charm. Nevertheless when the partridge came, Mr. Prohack acidly reflected:

"I'm offering this fellow a portion of my daughter's new frock on a charger!"

They talked of the club, Mr. Bishop as a former member being surely entitled to learn all about it, and then they talked about clubs in the United States, where Mr. Bishop had spent recent years. But Mr. Bishop persisted in giving no hint of his business.

"It must be something rather big and annoying," thought Mr. Prohack, and ordered another portion of his daughter's new frock in the shape of excellent cigars.

"You don't mean to say we can smoke *here*," exclaimed Mr. Bishop.

"Yes," said Mr. Prohack. "Not in the members' coffee-room, but we can here. Stroke of genius on the part of the Committee! You see it tends to keep guests out of the smoking-room, which for a long time has been getting uncomfortably full after lunch."

"Good God!" murmured Mr. Bishop simply.

IV

And he added at once, as he lighted the Corona Corona: "Well, I'd better tell you what I've come to see you about. You remember that chap, Silas Angmering?"

"Silas Angmering? Of course I do. Used to belong here. He cleared off to America ages ago."

"He did. And you lent him a hundred pounds to help him to clear off to America."

"Who told you?"

"He did," said Mr. Bishop, with a faint, mysterious smile.

"What's happened to him?"

"Oh! All sorts of things. He made a lot of money out of the war. He established himself in Cincinnati. And there were opportunities. . . ."

"How came he to tell you that I'd lent him anything?" Mr. Prohack interrupted sharply.

"I had business with him at one time—before the war and also just after the war began. Indeed I was in partnership with him." Mr. Bishop spoke with a measured soothing calmness.

"And you say he's made a lot of money out of the war. What do you mean—a lot?"

"Well," said Mr. Bishop, looking at the tablecloth through his glittering spectacles, "I mean a *lot*."

His tone was confidential; but then his tone was always confidential. He continued: "He's lost it all since."

"Pity he didn't pay me back my hundred pounds while he'd got it! How did he lose his money?"

"In the same way as most rich men lose their money," answered Mr. Bishop. "He died."

Although Mr. Prohack would have been capable of telling a similar story in a manner very similar to Mr. Bishop's, he didn't quite relish his guest's theatricality. It increased his suspicion of his guest, and checked the growth of friendliness which the lunch had favoured. Still, he perceived that there was a good chance of getting his hundred pounds back, possibly with interest—and the interest would mount up to fifty or sixty pounds. And a hundred and fifty pounds appeared to him to be an enormous sum. Then it occurred to him that probably Mr. Bishop was not indeed "after" anything and that he had been unjust to Mr. Bishop.

"Married?" he questioned, casually.

"Angmering? No. He never married. You know as well as anybody, I expect, what sort of a card he was. No relations, either."

"Then who's come into his money?"

"Well," said Mr. Bishop, with elaborate ease and smoothness of quiet delivery. "I've come into some of it. And there was a woman—actress sort of young thing—about whom perhaps the less said the better—she's come into some of it. And you've come into some of it. We share it in equal thirds."

"The deuce we do!"

"Yes."

"How long's he been dead?"

"About five weeks or less. I sailed as soon as I could after he was buried. I'd arranged before to come. I daresay I ought to have stayed a bit longer, as I'm the executor under the will, but I wanted to come, and I've got a very good lawyer over there—and over here too. I landed this morning, and here I am. Strictly speaking I suppose I should have cabled you. But it seemed to me that I could explain better by word of mouth."

"I wish you would explain," said Mr. Prohack. "You say he's been rich a long time, but he didn't pay his debt to me, and yet he goes and makes a will leaving me a third of his fortune. Wants some explaining, doesn't it?"

Mr. Bishop replied:

"It does and it doesn't. You know he was a champion postponer, poor old chap. Profoundly unbusinesslike. It's astonishing how unbusinesslike successful men are! He was always meaning to come to England to see you; but he never found time. He constantly talked of you—"

"But do you know," Mr. Prohack intervened, "that from that day to this I've never heard one single word from him? Not even a picture-postcard. And what's more I've never heard a single word *of* him."

"Just like Silas, that was! Just! . . . He died from a motor accident. He was perfectly conscious and knew he'd only a few hours to live. Spine. He made his will in hospital, and died about a couple of hours after he'd made it. I wasn't there myself. I was in New York."

"Well, well!" muttered Mr. Prohack. "Poor fellow! Well, well! This is the most amazing tale I ever heard in my life."

"It *is* rather strange," Mr. Bishop compassionately admitted.

A silence fell—respectful to the memory of the dead. The members' coffee-room seemed to Mr. Prohack to be a thousand miles off, and the chat with his cronies at the table in the window-embrasure to have happened a thousand years ago. His brain was in anarchy, and waving like a flag above the anarchy was the question: "How much did old Silas leave?" But the deceitful fellow would not permit the question to utter itself,—he had dominion over himself at any rate to that extent. He would not break the silence; he would hide his intense curiosity; he would force Softly Bishop to divulge the supreme fact upon his own initiative.

And at length Mr. Bishop remarked, musingly:

"Yes. Thanks to the exchange being so low, you stand to receive at the very least a hundred thousand pounds clear—after all deductions have been made."

"Do I really?" said Mr. Prohack, also musingly.

CHAPTER III

THE LAW

I

HIS tranquil tone disguised the immense anarchy within. Silas Angmering had evidently been what is called a profiteer. He had made his money "out of the war." And Silas was an Englishman. While Englishmen, and—later—Americans, had given up lives, sanity, fortunes, limbs, eyesight, health, Silas had gained riches. There was nothing highly unusual in this. Mr. Prohack had himself seen, in the very club in which he was now entertaining Softly Bishop, a man who had left an arm in France chatting and laughing with a man who had picked up over a million pounds by following the great principle that a commodity is worth what it will fetch when people want it very badly and there is a shortage of it. Mr. Prohack too had often chatted and laughed with this same picker-up of a million, who happened to be a quite jolly and generous fellow. Mr. Prohack would have chatted and laughed with Barabbas, convinced as he was that iniquity is the result of circumstances rather than of deliberate naughtiness. He seldom condemned. He had greatly liked Silas Angmering, who was a really educated and a well-intentioned man with a queer regrettable twist in his composition. That Silas should have profiteered when he got the chance was natural. Most men would do the same. Most heroes would do the same. The man with one arm would conceivably do the same.

But between excusing and forgiving a brigand (who has not despoiled *you*), and sharing his plunder, there was a gap, a chasm.

Few facts gave Mr. Prohack a more serene and proud satisfaction than the fact that he had materially lost through the war. He was positively glad that he had lost, and that the Government, his employer, had treated him badly. . . . And now to become the heir of a profiteer! Nor was that all! To become the co-heir with a woman of dubious renown, and with Mr. Softly Bishop! He knew nothing about the woman, and would think nothing. But he knew a little about Mr. Softly Bishop. Mr. Bishop, it used to be known and said in the club, had never had a friend. He had the usual number of acquaintances, but no relationship more intimate. Mr. Prohack, in the old days, had not for a long time actively disliked Mr. Bishop; but he had been surprised at the amount of active dislike which contact with Mr. Bishop engendered in other members of the club. Why such dislike? Was it due to his fat, red face, his spectacles, his conspiratorial manner, tone and gait, the evenness of his temper, his cautiousness, his mysteriousness? Nobody knew. In the end Mr. Prohack also had succeeded in disliking him. But Mr. Prohack produced a reason, and that reason was Mr. Bishop's first name. On it being pointed out to Mr. Prohack by argufiers that Mr. Bishop was not responsible for his first name, Mr. Prohack would reply that the mentality of parents capable of bestowing on an innocent child the Christian name of Softly was incomprehensible and in a high degree suspicious, and that therefore by the well-known laws of heredity there must be something devilish odd in the mentality of their offspring—especially seeing that the offspring pretended to glory in the Christian name as being a fine old English name. No! Mr. Prohack might stomach co-heirship with a far-off dubious woman; but could he stomach co-heirship with Softly Bishop? It would necessitate friendship with Mr. Bishop. It would bracket him for ever with Mr. Bishop.

These various considerations, however, had little to do with the immense inward anarchy that Mr. Prohack's tone had concealed as he musingly murmured: "Do I really?" The disturbance was due almost exclusively to a fierce imperial joy in the prospect of immediate wealth. The origin of the wealth scarcely affected him. The associations of the wealth scarcely affected him. He understood in a flash the deep wisdom of that old proverb (whose truth he had often hitherto denied) that money has no smell. Perhaps there might be forty good reasons against his accepting the inheritance, but they were all ridiculous. Was he to abandon his share of the money to Softly Bishop and the vampire-woman? Such a notion was idiotic. It was contrary to the robust and matter-of-fact commonsense which always marked his actions—if not his theories. No more should his wife be compelled to scheme out painfully the employment of her housekeeping allowance. Never again should there be a question about a new frock for his daughter. He was conscious, before anything else, of a triumphant protective and spoiling tenderness for his women. He would be absurd with his women. He would ruin their characters with kindness and with invitations to be capricious and exacting and expensive and futile. They nobly deserved it. He wanted to shout and to sing and to tell everybody that he would not in future stand any d——d nonsense from anybody. He would have his way.

"Why!" thought he, pulling himself up. "I've developed all the peculiarities of a millionaire in about a minute and a half."

And again, he cried to himself, in the vast and imperfectly explored jungle that every man calls his heart:

"Ah! I could not have borne to give up either of my clubs! No! I was deceiving myself. I could not have done it! I could not have done it! Anything rather than that. I see it now. . . . By the way, I wonder what all the fellows will say when they know! And how shall I break it to them? Not to-day! Not to-day! To-morrow!"

II

At the moment when Mr. Prohack ought to have been resuming his ill-remunerated financial toil for the nation at the Treasury, Bishop suggested in his offhand murmuring style that they might pay a visit to the City solicitor who was acting in England for him and the Angmering estate. Mr. Prohack opposingly suggested that national duty called him elsewhere.

"Does that matter—now?" said Bishop, and his accents were charged with meaning.

Mr. Prohack saw that it did not matter, and that in future any nation that did not like his office-hours would have to lump them. He feared greatly lest he might encounter some crony-member on his way out of the club with Bishop. If he did, what should he say, how should he carry off the situation? (For he was feeling mysteriously guilty, just as he had felt guilty an hour earlier. Not guilty as the inheritor of profiteering in particular, but guilty simply as an inheritor. It might have been different if he had come into the money in reasonable instalments, say of five thousand pounds every six months. But a hundred thousand unearned increment at one coup. . . !) Fortunately the cronies were still in the smoking-room. He swept Bishop from the club, stealthily, swiftly. Bishop had a big motor-car waiting at the door.

III

He offered no remark as to the car, and Mr. Prohack offered no remark. But Mr. Prohack was very interested in the car—he who had never been interested in cars. And he was interested in the clothes and in the deportment of the chauffeur. He was indeed interested in all sorts of new things. The window of a firm of house-agents who specialised in country houses, the jewellers' shops, the big hotels, the advertisements of theatres and concerts, the establishments of trunk-makers and of historic second-hand booksellers and of equally historic wine-merchants. He saw them all with a fresh eye. London suddenly opened to him its possibilities as a bud opens its petals.

"Not a bad car they hired out to me," said Bishop at length, with casual approval.

"You've hired it?"

"Oh, yes!"

And shortly afterwards Bishop said:

"It's fantastic the number of cars there are in use in America. You know it's a literal fact that almost every American family has a car. For instance, whenever there's a big meeting of strikers in New York, all the streets near the hall are blocked with cars."

Mr. Prohack had food for reflection. His outlook upon life was changed.

And later Bishop said, again apropos of nothing:

"Of course it's only too true that the value of money has fallen by about half. But on the other hand interest has about doubled. You can get ten per cent on quite safe security in these days. Even Governments have to pay about seven—as you know."

"Yes," concurred Mr. Prohack.

Ten thousand pounds a year!

And then he thought:

"What an infernal nuisance it would be if there was a revolution! Oh! But there couldn't be. It's unthinkable. Revolution everywhere, yes; but not in England or America!"

And he saw with the most sane and steady insight that the final duty of a Government was to keep order. Change there must be, but let change come gradually. Injustices must be remedied, naturally, but without any upheaval! Yet in the club some of the cronies (and he among them), after inveighing against profiteers and against the covetousness of trades unions, had often held that "a good red revolution" was the only way of knocking sense into the heads of these two classes.

The car got involved in a block of traffic near the Mansion House, and rain began to fall. The two occupants of the car watched each other surreptitiously, mutually suspicious, like dogs. Scraps of talk were separated by long intervals. Mr. Prohack wondered what the deuce Softly Bishop had done that Angmering should leave him a hundred thousand pounds. He tried to feel grief for the tragic and untimely death of his old friend Angmering, and failed. No doubt the failure was due to the fact that he had not seen Angmering for so many years.

At last Mr. Prohack, his hands in his pockets, his legs stretched out, his gaze uplifted, he said suddenly:

"I suppose it'll hold water?"

"What? The roof of the car?"

"No. The will."

Mr. Softly Bishop gave a short laugh, but made no other answer.

IV

The car halted finally before an immense new block of buildings, and the inheritors floated up to the fifth floor in a padded lift manned by a brilliantly-uniformed attendant. Mr. Prohack saw "Smathe and Smathe" in gilt on a glass door. The enquiry office resembled the ante-room of a restaurant, as the whole building resembled a fashionable hotel. Everywhere was mosaic flooring.

"Mr. Percy Smathe?" demanded Bishop of a clerk whose head glittered in the white radiance of a green-shaded lamp.

"I'll see, sir. Please step into the waiting-room." And he waved a patronising negligent hand. "What name?" he added.

"Have you forgotten my name already?" Mr. Bishop retorted sharply. "Bishop. Tell Mr. Percy Smathe I'm here. At once, please."

And he led Mr. Prohack to the waiting-room, which was a magnificent apartment with stained glass windows, furnished in Chippendale similar to, but much finer than, the furnishing of Mr. Prohack's own house. On the table were newspapers and periodicals. Not *The Engineering Times* of April in the previous year or a *Punch* of the previous decade, and *The Vaccination Record;* but such things as the current *Tatler, Times, Economist,* and *La Vie Parisienne.*

Mr. Prohack had uncomfortable qualms of apprehension. For several minutes past he had been thinking: "Suppose there *is* something up with that will!" He had little confidence in Mr. Softly Bishop. And now the aspect of the solicitors' office frightened him. It had happened to him, being a favourite trustee of his relations and friends, to visit the offices of some of the first legal firms in Lincoln's Inn Fields. You entered these lairs by a dirty door and a dirty corridor and another dirty door. You were interrogated by a shabby clerk who sat on a foul stool at a foul desk in a foul office. And finally after an interval in a cubby hole that could not boast even *The Anti-Vaccination Record,* you were driven along a dirtier passage into a dirtiest room whose windows were obscured by generations of filth, and in that room sat a spick and span lawyer of great name who was probably an ex-president of the Incorporated Law Society. The offices of Smathe and Smathe corresponded with alarming closeness to Mr. Prohack's idea of what a bucket-shop might be. Mr. Prohack had the gravest fears for his hundred thousand pounds.

"This is the solicitor's office new style," said Bishop, who seemed to have an uncanny gift of reading thoughts. "Very big firm. Anglo-American. Smathe and Smathe are two cousins. Percy's American. English mother. They specialise in what I may call the international complication business, pleasant and unpleasant."

Mr. Prohack was not appreciably reassured. Then a dapper, youngish man with a carnation in his buttonhole stepped neatly into the room, and greeted Bishop in a marked American accent.

"Here I am again," said Bishop curtly. "Mr. Prohack, may I introduce Mr. Percy Smathe?"

"Mr. Prohack, I'm delighted to make your acquaintance."

Mr. Prohack beheld the lawyer's candid, honest face, heard his tones of extreme deference, and noted that he had come to the enquiry room to fetch his clients.

"There's only one explanation of this," said Mr. Prohack to himself. "I'm a genuinely wealthy person."

And in Mr. Percy Smathe's private room he listened but carelessly to a long legal recital. Details did not interest him. He knew he was all right.

CHAPTER IV

EVE'S HEADACHE

I

THAT afternoon Mr. Prohack just got back to his bank before closing time. He had negligently declined to comprehend a very discreet hint from Mr. Percy Smathe that if he desired ready money he could have it—in bulk. Nevertheless he did desire to feel more money than usual in his pocket, and he satisfied this desire at the bank, where the September quarter of his annual salary lay almost intact. His bank was near Hanover Square, a situation inconvenient for him, but he had chosen that particular branch because its manager happened to be a friend of his. The Prohack account did no good to the manager personally, and only infinitesimal good to the vast corporation of which the branch-manager was the well-dressed, well-spoken serf. The corporation was a sort of sponge prodigiously absorbent but incapable of being squeezed. The manager could not be of the slightest use to Mr. Prohack in a financial crisis, for the reason that he was empowered to give no accommodation whatever without the consent of the head office. Still, Mr. Prohack, being a vigorous sentimentalist, as all truly wise men are, liked to bank with a friend. On the present occasion he saw the branch-manager, Insott by name, explained that he wanted some advice, and made an appointment to meet the latter at the latter's club, the Oriental, at six-thirty.

Thereupon he returned to the Treasury, and from mere high fantasy spread the interesting news that he had broken a back tooth at lunch and had had to visit his dentist at Putney. His colleague, Hunter, remarked to him that he seemed strangely gay for a man with a broken tooth, and Mr. Prohack answered that a philosopher always had resources of fortitude within himself. He then winked—a phenomenon hitherto unknown at the Treasury. He stayed so late at his office that he made the acquaintance of two charwomen, whom he courteously chaffed. He was defeated in the subsequent encounter, and acknowledged the fact by two half-crowns.

At the Oriental Club he told Insott that he might soon have some money to invest; and he was startled and saddened to discover that Insott knew almost nothing about exciting investments, or about anything at all, except the rigours of tube travel to Golder's Green. Insott had sunk into a deplorable groove. When, confidential, Insott told him the salary of a branch-manager of a vast corporation near Hanover Square, and incidentally mentioned that a bank-clerk might not marry without the consent in writing of the vast corporation, Mr. Prohack understood and pardoned the deep, deplorable groove. Insott could afford a club simply because his father, the once-celebrated authority on Japanese armour, had left him a hundred and fifty a year. Compared to the ruck of branch-managers Insott was a free and easy plutocrat.

As he departed from the Oriental Mr. Prohack sighed: "Poor Insott!" A sturdy and even exultant cheerfulness was, however, steadily growing in him. Poor Insott, unaware that he had been talking to a man with an assured income of ten thousand pounds a year, had unconsciously helped that man to realise the miracle of his own good fortune.

Mr. Prohack's route home lay through a big residential square or so and along residential streets of the first quality. All the houses were big, and they seemed bigger in the faint October mist. It was the hour after lighting up and before the drawing of blinds and curtains. Mr. Prohack had glimpses of enormous and magnificent interiors,—some right in the sky, some on the ground—with carved ceilings, rich candelabra, heavily framed pictures, mighty furniture, statuary, and superb and nonchalant menials engaged in the pleasant task of shutting away those interiors from the vulgar gaze. The spectacle continued furlong upon furlong, monotonously. There was no end to the succession of palaces of the wealthy. Then it would be interrupted while Mr. Prohack crossed a main thoroughfare, where scores of young women struggled against a few men for places in glittering motor-buses that were already packed with successful fighters for room in them. And then it would be resumed again in its majesty.

The sight of the street-travellers took Mr. Prohack's mind back to Insott. He felt a passionate sympathy for the Insotts of the world, and also for the Prohacks of six hours earlier. Once Mr. Prohack had been in easier circumstances; but those circumstances, thanks to the ambitions of statesmen and generals, and to the simplicity of publics, had gradually changed from easy to distressed. He saw with terrible clearness from what fate the Angmering miracle had saved him and his. He wanted to reconstruct society in the interest of those to whom no miracle had happened. He wanted to do away with all excessive wealth; and by "excessive" he meant any degree of wealth beyond what would be needed for the perfect comfort of himself, Mr. Prohack,—a reasonable man if ever there was one! Ought he not to devote his fortune to the great cause of reconstructing society? Could he enjoy his fortune while society remain unreconstructed? Well, societies were not to be reconstructed by the devoting of fortunes to the work. Moreover, if he followed such an extreme course he would be regarded as a crank, and he could not have borne to be regarded as a crank. He detested cranks more than murderers or even profiteers. As for enjoying his fortune in present circumstances, he thought that he might succeed in doing so, and that anyhow it was his duty to try. He was regrettably inconsistent.

II

Having entered his house as it were surreptitiously, and avoided his children, Mr. Prohack peeped through the half-open door between the conjugal bedroom and the small adjoining room, which should have been a dressing-room, but which Mrs. Prohack styled her boudoir. He espied her standing sideways in front of the long mirror, her body prettily curved and her head twisted over her shoulder so that she could see three-quarters of her back in the mirror. An attitude familiar to Mr. Prohack and one that he liked! She was wearing the Chinese garment of the morning, but he perceived that she had done something to it. He made a sharp noise with the handle of the door. She shrieked and started, and as soon as she had recovered she upbraided him, and as soon as she had upbraided him she asked him anxiously what he thought of the robe, explaining that it was really too good for a dressing-gown, that with careful treatment it would wear for ever, that it could not have been bought now for a hundred pounds or at least eighty, that it was in essence far superior to many frocks worn by women who had more money and less taste than herself, that she had transformed it into a dinner-dress for quiet evenings at home, and that she had done this as part of her part of the new economy scheme. It would save all her other frocks, and as for a dressing-gown, she had two old ones in her reserves.

Mr. Prohack kissed her and told her to sit down on the little sofa.

"To see the effect of it sitting down?" she asked.

"If you like," said he.

"Then you don't care for it? You think it's ridiculous?" said she anxiously, when she had sat down.

He replied, standing in front of her:

"You know that Oxford Concise Dictionary that I bought just before the war? Where is it?"

"Arthur!" she said. "What's the matter with you? You look so queer. I suppose the dictionary's where you keep it. *I* never touch it."

"I want you to be sure to remind me to cross the word 'economy' out of it to-night. In fact I think I'd better tear out the whole page."

"Arthur!" she exclaimed again. "Are you ill? Has anything serious happened? I warn you I can't stand much more to-day."

"Something very serious has happened," answered the incorrigible Mr. Prohack. "It may be all for the best; it may be all for the worst. Depends how you look at it. Anyway I'm determined to tell you. Of course I shouldn't dream of telling anybody else until I'd told you." He seated himself by her side. There was just space enough for the two of them on the sofa.

"Oh, dear!" sighed Mrs. Prohack, with apprehension, and instinctively she stretched her arm out and extinguished one of the lights.

He had been touched by her manœuvre, half economy and half coquetry, with the Chinese dress. He was still more touched by the gesture of extinguishing a light. For a year or two past Mrs. Prohack had been putting forward a theory that an average degree of illumination tried her eyes, and the household was now accustomed to twilit rooms in the evening. Mr. Prohack knew that the recent taste for obscurity had nothing to do with her eyes and everything to do with her years, but he pretended to be deceived by her duplicity. Not for millions would he have given her cause to suspect that he was not perfectly deceived. He understood and sympathised with her in all her manifestations. He did not select choice pieces of her character for liking, and dislike or disapprove of the rest. He took her undivided, unchipped, and liked the whole of her. It was very strange.

When he married her he had assumed, but was not sure, that he loved her. For thirteen or fourteen years she had endangered the bond between them by what seemed to him to be her caprices, illogicalities, perversities, and had saved it by her charming demonstrations of affection. During this period he had remained as it were neutral—an impassive spectator of her union with a man who happened to be himself. He had observed and weighed all her faults, and had concluded that she was not worse than other wives whom he respected. He continued to wonder what it was that held them together. At length, and very slowly indeed, he had begun to have a revelation, not of her but of himself. He guessed that he must be profoundly in love with her and that his original assumption was much more than accurate,—it was a bull's-eye. His love developed into a passion, not one of your eruptive, scalding affairs, but something as placid as an English landscape, with white heat far, far below the surface.

He felt how fine and amusing it was to have a genuine, incurable, illogical passion for a woman,—a passion that was almost an instinct. He deliberately cultivated it and dwelt on it and enjoyed it. He liked reflecting upon it. He esteemed that it must be about the most satisfying experience in the entire realm of sentiment, and that no other earthly experience of any sort could approach it. He made this discovery for himself, with the same sensations as if he had discovered a new star or the circulation of the blood. Of course he knew that two-thirds of the imaginative literature of the world was based on, and illustrative of, this great human discovery, and therefore that he was not exactly a pioneer. No matter! He was a pioneer all the same.

"Do you remember a fellow named Angmering?" he began, on a note of the closest confiding intimacy—a note which always flattered and delighted his wife.

"Yes."

"What was he like?"

"Wasn't he the man that started to run away with Ronnie Philps' wife and thought better of it and got her out of the train at Crewe and put her into the London train that was standing at the other platform and left her without a ticket? Was it Crewe or Rugby—I forget which?"

"No, no. You're all mixed up. That wasn't Angmering."

"Well, you have such funny friends, darling. Tell me, then."

"Angmering never ran away with anybody except himself. He went to America and before he left I lent him a hundred pounds."

"Arthur, I'll swear you never told me that at the time. In fact you always said positively you wouldn't lend money to anybody. You promised me. I hope he's paid you back."

"He hasn't. And I've just heard he's dead."

"I felt that was coming. Yes. I knew from the moment you began to talk that it was something of that kind. And just when we could do with that hundred pounds—heaven knows! Oh, Arthur!"

"He's dead," said Mr. Prohack clinchingly, "but he's left me ten thousand a year. Ha, ha!—Ha, ha!" He put his hand on her soft shoulder and gave a triumphant wink.

III

"Dollars, naturally," said Mrs. Prohack, after listening to various romantic details.

"No, pounds."

"And do you believe it? Are you sure this man Bishop isn't up to some game? You know anybody can get the better of you, sweetest."

"Yes," said Mr. Prohack. "I know I'm the greatest and sweetest imbecile that the Almighty ever created. But I believe it."

"But *why* should he leave you all this money? It doesn't stand to reason."

"It doesn't. But you see the poor fellow had to leave it to *some* one. And he'd no time to think. I expect he just did the first thing that came into his head and was glad to get it over. I daresay he rather enjoyed doing it, even if he was in great pain, which I don't think he was."

"And who do you say the woman is that's got as much as you have?"

"I don't say because I don't know."

"I guarantee *she* hadn't lent him a hundred pounds," said Mrs. Prohack with finality. "And you can talk as long as you like about real property in Cincinnati—what *is* real property? Isn't all property real?—I shall begin to believe in the fortune the day you give me a pearl necklace worth a thousand pounds. And not before."

"Lady," replied Mr. Prohack, "then I will never give you a pearl necklace."

Mrs. Prohack laughed.

"I know that," she said.

After a long meditative pause which her husband did not interrupt, she murmured: "So I suppose we shall be what you call rich?"

"Some people will undoubtedly call us rich. Others won't."

"You know we shan't be any happier," she warned him.

"No," Mr. Prohack agreed. "It's a great trial, besides being a great bore. But we must stick it."

"*I* shan't be any different. So you mustn't expect it."

"I never have expected it."

"I wonder what the children will say. Now, Arthur, don't go and tell them at dinner while the maid's there. I think I'll fetch them up now."

"You'll do nothing of the kind," said Mr. Prohack sharply.

"Why not?"

"Because I can't stand the strain of telling them to-night. Ha-ha!" He laughed. "I intend to think things over and tell them to-morrow. I've had quite enough strain for one day."

"Strain, darling?"

"Strain. These extremes of heat and cold would try a stronger man than me."

"Extremes of heat and cold, darling?"

"Well, just think how cold it was this morning and how warm it is to-night."

"You quaint boy!" she murmured, admiring him. "I quite understand. Quite. How sensitive you are! But then you always were. Now listen here. Shall *I* tell the children?" She gave him a long kiss.

"No," said he, making prods at her cheek with his finger, and smiling vaguely. "No. You'll do nothing of the kind. But there's something you *can* do for me."

"Yes?"

"Will you do it?"

"Yes."

"Whatever it is?"

"If you aren't going to play a trick on me."

"No. It's no trick.

"Very well, then."

"First, you must have one of your best headaches. Second, you must go to bed at once. Third, you must sprinkle some eau-de-cologne on the bed, to deceive the lower orders. Fourth, you must be content with some soup for your dinner, and I'll smuggle you up some dessert in my pocket if you're hungry. Fifth, you must send word to those children of yours that you don't wish to be disturbed."

"But you want to treat me like a baby."

"And supposing I do! For once, can't you be a baby to oblige me?"

"But it's too ridiculous! Why do you want me to go to bed?"

"You know why. Still, I'll tell you. You always like to be told what you know,—for instance, that I'm in love with you. I can't tell those kids to-night, and I'm not going to. The rumpus, the conflict of ideas, the atmospheric disturbance when they do get to know will be terrific, and I simply won't have it to-night. I must have a quiet evening to think in or else I shan't sleep. On the other hand, do you suppose I could sit through dinner opposite you, and you knowing all about it and me knowing all about it, and both of us pretending that there was nothing unusual in the air? It's impossible. Either you'd give the show away, or I should. Or I should burst out laughing. No! I can manage the situation alone, but I can't manage it if you're there. Hence, lady, you will keep your kind promise and hop into bed."

Without another word, but smiling in a most enigmatic manner, Mrs. Prohack passed into the bedroom. The tyrant lit a cigarette, and stretched himself all over the sofa. He thought: "She's a great woman. She understands. Or at any rate she acts as if she did. Now how many women in similar circumstances would have—" Etc. Etc.

He listened to her movements. He had not told her everything, for example, the profiteering origin of the fortune, and he wondered whether he had behaved quite nicely in not doing so.

"Arthur," she called from the bedroom.

"Hullo?"

"I do think this is really too silly."

"You're not paid to think, my girl."

A pause.

"Arthur," she called from the bedroom.

"Hullo?"

"You're sure you won't blurt it out to them when I'm not there?"

He only replied: "I'm sorry you've got such a frightful headache, Marian. You wouldn't have these headaches if you took my advice."

A pause.

"I'm in bed."

"All right. Stay there."

When he had finished his cigarette, he went into the bedroom. Yes, she was veritably in bed.

"You are a pig, Arthur. I wonder how many wives—"

He put his hand over her mouth.

"Stop," he said. "I'm not like you. I don't need to be told what I know already."

"But really—!" She dropped her head on one side and began to laugh, and continued to laugh, rather hysterically, until she could not laugh any more. "Oh, dear! We are the queerest pair!"

"It is possible," said he. "You've forgotten the eau-de-cologne."

He handed her the bottle. "It is quite possible that we're the queerest pair, but this is a very serious day in the history of the Prohack family. The Prohack family has been starving, and some one's given it an enormous beefsteak. Now it's highly dangerous to give a beefsteak to a starving person. The consequences might be fatal. That's why it's so serious. That's why I must have time to think."

The sound of Sissie playing a waltz on the piano came up from the drawing-room. Mr. Prohack started to dance all by himself in the middle of the bedroom floor.

CHAPTER V

CHARLIE

I

When Mr. Prohack, in his mature but still rich velvet jacket, came down to dinner, he found his son Charlie leaning against the mantelpiece in a new dark brown suit, and studying *The Owner-Driver*. Charlie seemed never to read anything but motor-car and light-car and side-car and motor-bicycle periodical literature; but he read it conscientiously, indefatigably, and completely—advertisements and all. He read it as though it were an endless novel of passion and he an idle woman deprived of the society her heart longed for. He possessed a motor-bicycle which he stabled in a mews behind the Square. He had possessed several such machines; he bought, altered, and sold them, apparently always with profit to himself. He had no interest in non-mechanical literature or in any of the arts.

"Your mother's gone to bed with a headache," said Mr. Prohack, with a fair imitation of melancholy.

"Oh!" said the young man apathetically. His face had a wearied, disillusioned expression.

"Is this the latest?" asked his father, indicating the new brown suit. "My respectful congratulations. Very smart, especially at the waist."

For a youth who had nothing in the world but what remained of his wound gratuity and other trifling military emoluments, and what he made out of commerce in motor-bicycles, Charlie spent a lot in clothes. His mother had advised his father to "speak to him about it." But his father had declined to offer any criticism, on the ground that Charlie had fought in Mesopotamia, Italy and France. Moreover, Charlie had scotched any possible criticism by asserting that good clothes were all that stood between him and the ruin of his career. "If I dressed like the dad," he had once grimly and gloomily remarked, "it would be the beginning of the end for me."

"Smart?" he now exclaimed, stepping forward. "Look at that." He advanced his right leg a little. "Look at that crease. See where it falls?" The trouser-crease, which, as all wise men know, ought to have fallen exactly on the centre of the boot-lacing, fell about an inch to the left thereof. "And I've tried this suit on four times! All the bally tailors in London seem to think you've got nothing else to do but call and try on and try on and try on. Never seems to occur to them that they don't know their business. It's as bad as staff work. However, if this fellow thinks I'm going to stick these trousers he'll have the surprise of his life to-morrow morning." The youth spoke in a tone of earnest disgust.

"My boy," said Mr. Prohack, "you have my most serious sympathy. Your life must be terribly complicated by this search for perfection."

"Yes, that's all very well," said Charlie.

"Where's Sissie?"

"Hanged if I know!"

"I heard her playing the piano not five minutes since."

"So did I."

Machin, the house-parlourmaid, then intervened:

"Miss Sissie had a telephone call, and she's gone out, sir."

"Where to?"

"She didn't say, sir. She only said she wouldn't be in for dinner, sir. I made sure she'd told you herself, sir."

The two men, by means of their eyes, transmitted to each other a unanimous judgment upon the whole female sex, and sat down to dine alone in the stricken house. The dinner was extremely frugal, this being the opening day of Mrs. Prohack's new era of intensive economy, but the obvious pleasure of Machin in serving only men brightened up somewhat its brief course. Charlie was taciturn and curt, though not impolite. Mr. Prohack, whose private high spirits not even the amazing and inexcusable absence of his daughter could impair, pretended to a decent woe, and chatted as he might have done to a fellow-clubman on a wet Sunday night at the Club.

At the end of the meal Charlie produced the enormous widow's cruse which he called his cigarette-case and offered his father a cigarette.

"Doing anything to-night?" asked Mr. Prohack, puffing.

"No," answered desperately Charlie, puffing.

"Ring the bell, will you?"

While Charlie went to the mantelpiece Mr. Prohack secreted an apple for his starving wife.

"Machin," said he to the incoming house-parlourmaid, "see if you can find some port."

Charlie raised his fatigued eyebrows.

"Yes, sir," said the house-parlourmaid, vivaciously, and whisked away her skirts, which seemed to remark:

"You're quite right to have port. I feel very sorry for you two attractive gentlemen taking a poor dinner all alone."

Charlie drank his port in silence and Mr. Prohack watched him.

II

Mr. Prohack's son was, in some respects, a great mystery to him. He could not understand, for instance, how his own offspring could be so unresponsive to the attractions of the things of the mind, and so interested in mere machinery and the methods of moving a living or a lifeless object from one spot on the earth's surface to another. Mr. Prohack admitted the necessity of machinery, but an automobile had for him the same status as a child's scooter and no higher. It was an ingenious device for locomotion. And there for him the matter ended. On the other hand, Mr. Prohack sympathised with and comprehended his son's general attitude towards life. Charlie had gone to war from Cambridge at the age of nineteen. He went a boy, and returned a grave man. He went thoughtless and light-hearted, and returned full of magnificent and austere ideals. Six months of England had destroyed these ideals in him. He had expected to help in the common task of making heaven in about a fortnight. In the war he had learnt much about the possibilities of human nature, but scarcely anything about its limitations. His father tried to warn him, but of course failed. Charlie grew resentful, then cynical. He saw in England nothing but futility, injustice and ingratitude. He refused to resume Cambridge, and was bitterly sarcastic about the generosity of a nation which, through its War Office, was ready to pay to studious warriors anxious to make up University terms lost in a holy war decidedly less than it paid to its street-sweepers. Having escaped from death, the aforesaid warriors were granted the right to starve their bodies while improving their minds. He might have had sure situations in vast corporations. He declined them. He spat on them. He called them "graves." What he wanted was an opportunity to fulfil himself. He could not get it, and his father could not get it for him. While searching for it, he frequently met warriors covered with ribbons but lacking food and shelter not only for themselves but for their women and children. All this, human nature being what it is, was inevitable, but his father could not convincingly tell him so. All that Mr. Prohack could effectively do Mr. Prohack did,—namely, provide the saviour of Britain with food and shelter. Charlie was restlessly and dangerously waiting for his opportunity. But he had not developed into a revolutionist, nor a communist, nor anything of the sort. Oh, no! Quite the reverse. He meditated a different revenge on society.

Mr. Prohack knew nothing of this meditated revenge, did not suspect it. If he had suspected it, he might have felt less compassion than, on this masculine evening with the unusual port, he did in fact feel. For he was very sorry for Charlie. He longed to tell him about the fortune, and to exult with him in the fortune, and to pour, as it were, the fortune into his lap. He did not care a fig, now, about advisable precautions. He did not feel the slightest constraint at the prospect of imparting the tremendous and gorgeous news to his son. He had no desire to reflect upon the proper method of telling. He merely and acutely wanted to tell, so that he might see the relief and the joyous anticipation on his son's enigmatic and melancholy face. But he could not tell because it had been tacitly agreed with his wife that he should not tell in her absence. True, he had given no verbal promise, but he had given something just as binding.

"Nothing exciting to-day, I suppose," he said, when the silence had begun to distress him in his secret glee.

"No," Charlie replied. "I got particulars of an affair at Glasgow, but it needs money."

"What sort of an affair?"

"Oh! Rather difficult to explain. Buying and selling. Usual thing."

"What money is needed?"

"I should say three hundred or thereabouts. Might as well be three thousand so far as I'm concerned."

"Where did you hear of it?"

"Club."

Charlie belonged to a little club in Savile Place where young warriors told each other what they thought of the nature of society.

Mr. Prohack drew in his breath with an involuntary gasp, and then said:

"I expect I could let you have three hundred."

"You couldn't!"

"I expect I could." Mr. Prohack had never felt so akin to a god. It seemed to him that he was engaged in the act of creating a future, yea, a man. Charlie's face changed. He had been dead. He was now suddenly alive.

"When?"

"Well, any time."

"Now?"

"Why not?"

Charlie looked at his watch.

"Well, I'm much obliged," he said.

III

Mr. Prohack had brought a new cheque-book from the Bank. It lay in his hip-pocket. He had no alternative but to write out a cheque. Three hundred pounds would nearly exhaust his balance, but that did not matter. He gave Charlie the cheque. Charlie offered no further information concerning the "affair" for which the money was required. And Mr. Prohack did not choose to enquire. Perhaps he was too proud to enquire. The money would probably be lost. And if it were lost no harm would be done. Good, rather, for Charlie would have gained experience. The lad was only a child, after all.

The lad ran upstairs, and Mr. Prohack sat solitary in delightful meditation. After a few minutes the lad re-appeared in hat and coat. Mr. Prohack thought that he had heard a bag dumped in the hall.

"Where are you off to?" he asked.

"Glasgow. I shall catch the night-train."

He rang the bell.

"Machin, run out and get me a taxi, sharp."

"Yes, sir." Machin flew. This was the same girl of whom Mrs. Prohack dared to demand nothing. Mr. Prohack himself would have hesitated to send her for a taxi. But Charlie ordered her about like a slave and she seemed to like it.

"Rather sudden this, isn't it?" said Mr. Prohack, extremely startled by the turn of events.

"Well, you've got to be sudden in this world, guv'nor," Charlie replied, and lit a fresh cigarette.

Mr. Prohack was again too proud to put questions. Still, he did venture upon one question:

"Have you got loose money for your fare?"

The lad laughed. "Oh, don't let that worry you, guv'nor . . . !" He looked at his watch once more. "I wonder whether that infernal girl is manufacturing that taxi or only fetching it."

"What must I say to your mother?" demanded Mr. Prohack.

"Give her my respectful regards."

The taxi was heard. Machin dashed into the house, and dashed out again with the bag. The lad clasped his father's hand with a warm vigour that pleased and reassured Mr. Prohack in his natural bewilderment. It was not consistent with the paternal dignity to leave the dining-room and stand, valedictory, on the front-doorstep.

"Well, I'm dashed!" Mr. Prohack murmured to himself as the taxi drove away. And he had every right to be dashed.

CHAPTER VI

SISSIE

I

"HAD any dinner?" Mr. Prohack asked his daughter.

"No."

"Aren't you hungry?"

"No, thanks."

Sissie seized the last remaining apple from the dessert-dish, and bit into it with her beautiful and efficient teeth. She was slim, and rather taller than necessary or than she desired to be. A pretty girl, dressed in a short-skirted, short-sleeved, dark blue, pink-heightened frock that seemed to combine usefulness with a decent perverse frivolity, and to carry forward the expression of her face. She had bright brown hair. She was perfectly mistress of the apple.

"Where's mother?"

"In bed with a headache."

"Didn't she have dinner with you?"

"She did not. And she doesn't want to be disturbed."

"Oh! I shan't disturb her, poor thing. I told her this afternoon she would have one of her headaches."

"Well," said Mr. Prohack, "that's one of the most remarkable instances of sound prophecy that I ever came across."

"Father, what's amusing you?"

"Nothing."

"Yes, something is. You've got your funny smile, and you were smiling all to yourself when I came in."

"I was thinking. My right to think is almost the only right I possess that hasn't yet been challenged in this house."

"Where's Charles?"

"Gone to Glasgow."

"Gone to *Glas*gow?"

"Yes."

"What, just now?"

"Ten minutes ago."

"Whatever has he gone to *Glas*gow for?"

"I don't know,—any more than I know why you went out before dinner and came back after dinner."

"Would you like to know why I went out?" Sissie spoke with sudden ingratiatingness.

"No, not at all. But I should like to know why you went out without telling anybody. When people are expected to dinner and fail to appear they usually give notice of the failure."

"But, father, I told Machin."

"I said 'anybody.' Don't you know that the whole theory of the society which you adorn is based on the assumption that Machin is nobody?"

"I was called away in a frightful hurry, and you and mother were gossiping upstairs, and it's as much as one's life is worth to disturb you two when you are together."

"Oh! That's news."

"Besides, I should have had to argue with mother, and you know what she is."

"You flatter me. I don't even know what *you* are, and you're elementary compared to your mother."

"Anyhow, I'm glad mother's in bed with a headache. I came in here trembling just now. Mother would have made such a tremendous fuss although she's perfectly aware that it's not the slightest use making a fuss. . . . Only makes me stupid and obstinate. Showers and showers of questions there'd have been, whereas you haven't asked a single one."

"Yes, you're rather upset by my lack of curiosity. But let me just point out that it is not consistent with my paternal duty to sit here and listen to you slanging your mother. As a daughter you have vast privileges, but you mustn't presume on them. There are some things I couldn't stand from any woman without protest."

"But you must admit that mother *is* a bit awful when she breaks loose."

"No. I've never known your mother awful, or even a bit awful."

"You aren't being intellectually honest, dad."

"I am."

"Ah! Well, of course she only shows her best side to *you*."

"She has no other side. In that sense she is certainly one-sided. Here! Have another." Mr. Prohack took the apple from his pocket, and threw it across the table to Sissie, who caught it.

II

Mr. Prohack was extremely happy; and Sissie too, in so far as concerned the chat with her father, was extremely happy. They adored each other, and they adored the awful woman laid low with a headache. Sissie's hat and cloak, which she had dropped carelessly on a chair, slipped to the floor, the hat carried away by the cloak. Mr. Prohack rose and picked them up, took them out of the room, and returned.

"So now you've straightened up, and you're pleased with yourself," observed Sissie.

"So now," said he. "Perhaps I may turn on my curiosity tap."

"Don't," said Sissie. "I'm very gloomy. I'm very disappointed. I might burst into tears at any moment. . . . Yes, I'm not joking."

"Out with it."

"Oh, it's nothing! It's only that I saw a chance of making some money and it hasn't come off."

"But what do you want to make money for?"

"I like that. Hasn't mother been telling me off and on all day that something will have to be done?"

"Done about what?"

"About economy, naturally." Sissie spoke rather sharply.

"But you don't mean your mother has spent the day in urging you to go forth and earn money!"

"Of course she hasn't, father. How absurd you are! You know very well mother would hate the idea of me earning money. Hate it! But I mean to earn some. Surely it's much better to bring more money in than to pinch and scrape. I loathe pinching and scraping."

"It's a sound loathing."

"And I thought I'd got hold of a scheme. But it's too big. I have fifty pounds odd of my own, but what use is fifty pounds when a hundred's needed? It's all off and I'm in the last stage of depression."

She threw away the core of the second apple.

"Is that port? I'll have some."

"So that you're short of fifty pounds?" said Mr. Prohack, obediently pouring out the port—but only half a glass. "Well, I might be able to let you have fifty pounds myself, if you would deign to accept it."

Sissie cried compassionately: "But you haven't got a cent, dad!"

"Oh! Haven't I? Did your mother tell you that?"

68/16606

"Well, she didn't exactly say so."

"I should hope not! And allow me to inform you, my girl, that in accusing me of not having a cent you're being guilty of the worst possible taste. Children should always assume that their fathers have mysterious stores of money, and that nothing is beyond their resources, and if they don't rise to every demand it's only because in their inscrutable wisdom they deem it better not to. Or it may be from mere cussedness."

"Yes," said Sissie. "That's what I used to think when I was young. But I've looked up your salary in *Whitaker's Almanac.*"

"It was very improper of you. However, nothing is secret in these days, and so I don't mind telling you that I've backed a winner to-day—not to-day, but some little time since—and I can if necessary and agreeable let you have fifty pounds."

Mr. Prohack as it were shook his crest in plenary contentment. He had the same sensation of creativeness as he had had a while earlier with his son,—a godlike sensation. And he was delighted with his girl. She was so young and so old. And her efforts to play the woman of the world with him were so comic and so touching. Only two or three years since she had been driving a motor-van in order to defeat the Germans. She had received twenty-eight shillings a week for six days of from twelve to fourteen hours. She would leave the house at eight and come back at eight, nine, or ten. And on her return, pale enough, she would laugh and say she had had her dinner and would go to bed. But she had not had her dinner. She was simply too tired and nervously exasperated to eat. And she would lie in bed and tremble and cry quietly from fatigue. She did not know that her parents knew these details. The cook, her confidante, had told them, much later. And Mr. Prohack had decreed that Sissie must never know that they knew. She had stuck to the task during a whole winter, skidding on glassy asphalt, slimy wood, and slithery stone-setts in the East End, and had met with but one accident, a minor affair. The experience seemed to have had no permanent effect on her, but it had had a permanent effect on her father's attitude towards her,—her mother had always strongly objected to what she called the "episode," had shown only relief when it concluded, and had awarded no merit for it.

"Can you definitely promise me fifty pounds, dad?" Sissie asked quietly.

Mr. Prohack made no articulate answer. His reply was to take out his cheque-book and his fountain-pen and fill in a cheque to Miss Sissie Prohack or order. He saw no just reason for differentiating between the sexes in his offspring. He had given a cheque to Charlie; he gave one to Sissie.

"Then you aren't absolutely stone-broke," said Sissie, smiling.

"I should not so describe myself."

"It's just like mother," she murmured, the smile fading.

Mr. Prohack raised a sternly deprecating hand. "Enough."

"But don't you want to know what I want the money for?" Sissie demanded.

"No! . . . Ha-ha!"

"Then I shall tell you. The fact is I must tell you."

III

"I've decided to teach dancing," said Sissie, beginning again nervously, as her father kept a notable silence.

"I thought you weren't so very keen on dancing."

"I'm not; but perhaps that's because I don't care much for the new fashion of dancing a whole evening with the same man. Still the point is that I'm a very fine dancer. Even Charlie will tell you that."

"But I thought that all the principal streets in London were full of dancing academies at the present time, chiefly for the instruction of aged gentlemen."

"I don't know anything about that," Sissie replied seriously. "What I do know is that now I can find a hundred pounds, I have a ripping chance of taking over a studio—at least part of one; and it's got quite a big connection already,—in fact pupils are being turned away."

"And this is all you can think of!" protested Mr. Prohack with melancholy. "We are living on the edge of a volcano—the country is, I mean—and your share in the country's work is to teach the citizens to dance!"

"Well," said Sissie. "They'll dance anyhow, and so they may as well learn to dance properly. And what else can I do? Have you had me taught to do anything else? You and mother have brought me up to be perfectly useless except as the wife of a rich man. That's what you've done, and you can't deny it."

"Once," said Mr. Prohack. "You very nobly drove a van."

"Yes, I did. But no thanks to you and mother. Why, I had even to learn to drive in secret, lest you should stop me! And I can tell you one thing—if I was to start driving a van now I should probably get mobbed in the streets. All the men have a horrid grudge against us girls who did their work in the war. If we want to get a job in these days we jolly well have to conceal the fact that we were in the W. A. A. C. or in anything at all during the war. They won't look at us if they find out that. Our reward! However, I don't want to drive a van. I want to teach dancing. It's not so dirty and it pays better. And if people feel like dancing, why shouldn't they dance? Come now, dad, be reasonable."

"That's asking a lot from any human being, and especially from a parent."

"Well, have you got any argument against what I say?"

"I prefer not to argue."

"That's because you can't."

"It is. It is. But what is this wonderful chance you've got?"

"It's that studio where Charlie and I went last night, at Putney."

"At *Putney?*"

"Well, why not Putney? They have a gala night every other week, you know. It belongs to Viola Ridle. Viola's going to get married and live in Edinburgh, and she's selling it. And Eliza asked me if I'd join her in taking it over. Eliza telephoned me about it to-night, and so I rushed across the Park to see her. But Viola's asking a hundred pounds premium and a hundred for the fittings, and very cheap it is too. In fact Viola's a fool, *I* think, but then she's fond of Eliza."

"Now, Eliza? Is that Eliza Brating, or am I getting mixed up?"

"Yes, it's Eliza Brating."

"Ah!"

"You needn't be so stuffy, dad, because her father's only a second-division clerk at the Treasury."

"Oh, I'm not. It was only this morning that I was saying to Mr. Hunter that we must always remember that second-division clerks are also God's creatures."

"Father, you're disgusting."

"Don't say that, my child. At my age one needs encouragement, not abuse. And I'm glad to be able to tell you that there is no longer any necessity either for you to earn money or to pinch and scrape. Satisfactory arrangements have been made. . . ."

"Really? Well, that's splendid. But of course it won't make any difference to me. There may be no necessity so far as you're concerned. But there's my inward necessity. I've got to be independent. It wouldn't make any difference if you had an income of ten thousand a year."

Mr. Prohack blenched guiltily.

"Er—er—what was I going to say? Oh, yes,—where's this Eliza of yours got her hundred pounds from?"

"I don't know. It's no business of mine."

"But do you insist—shall you—insist on introductions from your pupils?"

"Father, how you do chop about! No, naturally we shan't insist on introductions."

"Then any man can come for lessons?"

"Certainly. Provided he wears evening-dress on gala nights, and pays the fees and behaves properly. Viola says some of them prefer afternoon lessons because they haven't got any evening-dress."

"If I were you I shouldn't rush at it," said Mr. Prohack.

"But we must rush at it—or lose it. And I've no intention of losing it. Viola has to make her arrangements at once."

"I wonder what your mother will say when you ask her."

"I shan't ask her. I shall tell her. Nobody can decide this thing for me. I have to decide it for myself, and I've decided it. As for what mother says—" Sissie frowned and then smiled, "that's your affair."

"My affair!" Mr. Prohack exclaimed in real alarm. "What on earth do you mean?"

"Well, you and she are so thick together. You've got to live with her. I haven't got to live with her."

"I ask you, what on earth *do* you mean?"

"But surely you've understood, father, that I shall have to live at the studio. Somebody has to be on the spot, and there are two bedrooms. But of course you'll be able to put all that right with mother, dad. You'll do it for your own sake; but a bit for mine, too." She giggled nervously, ran round the table and kissed her parent. "I'm frightfully obliged for the fifty pounds," she said. "You and the mater will be fearfully happy together soon if Charlie doesn't come back. Ta-ta! I must be off now."

"Where?"

"To Eliza's of course. We shall probably go straight down to Putney together and see Viola and fix everything up. I know Viola's had at least one other good offer. I may sleep at the studio. If not, at Eliza's. Anyhow it will be too late for me to come back here."

"I absolutely forbid you to go off like this."

"Yes, do, father. You forbid for all you're worth if it gives you any pleasure. But it won't be much use unless you can carry me upstairs and lock me in my room. Oh! Father, you are a great pretender. You know perfectly well you're delighted with me."

"Indeed I'm not! I suppose you'll have the decency to see your mother before you go?"

"What! And wake her! You said she wasn't to be disturbed 'on any account.'"

"I deny that I said 'on any account.'"

"I shouldn't dream of disturbing her. And you'll tell her so much better than I could. You can do what you like with her."

IV

"Where's my dessert?" demanded Mrs. Prohack, anxiously and resentfully, when her husband at length reached the bedroom. "I'm dying of hunger, and I've got a real headache now. Oh! Arthur how absurd all this is! At least it would be if I wasn't so hungry."

"Sissie ate all the dessert," Mr. Prohack answered timidly. He no longer felt triumphant, careless and free. Indeed for some minutes he had practically forgotten that he had inherited ten thousand a year. "The child ate it every bit, so I couldn't bring any. Shall I ring for something else?"

"And why," Mrs. Prohack continued, "why have you been so long? And what's all this business of taxis rushing up to the door all the evening?"

"Marian," said Mr. Prohack, ignoring her gross exaggeration of the truth as to the taxis. "I'd better tell you at once. Charlie's gone to Glasgow on his own business and Sissie's just run down to Viola Ridle's studio about a new scheme of some kind that she's thinking of. For the moment we're alone in the world."

"It's always the same," she remarked with indignation, when with forced facetiousness he had given her an extremely imperfect and bowdlerized account of his evening. "It's always the same. As soon as I'm laid up in bed, everything goes wrong. My poor boy, I cannot imagine what you've been doing. I suppose I'm very silly, but I *can't* understand it."

Nor could Mr. Prohack himself, now that he was in the sane conjugal atmosphere of the bedroom.

CHAPTER VII

THE SYMPATHETIC QUACK

I

THE next morning Mr. Prohack had a unique shock, for he was awakened by his wife coming into the bedroom. She held a big piece of cake in her hand. Never before had Mrs. Prohack been known to rise earlier than her husband. Also, the hour was eight-twenty, whereas never before had Mr. Prohack been known, on a working-day, to rise later than eight o'clock. He realised with horror that it would be necessary for him to hurry. Still, he did not jump up. He was not a brilliant sleeper, and he had had a bad night, which had only begun to be good at the time when as as rule he woke finally for the day. He did not feel very well, despite the fine sensation of riches which rushed reassuringly into his arms the moment consciousness returned.

"Arthur," said Mrs. Prohack, who was in her Chinese robe, "do you know that girl hasn't been home all night. Her bed hasn't been slept in!"

"Neither has mine," answered Mr. Prohack. "What girl?"

"Sissie, of course."

"Ah! Sissie!" murmured Mr. Prohack as if he had temporarily forgotten that such a girl existed. "Didn't I tell you last night she mightn't be back?"

"No, you didn't! And you know very well you didn't!"

"Honestly," said Mr. Prohack (meaning "dishonestly" as most people do in similar circumstances), "I thought I did."

"Do you suppose I should have slept one wink if I'd thought Sissie wasn't coming *home?*"

"Yes, I do. The death of Nelson wouldn't keep you awake. And now either I shall be late at the office, or else I shall go without my breakfast. I think you might have wakened me."

Mrs. Prohack, munching the cake despite all her anxieties, replied in a peculiar tone:

"What does it matter if you are late for the office?"

Mr. Prohack reflected that all women were alike in a lack of conscience where the public welfare was concerned. He was rich:

therefore he was entitled to neglect his duty to the nation! A pleasing argument! Mr. Prohack sat up, and Mrs. Prohack had a full view of his face for the first time that morning.

"Arthur," she exclaimed, absolutely and in an instant forgetting both cake and daughter. "You're ill!"

He thought how agreeable it was to have a wife who was so marvellously absorbed in his being. There was something uncanny, something terrible, in it.

"Oh, no I'm not," he said. "I swear I'm not. I'm very tired, but I'm not ill. Get out of my way."

"But your face is as yellow as a cheese," protested Eve, frightened.

"It may be," said Mr. Prohack.

"You won't get up."

"I shall get up."

Eve snatched her hand-mirror from the dressing-table, and gave it to him with a menacing gesture. He admitted to himself that the appearance of his face was perhaps rather alarming at first sight; but really he did not feel ill; he only felt tired.

"It's nothing. Liver." He made a move to emerge from the bed. "Exercise is all I want."

He saw Eve's lips tremble; he saw tears hanging in her eyes; these phenomena induced in him the sensation of having somehow committed a solecism or a murder. He withdrew the move to emerge. She was hurt and desperate. He at once knew himself defeated. He thought how annoying it was to have a woman in the house who was so marvellously absorbed in his being. She was wrong; but her unreasoning desperation triumphed over his calm sagacity.

"Telephone for Dr. Veiga," said Mrs. Prohack to Machin, for whom she had rung. "V-e-i-g-a. Bruton Street. He's in the book. And ask him to come along as soon as he can to see Mr. Prohack."

Now Mr. Prohack had heard of, but never seen, Dr. Veiga. He had more than once listened to the Portuguese name on Eve's lips, and the man had been mentioned more than once at the club. Mr. Prohack knew that he was, if not a foreigner, of foreign descent, and hence he did not like him. Mr. Prohack took kindly to foreign singers and cooks, but not to foreign doctors. Moreover he had doubts about the fellow's professional qualifications. Therefore he strongly resented his wife's most singular and startling order to Machin, and as soon as Machin had gone he expressed himself:

"Anyway," he said curtly, after several exchanges, "I shall see my own doctor, if I see any doctor at all—which is doubtful."

Eve's response was to kiss her husband—a sisterly rather than a wifely kiss. And she said, in a sweet, noble voice:

"It's I that want Dr. Veiga's opinion about you, and I must insist on having it. And what's more, you know I've never cared for your friend Dr. Plott. He never seems to be interested. He scarcely listens to what you have to say. He scarcely examines you. He just makes you think your health is of no importance at all, and it doesn't really matter whether you're ill or well, and that you may get better or you mayn't, and that he'll humour you by sending you a bottle of something."

"Stuff!" said Mr. Prohack. "He's a first-rate fellow. No infernal nonsense about *him!* And what do *you* know about Veiga? I should like to be informed."

"I met him at Mrs. Cunliff's. He cured her of cancer."

"You told me Mrs. Cunliff hadn't got cancer at all."

"Well, it was Dr. Veiga who found out she hadn't, and stopped the operation just in time. She says he saved her life, and she's quite right. He's wonderful."

Mrs. Prohack was now sitting on the bed. She gazed at her husband's features with acute apprehension and yet with persuasive grace.

"Oh! Arthur!" she murmured, "you are a worry to me!"

Mr. Prohack, not being an ordinary Englishman, knew himself beaten—for the second time that morning. He dared not trifle with his wife in her earnest, lofty mood.

"I bet you Veiga won't come," said Mr. Prohack.

"He will come," said Mrs. Prohack blandly.

"How do you know?"

"Because he told me he'd come at once if ever I asked him. He's a perfect dear."

"Oh! I know the sort!" Mr. Prohack said sarcastically. "And you'll see the fee he'll charge!"

"When it's a question of health money doesn't matter."

"It doesn't matter when you've got the money. You'd never have dreamed of having Veiga this time yesterday. You wouldn't even have sent for old Plott."

Mrs. Prohack merely kissed her husband again, with a kind of ineffable resignation. Then Machin came in with her breakfast, and said that Dr. Veiga would be round shortly, and was told to telephone to the Treasury that her master was ill in bed.

"And what about my breakfast?" the victim enquired with irony. "Give me some of your egg."

"No, dearest, egg is the very last thing you should have with that colour."

"Well, if you'd like to know, I don't want any breakfast. Couldn't eat any."

"There you are!" Mrs. Prohack exclaimed triumphantly. "And yet you swear you aren't ill! That just shows. . . . It will be quite the best thing for you not to take anything until Dr. Veiga's been."

Mr. Prohack, helpless, examined the ceiling, and decided to go to the office in the afternoon. He tried to be unhappy but couldn't. Eve was too funny, too delicious, too exquisitely and ingenuously "firm," too blissful in having him at her mercy, for him to be unhappy. . . . To say nothing of the hundred thousand pounds! And he knew that Eve also was secretly revelling in the hundred thousand pounds. Dr. Veiga was her first bite at it.

II

Considering that he was well on the way to being a fashionable physician, Dr. Veiga arrived with surprising promptitude. Mr. Prohack wondered what hold Eve had upon him and how she had acquired it. He was prejudiced against the fellow before he came into the bedroom, simply because Eve, on hearing the noise of a car and a doorbell, had hurried downstairs, and a considerable interval had elapsed between the doctor's entrance into the house and his appearance at the bedside. Mr. Prohack guessed easily that those two had been plotting against him. Strange how Eve could be passionately loyal and basely deceitful simultaneously! The two-faced creature led the doctor forward with a candid smile that partook equally of the smile of a guardian angel and the smile of a cherub. She was an unparalleled comedian.

Dr. Veiga was fattish and rather shabby; about sixty years of age. He spoke perfectly correct English with a marked foreign accent. His demeanour was bland, slightly familiar, philosophical and sympathetic. Dr. Plott's eyes would have said: "This is my thirteenth visit this morning, and I've eighteen more to do, and it's all very tedious. Why *do* you people let yourselves get ill—if it's a fact that you really are ill? I don't think you are, but I'll see." Dr. Veiga's eyes said: "How interesting your case is! You've had no luck this time. We must make the best of things; but also we must face the truth. God knows I don't want to boast, but I expect I can put you right, with the help of your own strong commonsense."

Mr. Prohack, a connoisseur in human nature, noted the significances of the Veiga glance, but he suspected that there might also be something histrionic in it. Dr. Veiga examined heart, pulse, tongue. He tapped the torso. He asked many questions. Then he took an instrument out of a leather case which he carried, and fastened a strap round Mr. Prohack's forearm and attached it to the instrument, and presently Mr. Prohack could feel the strong pulsations of the blood current in his arm.

"Dear, dear!" said Dr. Veiga. "175. Blood pressure too high. Much too high! Must get that down."

Eve looked as though the end of the world had been announced, and even Mr. Prohack had qualms. Ten minutes earlier Mr. Prohack had been a strong, healthy man a trifle unwell in a bedroom. He was suddenly transformed into a patient in a nursing-home.

"A little catarrh," said Dr. Veiga.

"I've got no catarrh," said Mr. Prohack, with conviction.

"Yes, yes. Catarrh of the stomach. Probably had it for years. The duodenum is obstructed. A little accident that easily happens."

He addressed himself as it were privately to Mrs. Prohack. "The duodenum is no thicker than that." He indicated the pencil with which he was already writing in a pocket-book. "We'll get it right."

"What is the duodenum?" Mr. Prohack wanted to cry out. But he was too ashamed to ask. It was hardly conceivable that he, so wise, so prudent, had allowed over forty years to pass in total ignorance of this important item of his own body. He felt himself to be a bag full of disconcerting and dangerous mysteries. Or he might have expressed it that he had been smoking in criminal nonchalance for nearly half a century on the top of a powder magazine. He was deeply impressed by the rapidity and assurance of the doctor's diagnosis. It was wonderful that the queer fellow could in a few minutes single out an obscure organ no bigger than a pencil and say: "There is the ill." The fellow might be a quack, but sometimes quacks were men of genius. His shame and his alarm quickly vanished under the doctor's reassuring and bland manner. So much so that when Dr. Veiga had written out a prescription, Mr. Prohack said lightly:

"I suppose I can get up, though."

To which Dr. Veiga amiably replied:

"I shall leave that to you. Perhaps if I tell you you'll be lucky if you don't have jaundice . . . ! But I think you *will* be lucky. I'll try to look in again this afternoon."

These last words staggered both Mr. and Mrs. Prohack.

"I've been expecting this for years. I knew it would come." Mrs. Prohack breathed tragically.

And even Mr. Prohack reflected aghast:

"My God! Doctor calling twice a day!"

True, "duodenum" was a terrible word.

Mrs. Prohack gazed at Dr. Veiga as at a high priest, and waited to be vouchsafed a further message.

"Anyhow, if I find it impossible to call, I'll telephone in any case," said Dr. Veiga.

Some slight solace in this!

Mrs. Prohack, like an acolyte, personally attended the high priest as far as the street, listening with acute attention to his recommendations. When she returned she had put on a carefully bright face. Evidently she had decided, or had been told, that cheerfulness was essential to ward off jaundice.

"Now that's what I *call* a doctor," said she. "To think of your friend Plott. . . ! I've telephoned for a messenger boy to go to the chemist's."

"You're at liberty to call the man a doctor," answered Mr. Prohack. "And I'm at liberty to call him a fine character actor."

"I knew the moment you sat up it was jaundice," said Mrs. Prohack.

"Well," said Mr. Prohack. "I lay you five to one I don't have jaundice. Not that you'd ever pay me if you lost."

Mrs. Prohack said:

"When I saw you were asleep at after eight o'clock this morning I knew there must be something serious. I felt it. However, as the doctor says, if we *take* it seriously it will soon cease to be serious."

"He's not a bad phrase-maker," said Mr. Prohack.

In the late afternoon Dr. Veiga returned like an old and familiar acquaintance, with his confident air of saying: "We can manage this affair between us—I am almost sure." Mr. Prohack felt worse; and the room, lighted by one shaded lamp, had begun to look rather like a real sick-room. Mr. Prohack, though he mistrusted the foreign accent, the unprofessional appearance, and the adventurous manner, was positively glad to see his new doctor, and indeed felt that he had need of succour.

"Yes," said Dr. Veiga, after investigation. "My opinion is that you'll escape jaundice. In four or five days you ought to be as well as you were before the attack. I don't say *how* well you were before."

Mr. Prohack instantly felt better.

"It will be very awkward if I can't get back to the office early next week," said he.

"I'm sure it will," Dr. Veiga agreed. "And it might be still more awkward if you went back to the office early next week, and then never went any more."

"What do you mean?"

Dr. Veiga smiled understandingly at Mrs. Prohack, as though he and she were the only grown-up persons in the room.

"Look here," he addressed the patient. "I see I shall have to charge you a fee for telling you what you know as well as I do. The fact is I get my living by doing that. How old are you?"

"Forty-six."

"Every year of the war counts double. So you're over fifty. A difficult age. You can run an engine ten hours a day for fifty years. But it's worn; it's second-hand. And if you keep on running it ten hours a day you'll soon discover how worn it is. But you can run it five hours a day for another twenty years with reasonable safety and efficiency. That's what I wanted to tell you. You aren't the man you were, Mr. Prohack. You've lost the trick of getting rid of your waste products. You say you feel tired. Why do you feel tired? Being tired simply means being clogged. The moment you feel tired your waste products are beginning to pile up. Look at those finger joints! Waste products! Friction! Why don't you sleep well? You say the more tired you are the worse you sleep: and you seem surprised. But you're only surprised because you haven't thought it out. Morpheus himself wouldn't sleep if his body was a mass of friction-producing waste products from top to toe. You aren't a body and soul, Mr. Prohack. You're an engine—I wish you'd remember that and treat yourself like one. The moment you feel tired, stop the engine. If you don't, it'll stop itself. It pretty nearly stopped to-day. You need lubrication too. The best lubricant is a tumbler of hot water four times a day. And don't take coffee, or any salt except what your cook puts into the dishes. Don't try to be cleverer than nature. Don't think the clock is standing still. It isn't. If you treat yourself as well as you treat your watch, you'll bury me. If you don't, I shall bury you. All that I've told you I know by heart, because I'm saying it to men of your age every day of my life."

Mr. Prohack felt like a reprimanded schoolboy. He feared the wrath to come.

"Don't you think my husband ought to take a long holiday?" Eve put in.

"Well, *of course* he ought," said Dr. Veiga, opening both mouth and eyes in protest against such a silly question.

"Six months?"

"At least."

"Where ought he to go?"

"Doesn't matter. Portugal, the Riviera, Switzerland. But it's not the season yet for any of these places. If he wants to keep on pleasant terms with nature he'll get out his car and motor about his own country for a month or two. After that he might go to the Continent. But of course he won't. I know these official gentlemen. If you ask them to disturb their routine they'll die first. They really would sooner die. Very natural of course. Routine is their drug."

"My husband will take six months holiday," said Eve quietly. "I suppose you could give the proper certificate? You see in these Government departments . . ."

"I'll give you the certificate to-morrow."

Mr. Prohack was pretending to be asleep, or at least to be too fatigued and indifferent to take notice of this remarkable conversation. But as soon as Dr. Veiga had blandly departed under the escort of Eve, he slipped out of bed and cautiously padded to the landing where there was a bookcase.

"Duodenum. Duodenum. Must be something to do with twelve." Then he found a dictionary and brought it back into the bedroom and consulted it. "So it's twelve inches long, is it?" he murmured. He had just time to plunge into bed and pitch the dictionary under the bed before his wife returned.

III

She was bending over him.

"Darling!"

He opened his deceiving eyes. Her face was within a foot of his.

"How do you feel now?"

"I feel," said he, "that this is the darnedest swindle that ever was. If I hadn't come into a fortune I should have been back at the office the day after to-morrow. In about eight hours, with the help of that Portuguese mountebank, you've changed me from a sane normal man into a blooming valetudinarian who must run all over the earth in search of health. I've got to 'winter' somewhere, have I? You'll see. It's absolutely incredible. It's more like Maskelyne and Cook's than anything I ever came across." He yawned. He knew that it was the disturbed duodenum that caused him to yawn, and that also gave him a dry mouth and a peculiar taste therein.

"Yes, darling," Eve smiled above him the smile of her impenetrable angelicism. "Yes, darling. You're better."

The worst was that she had beaten him on the primary point. He had asserted that he was not ill. She had asserted that he was. She had been right; he wrong. He could not deny, even to himself, that he was ill. Not gravely, only somewhat. But supposing that he was gravely ill! Supposing that old Plott would agree with all that Veiga had said! It was conceivable. Misgivings shot through him.

And Eve had him at her sweet mercy. He was helpless. She was easily the stronger. He perceived then, what many a husband dies without having perceived, that his wife had a genuine individual existence and volition of her own, that she was more than his complement, his companion, the mother of his children.

She lowered her head further and gave him a long, fresh, damp kiss. They were very intimate, with an intimacy that her enigmatic quality could not impair. He was annoyed, aggrieved, rebellious, but extremely happy in a weak sort of way. He hated and loved her, he despised and adored her, he reprehended and admired her—all at once. What specially satisfied him was that he had her to himself. The always-impinging children were not there. He liked this novel solitude of two.

"Darling, where is Charlie staying in Glasgow?"

"Why?"

"I want to write to him."

"Post's gone, my poor child."

"Then I shall telegraph."

"What about?"

"Never mind."

"I shan't tell you the address unless you promise to show me the telegram. I intend to be master in my own house even if I am dying."

Thus he saw the telegram, which ran: "Father ill in bed what is the best motor car to buy. Love. Mother." The telegram astounded Mr. Prohack.

"Have you taken leave of your senses?" he cried. Then he laughed. What else was there to do? What else but the philosopher's laugh was adequate to the occasion?

While Eva with her own unrivalled hand was preparing the bedroom for the night, Machin came in with a telegram. Without being asked to do so Eve showed it to the sufferer: "Tell him to buck up. Eagle six cylinder. Everything fine here. Charles."

"I think he might have sent his love," said Eve.

Mr. Prohack no longer attempted to fight against the situation, which was like a net winding itself round him.

CHAPTER VIII

ISSIE'S BUSINESS

I

ONE evening, ten days later, Mr. Prohack slipped out of his own house as stealthily as a thief might have slipped into it. He was cured provisionally. The unseen, unfelt, sinister duodenum no longer mysteriously deranged his whole engine. Only a continual sensation of slight fatigue indicated all the time that he was not cleverer than nature and that he was not victoriously disposing of his waste products. But he could walk mildly about; his zest for smoking had in part returned; and to any uninstructed observer he bore a close resemblance to a healthy man.

Four matters worried him, of which three may be mentioned immediately. He could not go to the Treasury. His colleague Hunter had amiably called the day after his seizure, and Mrs. Prohack had got hold of Hunter. Her influence over sane and well-balanced males was really extraordinary. Mr. Prohack had remained in perfect ignorance of the machinations of these two for eight days, at the end of which period he received by post an official document informing him that My Lords of the Treasury had granted him six months' leave of absence for reasons of ill-health. Dr. Veiga had furnished the certificate unknown to the patient. The quick despatch of the affair showed with what celerity a government department can function when it is actuated from the inside. The leave of absence for reasons of ill-health of course prevented Mr. Prohack from appearing at his office. How could he with decency appear at his office seemingly vigorous when it had been officially decided that he was too ill to work? And Mr. Prohack desired greatly to visit the Treasury. The habit of a life-time had been broken in a moment, and since Mr. Prohack was the creature of that habit he suffered accordingly. He had been suffering for two days. This was the first matter that worried Mr. Prohack.

The second matter had to do with his clubs. He was cut off from his clubs. Partly for the same reason as that which cut him off from the Treasury—for both his clubs were full of Civil Servants—and partly because he was still somehow sensitive concerning the fact of his inheritance. He would have had a similar objection to entering his clubs in Highland kilt. The explanation was obvious. He hated to be conspicuous. His inheritance was already (through Mr. Softly Bishop) the talk of certain official and club circles, and Mr. Prohack apprehended that every eye would be curiously upon him if he should set foot in a club. He could not bear that, and he could not bear the questions and the pleasantries. One day he would have to bear them—but not yet.

The third matter that worried him was that he could not, even in secret, consult his own doctor. How could he go to old Plott and say: "Plott, old man, I've been ill and my wife insisted upon having another doctor, but I've come to ask you to tell me whether or not the other doctor's right?" The thing was impossible. Yet he badly wanted to verify Veiga by Plott. He still mistrusted Veiga, though his mistrust lessened daily, despite his wish to see it increase.

Mrs. Prohack had benevolently suggested that he should run down to his club, but on no account for a meal—merely "for a change." He had declined, without giving the reason, and she had admitted that perhaps he was right.

He attributed all the worries to his wife.

"I pay a fine price for that woman," he thought as he left the house, "a rare fine price!" But as for her price, he never haggled over it. She, just as she existed in her awful imperfection, was his first necessary of life. She had gone out after dinner to see an acquaintance about a house-maid (for already she was reorganising the household on a more specious scale); she was a mile off at least; but she would have disapproved of him breaking loose into his clubs at night, and so the Terror of the departments stole forth, instead of walking forth, intimidated by that moral influence which she left behind her. Undoubtedly since the revolt of the duodenum her grip of him had sensibly tightened.

Not that Mr. Prohack was really going to a club. He had deceitfully told himself that he *might* stroll down to his principal club, for the sake of exercise (his close friends among the members were lunchers not diners), but the central self within himself was aware that no club would see him that evening.

A taxi approached in the darkness; he knew by its pace that it was empty. He told the driver to drive to Putney. In the old days of eleven days ago he would not have dared to tell a taxi-driver to drive to Putney, for the fare would have unbalanced his dizzy private weekly budget; and even now he felt he was going the deuce of a pace. Even now he would prudently not have taken a taxi had not part of the American hundred thousand pounds already materialised. Mr. Softly Bishop had been to see him on the previous day, and in addition to being mysteriously sympathetic about his co-heir's ill-health had produced seven thousand pounds of the hundred thousand. A New York representative had cabled fourteen thousand, not because Mr. Prohack was in a hurry for seven, but because Mr. Softly Bishop was in a hurry for seven. And Mr. Softly Bishop had pointed out something which Mr. Prohack, Treasury official, had not thought of. He had pointed out that Mr. Prohack might begin immediately to spend just as freely as if the hundred thousand were actually in hand.

"You see," said he, "the interest has been accumulating over there ever since Angmering's death, and it will continue to accumulate until we get all the capital; and the interest runs up to about a couple of hundred a week for each of us."

Now Mr. Prohack had directed the taxi to his daughter's dance studio, and perhaps it was the intention to do so that had made him steal ignobly out of the house. For Eve would assuredly have rebelled. A state of war existed between Eve and her daughter, and Mr. Prohack's intelligence, as well as his heart, had ranged him on Eve's side. Since Sissie's departure, the girl had given no sign whatever to her parents. Mrs. Prohack had expected to see her on the next day after her defection. But there was no Sissie, and there was no message from Sissie. Mrs. Prohack bulged with astounding news for Sissie, of her father's illness and inheritance. But Mrs. Prohack's resentful pride would not make the first move, and would not allow Mr. Prohack to make it. They knew, at second-hand through a friend of Viola Ridle's, that Sissie was regularly active at the studio; also Sissie had had the effrontery to send a messenger for some of her clothes—without even a note! The situation was incredible, and waxed daily in incredibility. Sissie's behaviour could not possibly be excused.

This was the fourth and the chief matter that worried Mr. Prohack. He regarded it sardonically as rather a lark; but he was worried to think of the girl making a fool of herself with her mother. Her mother was demonstrably in the right. To yield to the chit's appalling heartlessness would be bad tactics and it would be humiliating. Nevertheless Mr. Prohack had directed the taxi-driver to the dance-studio at Putney. On the way it suddenly occurred to him, almost with a shock, that he was a rich man, secure from material anxieties, and that therefore he ought to feel light-hearted. He had been losing sight of this very important fact for quite some time.

II

The woman in the cubicle near the door was putting a fresh disc on to a gramophone and winding up the instrument. She was a fat, youngish woman, in a parlourmaid's cap and apron, and Mr. Prohack had a few days earlier had a glimpse of her seated in his own hall waiting for a package of Sissie's clothes.

"Very sorry, sir," said she, turning her head negligently from the gramophone and eyeing him seriously. "I'm afraid you can't go in if you're not in evening dress." Evidently from her firm, polite voice, she knew just what she was about, did that young woman. She added: "The rule's very strict on Fridays."

At the same moment a bell rang once. The woman immediately released the catch of the gramophone and lowered the needle on to the disc, and Mr. Prohack heard music, but not from the cubicle. There was a round hole in the match-board partition, and the trumpet attachment of the gramophone disappeared beyond the hole.

"This affair is organised," thought Mr. Prohack, decidedly impressed by the ingenuity of the musical arrangement and by the promptness of the orchestral director in obeying the signal of the bell.

"My name is Prohack," said he. "I'm Miss Prohack's father."

This important announcement ought to have startled the sang-froid of the guardian, but it did not. She merely said, with a slight mechanical smile:

"As soon as this dance is over, sir, I'll let Miss Prohack know she's wanted." She did not say: "Sir, a person of your eminence is above rules. Go right in."

Two girls in all-enveloping dark cloaks entered behind him. "Good-evening, Lizzie," one of them greeted the guardian. And Lizzie's face relaxed into a bright genuine smile.

"Good-evening, miss. Good-evening, miss."

The two girls vanished rustlingly through a door over which was hung a piece of cardboard with the written words: "Ladies' cloakroom." In a few moments they emerged, white and fluffy apparitions, eager, self-conscious, and they vanished through another door. Mr. Prohack judged from their bridling and from their whispers to each other that they belonged to the class which ministers to the shopping-class. He admitted that they looked very nice and attractive; but he had the sensation of having blundered into a queer, hitherto unknown world, and of astonishment and qualms that his daughter should be a ruler in that world.

Lizzie stood up and peeped through a little square window in the match-boarding. As soon as she had finished peeping Mr. Prohack took liberty to peep also, and the dance-studio was revealed to him. Somehow he could scarcely believe that it was not a hallucination, and that he was really in Putney, and that his own sober house in which Sissie had been reared still existed not many miles off.

For Mr. Prohack, not continuously but at intervals, possessed a disturbing faculty that compelled him to see the phenomena of human life as they actually were, and to disregard entirely the mere names of things,—which mere names by the magic power of mere names usually suffice to satisfy the curiosity of most people and to allay their misgivings if any. Mr. Prohack now saw (when he looked downwards) a revolving disc which was grating against a stationary needle and thereby producing unpleasant rasping sounds. But it was also producing a quite different order of sounds. He did not in the least understand, and he did not suppose that anybody in the dance-studio understood, the delicate secret mechanism by which these other sounds were produced. All he knew was that by means of the trumpet attachment they were transmitted through the wooden partition and let loose into the larger air of the studio, where the waves of them had a singular effect on the brains of certain bright young women and sombre young and middle-aged men who were arranged in clasped couples: with the result that the brains of the women and men sent orders to their legs, arms, eyes, and they shifted to and fro in rhythmical movements. Each woman placed herself very close—breast against breast—to each man, yielding her volition absolutely to his, and (if the man was the taller) often gazing up into his face with an ecstatic expression of pleasure and acquiescence. The physical relations between the units of each couple would have caused censorious comment had the couple been alone or standing still; but the movement and the association of couples seemed mysteriously to lift the whole operation above criticism and to endow it with a perfect propriety. The motion of the couples, and their manner of moving, over the earth's surface were extremely monotonous; some couples indeed only walked stiffly to and fro; on the other hand a few exhibited variety, lightness and grace, in manœuvres which involved a high degree of mutual trust and comprehension.

While only some of the faces were ecstatic, all were rapt. The ordinary world was shut out of this room, whose inhabitants had apparently abandoned themselves with all their souls to the performance of a complicated and solemn rite.

Odd as the spectacle was, Mr. Prohack enjoyed it. He enjoyed the youth and the prettiness and the litheness of the brightly-dressed girls and the stern masculinity of the men, and he enjoyed the thought that both girls and men had had the wit to escape from the ordinary world into this fantastic environment created out of four walls, a few Chinese lanterns, some rouge, some stuffs, some spangles, friction between two pieces of metal, and the profoundest instinct of nature. Beyond everything he enjoyed the sight of the lithest and most elegant of the girls, whom he knew to be Eliza Brating and who was dancing with a partner whose skill obviously needed no lessons. He would have liked to see his daughter Sissie in Eliza's place, but Sissie was playing the man's rôle to a stout and nearly middle-aged lady, whose chief talent for the rite appeared to be an iron determination.

Mr. Prohack was in danger of being hypnotised by the spectacle, but suddenly the conflict between the disc and the needle grew more acute, and Lizzie, the guardian, dragged the needle sharply from the bosom of its antagonist. The sounds ceased, and the brains of the couples in the studio, no longer inspired by the sounds, ceased to inspire the muscles of the couples, and the rite suddenly finished. Mr. Prohack drew breath.

"To think," he reflected, "that this sort of thing is seriously going on all over London at this very instant, and that many earnest persons are making a livelihood from it, and that nobody but me perceives how marvellous, charming, incomprehensible and disconcerting it is!"

He said to the guardian:

"There doesn't seem to be much 'lesson' about this business. Everybody here seems to be able to dance all right."

To which Lizzie replied with a sagacious, even ironic, smile:

"You see, sir, on these gala nights they all do their very best."

"Father!"

Sissie had arrived upon him. Clearly she was preoccupied, if not worried, and the unexpected sight of her parent forced her, as it were, unwillingly from one absorbing train of ideas into another. She was startled, self-conscious, nervous. Still, she jumped at him and kissed him,—as if in a dream.

"Nothing the matter, is there?"

"Nothing."

"I'm frightfully busy to-night. Just come in here, will you?"

And she took him into the ladies' cloakroom—an apartment the like of which he had never before seen. It had only one chair, in front of a sort of dressing-table covered with mysterious apparatus and instruments.

Mr. Prohack inspected his daughter as though she had been somebody else's daughter.

"Well," said he. "You look just like a real business woman, except the dress."

She was very attractive, very elegant, comically young (to him), and very business-like in her smart, short frock, stockings, and shoes.

"Can't you understand," she objected firmly, "that this *is* my business dress, just as much as a black frock and high collar would be in an office?"

He gave a short, gentle laugh.

"I don't know what you're laughing at, dad," she reproached him, not unkindly. "Anyhow, I'm glad some one's come at last. I was beginning to think that my home had forgotten all about me. Even when I sent up for some clothes no message came back."

The life-long experience of Mr. Prohack had been that important and unusual interviews rarely corresponded with the anticipation of them, and the present instance most sharply confirmed his experience. He had expected to be forgiving an apologetic daughter, but the reality was that he found himself in the dock. He hesitated for words, and Sissie went on:

"Here have I been working myself to death reorganising this place after Viola went—and I can tell you it needed reorganising! Haven't had a minute in the mornings, and of course there are the lessons afternoon and evening. And no one's been down to see how I was getting on, or even written. I do think it's a bit steep. Mother might have known that if I *had* had any spare time I should have run up."

"I've been rather queer," he excused himself and the family. "And your mother's been looking after me, and of course you know Charlie's still in Glasgow."

"I don't know anything," she corrected him. "But you needn't tell me that if you've been unwell mother's been looking after you. Does she ever do anything else? Are you better? What was it? You *look* all right."

"Oh! General derangement. I haven't been to the office since you decamped." He did not feel equal to telling her that he would not be returning to the office for months. She had said that he looked all right, and her quite honest if hasty verdict on his appearance gave him a sense of guilt, and also renewed suspicions of Dr. Veiga.

"Not been to the office!" The statement justly amazed the girl, almost shocked her. But she went on in a fresh, satirical accent recalling Mr. Prohack's own: "You *must* have been upset! But of course you're highly nervous, dad, and I expect the excitement of the news of your fortune was too much for you. I know exactly how you get when anything unusual happens."

She had heard of the inheritance!

"I was going to tell you about that little affair," he said awkwardly. "So you knew! Who told you?"

"Nobody in my family at any rate," she answered. "I heard of it from an outsider, and of course from sheer pride I had to pretend that I knew all about it. And what's more, father, you knew when you gave me that fifty pounds, only you wouldn't let on. Don't deny it. . . . Naturally I'm glad about it, very glad. And yet I'm not. I really rather regret it for you and mother. You'll never be as happy again. Riches will spoil my poor darling mother."

"That remains to be seen, Miss Worldly Wisemiss," he retorted with unconvincing lightness. He was disturbed, and he was impressed, by her indifference to the fortune. It appeared not to concern or to interest her. She spoke not merely as one who objected to unearned wealth but as one to whom the annals of the Prohack family were henceforth a matter of minor importance. It was very strange, and Mr. Prohack had to fight against a feeling of intimidation. The girl whom he had cherished for over twenty years and whom he thought he knew to the core, was absolutely astounding him by the revelation of her individuality. He didn't know her. He was not her father. He was helpless before her.

"How are things here?" he demanded, amiably inquisitive, as an acquaintance.

"Excellent," said she. "Jolly hard work, though."

"Yes, I should imagine so. Teaching men dancing! By Jove!"

"There's not so much difficulty about teaching men. The difficulty's with the women. Father, they're awful. You can't imagine their stupidity."

Lizzie glanced into the room. She simply glanced, and Sissie returned the glance.

"You'll have to excuse me a bit, father," said Sissie. "I'll come back as quick as I can. Don't go." She departed hurriedly.

"I'd better get out of this anyhow," thought Mr. Prohack, surveying the ladies' cloakroom. "If one of 'em came in I should have to explain my unexplainable presence in this sacred grot."

III

Having received no suggestion from his daughter as to how he should dispose of himself while awaiting her leisure, Mr. Prohack made his way back to the guardian's cubicle. And there he discovered a chubby and intentionally-young man in the act of gazing through the small window into the studio exactly as he himself had been gazing a few minutes earlier.

"Hel*lo*, Prohack!" exclaimed the chubby and intentionally-young man, with the utmost geniality and calmness.

"How d'ye do?" responded Mr. Prohack with just as much calmness and perhaps ten per cent less geniality. Mr. Prohack was a peculiar fellow, and that on this occasion he gave rather less geniality than he received was due to the fact that he had never before spoken to the cupid in his life and that he was wondering whether membership of the same club entirely justified so informal a mode of address—without an introduction and outside the club premises. For, like all modest men, Mr. Prohack had some sort of a notion of his own dignity, a sort of a notion that occasionally took him quite by surprise. Mr. Prohack did not even know the surname of his aggressor. He only knew that he never overheard other men call him anything but "Ozzie." Had not Mr. Prohack been buried away all his life in the catacombs of the Treasury and thus cut off from the great world-movement, he would have been fully aware that Oswald Morfey was a person of importance in the West End of London, that he was an outstanding phenomenon of the age, that he followed very closely all the varying curves of the great world-movement, that he was constantly to be seen on the pavements of Piccadilly, Bond Street, St. James's Street, Pall Mall and Hammersmith, that he was never absent from a good first night or a private view of very new or very old pictures or a distinguished concert or a poetry-reading or a fashionable auction at Christie's, that he received invitations to dinner for every night in the week and accepted all those that did not clash with the others, that in return for these abundant meals he gave about once a month a tea-party in his trifling Japanese flat in Bruton Street, where the sandwiches were as thin as the sound of the harpsichord which eighteenth century ladies played at his request; and that he was in truth what Mr. Asprey Chown called "social secretary" to Mr. Asprey Chown.

Mr. Prohack might be excused for his ignorance of this last fact, for the relation between Asprey Chown and Ozzie was never very clearly defined—at any rate by Ozzie. He had no doubt learned, from an enforced acquaintance with the sides of motor-omnibuses, that Mr. Asprey Chown was a theatre-manager of some activity, but he certainly had not truly comprehended that Mr. Asprey Chown was head of one of the two great rival theatrical combines and reputed to be the most accomplished showman in the Western hemisphere, with a jewelled finger in notable side-enterprises such as prize-fights, restaurants, and industrial companies. The knowing ones from whom naught is hidden held that Asprey Chown had never given a clearer proof of genius than in engaging this harmless and indefatigable parasite of the West End to be his social secretary. The knowing ones said further that whereas Ozzie was saving money, nobody could be sure that Asprey Chown was saving money. The engagement had a double effect—it at once put Asprey Chown into touch with everything that could be useful to him for the purposes of special booming, and it put Ozzie into touch with half the theatrical stars of London—in an age when a first-rate heroine of revue was worth at least two duchesses and a Dame in the scale of social values.

Mr. Oswald Morfey, doubtless in order to balance the modernity of his taste in the arts, wore a tight black stock and a wide eye-glass ribbon in the daytime, and in the evening permitted himself to associate a soft silk shirt with a swallow-tail coat. It was to Mr. Prohack's secondary (and more exclusive) club that he belonged. Inoffensive though he was, he had managed innocently to offend Mr. Prohack. "Who is the fellow?" Mr. Prohack had once asked a friend in the club, and having received no answer but "Ozzie," Mr. Prohack had added: "He's a perfect ass," and had given as a reason for this harsh judgment: "Well, I can't stick the way he walks across the hall."

In the precincts of the dance-studio Mr. Oswald Morfey said in that simple, half-lisping tone and with that wide-open child-like glance that characterised most of his remarks:

"A very prosperous little affair here!" Having said this, he let his eyeglass fall into the full silkiness of his shirt-front, and turned and smiled very amicably and agreeably on Mr. Prohack, who could not help thinking: "Perhaps after all you aren't such a bad sort of an idiot."

"Yes," said Mr. Prohack. "Do you often get as far as Putney?" For Mr. Oswald Morfey, enveloped as he unquestionably was in the invisible aura of the West End, seemed conspicuously out of place in a dance-studio in a side-street in Putney, having rather the air of an angelic visitant.

"Well, now I come to think of it, I don't!" Mr. Morfey answered nearly all questions as though they were curious, disconcerting questions that took him by surprise. This mannerism was universally attractive—until you got tired of it.

Mr. Prohack was now faintly attracted by it,—so that he said, in a genuine attempt at good-fellowship:

"You know I can't for the life of me remember your name. You must excuse me. My memory for names is not what it was. And I hate to dissemble, don't you?"

The announcement was a grave shock to Mr. Oswald Morfey, who imagined that half the taxi-drivers in London knew him by sight. Nevertheless he withstood the shock like a little man of the world, and replied with miraculous and sincere politeness: "I'm sure there's no reason why you should remember my name." And he vouchsafed his name.

"Of course! Of course!" exclaimed Mr. Prohack, with a politeness equally miraculous, for the word "Morfey" had no significance for the benighted official. "How stupid of me!"

"By the way," said Mr. Morfey in a lower, confidential tone. "Your Eagle will be ready to-morrow instead of next week."

"My Eagle?"

"Your new car."

It was Mr. Prohack's turn to be staggered, and to keep his nerve. Not one word had he heard about the purchase of a car since Charlie's telegram from Glasgow. He had begun to think that his wife had either forgotten the necessity of a car or was waiting till his more complete recovery before troubling him to buy it. And he had taken care to say nothing about it himself, for he had discovered, upon searching his own mind, that his interest in motor-cars was not an authentic interest and that he had no desire at all to go motoring in pursuit of health. And lo! Eve had been secretly engaged in the purchase of a car for him! Oh! A remarkable woman, Eve: she would stop at nothing when his health was in question. Not even at a two thousand pound car.

"Ah, yes!" said Mr. Prohack, with as much tranquillity as though his habit was to buy a car once a week or so. "To-morrow, you say? Good!" Was the fellow then a motor-car tout working on commission?

"You see," said Ozzie, "my old man owns a controlling interest in the Eagle Company. That's how I happen to know."

"I see," murmured Mr. Prohack, speculating wildly in private as to the identity of Ozzie's old man.

When Ozzie with a nod and a smile and a re-fixing of his monocle left the cubicle to enter the studio, he left Mr. Prohack freshly amazed at the singularities of the world and of women, even the finest women. How disturbing to come down to Putney in a taxicab in order to learn from a stranger that you have bought a two thousand pound car which is to come into your possession on the morrow! The dangerousness, the excitingness, of being rich struck Mr. Prohack very forcibly.

A few minutes later he beheld a sight which affected him more deeply, and less pleasantly, than anything else in an evening of thunderclaps. Through the little window he saw Sissie dancing with Ozzie Morfey. And although Sissie was not gazing upward ecstatically into Ozzie's face—she could not because they were of a size—and although her features had a rather stern, fixed expression, Mr. Prohack knew, from his knowledge of her, that Sissie was in a secret ecstasy of enjoyment while dancing with this man. He did not like her ecstasy. Was it possible that she, so sensible and acute, had failed to perceive that the fellow was a perfect ass? For in spite of his amiability, a perfect ass the fellow was. The sight of his Sissie held in the arms of Ozzie Morfey revolted Mr. Prohack. But he was once again helpless. And the most sinister suspicions crawled into his mind. Why was the resplendent, the utterly correct Ozzie dancing in a dancing studio in Putney? Certainly he was not there to learn dancing. He danced to perfection. The feet of the partners seemed to be married into a mystic unity of direction. The performance was entrancing to watch. Could it be possible that Ozzie was there because Sissie was there? Darker still, could it be possible that Sissie had taken a share in the studio for any reason other than a purely commercial reason?

"He thinks you're a darling," said Sissie to her father afterwards when he and she and Eliza Brating, alone together in the studio, were informally consuming buns and milk in the corner where the stove was.

The talk ran upon dancers, and whether Ozzie Morfey was not one of the finest dancers in London. Was Sissie's tone quite natural? Mr. Prohack could not be sure. Eliza Brating said she must go at once in order not to miss the last tram home. Mr. Prohack, without thinking, said that he would see her home in his taxi, which had been ruthlessly ticking his fortune away for much more than an hour.

"Kiss mother for me," said Sissie, "and tell her that she's a horrid old thing and I shall come along and give her a piece of my mind one of these days." And she gave him the kiss for her mother.

And as she kissed him, Mr. Prohack was very proud of his daughter—so efficient, so sound, so straight, so graceful.

"She's all right, anyway," he reflected. And yet she could be ecstatic in the arms of that perfect ass! And in the taxi: "Fancy me seeing home this dancing-mistress!" Eliza lived at Brook Green. She was very elegant, and quite unexceptionable until she opened her mouth. She related to him how her mother, who had once been a *premier sujet* in the Covent Garden ballet, was helpless from sciatica. But she related this picturesque and pride-causing detail in a manner very insipid, naïve, and even vulgar, (After all there was a difference between First Division and Second Division in the Civil Service!) She was boring him terribly before they reached Brook Green. She took leave with a deportment correct but acquired at an age too late. Still, he had liked to see her home in the taxi. She was young, and she was an object pleasing to the eye. He realised that he was not accustomed to the propinquity of young women. What would his cronies at the Club say to the escapade? . . . Odd, excessively odd, that the girl should be Sissie's partner, in a business enterprise of so odd a character! . . . The next thing was to meet Eve after the escapade. Should he keep to the defensive, or should he lead off with an attack apropos of the Eagle car?

CHAPTER IX

COLLISION

I

After an eventful night Mr. Prohack woke up late to breakfast in bed. Theoretically he hated breakfast in bed, but in practice he had recently found that the inconveniences to himself were negligible compared to the intense and triumphant pleasure which his wife took in seeing him breakfast in bed, in being fully dressed while he was in pyjamas and dressing-gown, and in presiding over the meal and over him. Recently Marian had formed the habit of rising earlier and appearing to be very busy upon various minute jobs at an hour when, a few weeks previously, she would scarcely have decided that day had given place to night. Mr. Prohack, without being able precisely to define it, thought that he understood the psychology of the change in this unique woman.

Under ordinary circumstances he would have been worried by his sense of fatigue, but now, as he had nothing whatever to do, he did not much care whether he was tired or not. Neither the office nor the State would suffer through his lack of tone.

The events of the night had happened exclusively inside Mr. Prohack's head. Nor were they traceable to the demeanour of his wife when he returned home from the studio. She had mysteriously behaved to him as though nocturnal excursions to disgraceful daughters in remote quarters of London were part of his daily routine. She had been very sweet and very incurious. Whereon Mr. Prohack had said to himself: "She has some diplomatic reason for being an angel." And even if she had not been an angel, even if she had been the very reverse of an angel, Mr. Prohack would not have minded, and his night would not have been thereby upset; for he regarded her as a beautiful natural phenomenon is regarded by a scientist, lovingly and wonderingly, and he was incapable of being irritated for more than a few seconds by anything that might be done or said by this forest creature of the prime who had strayed charmingly into the twentieth century. He was a very fortunate husband.

No! The eventfulness of the night originated in reflection upon the relations between Sissie and Ozzie Morfey. If thoughts could take physical shape and solidity, the events of the night would have amounted to terrible collisions and catastrophes in the devil-haunted abysses of Mr. Prohack's brain. The forces of evil were massacring all opponents between three and four a. m. It was at this period Mr. Prohack was convinced that Sissie, in addition to being an indescribably heartless daughter, was a perfect fool hoodwinked by a perfect ass, and that Ozzie's motive in the affair was not solely or chiefly admiration for Sissie, but admiration of the great fortune which, he had learnt, had fallen into the lap of Sissie's father. After five o'clock, according to the usual sequence, the forces of evil lost ground, and at six-thirty, when the oblong of the looking-glass glimmered faintly in the dawn, Mr. Prohack said roundly: "I am an idiot," and went to sleep.

"Now, darling," said Eve when he emerged from the bathroom. "Don't waste any more time. I want you to give me your opinion about something downstairs."

"Child," said Mr. Prohack. "What on earth do you mean—'wasting time'? Haven't you insisted, and hasn't your precious doctor insisted, that I must read the papers for an hour in bed after I've had my breakfast in bed? Talk about 'wasting time' indeed!"

"Yes, of course darling," Eve concurred, amazingly angelic. "I don't mean you've been wasting time; only I don't want you to waste any *more* time."

"My mistake," said Mr. Prohack.

From mere malice and wickedness he spun out the business of dressing to nearly its customary length, and twice Eve came uneasily into the bedroom to see if she could be of assistance to him. No nurse could have been so beautifully attentive. During one of her absences he slipped furtively downstairs into the drawing-room, where he began to strum on the piano, though the room was yet by no means properly warm. She came after him, admirably pretending not to notice that he was behaving unusually. She was attired for the street, and she carried his hat and his thickest overcoat.

"You're coming out," said she, holding up the overcoat cajolingly.

"That's just where you're mistaken," said he.

"But I want to show you something."

"What do you want to show me?"

"You shall see when you come out."

"Is it by chance the bird of the mountains that I am to see?"

"The bird of the mountains? My dear Arthur! What are you driving at now?"

"Is it the Eagle car?" And as she staggered speechless under the blow he proceeded: "Ah! Did you think you could deceive *me* with your infantile conspiracies and your tacit deceits and your false smiles?"

She blushed.

"Some one's told you. And I do think it's a shame!"

"And who should have told me? Who have I seen? I suppose you think I picked up the information at Putney last night. And haven't you opened all my letters since I was ill, on the pretext of saving me worry? Shall I tell you how I know? I knew from your face. Your face, my innocent, can't be read like a book. It can be read like a newspaper placard, and for days past I've seen on it, 'Extra special. Exciting purchase of a motor-car by a cunning wife.'" Then he laughed. "No, chit. That fellow Oswald Morfey, let it out last night."

When she had indignantly enquired how Oswald Morfey came to be mixed up in her private matters, she said:

"Well, darling, I hope I needn't tell you that my *sole* object was to save you trouble. The car simply had to be bought, and as quickly as possible, so I did it. Need I tell you—"

"You needn't, certainly," Mr. Prohack agreed, and going to the window he lifted the curtain. Yes. There stood a real car, a landaulette, with the illustrous eagle on the front of its radiator, and a real chauffeur by its side. The thing seemed entirely miraculous to Mr. Prohack; and he was rather impressed by his wife's daring and enterprise. After all, it was somewhat of an undertaking for an unworldly woman to go out alone into the world and buy a motor-car and engage a chauffeur, not to mention clothing the chauffeur. But Mr. Prohack kept all his imperturbability.

"Isn't it lovely?"

"Is it paid for?"

"Oh, no!"

"Didn't you have to pay any deposit?"

"Of course I didn't. I gave your name, and that was sufficient. We needn't keep it if we don't like it after the trial run."

"And is it insured?"

"Of course, darling."

"And what about the licence?"

"Oh! The Eagle Company saw to all those stupid things for me."

"And how many times have you forged my signature while I've been lying on a bed of pain?"

"The fact is, darling, I made the purchase in my own name. Now come *along*. We're going round the park."

The way she patted his overcoat when she had got it on to him . . . ! The way she took him by the hand and pulled him towards the drawing-room door . . . ! She had done an exceedingly audacious deed, and her spirits rose as she became convinced from his demeanour that she had not pushed audacity too far. (For she was never absolutely sure of him.)

"Wait one moment," said Mr. Prohack releasing himself and slipping back to the window.

"What's the matter?"

"I merely desired to look at the chauffeur's face. Is it a real chauffeur? Not an automaton?"

"Arthur!"

"You're sure he's quite human?" Mrs. Prohack closed the piano, and then stamped her foot.

"Listen," said Mr. Prohack. "I'm about to trust my life to the mysterious being inside that uniform. Did you imagine that I would trust my life to a perfect stranger? In another half hour he and I may be lying in hospital side by side. And I don't even know his name! Fetch him in, my dove, and allow me to establish relations with him. But confide to me his name first." The expression on Mrs. Prohack's features was one of sublime forbearance under ineffable provocation.

"This is Carthew," she announced, bringing the chauffeur into the drawing-room.

Carthew was a fairly tall, fairly full-bodied, grizzled man of about forty; he carried his cap and one gauntleted glove in one gloved hand, and his long, stiff green overcoat slanted down from his neck to his knees in an unbroken line. He had the impassivity of a policeman.

"Good morning, Carthew," Mr. Prohack began, rising. "I thought that you and I would like to make one another's acquaintance."

"Yes, sir."

Mr. Prohack held out his hand, which Carthew calmly took.

"Will you sit down?"

"Thank you, sir."

"Have a cigarette?" Carthew hesitated.

"Do you mind if I have one of my own, sir?"

"These are Virginian."

"Oh! Thank you, sir." And Carthew took a cigarette from Mr. Prohack's case.

"Light?"

"After you, sir."

"No, no."

"Thank you, sir."

Carthew coughed, puffed, and leaned back a little in his chair. At this point Mrs. Prohack left the room. (She said afterwards that she left the room because she couldn't have borne to be present when Carthew's back broke the back of the chair.)

Carthew sat silent.

"Well," said Mr. Prohack. "What do you think of the car? I ought to tell you I know nothing of motors myself, and this is the first one I've ever had."

"The Eagle is a very good car, sir. If you ask me I should say it was light on tyres and a bit thirsty with petrol. It's one of them cars as anybody can *drive*—if you understand what I mean. I mean anybody can make it *go*. But of course that's only the beginning of what I call driving."

"Just so," agreed Mr. Prohack, drawing by his smile a very faint smile from Carthew. "My son seems to think it's about the best car on the market."

"Well, sir, I've been mixed up with cars pretty well all my life—I mean since I was twenty—"

"Have you indeed!"

"I have, sir—" Carthew neatly flicked some ash on the carpet, and Mr. Prohack thoughtfully did the same—"I have, sir, and I haven't yet come across the best car on the market, if you understand what I mean."

"Perfectly," said Mr. Prohack.

Carthew sat silent.

"But it's a very good car. Nobody could wish for a better. I'll say that," he added at length.

"Had many accidents in your time?"

"I've been touched, sir, but I've never touched anything myself. You can have an accident while you're drawn up alongside the kerb. It rather depends on how many fools have been let loose in the traffic, doesn't it, sir, if you understand what I mean."

"Exactly," said Mr. Prohack.

Carthew sat silent.

"I gather you've been through the war," Mr. Prohack began again.

"I was in the first Territorial regiment that landed in France, and I got my discharge July 1919."

"Wounded?"

"Well, sir, I've been blown up twice and buried once and pitched into the sea once, but nothing ever happened to me."

"I see you don't wear any ribbons."

"It's like this, sir. I've seen enough ribbons on chests since the armistice. It isn't as if I was one of them conscripts."

"No," murmured Mr. Prohack thoughtfully; then brightening: "And as soon as you were discharged you went back to your old job?"

"I did and I didn't, sir. The fact is, I've been driving an ambulance for the City of London, but as soon as I heard of something private I chucked that. I can't say as I like these Corporations. There's a bit too much stone wall about them Corporations, for my taste."

"Family man?" asked Mr. Prohack lightly. "I've two children myself and both of them can drive."

"Really, sir, I am a family man, as ye might say, but my wife and me, we're best apart."

"Sorry to hear that. I didn't want to—"

"Oh, not at all, sir! That's all right. But you see—the war—me being away and all that—I've got the little boy. He's nine."

"Well," said Mr. Prohack, jumping up nervously, "suppose we go and have a look at the car, shall we?"

"Certainly, sir," said Carthew, throwing the end of his cigarette into the fender, and hastening.

"My dove," said Mr. Prohack to his wife in the hall. "I congratulate you on your taste in chauffeurs. Carthew and I have laid the foundations of a lasting friendship."

"I really wonder you asked him to smoke in the drawing-room," Mrs. Prohack critically observed.

"Why? He saved England for me; and now I'm trusting my life to him."

"I do believe you'd *like* there to be a revolution in this country."

"Not at all, angel! And I don't think there'll be one. But I'm taking my precautions in case there should be one."

"He's only a chauffeur."

"That's very true. He was doing some useful work. driving an ambulance to hospitals. But we've stopped that. He's now only a chauffeur to the idle rich."

"Oh, Arthur! I wish you wouldn't try to be funny on such subjects. You know you don't mean it."

Mrs. Prohack was now genuinely reproachful, and the first conjugal joy-ride might have suffered from a certain constraint had it taken place. It did not, however, take place. Just as Carthew was holding out the rug (which Eve's prodigious thoroughness had remembered to buy) preparatory to placing it on the knees of his employers, a truly gigantic automobile drove up to the door, its long bonnet stopping within six inches of the Eagle's tail-lantern. The Eagle looked like nothing at all beside it. Mr. Prohack knew that leviathan. He had many times seen it in front of the portals of his principal club. It was the car of his great club crony, Sir Paul Spinner, the "city magnate."

Sir Paul, embossed with carbuncles, got out, and was presently being presented to Eve,—for the friendship between Mr. Prohack and Sir Paul had been a purely club friendship. Like many such friendships it had had no existence beyond the club, and neither of the cronies knew anything of real interest about the domestic circumstances of the other. Sir Paul was very apologetic to Eve, but he imperiously desired an interview with Mr. Prohack at once. Eve most agreeably and charmingly said that she would take a little preliminary airing in the car by herself, and return for her husband. Mr. Prohack would have preferred her to wait for him; but, though Eve was sagacious enough at all normal times, when she got an idea into her head that idea ruthlessly took precedence of everything else in the external world. Moreover the car was her private creation, and she was incapable of resisting its attractions one minute longer.

II

"I hear you've come into half a million, Arthur," said Paul Spinner, after he had shown himself very friendly and optimistic about Mr. Prohack's health and given the usual bulletin about his own carbuncles and the shortcomings of the club.

"But you don't believe it, Paul."

"I don't," agreed Paul. "Things get about pretty fast in the City and we can size them up fairly well; and I should say, putting two and two together, that a hundred and fifty thousand would be nearer the mark."

"It certainly is," said Mr. Prohack.

If Paul Spinner had suggested fifty thousand, Mr. Prohack would have corrected him, but being full of base instincts he had no impulse to correct the larger estimate, which was just as inaccurate.

"Well, well! It's a most romantic story and I congratulate you on it. No such luck ever happened to me." Sir Paul made this remark in a tone to indicate that he had had practically no luck himself. And he really believed that he had had no luck, though the fact was that he touched no enterprise that failed. Every year he signed a huger cheque for super-tax, and every year he signed it with a gesture signifying that he was signing his own ruin.

This distressing illusion of Sir Paul's was probably due to his carbuncles, which of all pathological phenomena are among the most productive of a pessimistic philosophy. The carbuncles were well known up and down Harley Street. They were always to be cured and they never were cured. They must have cost their owner about as much as his motor-car for upkeep—what with medical fees, travelling and foreign hotels—and nobody knew whether they remained uncured because they were incurable or because the medical profession thought it would be cruel at one stroke to deprive itself of a regular income and Sir Paul of his greatest hobby. The strange thing was that Sir Paul with all his powerful general sagacity and shrewdness, continued firmly, despite endless disappointments, in the mystical faith that one day the carbuncles would be abolished.

"I won't beat about the bush," said he. "We know one another. I came here to talk frankly and I'll talk frankly."

"You go right ahead," Mr. Prohack benevolently encouraged him.

"First of all I should like to give you just the least hint of warning against that fellow Softly Bishop. I daresay you know something about him—"

"I know nothing about him, except the way he looks down his nose. But no man who looks down his nose the way he looks down his nose is going to influence me in the management of my financial affairs. I'm only an official; I should be a lamb in the City; but I have my safeguards, old chap. Thanks for the tip all the same."

Sir Paul Spinner laughed hoarsely, as Mr. Prohack had made him laugh hundreds of times in the course of their friendship. And Mr. Prohack was aware of a feeling of superiority to Sir Paul. The feeling grew steadily in his breast, and he was not quite sure how it originated. Perhaps it was due to a note of dawning obsequiousness in Sir Paul's laugh, reminding Mr. Prohack of the ancient proverb that the jokes of the exalted are always side-splitting.

"As I say," Sir Paul proceeded, "you and I know each other."

Mr. Prohack nodded, with a trace of impatience against unnecessary repetition. Yet he was suddenly struck with the odd thought that Sir Paul certainly did not know him, but only odd bits of him; and he was doubtful whether he knew Sir Paul. He saw an obese man of sixty sitting in the very chair that a few moments ago had been occupied by Carthew the chauffeur, a man with big purplish features and a liverish eye, a man smoking a plutocratic and heavenly cigar and eating it at the same time, a man richly dressed and braided and jewelled, a man whose boots showed no sign of a crease, an obvious millionaire of the old type, in short a man who was practically all prejudices and waste-products. And he wondered why and how that man had become his friend and won his affection. Sir Paul looked positively coarse in Mr. Prohack's frail Chippendale drawing-room, seeming to need for suitable environment the pillared marble and gilt of the vast Club. Well, after having eaten many hundreds of meals and drunk many hundreds of cups of coffee in the grunting society of Sir Paul, all that Mr. Prohack could be sure of knowing about Sir Paul was, first, that he had an absolutely unspotted reputation; second, that he was a very decent, simple-minded, kindly, ignorant fellow (ignorant, that is, in the matters that interested Mr. Prohack); third, that he instinctively mistrusted intellect and brilliance; fourth, that for nearly four years he had been convinced that Germany would win the war, and fifth, that he was capable of astounding freaks of generosity. Stay, there was another item,—Sir Paul's invariable courtesy to the club servants, which courtesy he somehow contrived to combine with continual grumbling. The club servants held him in affection. It was probably this sixth item that outweighed any of the others in Mr. Prohack's favourable estimate of the financier.

And then Mr. Prohack, as in a dream, heard from the lips of Paul Spinner the words, "oil concessions in Roumania." In a flash, in an earthquake, in a blinding vision, Mr. Prohack instantaneously understood the origin of his queer nascent feeling of superiority to old Paul. What he had previously known subconsciously he now knew consciously. Old Paul who had no doubt been paying in annual taxes about ten times the amount of Mr. Prohack's official annual salary; old Paul whose name was the synonym for millions and the rumours of whose views on the stock-markets caused the readers of financial papers to tremble; old Paul was after Mr. Prohack's money! Marvellous, marvellous, thrice marvellous money! . . . It was the most astounding, the most glorious thing that ever happened. Mr. Prohack immediately began to have his misgivings about Sir Paul Spinner. Simultaneously he felt sorry for old Paul. And such was his constraint that he made the motion of swallowing, and had all he could do not to blush.

Mr. Prohack might be a lamb in the City, but he had a highly trained mind, and a very firm grasp of the mere technique of finance. Therefore Sir Paul could explain himself succinctly and precisely in technical terms, and he did so—with much skill and a sort of unconsidered persuasiveness, realising in his rough commonsense that there was no need to drive ideas into Mr. Prohack's head with a steam-hammer, or to intoxicate him with a heady vapour of superlatives.

In a quarter of an hour Mr. Prohack learnt that Sir Paul was promoting a strictly private syndicate as a preliminary to the formation of a big company for the exploitation of certain options on Roumanian oil-territory which Sir Paul held. He learnt about the reports of the trial borings. He learnt about the character and the experience of the expert whom Sir Paul had sent forth to Roumania. He learnt about the world-supply of oil and the world-demand for oil. He learnt about the great rival oil-groups that were then dividing the universe of oil. He had the entire situation clearly mapped on his brain. Next he obtained some startling inside knowledge about the shortage of liquid capital in the circles of "big money," and then followed Sir Paul's famous club disquisition upon the origin of the present unsaleableness of securities and the appalling uneasiness, not to say collapse, of markets.

"What we want is stability, old boy. We want to be left alone. We're being governed to death. Social reform is all right. I believe in it, but everything depends on the pace. Change there ought to be, but it mustn't be like a transformation scene in a pantomime."

And so on.

Mr. Prohack was familiar with it all. He expected the culminating part of the exposition. But Sir Paul curved off towards the navy and the need of conserving in British hands a more than adequate gush of oil for the navy. Mr. Prohack wished that Sir Paul could have left out the navy. And then the Empire was reached. Mr. Prohack wished that Sir Paul could have left out the Empire. Finally Sir Paul arrived at the point.

"I've realised all I can in reason and I'm eighty thousand short. Of course I can get it, get it easily, but not without giving away a good part of my show in quarters that I should prefer to keep quite in the dark. I thought of you—you're clean outside all that sort of thing, and also I know you'd lie low. You might make a hundred per cent; you might make two hundred per cent. But I'll guarantee you this—you won't lose, whatever happens. Of course your capital may not be liquid. You mayn't be able to get at it. I don't know. But I thought it was just worth mentioning to you, and so I said to myself I'd look in here on my way to the City."

Sir Paul Spinner touting for a miserable eighty thousand pounds!

"Hanged if I know *how* my capital is!" said Mr. Prohack.

"I suppose your lawyer knows. Smathe, isn't it? . . . I heard so."

"How soon do you want an answer, yes or no?" Mr. Prohack asked, with a feeling that he had his back to the wall and old Paul had a gun.

"I don't want an answer now, anyhow, old boy. You must think it over. You see, once we've got the thing, I shall set the two big groups bidding against each other for it, and we shall see some fun. And I wouldn't ask them for cash payments. Only for payment in their own shares—which are worth more than money."

"Want an answer to-morrow?"

"Could you make it to-night?" Sir Paul surprisingly answered. "And assuming you say yes—I only say assuming—couldn't you run down with me to Smathe's now and find out about your capital? That wouldn't bind you in any way. I'm particularly anxious you should think it over very carefully. And, by the way, better keep these papers to refer to. But if you can't get at your capital, no use troubling further. That's the first thing to find out."

"I can't go to Smathe's now," Mr. Prohack stammered.

"Why not?"

"Because I'm going out with my wife in the car."

"But, my dear old boy, it's a big thing, and it's urgent."

"Yes, I quite see that. But I've got to go with Marian. I'll tell you what I can do. I'll telephone Smathe that you're coming down to see him yourself, and he must tell you everything. That'll be best. Then I'll let you know my decision later."

As they parted, Sir Paul said:

"We know each other, and you may take it from me it's all right. I'll say no more. However, you think it over."

"Oh! I will!"

Old Paul touting for eighty thousand pounds! A wondrous world! A stupefying world!

Mr. Prohack, who didn't know what to do with a hundred thousand pounds, saw himself the possessor of a quarter of a million, and was illogically thrilled by the prospect. But the risk! Supposing that honest Paul was wrong for once, or suppose he was carried off in the night by a carbuncle,—Mr. Prohack might find himself a pauper with a mere trifle of twenty thousand pounds to his name.

As soon as he had telephoned he resumed his hat and coat and went out on to the pavement to look for his car, chauffeur and wife. There was not a sign of them.

III

Mr. Prohack was undeniably a very popular man. He had few doubts concerning the financial soundness of old Paul's proposition; but he hesitated, for reasons unconnected with finance or with domesticity, about accepting it. And he conceived the idea (which none but a very peculiar man would have conceived) of discussing the matter with some enemy of old Paul's. Now old Paul had few enemies. Mr. Prohack, however, could put his hand on one,—Mr. Francis Fieldfare—the editor of an old-established and lucrative financial weekly, and familiar to readers of that and other organs as "F. F." Mr. Fieldfare's offices were quite close to Mr. Prohack's principal club, of which Mr. Fieldfare also was a member, and Mr. Fieldfare had the habit of passing into the club about noon and reading the papers for an hour, lunching early, and leaving the club again just as the majority of the members were ordering their after-lunch coffee. Mr. Fieldfare pursued this course because he had a deep instinct for being in the minority. Mr. Prohack looked at his watch. The resolution of every man is limited in quantity. Only in mad people is resolution inexhaustible. Mr. Prohack had no more resolution than becomes an average sane fellow, and his resolution to wait for his wife had been seriously tried by the energetic refusal to go with Spinner to see Smathe. It now suddenly gave out.

"Pooh!" said Mr. Prohack. "I've waited long enough for her. She'll now have to wait a bit for me."

And off he went by taxi to his club. The visit, he reflected, would serve the secondary purpose of an inconspicuous re-entry into club-life after absence from it.

He thought:

"They may have had an accident with that car. One day she's certain to have an accident anyhow,—she's so impulsive."

Of course Mr. Fieldfare was not in the morning-room of the club as he ought to have been. That was bound to happen. Mr. Prohack gazed around at the monumental somnolence of the great room, was ignored, and backed out into the hall, meaning to return home. But in the hall he met F. F. just arriving. It surprised and perhaps a little pained Mr. Prohack to observe that F. F. had evidently heard neither of his illness nor of his inheritance.

Mr. Fieldfare was a spare, middle-aged man, of apparently austere habit; short, shabby; a beautiful, resigned face, burning eyes, and a soft voice. He was weighed down, and had been weighed down for thirty years, by a sense of the threatened immediate collapse of society—of all societies, and by the solemn illusion that he more clearly than anybody else understood the fearful trend of events.

Mr. Prohack had once, during the war, remarked on seeing F. F. glance at the tape in the Club: "Look at F. F. afraid lest there may be some good news." Nevertheless he liked F. F.

As editor of a financial weekly, F. F. naturally had to keep well under control his world-sadness. High finance cannot prosper in an atmosphere of world-sadness, and hates it. F. F. ought never to have become the editor of a financial weekly; but he happened to be an expert statistician, an honest man and a courageous man, and an expert in the pathology of stock-markets, and on this score his proprietors excused the slight traces of world-sadness occasionally to be found in the paper. He might have left his post and obtained another; but to be forced by fate to be editor of a financial weekly was F. F.'s chief grievance in life, and he loved a good grievance beyond everything.

"But, my dear fellow," said F. F. with his melancholy ardent glance, when Mr. Prohack had replied suitably to his opening question. "I'd no idea you'd been unwell. I hope it isn't what's called a breakdown."

"Oh, no!" Mr. Prohack laughed nervously. "But you know what doctors are. A little rest has been prescribed."

F. F. gazed at him softly compassionate, as if to indicate that nothing but trouble could be expected under the present political régime. They examined the tape together.

"Things can't go on much longer like this," observed F. F. comprehensively, in front of the morning's messages from the capitals of the world.

"Still," said Mr. Prohack, "we've won the war, haven't we?"

"I suppose we have," said F. F. and sighed.

Mr. Prohack felt that he had no more time for preliminaries, and in order to cut them short started some ingenious but quite inexcusable lying.

"You didn't chance to see old Paul Spinner going out as you came in?"

"No," answered F. F. "Why?"

"Nothing. Only a man in the morning-room was wanting to know if he was still in the Club, and I told him I'd see."

"I hear," said F. F. after a moment, and in a lower voice, "I hear he's getting up some big new oil scheme."

"Ah!" murmured Mr. Prohack, delighted at so favourable a coincidence, with a wonderful imitation of casualness. "And what may that be?"

"Nobody knows. Some people would give a good deal to know. But if I'm any judge of my Spinner they won't know till he's licked off all the cream. It's marvellous to me how Spinner and his sort can keep on devoting themselves to the old ambitions while the world's breaking up. Marvellous!"

"Money, you mean?"

"Personal aggrandisement."

"Well," answered Mr. Prohack, with a judicial, detached air. "I've always found Spinner a very decent agreeable chap."

"Oh, yes! Agreed! Agreed! They're all too confoundedly agreeable for anything, all that lot are."

"But surely he's honest?"

"Quite. As straight a man as ever breathed, especially according to his own lights. All his enterprises are absolutely what is known as 'sound.' They all make rich people richer, and in particular they make *him* richer, though I bet even he's been feeling the pinch lately. They all have."

"Still, I expect old Spinner desires the welfare of the country just as much as any one else. It's not all money with him."

"No. But did you ever know Spinner touch anything that didn't mean money in the first place? I never did. What he and his lot mean by the welfare of the country is the stability of the country *as it is*. They see the necessity for development, improvement in the social scheme. Oh, yes! They see it and admit it. Then they go to church, or they commune with heaven on the golf-course, and their prayer is: 'Give us needed change, O Lord, but not just yet.'"

The pair moved to the morning-room.

"Look here," said Mr. Prohack, lightly, ignoring the earnestness in F. F.'s tone. "Supposing you had a bit of money, say eighty thousand pounds, and the chance to put it into one of old who-is-it's schemes, what would you do?"

"I should be ashamed to have eighty thousand pounds," F. F. replied with dark whispering passion. "And in any case nothing would induce me to have any dealings with the gang."

"Are they all bad?"

"They're all bad, all! They are all anti-social. All! They are all a curse to the country and to all mankind." F. F. had already rung the bell, and he now beckoned coldly to the waitress who entered the room. "Everybody who supports the present Government is guilty of a crime against human progress. Bring me a glass of that brown sherry I had yesterday—you know the one—and three small pieces of cheese."

Mr. Prohack went away to the telephone, and got Paul Spinner at Smathe's office.

"I only wanted to tell you that I've decided to come into your show, if Smathe can arrange for the money. I've thought it all over carefully, and I'm yours, old boy."

He hung up the receiver immediately.

IV

The excursion to the club had taken longer than Mr. Prohack had anticipated, and when he got back home it was nearly lunch-time. No sign of an Eagle car or any other car in front of the house! Mr. Prohack let himself in. The sounds of a table being set came from the dining-room. He opened the door there. Machin met him at the door. Each withdrew from the other, avoiding a collision.

"Your mistress returned?"

"Yes, sir." Machin seemed to hesitate, her mind disturbed.

"Where is she?"

"I was just coming to tell you, sir. She told me to say that she was lying down."

"Oh!"

Disdaining further to interrogate the servant, he hurried upstairs. He had to excuse himself to Eve, and he had also to justify to her the placing of eighty thousand pounds in a scheme which she could not possibly understand and for which there was nothing whatever to show. She would approve, of course; she would say that she had complete confidence in his sagacity, but all the inflections of her voice, all her gestures and glances, would indicate to him that in her opinion he was a singularly ingenuous creature, the natural prey of sharpers, and that the chances of their not being ruined by his incurable simplicity were exceedingly small.

His immense reputation in the Treasury, his sinister fame as the Terror of the departments, would not weigh an atom in her general judgment of the concrete case affecting the fortunes of the Prohack family. Then she would be brave; she would be bravely resigned to the worst. She would kiss his innocence. She would quite unconvincingly assure him, in her own vocabulary, that he was a devil of a fellow and the smartest man in the world.

Further, she would draw in the horns of her secret schemes of expenditure. She would say that she had intended to do so-and-so and to buy so-and-so, but that perhaps it would be better, in view of the uncertainties of destiny, neither to do nor to buy so-and-so. In short, she would succeed in conveying to him the idea that to live with him was like being in an open boat with him adrift in the middle of the stormy Atlantic. She loved to live with him, the compensations were exquisite, and moreover what would be his fate if he were alone? Still, it was like being in an open boat with him adrift in the middle of the stormy Atlantic. And she would cling closer to him and point to the red sun setting among black clouds of tempest. And this would continue until he could throw say about a hundred and sixty thousand pounds into her lap, whereupon she would calmly assert that in her opinion he and she had really been safe all the while on the glassy lake of the Serpentine in a steamer.

"I ought to have thought of all that before," he said to himself. "And if I had I should have bought houses, something for her to look at and touch. And even then she would have suggested that if I hadn't been a coward I could have done better than houses. She would have found in *The Times* every day instances of companies paying twenty and thirty per cent . . . No! It would have been impossible for me to invest the money without losing her esteem for me as a man of business. I wish to heaven I hadn't got any money. So here goes!"

And he burst with assumed confidence into the bedroom. And simultaneously, to intensify his unease, the notion that profiteering was profiteering, whether in war or in peace, and the notion that F. F. was a man of lofty altruistic ideals, surged through his distracted mind.

Eve was lying on the bed. She looked very small on the bed, smaller than usual. At the sound of the door opening she said, without moving her head—he could not see her face from the door:

"Is that you, Arthur?"

"Yes, what's the matter?"

"Just put my cloak over my feet, will you?"

He came forward and took the cloak off a chair.

"What's the matter?" he repeated, arranging the cloak.

"I'm not hurt, dearest, I assure you I'm not—not at all." She was speaking in a faint, weak voice, like a little child's.

"Then you've had an accident?"

She glanced up at him sideways, timidly, compassionately, and nodded.

"You mustn't be upset. I told Machin to go on with her work and not to say anything to you about it. I preferred to tell you myself. I know how sensitive you are where I'm concerned."

Mr. Prohack had to adjust his thoughts, somewhat violently, to the new situation, and he made no reply; but he was very angry about the mere existence of motor-cars. He felt that he had always had a prejudice against motor-cars, and that the prejudice was not a prejudice because it was well-founded.

"Darling, don't look so stern. It wasn't Carthew's fault. Another car ran into us. I told Carthew to drive in the Park, and we went right round the Park in about five minutes. So as I felt sure you'd be a long time with that fat man, I had the idea of running down to Putney—to see Sissie." Eve laughed nervously. "I thought I might possibly bring her home with me. . . . After the accident Carthew put me into a taxi and I came back. Of course he had to stay to look after the car. And then you weren't here when I arrived! Where are you going, dearest?"

"I'm going to telephone for the doctor, of course," said Mr. Prohack quietly, but very irritably.

"Oh, darling! I've sent for the doctor. He wasn't in, they said, but they said he'd be back quite soon and then he'd come at once. I don't really need the doctor. I only sent for him because I knew you'd be so frightfully angry if I didn't."

Mr. Prohack had returned to the bed. He took his wife's hand.

"Feel my pulse. It's all right, isn't it?"

"I can't feel it at all."

"Oh, Arthur, you never could! I can feel your hand trembling, that's what I can feel. Now please don't be upset, Arthur."

"I suppose the car's smashed?"

She nodded:

"It's a bit broken."

"Where was it?"

"It was just on the other side of Putney Bridge, on the tram-lines there."

"Carthew wasn't hurt?"

"Oh, no! Carthew was simply splendid."

"How did it happen, exactly?"

"Oh, Arthur, you with your 'exactlys'! Don't ask me. I'm too tired. Besides, I didn't see it. My eyes were shut." She closed her eyes.

Suddenly she sat up and put her hand on his shoulder, in a sort of appeal, vaguely smiling. He tried to smile, but could not. Then her hand dropped. A totally bewildered expression veiled the anxious kindness in her eyes. The blood left her face until her cheeks were nearly as white as the embroidered cloth on the night-table. Her eyes closed. She fell back. She had fainted. She was just as if dead. Her hand was as cold as the hand of a corpse.

Such was Mr. Prohack's vast experience of life that he had not the least idea what to do in this crisis. But he tremendously regretted that Angmering, Bishop, and the inventor of the motor-car had ever been born. He rushed out on to the landing and loudly shouted: "Machin! Machin! Ring up that d——d doctor again, and if he can't come ring up Dr. Plott at once."

"Yes, sir. Yes, sir."

He rushed back into the bedroom, discovered Eve's smelling-salts, and held them to her nose. Already the blood was mounting again.

"Well, she's not dead, anyway!" he said to himself grimly.

He could see the blood gently mounting, mounting. It was a wonderful, a mysterious and a reassuring sight.

"I don't care so long as she isn't injured internally," he said to himself.

Eve opened her eyes in a dazed look. Then she grinned as if apologetically. Then she cried copiously.

Mr. Prohack heard a car outside. It was Dr. Veiga's. The mere sound of Dr. Veiga's car soothed Mr. Prohack, accused him of losing his head, and made a man of him.

Dr. Veiga entered the bedroom in exactly the same style as on his first visit to Mr. Prohack himself. He had heard the nature of the case from Machin on his way upstairs. He listened to Mr. Prohack, who spoke, in the most deceitful way, as if he had been through scores of such affairs.

"Exactly," said Dr. Veiga, examining Eve summarily. "She sat up. The blood naturally left her head, and she fainted. Fainting is nothing but a withdrawing of blood from the head. Will you ring for that servant of yours, please?"

"I'm positive I'm quite all right, Doctor," Eve murmured.

"Will you kindly not talk," said he. "If you're so positive you're all right, why did you send for me? Did you walk upstairs? Then your legs aren't broken, at least not seriously." He laughed softly.

But shortly afterwards, when Mr. Prohack, admirably dissembling his purposes, crept with dignity out of the room, Dr. Veiga followed him, and shut the door, leaving Machin busy within.

"I don't think that there is any internal lesion," said Dr. Veiga, with seriousness. "But I will not yet state absolutely. She has had a very severe shock and her nerves are considerably jarred."

"But it's nothing physical?"

"My dear sir, of course it's physical. Do you conceive the nerves are not purely physical organs? I can't conceive them as anything but physical organs. Can you?"

Mr. Prohack felt schoolboyish.

"It's you that she's upset about, though. Did you notice she motioned me to give you some of the brandy she was taking? Very sweet of her, was it not? . . . What are you going to do now?"

"I'm going to fetch my daughter."

"Excellent. But have something before you go. You may not know it, but you have been using up nervous tissue, which has to be replaced."

As he was driving down to Putney in a taxi, Mr. Prohack certainly did feel very tired. But he was not so tired as not to insist on helping the engine of the taxi. He pushed the taxi forward with all his might all the way to Putney. He pushed it till his arms ached, though his hands were in his pockets. The distance to Putney had incomprehensibly stretched to nine hundred and ninety-nine miles.

He found Sissie in the studio giving a private lesson to a middle-aged gentleman who ought, Mr. Prohack considered, to have been thinking of his latter end rather than of dancing. He broke up the lesson very abruptly.

"Your mother has had a motor accident. You must come at once."

Sissie came.

"Then it must have been about here," said she, as the taxi approached Putney Bridge on the return journey.

So it must. He certainly had not thought of the *locus* of the accident. He had merely pictured it, in his own mind, according to his own frightened fancy. Yes, it must have been just about there. And yet there was no sign of it in the roadway. Carthew must have had the wounded Eagle removed. Mr. Prohack sat stern and silent. A wondrous woman, his wife! Absurd, possibly, about such matters as investments; but an angel! Her self-forgetfulness, her absorption in *him,*—staggering! The accident was but one more proof of it. He was greatly alarmed about her, for the doctor had answered for nothing. He seemed to have a thousand worries. He had been worried all his life, but the worries that had formed themselves in a trail to the inheritance were worse worries than the old simple ones. No longer did the thought of the inheritance brighten his mind. He somehow desired to go back to former days. Glancing askance at Sissie, he saw that she too was stern. He resumed the hard pushing of the taxi. It was not quite so hard as before, because he knew that Sissie also was pushing her full share.

CHAPTER X

THE THEORY OF IDLENESS

I

WITHIN the next seven days Mr. Prohack had reason to lose confidence in himself as an expert in human nature. "After all," he reflected, "I must have been a very simple-minded man to have thought that I thoroughly understood another human being. Every human being is infinite, and will beat your understanding in the end."

The reference of course was to his wife. Since the automobile accident she had become another person and a more complex person. The climax, or what seemed to be the climax, came one cold morning when she and Mr. Prohack and Sissie and Dr. Veiga were sitting together in the little boudoir beyond the bedroom. They were packed in there because Eve (otherwise Marian) had taken a fancy to the sofa.

Eve was relating to the admired and trusted doctor all her peculiar mental and moral symptoms. She was saying that she could no longer manage the house, could not concentrate her mind on anything, could not refrain from strange caprices, could not remain calm, could not keep her temper, and was the worst conceivable wife for such a paragon as Arthur Prohack. Her daughter alone had saved the household organism from a catastrophe; her daughter Sissie—

"Come here, Sissie!"

Sissie obeyed the call and was suddenly embraced by her mother with deep tenderness. This in front of the doctor! Still more curious was the fact that Sissie, of late her mother's frigid critic, came forward and responded to the embrace almost effusively. The spectacle was really touching. It touched Mr. Prohack, who yet felt as if the floor had yielded under his feet and he was falling into the Tube railway underground. Indeed Mr. Prohack had never had such sensations as drew and quartered him then.

"Well," said Dr. Veiga to Mrs. Prohack in his philosophical-realistic manner, "I've been marking time for a week. I shall now proceed to put you right. You can't sleep. You will sleep to-night—I shall send you something. I suppose it isn't your fault that you've been taking the digestive tonic I sent you last thing at night under the impression that it was a sedative, in spite of the label. But it is regrettable. As for your headaches, I will provide a pleasing potion. As for this sad lack of application, don't attempt application. As for your strange caprices, indulge them. One thing is essential. You must go away to the sea. You must go to Frinton-on-Sea. It is an easy journey. There is a Pullman car on the morning train, and the air is unrivalled for your—shall I say?—idiosyncrasy."

"Yes, darling mother," said Sissie. "You must go away, and father and I will take you."

"Of course!" confirmed Mr. Prohack, with an imitation of pettishness, as though he had been steadily advocating a change of scene for days past; but he had done nothing of the kind.

"Oh!" Eve cried piteously, "that's the one thing I can't do!"

Dr. Veiga laughed. "Afraid of the expense, I suppose?"

"No," Eve answered with seriousness. "My husband has just made a very fortunate investment, which means a profit of at least a hundred thousand pounds—like that!" She snapped her fingers and laughed lightly.

Here was another point to puzzle an expert in human nature. Instead of being extremely incredulous and apprehensive about the vast speculation with Sir Paul, Eve had in truth accepted it for a gold-mine. She did not assume satisfaction; she really was satisfied. Her satisfaction was absurd, and nothing that Mr. Prohack could say would diminish it. She had already begun to spend the financial results of the speculation with enormous verve. For instance, she had hired another Eagle to take the place of the wounded Eagle, without uttering a word to her husband of what she had done. Mr. Prohack could see the dregs of his bank-balance; and in a dream he had had glimpses of a sinister edifice at the bottom of a steep slope, the building being the Bankruptcy Court.

"Is it a railway strike you're afraid of?" demanded Dr. Veiga cruelly.

And Eve replied with sweetness:

"I can't leave London until my son Charlie comes back from Glasgow, and he's written me to say he'll be here next week."

A first-rate example, this, of her new secretiveness! She had said absolutely nothing to Mr. Prohack about a letter from Charlie.

"When did you hear that?" Mr. Prohack might well have asked; but he was too loyal to her to betray her secretiveness by such a question. He did not wish the Portuguese quack to know that he, the husband, was kept in the dark about anything whatever. He had his ridiculous dignity, had Mr. Prohack, and all his motives were mixed motives. Not a perfectly pure motive in the whole of his volitional existence!

However, Sissie put the question in her young blundering way. "Oh, mother dear! You never told us!"

"I received the letter the day before yesterday," Eve continued gravely. "And Charlie is certainly not coming home to find me away."

For two entire days she had had the important letter and had concealed it. Mr. Prohack was disturbed.

"Very well," Dr. Veiga concurred. "It doesn't really matter whether you go to Frinton now or next month, or even next year but one. You're a powerful woman and you'll last a long time yet, especially if you don't worry. I won't call for about a week, and if you'd like to consult another doctor, do." He smiled on her in an avuncular manner, and rose.

Whereupon Mr. Prohack also jumped up.

"I'm not worrying," she protested, with a sweet, pathetic answering smile. "Yes, I am. Yes, I am. I'm worrying because I know I'm worrying my poor husband." She went quickly to her poor husband and kissed him lavishly. Eve was an artist in kissing, and never a greater artist than at that moment. And now Mr. Prohack, though still to the physical eye a single individual, became two Mr. Prohacks. There was the Mr. Prohack who strongly deprecated this departure from the emotional reserve which is one of the leading and sublimest characteristics of the British governing-class. And there was the Mr. Prohack, all nerves and heart and humanity, who profoundly enjoyed the demonstration of a woman's affection, disordered and against the rules though the demonstration might be. The first Mr. Prohack blushed and hated himself for blushing. The second was quite simply enraptured and didn't care who knew it.

"Dr. Veiga," Eve appealed, clinging to Mr. Prohack's coat. "It is my husband who needs looking after. He is not making any progress, and it is my fault. And let me tell you that you've been neglecting him for me."

She was a dramatic figure of altruism, of the everlasting sacrificial feminine. She was quite possibly absurd, but beyond doubt she was magnificent. Mr. Prohack felt ashamed of himself, and the more ashamed because he considered that he was in quite tolerable health.

"Mother," murmured Sissie, with a sweetness of which Mr. Pro-

HARRIS PUBLIC LIBRARY PRESTON

hack had imagined her to be utterly incapable. "Come and sit down."

And Eve, guided by her daughter, the callous, home-deserting dancing-mistress, came and sat down.

II

"My dear sir," said Dr. Veiga. "There is nothing at all to cause alarm. She will gradually recover. Believe me."

He and Mr. Prohack and Sissie were conspiring together in the dining-room, the drawing-room being at that hour and on that day under the dominion of servants with brushes.

"But what's the matter with her? What is it?"

"Merely neurasthenia—traumatic neurasthenia."

"But what's that?" Mr. Prohack spoke low, just as though his wife could overhear from the boudoir above and was listening to them under the impression that they were plotting against her life.

"It's a morbid condition due to a violent shock."

"But how? You told me the other day that it was purely physical."

"Well," said Dr. Veiga. "It is, because it must be. But I assure you that if a post-mortem were to be held on Mrs. Prohack—"

"Oh, doctor, please!" Sissie stopped him resentfully.

The doctor paused and then continued: "There would be no trace of any morbid condition in any of the organs."

"Then how do you explain it?"

"We don't explain it," cried Dr. Veiga, suddenly throwing the onus on the whole medical profession. "We can't. We don't know."

"It's very, very unsatisfactory, all this ignorance."

"It certainly is. But did you suppose that medical science, alone among all sciences, had achieved finality and omniscience? We've reached the state of knowing that we don't know, and that's something. I hope I'm not flattering you by talking like this. I only do it to people whom I suspect to be intelligent. But of course if you'd prefer the omniscient bedside manner you can have it without extra charge."

Mr. Prohack thought, frightened: "I shall be making a friend of this quack soon, if I'm not careful."

"And by the way, about *your* health," Dr. Veiga proceeded, after having given further assurances as to his other patient. "Mrs. Prohack was perfectly correct. You're not making progress. The fact is, you're bored. You haven't organised your existence, and the lack of organisation is reacting on your health."

"Something is reacting on his health," Sissie put in. "I'm not at all pleased." She was now not Mr. Prohack's daughter but his aunt.

"How can I organise my existence?" Mr. Prohack burst out crossly. "I haven't got any existence to organise. I haven't got anything to do. I thought I had too much to do, the other day. Illusion. Of course I'm bored. I feel all right, but bored I am. And it's your fault."

"It is," the doctor admitted. "It is my fault. I took you for a person of commonsense, and so I didn't tell you that two and two make four and a lot more important things of the same sort. I ought to have told you. You've taken on the new profession of being idle—it's essential for you—but you aren't treating it seriously. You have to be a *professionally* idle man. Which means that you haven't got a moment to spare. When I advised you to try idleness, I didn't mean you to be idle idly. That's worse than useless. You've got to be idle busily. You aren't doing half enough. Do you ever have a Turkish bath?"

"No. Never could bear the idea of them."

"Well, you will kindly take two Turkish baths a week. You can be massaged at the same time. A Turkish bath is as good as a day's hunting, as far as exercise goes, but you must have more exercise. Do you dance? I see you don't. You had better begin dancing. There is no finer exercise. I absolutely prescribe it."

At this juncture Mr. Prohack was rather relieved that the sound of an unaccustomed voice in the hall drew his daughter out of the dining-room. When she had gone Dr. Veiga went on, in a more confidential tone:

"There's another point. An idle man who really knows his business will visit his tailor's, his hosier's, his bootmaker's, his barber's much oftener and much more conscientiously than you do. You've got a mind above clothes—of course. So have I. I take a wicked pleasure in being picturesquely untidy. But I'm not a patient. My life is a great lark. Yours isn't. Yours is serious. You have now a serious profession, idleness. Bring your mind down to clothes. I say this, partly because to be consistently well-dressed means much daily expenditure of time, and partly because really good clothes have a distinctly curative effect on the patient who wears them. Then again—"

Mr. Prohack was conscious of a sudden joyous uplifting of the spirit.

"Here!" said he, interrupting Dr. Veiga with a grand gesture. "Have a cigar."

"I cannot, my friend." Dr. Veiga looked at his watch.

"You must. Have a corona." Mr. Prohack moved to the cigar cabinet which he had recently purchased.

"No. My next patient is awaiting me in Hyde Park Gardens at this moment."

"Let him die!" exclaimed Mr. Prohack ruthlessly. "You've got to have a cigar with me. Look. I'll compromise. I'll make it a half-corona. You can charge me as if for another consultation."

The doctor's foreign eyes twinkled as he sat down and struck a match.

"You thought I was a quack," he said maliciously, and maliciously he seemed to intensify his foreign accent.

"I did," admitted Mr. Prohack with candour.

"So I am," said Dr. Veiga. "But I'm a fully qualified quack, and all really good doctors are quacks. They have to be. They wouldn't be worth anything if they weren't. Medicine owes a great deal to quacks."

"Tell me something about some of your cases," said Mr. Prohack imperatively. "You're one of the most interesting men I've ever met. So now you know. We want some of your blood transfused. into the English character. You've got a soul above medicine as well as clothes."

"All good doctors have," said Dr. Veiga. "My life is a romance."

"And so shall mine be," said Mr. Prohack.

III

When at length Mr. Prohack escorted Dr. Veiga out into the hall he saw Sissie kissing Eliza Brating with much affection on the front-door step. They made an elegant group for a moment and then Eliza Brating departed hurriedly, disappearing across the street behind Dr. Veiga's attendant car.

"Now I'll just repeat once more to both of you," resumed Dr. Veiga, embracing father and daughter in one shrewd glance. "You've nothing to worry about upstairs." He indicated the boudoir by a movement of his somewhat tousled head. "But you've got just a little to worry about here." And he indicated Mr. Prohack.

"I know," said Sissie with assurance. "But I shall look after him, doctor. You can rely on me. I understand—both cases."

"Well, there's one good thing," said Sissie, following her father into the dining-room after the doctor had gone. "I've done with that foolish Eliza. I knew it couldn't last and it hasn't. Unless I'm there all the time to keep my eye on everything—of course it all goes to pieces. That girl is the biggest noodle . . . !"

"But haven't I just seen you and her joined in the deepest affection?"

"Naturally I had to kiss her. But I've finished with her. And what's more, she knows what I think of her. She never liked me."

"Sissie," said Mr. Prohack, "you shock me." And indeed he was genuinely shocked, for he had always thought that Sissie was different from other girls; that she had all the feminine qualities without any of the feminine defects. Yes, he had thought that she might develop into a creature more perfect even than Marian. And here she was talking and behaving exactly as men at the club would relate of their own conventional women.

Sissie gazed firmly at her father, as it were half in pity and half in disdain. Did the innocent fellow not then understand the nature of women? Or was he too sentimental to admit it, too romantic to be a realist?

"Would you believe," said Sissie, "that although I was there last night and told her exactly what to do, she's had a quarrel this morning with the landlord of the studio? Well, she has. You know the A. R. A. on the first floor has been making a lot of silly complaints about the noise—music and so on—every night. And some other people have complained. *I* could have talked the landlord round in ten minutes! Eliza doesn't merely not talk him round,—she quarrels with him! Of course it's all up. And as if that wasn't enough, a County Council inspector has been round asking about a music and dancing licence. We shall either have to give up business altogether or else move somewhere else. Eliza says she knows of another studio. Well, I shall write her to-night and tell her she can have my share of the fittings and furniture and go where she likes, but I shan't go with her. And if she never liked me I can honestly say I never liked her. And I don't want to run a dancing studio any more, either. Why should I, after all? We *were* the new poor. Now we're the new rich. Well, we may as well *be* the new rich."

Mr. Prohack was now still more shocked. Nay, he was almost frightened. And yet he wasn't either shocked or frightened, in the centre of his soul. He was rather triumphant,—not about his daughter with the feet of clay, but about himself.

"But I shan't give up teaching dancing entirely," said Sissie.

"No?" He wondered what would come next.

"No! I shall teach you."

"Indeed you won't!" He instinctively recoiled.

"Yes, I shall. I promised the doctor he could rely on me. You'll buy a gramophone, and we'll have the carpet up in the drawing-room. Oh! You startled deer, do you want to run back into the depths of the forest? . . . Father, you are the funniest father that ever was." She marched to him and put her hand on his shoulder and just twitched his beard. "I can look after you quite as well as mother can. We're pals, aren't we?"

"Yes. Like the tiger and the lamb. You've got hold of my silky fleece already."

IV

Mr. Prohack sat in the dining-room alone. The room was now heated by an electric radiator which Eve had just bought for the sake of economy. But her economy was the economy of the rich, for the amount of expensive current consumed by that radiator was prodigious, while the saving it effected in labour, cleanliness and atmospheric purity could certainly not have been measured without a scientific instrument adapted to the infinitely little. (Still, Machin admired and loved it.) Mr. Prohack perceived that all four bars of it were brightly incandescent, whereas three bars would have been ample to keep the room warm. He ought to get up and turn a bar off. . . . He had a hundred preoccupations. His daughter had classed him with the new rich. He resented the description, but could he honestly reject it? All his recent troubles sprang from the new riches. If he had not inherited from a profiteer he would assuredly have been at his office in the Treasury, earning an honest living, at that very moment. For only sick persons of plenteous independent means are ever prescribed for as he had been prescribed for; the others either go on working and making the best of such health as is left to them, or they die. If he had not inherited from a profiteer he would not have had a car and the car would not have had an accident and he would not have been faced with the prospect (as he was faced with it) of a legal dispute, to be fought by him on behalf of the insurance company, with the owner of the colliding car. (The owner of the colliding car was a young woman as to whose veracity Carthew had had some exceedingly hard things to say.) Mr. Prohack would have settled the matter, but neither Eve nor the insurance company would let him settle it. And if the car had not had an accident Eve would not have had traumatic neurasthenia, with all its disconcerting reactions on family life. And if he had not inherited from a profiteer, Charlie would not have gone off to Glasgow,—he had heard odds and ends of strange tales as to Charlie's doings in Glasgow,—not in the least reassuring! And if he had not inherited from a profiteer Sissie would not have taken a share in a dancing studio and might never have dangerously danced with that worm Oswald Morfey. And if he had not inherited from a profiteer he would not have been speculating, with a rich chance of more profiteering, in Roumanian oil with Paul Spinner. In brief—well, he ought to get up and turn off a bar of that wasteful radiator.

Yet he was uplifted, happy. Not because of his wealthy ease. No! A week or two ago he had only to think of his fortune to feel uplifted and happy. But now!

No! He was uplifted and happy now for the simple reason that he had caught the romance of the doctor's idea of taking idleness seriously and practising it as a profession. If circumstances forced him to be idle, he would be idle in the grand manner. He would do everything that the doctor had suggested, and more. (The doctor saw life like a poet. He might be a cross between a comedian and a mountebank, but he was a great fellow.) Every species of idleness should have its appointed hour. In the pursuit of idleness he would become the busiest man in London. A definite programme would be necessary. Strict routine would be necessary. No more loafing about! He hankered after routine as the drunkard after alcohol. Routine was what he had been missing. The absence of routine, and naught else, was retarding his recovery. (Yes, he knew in his heart that what they all said was true,—he was not getting better.) His own daughter had taught him wisdom. Inevitably, unavoidably, he was the new rich. Well, he would be the new rich thoroughly. No other aim was logical. . . . Let the radiator burn!

CHAPTER XI

NEURASTHENIA CURED

I

THREE days later Mr. Prohack came home late with his daughter in the substituted car. He had accompanied Sissie to Putney for the final disposition of the affairs of the dance-studio, and had witnessed her blighting politeness to Eliza Brating and Eliza Brating's blighting politeness to her. The last kiss between these two young women would have desolated the heart of any man whose faith in human nature was less strong than Mr. Prohack's. "I trust that the excellent Eliza is not disfigured for life," he had observed calmly in the automobile. "What are you talking about, father?" Sissie had exclaimed, suspicious. "I was afraid her lips might be scorched. You feel no pain yourself, my child, I hope?" He made the sound of a kiss. After this there was no more conversation in the car during the journey. Arrived home, Sissie said nonchalantly that she was going to bed.

"Burn my lips first," Mr. Prohack implored.

"Father!" said she, having kissed him. "You are simply terrible."

"I am a child," he replied. "And you are my grandmother."

"You wait till I give you your next dancing-lesson," Sissie retorted, turning and threatening him from the stairs. "It won't be as mild as this afternoon's."

He smiled, giving an imitation of the sphinx. He was happy enough as mortals go. His wife was perhaps a little better. And he was gradually launching himself into an industrious career of idleness. Also, he had broken the ice,—the ice, that is to say, of tuition in dancing. Not a word had been spoken abroad in the house about the first dancing-lesson. He had had it while Mrs. Prohack was, in theory at least, paying calls; at any rate she had set forth in the car. Mr. Prohack and Sissie had rolled up the drawing-room carpet and moved the furniture themselves. Mr. Prohack had unpacked the gramophone in person. They had locked the drawing-room door. At the end of the lesson they had relaid the carpet and replaced the furniture and enclosed the gramophone and unlocked the door, and Mr. Prohack had issued from the drawing-room like a criminal. The thought in his mind had been that he was no end of a dog and of a brave dog at that. Then he sneered at himself for thinking such a foolish thought. After all, what was there in learning to dance? But the sneer was misplaced. His original notion that he had done something courageous and wonderful was just a notion.

The lesson had favoured the new nascent intimacy with his daughter. Evidently she was a born teacher as well as a born dancer. He perceived in two minutes how marvellous her feet were. She guided him with pressures light as a feather. She allowed herself to be guided with an intuitive responsiveness that had to be felt to be believed. Her exhortations were delicious, her reprimands exquisite, her patience was infinite. Further, she said that he had what she called "natural rhythm," and would learn easily and satisfactorily. Best of all, he had been immediately aware of the physical benefit of the exercise. The household was supposed to know naught of the affair, but the kitchen knew a good deal about it somehow; the kitchen was pleasantly and rather condescendingly excited, and a little censorious, for the reason that nobody in the kitchen had ever before lived in a house the master of which being a parent of adult children took surreptitious lessons in dancing; the thing was unprecedented, and therefore of course intrinsically reprehensible. Mr. Prohack guessed the attitude of the kitchen, and had met Machin's respectful glance with a self-conscious eye.

He now bolted the front-door and went upstairs extinguishing the lights after him. Eve had told her husband and child that she should go to bed early. He meant to have a frolicsome, teasing chat with her, for the doctor had laid it down that light conversation would assist the cure of traumatic neurasthenia. She would not be asleep, and even if she were asleep she would be glad to awaken, because she admired his style of gossip when both of them were in the vein for it. He would describe for her the evening at the studio humorously, in such a fashion as to confirm her in her righteous belief that the misguided Sissie had seen the maternal wisdom and quitted dance-studios for ever.

The lamps were out in the bedroom. She slept. He switched on a light, but her bed was empty; it had not been occupied!

"Marian!" he called in a low voice, thinking that she might be in the boudoir.

And if she was in the boudoir she must be reclining in the dark there. He ascertained that she was not in the boudoir. Then he visited both the drawing-room and the dining-room. No Marian anywhere! He stood a moment in the hall and was in a mind to ring for Machin—he could see from a vague illumination at the entrance to the basement steps that the kitchen was still inhabited —but just then all the servants came upwards on the way to the attics, and at the strange spectacle of their dancing master in the hall they all grew constrained and either coughed or hurried as though they ought not to be caught in the act of retiring to bed.

Mr. Prohack, as it were, threw a lasso over Machin, who was the last of the procession.

"Where is your mistress, Machin?" He tried to be matter-of-fact, but something unusual in his tone apparently started her.

"She's gone to bed, sir. She told me to put her hot-water bag in the bed early."

"Oh! Thanks! Good-night."

"Good-night, sir."

He could not persuade himself to call an alarm. He could not even inform Machin that she was mistaken, for to do so would have been equivalent to calling an alarm. Hesitating and inactive he allowed the black-and-white damsels and the blue cook to disappear. Nor would he disturb Sissie—yet. He had first to get used to the singular idea that his wife had vanished from home. Could this vanishing be one of the effects of traumatic neurasthenia? He hurried about and searched all the rooms again, looking with absurd carefulness, as if his wife were an insignificant object that might have dropped unperceived under a chair or behind a couch.

Then he telephoned to her sister, enquiring in a voice of studied casualness. Eve was not at her sister's. He had known all the while that she would not be at her sister's. Being unable to recall the number, he had had to consult the telephone book. His instinct now was to fetch Sissie, whose commonsense had of late impressed him more and more; but he repressed the instinct, holding that he ought to be able to manage the affair alone. He could scarcely say to his daughter: "Your mother has vanished. What am I to do?" Moreover, feeling himself to be the guardian of Marian's reputation for perfect sanity, he desired not to divulge her disappearance, unless obliged to do so. She might return at any moment. She must return very soon. It was inconceivable that anything should have "happened" in the Prohack family. . . .

Almost against his will he looked up "Police Stations" in the telephone-book. There were scores of police stations. The nearest seemed to be that of Mayfair. He demanded the number. To demand the number of the police station was like jumping into bottomless cold water. In a detestable dream he gave his name and address and asked if the police had any news of a street accident. Yes, several. He described his wife. He said, reflecting wildly, that she was not very tall and rather plump; dark hair. Dress? Dark blue. Hat and mantle? He could not say. Age? A queer impulse here. He knew that she hated the mention of her real age, and so he said thirty-nine. No! The police had no news of such a person. But the polite firm voice on the wire said that it would telephone to other stations and would let Mr. Prohack hear immediately if there was anything to communicate. Wonderful organisation, the London police force!

As he hung up the receiver he realised what had occurred and what he had done. Marian had mysteriously disappeared and he had informed the police,—he, Arthur Prohack, C. B. What an awful event!

His mind ran on the consequences of traumatic neurasthenia. He put on his hat and overcoat and unbolted the front-door as silently as he could—for he still did not want anybody in the house to know the secret—and went out into the street. What to do? A ridiculous move! Did he expect to find her lying in the gutter? He walked to the end of the dark street and peered into the cross-street, and returned. He had left the front-door open. As he re-entered the house he descried in a corner of the hall, a screwed-up telegraph-envelope. Why had he not noticed it before? He snatched at it. It was addressed to "Mrs. Prohack."

Mr. Prohack's soul was instantaneously bathed in heavenly solace. Traumatic neurasthenia had nothing to do with Eve's disappearance! His bliss was intensified by the fact that he had said not a word to the servants and had not called Sissie. And it was somewhat impaired by the other fact that he had been ass enough to tell the police. He was just puzzling his head to think what misfortune could have called his wife away—not that the prospect of any misfortune much troubled him now that Eve's vanishing was explained—when through the doorway he saw a taxi drive up. Eve emerged from the taxi.

II

He might have gone out and paid the fare for her, but he stayed where he was, in the doorway, thinking with beatific relief that after all nothing had "happened" in the family.

"Ah!" he said, in the most ordinary, complacent, quite undisturbed tone, "I was just beginning to wonder where you'd got to. We've been back about five minutes, Sissie and I, and Sissie's gone to bed. I really don't believe she knows you were out."

Mrs. Prohack came urgently towards him, pushing the door to behind her with a careless loud bang. The bang might waken the entire household, but Mrs. Prohack did not care. Mrs. Prohack kissed him without a word. He possessed in his heart a barometric scale of her kisses, and this was a set-fair kiss, a kiss with a somewhat violent beginning and a reluctant close. Then she held her cheek for him to kiss. Both cheek and lips were freshly cold from the night air. Mr. Prohack was aware of an immense romantic felicity. And he immediately became flippant, not aloud, but secretly, to hide himself from himself.

He thought:

"It's a positive fact that I've been kissing this girl of a woman for a quarter of a century, and she's fat."

But beneath his flippancy and beneath his felicity there was a lancinating qualm, which, if he had expressed it he would have expressed thus:

"If anything *did* happen to her, it would be the absolute ruin of me."

The truth was that his felicity frightened him. Never before had he been seriously concerned for her well-being. The reaction from grave alarm lighted up the interior of his mysterious soul with a revealing flash of unique intensity.

"What are all these lights burning for?" she murmured. Lights were indeed burning everywhere. He had been in a mood to turn on but not to turn off.

"Oh!" he said. "I was just wandering about."

"I'll go straight upstairs," she said, trying to be as matter-of-fact as her Arthur appeared to be.

When he had leisurely set the whole of the ground-floor to rights, he followed her. She was waiting for him in the boudoir. She had removed her hat and mantle, and lighted one of the new radiators, and was sitting on the sofa.

"There came a telegram from Charlie," she began. "I was crossing the hall just as the boy reached the door. So I opened the door myself. It was from Charlie to say that he would be at the Grand Babylon Hotel to-night."

"Charlie! The Grand Babylon! . . . Not Buckingham Palace."

Eve ignored his crude jocularity.

"It seems I ought to have received it early in the afternoon. I was so puzzled I didn't know what to do—I just put my things on and went off to the hotel at once. It wasn't till after I was in the taxi that I remembered I ought to have told the servants where I was going. That's why I hurried back. I wanted to get back before you did. Charlie suggested telephoning from the hotel, but I wouldn't let him on any account."

"Why not?"

"Well, I thought you might be upset and wonder what on earth was going on."

"What was going on?" Mr. Prohack repeated, gazing at her childlike maternal serious face, whose wistfulness affected him in an extraordinary way. "What on earth are you insinuating?"

No! It was inconceivable that this pulsating girl perched on the sofa should be the mother of the mature and independent Charles.

"Charlie's *staying* at the Grand Babylon Hotel," said Eve, as though she were saying that Charlie had forged a cheque or blown up the Cenotaph.

Even the imperturbable man of the world in front of her momentarily blenched at the news.

"More fool him!" observed Mr. Prohack.

"Yes, and he's got a bedroom and a private sitting-room and a bathroom, and a room for a secretary—"

"Hence a secretary," Mr. Prohack put in.

"Yes, and a secretary. And he dictates things to the secretary all the time, and the telephone's always going,—yes, even at this time of night. He must be spending enormous sums. So of course I hurried back to tell you."

"You did quite right, my pet," said Mr. Prohack. "A good wife should share these tit-bits with her husband at the earliest possible moment."

He was really very like what in his more conventional moments he would have said a woman was like. If Eve had taken the affair lightly he would without doubt have remonstrated, explaining that such an affair ought by no means to be taken lightly. But seeing that she took it very seriously, his instinct was to laugh at it, though in fact he was himself extremely perturbed by this piece of news, which confirmed, a hundredfold and in the most startling manner, certain sinister impressions of his own concerning Charlie's deeds in Glasgow. And he assumed the gay attitude, not from a desire to reassure his wife, but from mere contrariness. Positively the strangest husband that ever lived, and entirely different from normal husbands!

Then he saw tears hanging in Eve's eyes,—tears not of resentment against his lack of sympathy, tears of bewilderment and perplexity. She simply did not understand his attitude. And he sat down close by her on the sofa and solaced her with three kisses. She was singularly attractive in her alternations of sagacity and helplessness.

"But it's awful," she whimpered. "The boy must be throwing money away at the rate of twenty or twenty-five pounds a day."

"Very probably," Mr. Prohack agreed.

"Where's he getting it from?" she demanded. "He must be getting it from somewhere."

"I expect he's made it. He's rather clever, you know."

"But he can't have made money like that."

"People do, sometimes."

"Not honestly,—you know what I mean, Arthur!" This was an earthquaking phrase to come from a mother's lips.

"And yet," said Mr. Prohack, "everything Charlie did used to be right for you."

"But he's carrying on just like an adventurer! I've read in reports of trials about people carrying on just like that. A fortnight ago he hadn't got fifty pounds cash in the world, and now he's living like a millionaire at the Grand Babylon Hotel! Arthur, what are you going to do about it? Couldn't you go and see him to-night?"

"Now listen to me," Mr. Prohack began in a new tone, taking her hands. "Supposing I did go and see him to-night, what could I say to him?"

"Well, you're his father."

"And you're his mother. What did *you* say to him?"

"Oh! I didn't say anything. I only said I should have been very glad if he could have arranged to sleep at home as usual, and he said he was sorry he couldn't because he was so busy."

"You didn't tell him he was carrying on like an adventurer?"

"Arthur! How could I?"

"But you'd like *me* to tell him something of the sort. All that I can say, you could say—and that is, enquire in a friendly way what he has done, is doing, and hopes to do."

"But—"

"Yes, my innocent creature. You may well pause." He caressed her, and she tried to continue in unhappiness, but could not. "You pause because there is nothing to say."

"You're his father at any rate," she burst out triumphantly.

"That's not his fault. You ought to have thought of all this over twenty years ago, before Charlie was born, before we were married, before you met me. To become a parent is to accept terrible risks. I'm Charlie's father. What then? Am I to give him orders as to what he must do and what he mustn't? This isn't China and it isn't the eighteenth century. He owes nothing whatever to me, or to you. If we were starving and he had plenty, he would probably consider it his duty to look after us; but that's the limit of what he owes us. Whereas nothing can put an end to our responsibility towards him. You see, we brought him here. We thought it would be so nice to have children, and so Charlie arrived. He didn't choose his time, and he didn't choose his character, nor his education, nor his chance. If he had his choice you may depend he'd have chosen differently. Do you want me, on the top of all that, to tell him that he must obediently accept something else from us—our code of conduct? It would be mere cheek, and with all my shortcomings I'm incapable of impudence, especially to the young. He was our slave for nearly twenty years. We did what we liked with him; and if Charlie fails now it simply means that we've failed. Besides, how can you be sure that he's carrying on like an adventurer? He may be carrying on like a financial genius. Perhaps we have brought a giant to earth. We can't believe it of course, because we haven't got enough faith in ourselves, but later on we may be compelled to believe it. Naturally if Charlie crashes after a showy flight, then he won't be a financial genius,—he'll only be an adventurer, and there may be some slight trouble in the law courts,—there usually is. That is where we shall have to come forward and pay for the nice feeling of having children. And, remember, we shan't be in a position to upbraid Charlie. He could silence us with one question, to which we could find no answer: 'Why did you get married, you two?' However, my pet, let us hope for the best. It's not yet a crime to live at great price at the Grand Babylon Hotel. Quite possibly your son has not yet committed any crime, whatever. If he succeeds in making a huge fortune and in keeping it, he will not commit any crime. Rich men never do. They can't. They never even commit murder. There is no reason why they should. Whatever they do, it is no worse than an idiosyncrasy. Now tell me what our son talked about."

"Well, he didn't talk much. He—he wasn't expecting me."

"Did he ask after me?"

"I told him about you. He asked about the car."

"He didn't ask after me, but he asked after the car. Nothing very original there, is there? Any son would behave like that. He must do better than that if he doesn't mean to end as an adventurer. I must go and see him, and offer him, very respectfully, some advice."

"Arthur, I insist that he shall come here. It is not proper that you should go running after *him*."

"Pooh, my dear! I'm rich enough myself to run after him without being accused of snobbishness or lion-hunting or anything of that kind."

"Oh! Arthur!" sobbed Eve. "Don't you think you've been funny quite long enough?" She then openly wept.

The singular Mr. Prohack was apparently not in the least moved by his wife's tears. He and she alone in the house were out of bed; there was no chance of their being disturbed. He did not worry about his adventurous son. He did not worry about the possibility of Oswald Morfey having a design to convert his daughter into Mrs. Oswald Morfey. He did not worry about the fate of the speculation in which he had joined Sir Paul Spinner. Nor did he worry about the malady called traumatic neurasthenia. As for himself he fancied that he had not for years felt better than he felt at that moment. He was aware of the most delicious sensation of sharing a perfect nocturnal solitude with his wife. He drew her towards him until her acquiescent head lay against his waistcoat. He held her body in his arms, and came deliberately to the conclusion that to be alive was excellent.

Eve's body was as yielding as that of a young girl. To Mr. Prohack, who of course was the dupe of an illusion, it had an absolutely enchanting girlishness. She sobbed and she sobbed, and Mr. Prohack let her sob. He loosed the grip of his arms a little, so that her face, free of his waistcoat, was turned upwards in the direction of the ceiling; and then he very caressingly wiped her eyes with his own handkerchief. He gave an elaborate care to the wiping of her eyes. For some minutes it was a Sisyphean labour, for what he did she immediately undid; but after a time the sobs grew less frequent, and at length they ceased; only her lips trembled at intervals.

Mr. Prohack said ingratiatingly:

"And whose fault is it if I'm funny? Answer, you witch."

"I don't know," Eve murmured tremblingly and not quite articulately.

"It's your fault. Do you know that you gave me the fright of my life to-night, going out without saying where you were going to? Do you know that you put me into such a state that I've been telephoning to police-stations to find out whether there'd been any street accidents happening to a woman of your description? I was so upset that I daren't even go upstairs and call Sissie."

"You said you'd only been back five minutes when I came," Eve observed in a somewhat firmer voice.

"I did," said Mr. Prohack. "But that was neither more nor less than a downright lie. You see I was in such a state that I had to pretend, to both you and myself, that things aren't what they are. . . . And then, without the slightest warning, you suddenly arrive without a scratch on you. You aren't hurt. You aren't even dead. It's a scandalous shame that a woman should be able, by merely arriving in a taxi, to put a sensible man into such a paroxysm of satisfaction as you put me into a while ago. It's not right. It's not fair. Then you try to depress me with bluggy stories of your son's horrible opulence, and when you discover you can't depress me you burst into tears and accuse me of being funny. What did you expect me to be? Did you expect me to groan because you aren't lying dead in a mortuary? If I'm funny, you are at liberty to attribute it to hysteria, the hysteria of joy. But I wish you to understand that these extreme revulsions of feeling which you impose on me are very dangerous for a plain man who is undergoing a rest-cure."

Eve raised her arms about Mr. Prohack's neck, lifted herself up by them, and silently kissed him. Then she sank back to her former position.

"I've been a great trial to you lately, haven't I?" she breathed.

"Not more so than usual," he answered. "You know you always abuse your power."

"But I *have* been queer?"

"Well," judicially, "perhaps you have. Perhaps five per cent or so above your average of queerness."

"Didn't the doctor say what I'd got was traumatic neurasthenia?"

"That or something equally absurd."

"Well, I haven't got it any more. I'm cured. You'll see."

Just then the dining-room clock entered upon its lengthy business of chiming the hour of midnight. And as it faintly chimed Mr. Prohack, supporting his wife, had a surpassing conviction of the beauty of existence and in particular of his own good fortune—though the matter of his inheritance never once entered his mind. He gazed down at Eve's ingenuous features, and saw in them the fastidious fineness which had caused her to recoil so sensitively from her son's display at the Grand Babylon. Yes, women had a spiritual beauty to which men could not pretend.

"Arthur," said she, "I never told you that you'd forgotten to wind up that clock on Sunday night. It stopped this evening while you were out, and I had to wind it and I only guessed what the time was."

CHAPTER XII

THE PRACTICE OF IDLENESS

I

At ten minutes to eleven the next morning Mr. Prohack rushed across the pavement, and sprang head-first into the original Eagle (now duly repaired) with the velocity and agility of a man long accustomed to the fact that seconds are more precious than sixpences and minutes than banknotes. And Carthew slammed the door on him like a conjuror performing the final act of a trick before an audience of three thousand people.

Mr. Prohack was late. He was late on this the first full day of his career as a consciously and scientifically idle man. Carthew knew that his employer was late; and certainly the people in his house knew that he was late. Mr. Prohack's breakfast in bed had been late, which meant that his digestive and reposeful hour of newspaper reading was thrown forward. And then he had actually been kept out of his own bathroom, through the joint fault of Sissie and her mother, who had apparently determined to celebrate Sissie's definite release from the dance-studio, and Mrs. Prohack's astonishing recovery from traumatic neurasthenia, by a thorough visitation and reorganisation of the house and household. Those two, re-established in each other's affection, had been holding an inquisition in the bathroom, of all rooms, at the very moment when Mr. Prohack needed the same, with the consequence that he found the bath empty instead of full, and the geyser not even lighted. Yet they well knew that he had a highly important appointment at the tailor's at ten forty-five, followed by other just as highly important appointments! The worst of it was that he could not take their crime seriously because he was on such intimate and conspiratorial terms with each of them separately. On the previous evening he had exchanged wonderful and rather dangerous confidences with his daughter, and, further on in the night he and her mother had decided that the latter's fantastic excursion to the Grand Babylon Hotel should remain a secret. And Sissie, as much as her mother, had taken advantage of his helplessness in the usual unscrupulous feminine manner. They went so far as to smile quasi-maternally at his boyish busy-ness.

Now no sooner had Carthew slamed the door of the Eagle and got into the driving-seat than a young woman, a perfect stranger to Mr. Prohack, appeared, and through the open window asked in a piteous childlike voice if Mr. Prohack was indeed Mr. Prohack, and, having been informed that this was so, expressed the desire to speak with him. Mr. Prohack was beside himself with annoyance and thwarted energy. Was the entire universe uniting against the execution of his programme?

"I have a most important appointment," said he, raising his hat and achieving politeness by an enormous effort, "and if your business is urgent you'd better get into the car. I'm going to Conduit Street."

She slipped into the car like a snake, and Carthew, beautifully unaware that he had two passengers, simultaneously drove off.

If a snake, she was a very slim, blushing and confused snake,—short, too, for a python. And she had a turned-up nose, and was quite young. Her scales were stylish. And, although certainly abashed, apprehensive and timorous, she yet had, about her delicate mouth, the signs of terrible determination, of ruthlessness, of an ambition that nothing could thwart. Mr. Prohack might have been alarmed, but fortunately he was getting used to driving in closed cars with young women, and so could keep his nerve. Moreover, he enjoyed these experiences, being a man of simple tastes and not too analytical of good fortune when it came his way.

"It's very good of you to see me like this," said the girl, in the voice of a rapid brook with a pebbly bed. "My name is Winstock, and I've called about the car."

"The car? What car?"

"The motor-car accident at Putney, you know."

"Ah!"

"Yes."

"Just so. Just so. You are the owner-driver of the other car."

"Yes."

"I think you ought to have seen my wife. It is really she who is the owner of this car. As you are aware, I wasn't in the accident myself, and I don't know anything about it. Besides, it's entirely in the hands of the insurance company and the solicitors. You are employing a solicitor, aren't you?"

"Oh, yes."

"Then I suppose it's by his advice that you've come to see me."

"Well, I'm afraid it isn't."

"What!" cried Mr. Prohack. "If it isn't by his advice you may well be afraid. Do you know you've done a most improper thing? Most improper. I can't possibly listen to you. *You* may go behind your lawyer's back. But I can't. And also there's the insurance company." Mr. Prohack lifted the rug which had fallen away from her short skirts.

"I think solicitors and companies and things are so silly," said Miss Winstock, whose eyes had not moved from the floor-mat. "Thank you." The 'thank you' was in respect to the rug.

"So they are," Mr. Prohack agreed.

"That was why I thought it would be better to come straight to you." For the first time she glanced at him; a baffling glance, a glance that somehow had the effect of transferring some of the apprehension in her own breast to that of Mr. Prohack.

"Well," said he, in a departmental tone recalling Whitehall. "Will you kindly say what you have to say?"

"Can I speak confidentially?"

Mr. Prohack raised his hands and laughed in what he hoped was a sardonic manner.

"I give you young women up," he murmured. "Yes, I give you up. You're my enemy. We're at law. And you want to talk confidentially! How can I tell whether I can let you talk confidentially until I've heard what you're going to say?"

"Oh! I was only going to say that I'm not really the owner-driver of the car. I'm personal secretary to Mr. Carrel Quire, and it's really his car. You see he has three cars, but as there's been such a fuss about waste lately and he's so prominent in the anti-squandermania campaign, he prefers to keep only one car in his own name."

"You don't mean to sit there and tell me you're talking about the Secretary for Foreign Affairs!"

"Yes, of course. Who else? You know he's on the continent at present. He wouldn't take me with him because he wanted to create an effect of austerity in Paris—that's what he said; and I must get this accident affair settled up before he comes back, or he *may* dismiss me. I don't think he will, because I'm a cousin of the late Lady Queenie Paulle—that's how I got the place—but he may. And then where should I be? I was told you were so kind and nice—that's why I came."

"I am not kind and I am not nice," remarked Mr. Prohack, in an acid tone, but laughing to himself because the celebrated young statesman, Mr. Carrel Quire (bald at thirty-five) was precisely one of the ministers who, during the war, had defied and trampled upon the Treasury. He now almost demoniacally contemplated the ruin of Mr. Carrel Quire.

"You have made a serious mistake in coming to me. Unfortunately you cannot undo it. Be good enough to understand that you have not been talking confidentially."

Miss Winstock ought to have been intimidated and paralysed by the menacing manner of the former Terror of the Departments. But she was not.

"Please, please, Mr. Prohack," she said calmly, "don't talk in that strain. I distinctly told you I was talking confidentially, and I'm sure I can rely on you—unless all that I've heard about you is untrue; which it can't be. I only want matters to be settled quietly, and when Mr. Quire returns he will pay anything that has to be paid—if it isn't too much."

"My chauffeur asserts that you have told a most naughty untruth about the accident. You say that he ran into you, whereas the fact is that he was nearly standing still while you were going too fast and you skidded badly into him off the tramlines. And he's found witnesses to prove what he says."

"I may have been a little mistaken," Miss Winstock admitted with light sadness. "I won't say I wasn't. You know how you are in an accident."

"I've never been in an accident in my life," Mr. Prohack objected.

"If you had, you'd sympathise with me."

At this moment the Eagle drew up at the desired destination in Conduit Street. Mr. Prohack looked at his watch.

"I'm sorry to seem inhospitable," he said, "but my appointment is extremely important. I cannot wait."

"Can *I* wait?" Miss Winstock suggested. "I'm quite used to waiting for Mr. Carrel Quire. If I might wait in the car till you came out. . . . You see I want to come to an understanding."

"I don't know how long I shall be."

"That doesn't matter, truly. I haven't got anything else in the world to do, as Mr. Carrel Quire is away."

Mr. Prohack left Miss Winstock in the car.

II

The establishment into which Mr. Prohack disappeared was that of his son's tailors. He slipped into it with awe, not wholly because the tailors were his son's tailors, but in part because they were tailors to various august or once-august personages throughout

Europe. Till that day Mr. Prohack had bought his clothes from an insignificant though traditional tailor in Maddox Street, to whom he had been taken as a boy by his own father. And he had ordered his clothes hastily, negligently, anyhow, in intervals snatched from meal-hours or on the way from one more important appointment to another more important appointment. Indeed he had thought no more of ordering a suit than of ordering a whiskey and soda. Nay, he had on one occasion fallen incredibly low, and his memory held the horrid secret for ever,—on one occasion he had actually bought a ready-made suit. It had fitted him, for he was slimmish and of a good stock size, but he had told nobody, not even his wife, of this shocking defection from the code of true British gentlemanliness,—and he had never repeated the crime; the secret would die with him. And now he was devoting the top of the morning to the commandment of a suit. The affair was his chief business, and he had come to it in a great car whose six cylinders were working harmoniously for nothing else, and with the aid of an intelligent and experienced and expert human being whose sole object in life that morning was to preside over Mr. Prohack's locomotion to and from the tailors'!

Mr. Prohack perceived that he was only beginning to comprehend the wonder of existence. The adepts at the tailors', however, seemed to see nothing wonderful in the matter. They showed no surprise that he had written to make an appointment with a particular adept named Melchizidek, who had been casually mentioned weeks earlier by Charles as the one man in London who really comprehended waistcoats. They took it as a matter of course that Mr. Prohack had naught else to do with the top of the morning but order clothes, and that while he did so he should keep a mature man and a vast and elaborate machine waiting for him in the street outside. And Mr. Melchizidek's manner alone convinced Mr. Prohack that what he had told his family, and that what he had told Miss Winstock in the car, was strictly true and not the invention of his fancy—namely that the appointment was genuinely of high importance.

Mr. Melchizidek possessed the strange gift of condescending majestically to Mr. Prohack while licking his boots. He listened to Mr. Prohack as to an autocrat while giving Mr. Prohack to understand that Mr. Prohack knew not the first elements of sartorial elegance. At intervals he gazed abstractedly at the gold framed and crowned portraits that hung on the walls and at the inscriptions similarly framed and crowned and hung, and it was borne in upon Mr. Prohack that the inscriptions in actual practice referred to Mr. Melchizidek, and that this same Melchizidek, fawning and masterful, had seen monarchs in their shirt sleeves and spoken to princes with pins in his mouth, and made marks in white chalk between the shoulder-blades of grand-dukes; and that revolutions and cataclysms were nothing to Mr. Melchizidek.

When Mr. Melchizidek had decided by hypnotic suggestion and magic power what Mr. Prohack desired in the way of stuffs and patterns, he led Mr. Prohack mysteriously to a small chamber, and a scribe followed them carrying pencil and paper, and Mr. Prohack removed, with assistance, his shabby coat and his waistcoat, and Mr. Melchizidek measured him in unexampled detail and precision, and the scribe, writing, intoned aloud all Mr. Prohack's dimensions. And all the time Mr. Prohack was asking in his heart: "How much will these clothes cost?" And he, once the Terror of the departments, who would have held up the war to satisfy his official inquisitiveness on a question of price,—he dared not ask how much the clothes would cost. He felt that in that unique establishment money was simply not mentioned,—it could never be more than the subject of formal and stately correspondence.

During the latter part of the operation Mr. Prohack heard, outside in the shop, the sharp sounds of an imperial and decisive voice, and he was thereby well-nigh thunderstruck. And even Mr. Melchizidek seemed to be similarly affected by the voice,—so much so that the intimate of sovereigns unaffectedly hastened the business of enduing Mr. Prohack into the shameful waistcoat and coat, and then, with a gesture of apology, passed out of the cubicle, leaving Mr. Prohack with the attendant scribe.

Mr. Prohack, pricked by a fearful curiosity, followed Mr. Melchizidek; and the voice was saying:

"Oh! You're there, Melchizidek. Just come and look at this crease."

Mr. Melchizidek, pained, moved forward. Three acolytes were already standing in shocked silence round about a young man who stretched forth one leg so that all might see.

"I ask you," the young man proceeded, "is it an inch out or isn't it? And how many times have I tried these things on? I'm a busy man, and here I have to waste my time coming here again and again to get a thing right that ought to have been right the first time. And you call yourselves the first tailors in Europe. . . . Correct me if I'm inaccurate in any of my statements."

Mr. Melchizidek, who unlike an Englishman knew when he was beaten, said in a solemn bass:

"When can I send for them, sir?"

"You can send for them this afternoon at the Grand Babylon, and be sure that I have them back to-morrow night."

"Certainly, sir. It's only fair to ourselves, sir, to state that we have a great deal of trouble with our workmen in these days."

"No doubt. And I have a great deal of trouble to find cash in these days, but I don't pay your bills with bad money, I think."

A discreet sycophantic smile from the group at this devastating witticism!

Mr. Prohack cautiously approached; the moment had awkwardness, but Mr. Prohack owed it to himself to behave with all presence of mind.

"Hullo, Charlie!" said he casually.

"Hel*lo*, dad! How are you?" And Charlie, wearing the very suit in which he had left home for Glasgow, shook hands boyishly.

Looking into his firm, confident eyes, Mr. Prohack realised, perhaps for the first time, that the fruit of his loins was no common boy. The mere fact that as an out-of-work ex-officer, precariously making a bit in motor-bicycle deals, he had dared to go to Melchizidek's firm for clothes, and that he was now daring to affront Melchizidek,—this sole fact separated him from the ruck of sons.

"I warn you, dad, that if you're ordering clothes here you're ordering trouble."

Mr. Melchizidek's interjected remarks fitted to the occasion. The group dissipated. The males of the Prohack family could say nothing interesting to each other in such a situation. They could only pretend that their relations were purely normal; which they did quite well.

"I say, dad, I'm awfully busy this morning. I can't stop now. I've telephoned the mater and she's coming to the Grand Babylon for lunch—one thirty. Sis too, I think. Do come. You haven't got anything else to do." The boy murmured all this.

"Oh! Haven't I! I'm just as busy as you are, and more."

However, Mr. Prohack accepted the invitation. Charlie went off in haste. Mr. Prohack arrived on the pavement in time to see him departing in an open semi-racing car driven by a mature, handsome and elegant woman, with a chauffeur sitting behind. Mr. Prohack's mind was one immense interrogation concerning his son. He had seen him, spoken with him, and—owing to the peculiar circumstances—learnt nothing whatever. Indeed, the mystery of Charlie was deepened. Had Charles hurried away in order to hide the mature handsome lady from his father? . . . Mr. Prohack might have moralised, but he suddenly remembered that he had a lady in his own car, and that the disparity between their ages was no less than the disparity between the ages of the occupants of the car in which Charles had fled.

III

Turning to his own car, he observed with a momentary astonishment that Carthew, the chauffeur, leaning a little nonchalantly through the open off-window of the vehicle, was engaged in conversation with Miss Winstock. The astonishment passed when he reflected that as these two had been in the enforced intimacy of an accident together they were necessarily on some kind of speaking terms. Before Carthew had noticed Mr. Prohack, Mr. Prohack noticed that Carthew's attitude to Miss Winstock showed a certain tolerant condescension, while Miss Winstock's girlish gestures were of a subtly appealing nature. Then in an instant Carthew, the easy male tolerator of inaccurate but charming young women, disappeared from the window—disappeared indeed, entirely from the face of the earth—and a perfectly non-human, impassive automaton emerged from behind the back of the car and stood attentive at the door, holding the handle thereof. Mr. Prohack, with a gift of dissimulation equal to Carthew's own, gave him an address in Bond Street.

"I have another very urgent appointment," said Mr. Prohack to Miss Winstock as he sat down beside her. And he took his diary from his pocket and gazed at it intently, frowning, though there was nothing whatever on its page except the printed information that the previous Sunday was the twenty-fourth after Trinity, and a warning: "If you have omitted to order your new diary it would be well to do so NOW to prevent disappointment."

"It's awfully good of you to have me here," said Miss Winstock.

"It is," Mr. Prohack admitted. "And so far as I can see you've done nothing to deserve it. You were very wrong to get chatting with my chauffeur, for example."

"I felt that all the time. But he has such a powerful individuality."

"He may have. But what I pay him for is to drive my car, not to put his passengers into a semi-hypnotic state. Do you know why I am taking you about like this?"

"I hope it's because you are kind-hearted."

"Not at all. Do you think I should do it if you were fifty, fat and a fright? Of course I shouldn't. And no one knows that better than you. I'm doing it because you're young and charming and slim and attractive and smart. Though forty-six, I am still a man. The chief difference between me and most other men is that I know and openly admit my motives. That's what makes me so dangerous. You should beware of me. Take note that I haven't asked you what you've been saying to Carthew. Nor shall I ask him. Now what exactly do you want me to do?"

"Only not to let the law case about the accident go any further."

"And are you in a position to pay the insurance company for the damage to my car?"

"Oh! Mr. Carrel Quire will pay."

"Are you sure? Are you quite sure that Mr. Carrel Quire is not spending twice as much as his ministerial salary, that salary being the whole of his financial resources except loans from millionaires who will accept influence instead of interest? I won't enquire whether Mr. Carrel Quire pays your salary regularly. If he does, it furnishes the only instance of regularity in the whole of his gorgeous career. If our little affair becomes public it might ruin Mr. Carrel Quire as a politician—at the least it would set him back for ten years. And I am particularly anxious to ruin Mr. Carrel Quire. In doing so I shall accomplish a patriotic act."

"Oh, Mr. Prohack!"

"Yes. Mr. Carrel Quire may be—probably is—a delightful fellow, but he is too full of brains, and he constitutes the gravest danger that has threatened the British Empire for a hundred years. Hence it is my duty to ruin him if I get the chance; and I've got the chance. I don't see how he could survive the exposure of the simple fact that while preaching anti-waste he is keeping motor-cars in the names of young women."

The car had stopped in front of a shop over whose door a pair of gilded animals like nothing in zoology were leaping amiably at each other. Miss Winstock began to search neurotically in a bag for a handkerchief.

"This is the scene of my next appointment," Mr. Prohack continued. "Would you prefer to leave me at once or will you wait again?"

Miss Winstock hesitated.

"You had better wait," Mr. Prohack decided. "You'll be crying in fifteen seconds and your handkerchief is sadly inadequate to the crisis. Try a little self-control, and don't let Carthew hypnotise you. I shan't be surprised if you're gone when I come back."

A commissionaire was now holding open the door of the car.

"Carthew," said Mr. Prohack privily, after he had got out. "Oblige me by imagining that during my absence the car is empty."

Carthew quivered for a fraction of eternity, but was exceedingly quick to recover.

"Yes, sir."

The shop was all waxed parquetry, silks, satins, pure linen and pure wool, diversified by a few walking-sticks and a cuff link or so. Faced by a judge-like middle-aged authority in a frock-coat, Mr. Prohack suddenly lost the magisterial demeanour which he had exhibited to a defenceless girl in the car. He comprehended in a flash that suits of clothes were a detail in the existence of an idle man and that neckties and similar supremacies alone mattered.

"I want a necktie," he began gently.

"Certainly, sir," said the judge. But the judge's eyes, fixed on Mr. Prohack's neck, said: "I should just think you did."

Life was enlarged to a bewildering, a maddening maze of neckties. Mr. Prohack considered in his heart that one of the needs of the day was an encyclopædia of neckties. As he bought neckties he felt as foolish as a woman buying cigars. Any idiot could buy a suit, but neckties baffled the intelligence of the Terror of the departments, though he had worn something in the nature of a necktie for forty years. The neckties which he bought inspired him with fear—the fear lest he might lack the courage to wear them. In a nightmare he saw himself putting them on in his bedroom and proceeding downstairs to breakfast, and then, panic-stricken, rushing back to the bedroom to change into one of his old neckties.

And when he had bought neckties he apprehended that neckties without shirts were like butter without bread, and he bought shirts. And then he surmised that shirts without collars would be indecent. And when he had bought collars a still small voice told him that the logical foundation of all things was socks, and that really he had been trying to build a house from the fourth story downwards. Fortunately he had less hesitation about the socks, for he could comfort himself with the thought that socks did not jump to the eye as neckties did, and that by constant care their violence might even be forever concealed from the gaze of his household. He sighed with relief at the end of the sock episode. But he had forgotten braces, as to which he surrendered unconditionally to the frock-coated judge. He brooked the most astounding braces, for none but Eve would see them, and he could intimidate Eve.

"Shall we make you a quarter of a dozen pairs to measure, sir?"

This extraordinary question miraculously restored all Mr. Prohack's vanished aplomb. That at the end of the greatest war in the history of the earth, amid decapitated empires and cities of starvation, braces should be made to measure,—this was too much for Mr. Prohack, who had not dreamed that braces ever had been made to measure. It shocked him back into sense.

"No!" he said coldly, and soon afterwards left the shop.

Miss Winstock, in the car, sat for the statue of wistful melancholy.

"Heavens!" breathed Mr. Prohack to himself. "The little thing is taking me seriously. With all her experience of the queer world, and all her initiative and courage, she is taking me seriously!" He was touched; his irony became sympathetic, and he thought: "How young the young are!"

Her smile as he rejoined her had pathos in it. The totality of her was delicious.

"You cannot be all bad, Miss Winstock," said he to her, after instructing the chauffeur, "because nobody is. You are undisciplined. You do wild and rash things—you have already accomplished several this morning. But you have righteous instincts, though not often enough. Of course, with one word to the insurance company I could save you. The difficulty is that I could not save you without saving Mr. Carrel Quire also. And it would be very wrong of me to save Mr. Carrel Quire, for to save him would be to jeopardise the future of the British Empire, because unless he is scotched, that man's frantic egotism and ruthless ambition will achieve political disaster for four hundred million human beings. I should like to save you. But can I weigh you in the balance against an Empire? Can I, I say?"

"No," answered Miss Winstock weakly but sincerely.

"That's just where you're wrong," said Mr. Prohack. "I can. And you are shamefully ignorant of history. Never yet when empire, any empire, has been weighed in the balance against a young and attractive woman has the young woman failed to win! That is a dreadful fact, but men are thus constituted. Had you been a hag, I should not have hesitated to do my duty to my country. But as you are what you are, and sitting so agreeably in my car, I will save you and let my country go."

"Oh! Mr. Prohack, you are very kind—but every one told me you were."

"No! I am a knave. Also there is a condition."

"I will agree to anything."

"You must leave Mr. Carrel Quire's service. That man is dangerous not only to empires. The entire environment is the very worst decently possible for a girl like you. Get away from it. If you don't undertake to give him notice at once, and withdraw entirely from his set, then I will ruin both you and him."

"But I shall starve," cried Miss Winstock. "I shall never find another place without influence, and I have no more influence."

"Have the Winstocks no money?"

"Not a penny."

"And have the Paulles no money?"

"None for me."

"You are the ideal programme-girl in a theatre," said Mr. Prohack. "You will never starve. Excuse me for a few minutes. I have another very important appointment," he added, as the car stopped in Piccadilly.

After a quarter of an hour spent in learning that suits were naught, neckties were naught, shirts, collars, socks and even braces were naught, but that hats alone made a man of fashion and idleness, Mr. Prohack returned to Miss Winstock and announced:

"I will engage you as my private secretary. I need one very badly indeed. In fact I cannot understand how, with all my engagements, I have been able to manage without one so long. Your chief duties will be to keep on good terms with my wife and daughter, and not to fall in love with my son. If you were not too deeply preoccupied with my chauffeur, you may have noticed a young man who came out of the tailors' just before I did. That was my son."

"Oh!" exclaimed Miss Winstock, "the boy who drove off in Lady Massulam's car?"

"Was that Lady Massulam?" asked Mr. Prohack before he had had time to recover from the immense effect of hearing the startling, almost legendary name of Lady Massulam in connection with his son.

"Of course," said Miss Winstock. "Didn't you know?"

Mr. Prohack ignored her pertness.

"Well," he proceeded, having now successfully concealed his emotion, "after having dealt as I suggest with my wife and children, you will deal with my affairs. You shall have the same salary as Mr. Carrel Quire paid—or forgot to pay. Do you agree or not?"

"I should love it," replied Miss Winstock with enthusiasm.

"What is your Christian name?"

"Mimi."

"So it is. I remember now. Well, it won't do at all. Never mention it again, please."

When he had accompanied Mimi to a neighbouring post office and sent off a suitable telegram of farewell to Mr. Carrel Quire in her name, Mr. Prohack abandoned her till the morrow, and drove off quickly to pick up his wife for the Grand Babylon lunch.

"I am a perfect lunatic," said he to himself. "It must be the effect of riches. However, I don't care."

He meant that he didn't care about the conceivable consequences of engaging Mimi Winstock as secretary. But what he did care about was the conjuncture of Lady Massulam and Charlie.

CHAPTER XIII

FURTHER IDLENESS

I

STRANGE, inconceivable as it may appear to people of the great world and readers of newspapers, Mr. Prohack, C. B., had never in his life before been inside the Grand Babylon Hotel. Such may be the narrow and mean existence forced by circumstances upon secretly powerful servants of the Crown. He arrived late, owing to the intricate preparations of his wife and daughter for Charlie's luncheon. These two were unsuccessfully pretending not to be nervous, and their nervousness reacted upon Mr. Prohack, who perceived with disgust that his gay and mischievous mood of the morning was slipping away from him despite his efforts to retain it. He knew now definitely that his health had taken the right turn, and yet he could not prod the youthful Sissie as he had prodded the youthful Mimi Winstock. Moreover Mimi was a secret which would have to be divulged, and this secret not only weighed heavy within him, but seemed disturbingly to counterbalance the secrets that Charlie was withholding.

On the present occasion he saw little of the Grand Babylon, for as soon as he mentioned his son's name to the nonchalant official behind the enquiry counter the official changed like lightning into an obsequious courtier, and Charles's family was put in charge of a hovering attendant boy, who escorted it in a lift and along a mile of corridors, and Charlie's family was kept waiting at a door until the voice of Charlie permitted the boy to open the door. A rather large parlour set with a table for five; a magnificent view from the window of a huge white-bricked wall and scores of chimney pots and electric wires, and a moving grey sky above! Charlie, too, was unsuccessfully pretending not to be nervous.

"Hullo, kid!" he greeted his sister.

"Hullo yourself," responded Sissie.

They shook hands. (They very rarely kissed. However, Charlie kissed his mother. Even he would not have dared not to kiss her.)

"Mater," said he, "let me introduce you to Lady Massulam.

Lady Massulam had been standing in the window. She came

forward with a pleasant, restrained smile and made the acquaintance of Charlie's family; but she was not talkative. Her presence, coming as a terrific surprise to the ladies of the Prohack family, and as a fairly powerful surprise to Mr. Prohack, completed the general constraint. Mrs. Prohack indeed was somewhat intimidated by it. Mrs. Prohack's knowledge of Lady Massulam was derived exclusively from *The Daily Picture,* where her portrait was constantly appearing, on all sorts of pretexts, and where she was described as a leader of London society. Mr. Prohack knew of her as a woman credited with great feats of war-work, and also with a certain real talent for organisation; further, he had heard that she had a gift for high finance, and exercised it not without profit. As she happened to be French by birth, no steady English person was seriously upset by the fact that her matrimonial career was obscure, and as she happened to be very rich everybody raised sceptical eyebrows at the assertion that her husband (a knight) was dead; for *The Daily Picture* implanted daily in the minds of millions of readers the grand truth that to the very rich nothing can happen simply. The whole *Daily Picture* world was aware that of late she had lived at the Grand Babylon Hotel in permanence. That world would not have recognised her from her published portraits, which were more historical than actual. Although conspicuously anti-Victorian she had a Victorian beauty of the impressive kind; she had it still. Her hair was of a dark lustrous brown and showed no grey. In figure she was tall, and rather more than plump and rather less than fat. Her perfect and perfectly worn clothes proved that she knew just how to deal with herself. She would look forty in a theatre, fifty in a garden, and sixty to her maid at dawn.

This important person spoke, when she did speak, with a scarcely perceptible French accent in a fine clear voice. But she spoke little and said practically nothing: which was a shock to Marian Prohack, who had imagined that in the circles graced by Lady Massulam conversation varied from badinage to profundity and never halted. It was not that Lady Massulam was tongue-tied, nor that she was impolite; it was merely that with excellent calmness she did not talk. If anybody handed her a subject, she just dropped it; the floor around her was strewn with subjects.

The lunch was dreadful, socially. It might have been better if Charlie's family had not been tormented by the tremendous question: what had Charlie to do with Lady Massulam? Already Charlie's situation was sufficient of a mystery, without this arch-mystery being spread all over it. And inexperienced Charlie was a poor host; as a host he was positively pathetic, rivalling Lady Massulam in taciturnity.

Sissie took to chaffing her brother, and after a time Charlie said suddenly, with curtness:

"Have you dropped that silly dance-scheme of yours, kid?"

Sissie was obliged to admit that she had.

"Then I tell you what you might do. You might come and live here with me for a bit. I want a hostess, you know."

"I will," said Sissie, straight. No consultation of parents!

This brief episode overset Mrs. Prohack. The lunch worsened, to such a point that Mr. Prohack began to grow light-hearted, and chaffed Charlie in his turn. He found material for chaff in the large number of newly bought books that were lying about the room. There was even the *Encyclopaedia of Religion and Ethics* in eleven volumes. Queer possessions for a youth who at home had never read aught but the periodical literature of automobilism! Could this be the influence of Lady Massulam? Then the telephone bell rang, and it was like a signal of salvation. Charlie sprang at the instrument.

"For you," he said, indicating Lady Massulam, who rose.

"Oh!" said she. "It's Ozzie."

"Who's Ozzie?" Charlie demanded, without thought.

"No doubt Oswald Morfey," said Mr. Prohack, scoring over his son.

"He wants to see me. May I ask him to come up for coffee?"

"Oh! Do!" said Sissie, also without thought. She then blushed.

Mr. Prohack thought suspiciously and apprehensively:

"I bet anything he's found out that my daughter is here."

Ozzie transformed the final act of the luncheon. An adept conversationalist, he created conversationalists on every side. Mrs. Prohack liked him at once. Sissie could not keep her eyes off him. Charlie was impressed by him. Lady Massulam treated him with the familiarity of an intimate. Mr. Prohack alone was sinister in attitude. Ozzie brought the great world into the room with him. In his simpering voice he was ready to discuss all the pheuomena of the universe; but after ten minutes Mr. Prohack noticed that the fellow had one sole subject on his mind. Namely, a theatrical first-night, fixed for that very evening; a first-night of the highest eminence; one of Mr. Asprey Chown's first-nights, boomed by the marvellous showmanship of Mr. Asprey Chown into a mighty event. The competition for seats was prodigious, but of course Lady Massulam had obtained her usual stall.

"What a pity we can't go!" said Sissie simply.

"Will you all come in my box?" astonishingly replied Mr. Oswald Morfey, embracing in his weak glance the entire Prohack family.

"The fellow came here on purpose to fix this," said Mr. Prohack to himself as the matter was being effusively clinched.

"I must go," said he aloud, looking at his watch. "I have a very important appointment."

"But I wanted to have a word with you, dad," said Charlie, in quite a new tone across the table.

"Possibly," answered the superior ironic father in Mr. Prohack, who besides being sick of the luncheon party was determined that nothing should interfere with his Median and Persian programme. "Possibly. But that will be for another time."

"Well, to-night then," said Charlie, dashed somewhat.

"Perhaps," said Mr. Prohack. Yet he was burning to hear his son's word.

II

However, Mr. Prohack did not succeed in loosing himself from the embraces of the Grand Babylon Hotel for another thirty minutes. He offered to abandon the car, to abandon everything to his wife and daughter, and to reach his next important appointment by the common methods of conveyance employed by common people; but the ladies would permit no such thing; they announced their firm intention of personally escorting him to his destination. The party seemed to be unable to break up. There was a considerable confabulation between Eve and Lady Massulam at the entrance to the lift.

Mr. Prohack noticed anew that Eve's attitude to Lady Massulam was still a flattering one. Indeed Eve showed that in her opinion the meeting with so great a personage as Lady Massulam was not quite an ordinary episode in her simple existence. And Lady Massulam was now talking with a free flow to Eve. As soon as the colloquy had closed and Eve had at length joined her simmering husband in the lift, Charlie must have a private chat with Lady Massulam, apart, mysterious, concerning their affairs, whatever their affairs might be! In spite of himself, Mr. Prohack was impressed by the demeanour of the young man and the mature blossom of womanhood to each other. They exhibited a mutual trust; they understood each other; they liked each other. She was more than old enough to be his mamma, and yet as she talked to him she somehow became a dignified girl. Mr. Prohack was disturbed in a manner which he would never have admitted,—how absurd to fancy that Lady Massulam had in her impressive head a notion of marrying the boy! Still, such unions had occurred! —but he was pleasantly touched, too.

Then Oswald Morfey and Sissie made another couple, very different, more animated, and equally touching. Ozzie seemed to grow more likeable, and less despicable, under the honest and frankly ardent gaze of Miss Prohack; and Mr. Prohack was again visited by a doubt whether the fellow was after all the perfectly silly ass which he was reputed to be.

In the lift, Lady Massulam having offered her final adieux, Ozzie opened up to Mrs. Prohack the subject of an organisation called the United League of all the Arts. Mr. Prohack would not listen to this. He hated leagues, and especially leagues of arts. He knew in the marrow of his spine that they were preposterous; but Mrs. Prohack and Sissie listened with unfeigned eagerness to the wonderful tale of the future of the United League of all the Arts. And when, emerging from the lift, Mr. Prohack strolled impatiently on ahead, the three stood calmly moveless to converse, until Mr. Prohack had to stroll impatiently back again. As for Charlie, he stood by himself; there was leisure for the desired word with his father, but Mr. Prohack had bluntly postponed that, and thus the leisure was wasted.

Without consulting Mr. Prohack's wishes, Ozzie drew the ladies towards the great lounge, and Mr. Prohack at a distance unwillingly after them. In the lounge so abundantly enlarged and enriched since the days of the celebrated Felix Babylon, the founder of the hotel, post-lunch coffee was merging into afternoon tea. The number of idle persons in the world, and the number of busy persons who ministered to them, and the number of artistic persons who played voluptuous music to their idleness, struck Mr. Prohack as merely prodigious. He had not dreamed that idleness on so grandiose a scale flourished in the city which to him had always been a city of hard work and limited meal-hours. He saw that he had a great deal to learn before he could hope to be as skilled in idleness as the lowest of these experts in the lounge. He tapped his foot warningly. No effect on his women. He tapped more loudly, as the hatred of being in a hurry took possession of him. Eve looked round with a delightful placatory smile which conjured an answering smile into the face of her husband.

He tried to be irritated after smiling, and advancing said in a would-be fierce tone:

"If this lunch lasts much longer I shall barely have time to dress for dinner."

But the effort was a failure—so complete that Sissie laughed at him.

He had expected that in the car his women would relate to him the sayings and doings of Ozzie Morfey in relation to the United League of all the Arts. But they said not a syllable on the matter. He knew they were hiding something formidable from him. He might have put a question, but he was too proud to do so. Further, he despised them because they essayed to discuss Lady Massulam impartially, as though she was just a plain body, or nobody at all. A nauseating pretence on their part.

Crossing a street, the car was held up by a procession of unemployed, with guardian policemen, a band consisting chiefly of drums, and a number of collarless powerful young men who shook white boxes of coppers menacingly in the faces of passers-by.

"Instead of encouraging them, the police ought to forbid these processions of unemployed," said Eve gravely. "They're becoming a perfect nuisance."

"Why!" said Mr. Prohack, "this car of yours is a procession of unemployed."

This sardonic pleasantry pleased Mr. Prohack as much as it displeased Mrs. Prohack. It seemed to alleviate his various worries, and the process of alleviation went further when he remembered that, though he would be late for his important appointment, he had really lost no time because Dr. Veiga had forbidden him to keep this particular appointment earlier than two full hours after a meal.

"Don't take cold, darling," Eve urged with loving solicitude as he left the car to enter the place of rendezvous. Sissie grinned at him mockingly. They both knew that he had never kept such an appointment before.

III

Solemnity, and hush, and antique menials stiff with tradition, surrounded him. As soon as he had paid the entrance fee and deposited all his valuables in a drawer of which the key was formally delivered to him, he was motioned through a turnstile and requested to permit his boots to be removed. He consented. White linens were then handed to him.

"See here," he said with singular courage to the attendant. "I've never been into one of these resorts before. Where do I go?"

The attendant, who was a bare-footed mild child dressed in the Moorish mode, reassuringly charged himself with Mr. Prohack's well-being, and led the aspirant into a vast mosque with a roof of domes and little glowing windows of coloured glass. In the midst of the mosque was a pale green pool. White figures reclined in alcoves, round the walls. A fountain played—the only orchestra. There was an eastern sound of hands clapped, and another attendant glided across the carpeted warm floor. Mr. Prohack understood that, in this immense seclusion, when you desired no matter what you clapped your hands and were served. A beautiful peace descended upon him and enveloped him; and he thought: "This is the most wonderful place in the world. I have been waiting for this place for twenty years."

He yielded without reserve to its unique invitation. But some time elapsed before he could recover from the unquestionable fact that he was still within a quarter of a mile of Piccadilly Circus.

From the explanations of the attendant and from the precise orders which he had received from Dr. Veiga regarding the right method of conduct in a Turkish bath, Mr. Prohack, being a man of quick mind, soon devised the order of the ceremonial suited to his case, and began to put it into execution. At first he found the ceremonial exacting. To part from all his clothes and to parade through the mosque in attire of which the principal items were a towel and the key of his valuables (adorning his wrist) was ever so slightly an ordeal to one of his temperament and upbringing. To sit unsheltered in blinding steam was not amusing, though it was exciting. But the steam-chapel (as it might be called) of the mosque was a delight compared to the second next chapel further on, where the woodwork of the chairs was too hot to touch and where a gigantic thermometer informed Mr. Prohack that with only another fifty degrees of heat he would have achieved boiling point.

He remembered that it was in this chamber he must drink iced tonic water in quantity. He clapped his streaming hands clammily, and a tall, thin, old man whose whole life must have been lived near boiling point, immediately brought the draught. Short of the melting of the key of his valuables everything possible happened in this extraordinary chamber. But Mr. Prohack was determined to shrink from naught in the pursuit of idleness.

And at length, after he had sat in a less ardent chapel, and in still another chapel been laid out on a marble slab as for an autopsy and, defenceless, attacked for a quarter of an hour by a prize-fighter, and had jumped desperately into the ice-cold lake and been dragged out and smothered in thick folds of linen, and finally reposed horizontal in his original alcove,—then he was conscious of an inward and profound conviction that true, perfect, complete and supreme idleness had been attained. He had no care in the world; he was cut off from the world; he had no family; he existed beatifically and individually in a sublime and satisfied egotism.

But, such is the insecurity of human organisms and institutions, in less than two minutes he grew aware of a strange sensation within him, which sensation he ultimately diagnosed as hunger. To clap his hands was the work of an instant. The oncoming attendant recited a catalogue of the foods at his disposal; and the phrase "welsh rarebit" caught his attention. He must have a welsh rarebit; he had not had a welsh rarebit since he was at school. It magically arrived, on an oriental tray, set on a low Moorish table.

Eating the most wonderful food of his life and drinking tea, he looked about and saw that two of the unoccupied sofas in his alcove were strewn with garments; the owners of the garments had doubtlessly arrived during his absence in the chapels and were now in the chapels themselves. He lay back; earthly phenomena lost their hard reality. . . .

When he woke up the mosque was a pit of darkness glimmering with sharp points of electric light. He heard voices, the voices of two men who occupied the neighbouring sofas. They were discoursing to each other upon the difficulties of getting good whiskey in Afghanistan and in Rio de Janeiro respectively. From whiskey they passed to even more interesting matters, and Mr. Prohack, for the first time, began to learn how the other half lives, to such an extent that he thought he had better turn on the lamp over his head. Whereupon the conversation on the neighbouring sofas curved off to the English weather in late autumn.

Then Mr. Prohack noticed a deep snore. He perceived that the snore originated in a considerable figure that, wrapped in white and showing to the mosque only a venerable head, was seated in one of the huge armchairs which were placed near the entrance to every alcove. It seemed to him that he recognised the snore, and he was not mistaken, for he had twice before heard it on Sunday afternoons at his chief club. The head was the head of Sir Paul Spinner. Mr. Prohack recalled that old Paul was a devotee of the Turkish bath.

Now Mr. Prohack was exceedingly anxious to have speech with old Paul, for he had heard very interesting rumours of Paul's activities. He arose softly and approached the easy-chair and surveyed Sir Paul, who in his then state looked less like a high financier and more like something chipped off the roof of a cathedral than anything that Mr. Prohack had ever seen.

But Paul did not waken. A bather plunged into the pool with a tremendous splash, but Paul did not waken. And Mr. Prohack felt that it would be contrary to the spirit of the ritual of the mosque to waken him. But he decided that if he waited all night he would wait until old Paul regained consciousness.

At that moment an attendant asked Mr. Prohack if he desired the attentions of the barber, the chiropodist, or the manicurist. New vistas opened out before Mr. Prohack. He said yes. After the barber, he padded down the stairs from the barber's chapel (which was in the upper story of the mosque), to observe if there was any change in old Paul's condition. Paul still slept. Mr. Prohack did similarly after the chiropodist. Paul still slept. Then again after the manicurist. Paul still slept. Then a boyish attendant hurried forward and in a very daring manner shook the monumental Paul by the shoulder.

"You told me to wake you at six, Sir Paul." And Paul woke.

"How simple," reflected Mr. Prohack, "are the problems of existence when they are tackled with decision! Here have I been ineffectively trying to waken the fellow for the past hour. But I forgot that he who wishes the end must wish the means, and my regard for the ritual of the mosque was absurd."

He retired into the alcove to dress, keeping a watchful eye upon old Paul. He felt himself to be in the highest state of physical efficiency. From head to foot he was beyond criticism. When Mr. Prohack had got as far as his waistcoat Sir Paul uprose ponderously from the easy-chair.

"Hi, Paul!"

The encounter between the two friends was one of those affectionate and ecstatic affairs that can only happen in a Turkish Bath.

"I've been trying to get you on the 'phone half the day," grunted Paul Spinner, subsiding on to Mr. Prohack's sofa.

"I've been out all day. Horribly busy," said Mr. Prohack. "What's wrong? Anything wrong?"

"Oh, no! Only I thought you'd like to know I've finished that deal."

"I did hear some tall stories, but not a word from you, old thing." Mr. Prohack tried to assume a tranquillity which he certainly did not feel.

"Well, I never sing until I'm out of the wood. But this time I'm out sooner than I expected."

"Any luck?"

"Yes. But I dictated a letter to you before I came here."

"I suppose you can't remember what there was in it."

"I shall get the securities next week."

"What securities?"

"Well, you'll receive"—here Paul dropped his voice—"three thousand short of a quarter of a million in return for what you put in, my boy."

"Then I'm worth over two hundred and fifty thousand pounds!" murmured Mr. Prohack feebly. And he added, still more feebly: "Something will have to be done about this soon." His heart was beating against his waistcoat like an engine.

CHAPTER XIV

END OF AN IDLE DAY

I

It is remarkable that even in the most fashionable shopping thoroughfares certain shops remain brilliantly open, exposing plush-cushioned wares under a glare of electricity in the otherwise darkened street, for an hour or so after all neighbouring establishments have drawn down their blinds and put up their shutters. An interesting point of psychology is involved in this phenomenon.

On his way home from the paradise of the mosque, Mr. Prohack, afoot and high-spirited, and energised by a long-forgotten sensation of physical well-being, called in at such a shop, and, with the minimum of parley, bought an article enclosed in a rich case. A swift and happy impulse on his part! The object was destined for his wife, and his intention in giving it was to help him to introduce more easily to her notice the fact that he was now, or would shortly be, worth over quarter of a million of money. For he was a strange, silly fellow, and just as he had been conscious of a certain false shame at inheriting a hundred thousand pounds, so now he was conscious of a certain false shame at having increased his possessions to two hundred and fifty thousand pounds.

The Eagle was waiting in front of Mr. Prohack's door; he wondered what might be the latest evening project of his women, for he had not ordered the car so early; perhaps the first night had been postponed; however, he was too discreet, or too dignified, to make any enquiry from the chauffeur; too indifferent to the projects of his beloved women. He would be quite content to sit at home by himself, reflecting upon the marvels of existence and searching among them for his soul.

Within the house, servants were rushing about in an atmosphere of excitement and bell-ringing. He divined that his wife and daughter were dressing simultaneously for an important occasion—either the first night or something else. In that feverish environment he forgot the form of words which he had carefully prepared for the breaking to his wife of the great financial news. Fortunately she gave him no chance to blunder.

"Oh, Arthur, Arthur!" she cried, sweetly reproachful, as with an assumed jauntiness he entered the bedroom. "How late you are! I expected you back an hour ago at least. Your things are laid out in the boudoir. You haven't got a moment to spare. We're late as it is." She was by no means dressed, and the bedroom looked as if it had been put to the sack; nearly every drawer was ajar, and the two beds resembled a second-hand shop.

Mr. Prohack's self-protective instinct at once converted him into a porcupine. An attempt was being made to force him into a hurry, and he loathed hurry.

"I'm not late," said he, "because I didn't say when I should return. It won't take me more than a quarter of an hour to eat, and we've got heaps of time for the theatre."

"I'm giving a little dinner in the Grand Babylon restaurant," said Eve, "and of course we must be there first. Sissie's arranged it for me on the 'phone. It'll be much more amusing than dining here, and it saves the servants." Yet the woman had recently begun to assert that the servants hadn't enough to do!

"Ah!" said Mr. Prohack, startled. "And who are the guests?"

"Oh! Nobody! Only us and Charlie, of course, and Oswald Morfey, and perhaps Lady Massulam. I've told Charlie to do the ordering."

"I should have thought one meal per diem at the Grand Babylon would have been sufficient."

"But this is in the *restaurant,* don't I tell you? Oh, dear! That's three times I've tried to do my hair. It's always the same when I want it nice. Now do get along, Arthur!"

"Strange!" said he with a sardonic blitheness. "Strange how it's always my fault when your hair goes wrong!" And to himself he said: "All right! All right! I just shan't inform you about that quarter of a million. You've no leisure for details to-night, my girl."

And he went into the boudoir.

His blissful serenity was too well established to be overthrown by anything short of a catastrophe. Nevertheless it did quiver slightly under the shock of Eve's new tactics in life. This was the woman who, on only the previous night, had been inveighing against the ostentation of her son's career at the Grand Babylon. Now she seemed determined to rival him in showiness, to be the partner of his alleged vulgarity. That the immature Sissie should suddenly drop the ideals of the new poor for the ideals of the new rich was excusable. But Eve! But that modest embodiment of shy and quiet commonsense! She, who once had scorned the world of *The Daily Picture,* was more and more disclosing a desire for that world. And where now were her doubts about the righteousness of Charlie's glittering deeds? And where was the ancient sagacity which surely should have prevented her from being deceived by the superficialities of an Oswald Morfey? Was she blindly helping to prepare a disaster for her blind daughter? Was the explanation that she had tasted of the fruit? The horrid thought crossed Mr. Prohack's mind: *All women are alike.* He flung it out of his loyal mind, trying to substitute: All women except Eve are alike. But it came back in its original form. . . . Not that he cared, really. If Eve had transformed herself into a Cleopatra his ridiculous passion for her would have suffered no modification.

Lying around the boudoir were various rectangular parcels, addressed in flowing calligraphy to himself: the first harvest-loads of his busy morning. The sight of them struck his conscience. Was not he, too, following his wife on the path of the new rich? No! As ever he was blameless. He was merely executing the prescription of his doctor, who had expounded the necessity of scientific idleness and the curative effect of fine clothes on health. True, he knew himself to be cured, but if nature had chosen to cure him too quickly, that was not his fault. . . . He heard his wife talking to Machin in the bedroom, and Machin talking to his wife; and the servant's voice was as joyous and as worried as if she herself, and not Eve, were about to give a little dinner at the Grand Babylon. Queer! Queer! The phrase 'a quarter of a million' glinted and flashed in the circumambient air. But it was almost a meaningless phrase. He was like a sort of super-savage and could not count beyond a hundred thousand. And, quite unphilosophical, he forgot that the ecstasy produced by a hundred thousand had passed in a few days, and took for granted that the ecstasy produced by two hundred and fifty thousand would endure for ever.

"Take that thing off, please," he commanded his wife when he returned to the bedroom in full array. She was by no means complete, but she had achieved some progress, and was trying the effect of her garnet necklace.

"But it's the best I've got," said she.

"No, it isn't," he flatly contradicted her, and opened the case so newly purchased.

"Arthur!" she gasped, spellbound, entranced, enchanted.

"That's my name."

"Pearls! But—but—this must have cost thousands!"

"And what if it did?" he enquired placidly, clasping the thing with much delicacy round her neck. His own pleasure was intense, and yet he severely blamed himself. Indeed he called himself a criminal. Scarcely could he meet her gaze when she put her hands on his shoulders, after a long gazing into the mirror. And when she kissed him and said with frenzy that he was a dear and a madman, he privately agreed with her. She ran to the door.

"Where are you going?"

"I must show Sissie."

"Wait a moment, child. Do you know why I've bought that necklace? Because the affair with Spinner has come off." He then gave her the figures.

She observed, not unduly moved:

"But I knew *that* would be all right."

"How did you know?"

"Because you're so clever. You always get the best of everybody."

He realised afresh that she was a highly disturbing woman. She uttered highly disturbing verdicts without thought and without warning. You never knew what she would say.

"I think," he remarked, calmly pretending that she had said something quite obvious, "that it would be as well for us not to breathe one word to anybody at all about this new windfall."

She eagerly agreed.

"But we must really begin to spend—I mean spend regularly."

"Yes, of course," he admitted.

"Otherwise it would be absurd, wouldn't it?"

"Yes, of course."

"Arthur."

"Yes."

"How much will it be—in income?"

"Well, I'm not going in for any more flutters. No! I've done absolutely with all speculating idiocies. Providence has watched over us. I take the hint. Therefore my investments will all have to be entirely safe and sound. No fancy rates of interest. I should say that by the time old Paul's fixed up my investments we shall have a bit over four hundred pounds a week coming in—if that's any guide to you."

"Arthur, isn't it *wicked!*"

She examined afresh the necklace.

By the time they were all three in the car, Mr. Prohack had become aware of the fact that in Sissie's view he ought to have bought two necklaces while he was about it.

Sissie's trunks were on the roof of the car. She had decided to take up residence at the Grand Babylon that very night. The rapidity and the uncontrollability of events made Mr. Prohack feel dizzy.

"I hope you've brought some money, darling," said his wife.

II

"Lend me some money, will you?" murmured Mr. Prohack lightly to his splendid son, after he had glanced at the bill for Eve's theatre dinner at the Grand Babylon. Mr. Prohack had indeed brought some money with him, but not enough. "Haven't got any," said Charlie, with equal lightness. "Better give me the bill. I'll see to it." Whereupon Charlie signed the bill, and handed the bowing waiter five ten shilling notes.

"That's not enough," said Mr. Prohack.

"Not enough for the tip. Well, it'll have to be. I never give more than ten per cent."

Mr. Prohack strove to conceal his own painful lack of worldliness. He had imagined that he had in his pockets heaps of money to pay for a meal for a handful of people. He was mistaken; that was all, and the incident had no importance, for a few pounds more or less could not matter in the least to a gentleman of his income. Yet he felt guilty of being a waster. He could not accustom himself to the scale of expenditure. Barely in the old days could he have earned in a week the price of the repast consumed now in an hour. The vast apartment was packed with people living at just that rate of expenditure and seeming to think naught of it. "But do two wrongs make a right?" he privately demanded of his soul. Then his soul came to the rescue with its robust commonsense and replied:

"Perhaps two wrongs don't make a right, but five hundred wrongs positively must make a right." And he felt better.

And suddenly he understood the true function of the magnificent orchestra that dominated the scene. It was the function of a brass band at a quack-dentist's booth in a fair,—to drown the cries of the victims of the art of extraction.

"Yes," he reflected, full of health and carelessness. "This is a truly great life."

The party went off in two automobiles, his own and Lady

Massulam's. Cars were fighting for room in front of the blazing façade of the Metropolitan Theatre, across which rose in fire the title of the entertainment, *Smack Your Face,* together with the names of Asprey Chown and Eliza Fiddle. Car after car poured out a contingent of glorious girls and men and was hustled off with ferocity by a row of gigantic and implacable commissionaires. Mr. Oswald Morfey walked straight into the building at the head of his guests. Highly expensive persons were humbling themselves at the little window of the box office, but Ozzie held his course, and officials performed obeisances which stopped short only at falling flat on their faces at the sight of him. Tickets were not for him.

"This is a beautiful box," said Eve to him, amazed at the grandeur of the receptacle into which they had been ushered.

"It's Mr. Chown's own box."

"Then isn't Mr. Chown to be here to-night?"

"No! He went to Paris this morning for a rest. The acting manager will telephone to him after each act. That's how he always does, you know."

"When the cat's away the mice will play," thought Mr. Prohack uncomfortably, with the naughty sensations of a mouse. The huge auditorium was a marvellous scene of excited brilliance. As the stalls filled up a burst of clapping came at intervals from the unseen pit.

"What are they clapping for?" said the simple Eve, who, like Mr. Prohack, had never been to a first-night before, to say nothing of such a super-first-night as this.

"Oh!" replied Ozzie negligently. "Some one they know by sight just come into the stalls. The *chic* thing in the pit is to recognise, and to show by applause that you have recognised. The one that applauds the oftenest wins the game in the pit."

At those words and their tone Mr. Prohack looked at Ozzie with a new eye, as who should be thinking: "Is Sissie right about this fellow after all?"

Sissie sat down modestly and calmly next to her mother. Nobody could guess from her apparently ingenuous countenance that she knew that she, and not the Terror of the departments and his wife, was the originating cause of Mr. Morfey's grandiose hospitality.

"I suppose the stalls are full of celebrities?" said Eve.

"They're full of people who've paid twice the ordinary price for their seats," answered Ozzie.

"Who's that extraordinary old red-haired woman in the box opposite?" Eve demanded.

"That's Enid."

"Enid?"

"Yes. You know the Enid stove, don't you? All ladies know the Enid stove. It's been a household word for forty years. That's the original Enid. Her father invented the stove, and named it after her when she was a girl. She never misses a first-night."

"How extraordinary! Is she what you call a celebrity?"

"Rather!"

"Now," said Mr. Prohack. "Now, at last I understand the real meaning of fame."

"But that's Charlie down there!" exclaimed Eve, suddenly, pointing to the stalls and then looking behind her to see if there was not another Charlie in the box.

"Yes," Ozzie agreed. "Lady Massulam had an extra stall, and as five's a bit of a crowd in this box. . . . I thought he'd told you."

"He had not," said Eve.

The curtain went up, and this simple gesture on the part of the curtain evoked enormous applause. The audience could not control the expression of its delight. A young lady under a sunshade appeared; the mere fact of her existence threw the audience into a new ecstasy. An old man with a red nose appeared: similar demonstrations from the audience. When these two had talked to each other and sung to each other, the applause was tripled, and when the scene changed from Piccadilly Circus at 4 a. m. to the interior of a Spanish palace inhabited by illustrious French actors and actresses who proceeded to play an act of a tragedy by Corneille, the applause was quintupled. At the end of the tragedy the applause was decupled. Then the Spanish palace dissolved into an Abyssinian harem, and Eliza Fiddle in Abyssinian costume was discovered lying upon two thousand cushions of two thousand colours, and the audience rose at Eliza and Eliza rose at the audience, and the resulting frenzy was the sublimest frenzy that ever shook a theatre. The piece was stopped dead for three minutes while the audience and Eliza protested a mutual and unique passion. From this point onwards Mr. Prohack lost his head. He ran to and fro in the bewildering glittering maze of the piece, seeking for an explanation, for a sign-post, for a clue, for the slightest hint, and found nothing. He had no alternative but to cling to Eliza Fiddle, and he clung to her desperately. She was willing to be clung to. She gave herself, not only to Mr. Prohack, but to every member of the audience separately; she gave herself in the completeness of all her manifestations. The audience was rich in the possession of the whole of her individuality, which was a great deal. She sang, danced, chattered, froze, melted, laughed, cried, flirted, kissed, kicked, cursed, and turned somersaults with the fury of a dervish, the languor of an odalisque, and the inexhaustibility of a hot-spring geyser. . . . And at length Mr. Prohack grew aware of a feeling within himself that was at war with the fresh, fine feeling of physical well-being. "I have never seen a revue before," he said in secret. "Is it possible that I am bored?"

III

"Would you care to go behind and be introduced to Miss Fiddle?" Ozzie suggested at the interval after the curtain had been raised seventeen times in response to frantic shoutings, cheerings, thumpings and clappings, and the mighty tumult of exhilaration had subsided into a happy buzz that arose from all the seats in the entire orange-tinted brilliant auditorium. The ladies would not go; the ladies feared, they said, to impose their company upon Miss Fiddle in the tremendous strain of her activities. They spoke primly and decisively. It was true that they feared; but their fear was based on consideration for themselves rather than on consideration for Miss Fiddle. Ozzie was plainly snubbed. He had offered a wonderful privilege, and it had been disdained.

Mr. Prohack could not bear the spectacle of Ozzie's discomfiture. His sad weakness for pleasing people overcame him, and, putting his hand benevolently on the young man's shoulder, he said:

"My dear fellow, personally I'm dying to go."

They went by strangely narrow corridors and through iron doors across the stage, whose shirt-sleeved, ragged population seemed to be behaving as though the last trump had sounded, and so upstairs and along a broad passage full of doors ajar from which issued whispers and exclamations and transient visions of young women. From the star's dressing-room, at the end, a crowd of all sorts and conditions of persons was being pushed. Mr. Prohack trembled with an awful apprehension, and asked himself vainly what in the name of commonsense he was doing there, and prayed that Ozzie might be refused admission. The next moment he was being introduced to a middle-aged woman in a middle-aged dressing-gown. Her face was thickly caked with paint and powder, her eyes surrounded with rings of deepest black, her finger-nails red. Mr. Prohack, not without difficulty, recognised Eliza. A dresser stood on either side of her. Blinding showers of electric light poured down upon her defenceless but hardy form. She shook hands, but Mr. Prohack deemed that she ought to bear a notice: "Danger. Visitors are requested not to touch."

"So good of you to come round," she said, in her rich and powerful voice, smiling with all her superb teeth. Mr. Prohack, entranced, gazed, not as at a woman, but as at a public monument. Nevertheless he thought that she was not a bad kind, and well suited for the rough work of the world.

"I hope you're all coming to my ball to-night," said she. Mr. Prohack had never heard of any ball. In an instant she told him that she had remarked two most charming ladies with him in the box—(inordinate faculty of observation, mused Mr. Prohack)—and in another instant she was selling him three two guinea tickets for a grand ball and rout in aid of the West End Chorus Girls' Aid Association. Could he refuse, perceiving so clearly as he did that within the public monument was hiding a wistful creature, human like himself, human like his wife and daughter? He could not.

"Now you'll *come?*" said she.

Mr. Prohack swore that he would come, his heart sinking as he realised the consequence of his own foolish weakness. There was a knock at the door.

"Did you want me, Liza?" said a voice, and a fat gentleman, clothed with resplendent correctness, stepped into the room. It was the stage-manager, a god in his way.

Eliza Fiddle became a cyclone.

"I should think I did want you," she said passionately. "That's why I sent for you, and next time I'll ask you to come quicker. I'm not going to have that squint-eyed girl on the stage any more to-night. You know, the one at the end of the row. Twice she spoiled my exit by getting in the way. And you've got to throw her out, and take it from me. She does it on purpose."

"I can't throw her out without Mr. Chown's orders, and Mr. Chown's in Paris."

"Then you refuse?"

A pause.

"Yes."

"Then I'm not going on again to-night, not if I know it. I'm not going to be insulted in my own theatre."

"It's not the girl's fault. You know they haven't got room to move."

"I don't know anything about that and I don't care. All I know is that I've finished with that squint-eyed woman, and you can choose right now between her and me. And so that's that."

Miss Fiddle's fragile complexion had approached to within six inches of the stage-manager's broad and shiny features, and it had little resemblance to any of the various faces which audiences associated with the figure of Eliza Fiddle; it was a face voluptuously distorted by the violence of emotion. As Miss Fiddle appeared to be under the impression that she was alone with the stage-manager, Mr. Prohack rendered justice to that impression by softly departing. Ozzie followed. The stage-manager also followed. "Where are you going?" they heard Eliza's voice behind them addressing the stage-manager.

"I'm going to tell your under-study to get ready quick."

An enormous altercation uprose, and faces peeped from every door in the corridor; but Mr. Prohack stayed not. Ozzie led him to Mr. Asprey Chown's private room. The Terror of the departments was shaken. Ozzie laughed gently as he shut the door.

"What will happen?" asked Mr. Prohack, affecting a gaiety he did not feel.

"What do you think will happen?" simpered Ozzie blandly, "having due regard to the fact that Miss Fiddle has to choose between three hundred and fifty pounds a week and a law-suit with Chown involving heavy damages? I must say there's nobody like Blaggs for keeping these three hundred and fifty pound a week individuals in order. Chown would sooner lose forty of them than lose Blaggs. And Eliza knows it. By the way, what do you think of the show?"

"Will it succeed?"

"You should see the advance booking. There's a thousand pounds in the house to-night. Chown will be clearing fifteen hundred a week when he's paid off his production."

"Well, it's marvellous."

"You don't mean the show?"

"No. The profit."

"I agree," simpered Ozzie.

"I'm beginning to like this sizzling idiot," thought Mr. Prohack, as it were regretfully. They left the imperial richness of Mr. Chown's private room like brothers.

IV

When Mr. Prohack touched the handle of the door of the box, he felt as though he were returning to civilisation; he felt less desolated by the immediate past and by the prospect of the immediate future; he was yearning for the society of mere women after his commerce with a star at three hundred and fifty pounds a week. True, he badly wanted to examine his soul and enquire into his philosophy of life, but he was prepared to postpone that inquest until the society of mere women had had a beneficial effect on him.

Charlie, who had been paying a state visit to his mother and sister was just leaving the box and the curtain was just going up.

"Hullo, dad!" said the youth, "you're the very man I was looking for," and he drew his father out into the corridor. "You've got two of the finest ballroom dancers I ever saw," he added to Ozzie.

"Haven't we!" Ozzie concurred, with faint enthusiasm.

"But the rest of the show . . ." Charlie went on, ruthless. "Well, if Chown's shows were only equal to his showmanship . . . ! Only they aren't!"

Ozzie raised his eyebrows—a skilful gesture that at once defended his employer and agreed with Charles.

"By the way, dad, I've got a house for you. I've told the mater about it and she's going to see it to-morrow morning."

"A house!" Mr. Prohack exclaimed weakly, foreseeing new vistas of worry. "I've got one. I can't live in two."

"But this one's a *house*. You know about it, don't you, Morfey?"

Ozzie gave a nod and a vague smile.

"See here, dad! Come out here a minute."

Ozzie discreetly entered the box and closed the door.

"What is it?" asked Mr. Prohack.

"It's this," Charlie replied, handing his parent a cheque. "I've deducted what I paid for you to-night from what you lent me not long since. I've calculated interest on the loan at ten per cent. You can get ten practically anywhere in these days, worse luck."

"But I don't want this, my boy," Mr. Prohack protested, holding the cheque as he might have held a lady's handkerchief retrieved from the ground.

"Well, I'm quite sure I don't," said Charlie, a little stiffly.

There was a pause.

"As you please," said Mr. Prohack, putting the cheque—interest and all—into his pocket.

"Thanks," said Charlie. "Much obliged. You're a noble father, and I shouldn't be a bit surprised if you've laid the foundation of my fortunes. But of course you never know—in my business."

"What *is* your business?" Mr. Prohack asked timidly, almost apologetically. He had made up his mind on the previous evening that he would talk to Charlie as a father ought to talk to a son, that is to say, like a cross-examining barrister and a moralist combined. He had decided that it was more than his right—it was his duty to do so. But now the right, if not the duty, seemed less plain, and he remembered what he had said to Eve concerning the right attitude of parents to children. And chiefly he remembered that Charlie was not in his debt.

"I'm a buyer and seller. I buy for less than I sell for. That's how I live."

"It appears to be profitable."

"Yes. I made over ten thousand in Glasgow, buying an option on an engineering business—with your money—from people who wanted to get rid of it, and then selling what I hadn't paid for to people in London who wanted to get hold of an engineering business up there. Seems simple enough, and the only reason everybody isn't doing it is that it isn't as simple as it seems. At least, it's simple, but there's a knack in it. I found out I'd got the knack through my little deals in motor-bikes and things. As a matter of fact I didn't find out,—some one told me, and I began to think. . . . But don't be alarmed if I go bust. I'm on to a much bigger option now, in the City. Oh! Very much bigger. If it comes off . . . you'll see. Lady Massulam is keen on it, and she's something of a judge. . . . Any remarks?"

Mr. Prohack looked cautiously at the young man, his own creation, to whom, only the other day as it seemed, he had been in the habit of giving one pound per school-term for pocket-money. And he was affrighted—not by what he had created, but by the astounding possibilities of fatherhood, which suddenly presented itself to him as a most dangerous pursuit.

"No remarks," said he, briefly. What remarks indeed could he offer? Wildly guessing at the truth about his son, in that conversation with Eve on the previous evening, he had happened to guess right. And his sermon to Eve prevented now the issue of remarks.

"Oh! Of course!" Charlie burst out. "You can't tell me anything I don't know already. I'm a pirate. I'm not producing. All the money I make has to be earned by somebody else before

I get hold of it. I'm not doing any good to my beautiful country. But I did try to find a useful job, didn't I? My beautiful country wouldn't have me. It only wanted me in the trenches. Well, it's got to have me. I'll jolly well make it pay now. I'll squeeze every penny out of it. I'll teach it a lesson. And why not? I shall only be shoving its own ideas down its throat. Supposing I hadn't got this knack and I hadn't had *you*. I might have been wearing all my ribbons and playing a barrel organ in Oxford Street to-day instead of living at the Grand Babylon."

"You're becoming quite eloquent in your old age," said Mr. Prohack, tremulously jocular while looking with alarm into his paternal heart. Was not he himself a pirate? Had not the hundred and fifty thousand that was coming to him had to be earned by somebody else? Money did not make itself.

"Well," retorted Charlie, with a grim smile. "There's one thing to be said for me. When I *do* talk, I talk."

"And so at last you've begun to read?"

"I'm not going to be the ordinary millionaire. No fear! Make your mind easy on that point. Besides, reading isn't so bad after all."

"And what about that house you were speaking of? You aren't going to plant any of your options on me."

"We'll discuss that to-morrow. I must get back to my seat," said Charlie firmly, moving away. "So long."

"I say," Mr. Prohack summoned him to return. "I'm rather curious about the methods of you millionaires. Just when did you sign that cheque for me? You only lent me the money as we were leaving the hotel."

"I made it out while I was talking to the mater and Sis in your box, of course."

"How simple are the acts of genius—after they're accomplished!" observed Mr. Prohack. "Naturally you signed it in the box."

As he rejoined his family he yawned, surprising himself. He began to feel a mysterious fatigue. The effect of the Turkish bath, without doubt! The remainder of the evening stretched out in front of him, interminably tedious. The title of the play was misleading. He could not smack his face. He wished to heaven he could. . . . And then, after the play, the ball! Eliza might tell him to dance with her. She would be quite capable of such a deed. And by universal convention her suggestions were the equivalent of demands. Nobody ever could or would refuse to dance with Eliza. . . . There she was, all her four limbs superbly displayed, sweetly smiling with her enormous mouth, just as if the relations between Blaggs and herself were those of Paul and Virginia. The excited audience, in the professional phrase, was "eating" her.

V

Mr. Prohack was really a most absurd person. *Smack Your Face,* when it came to an end, towards midnight, had established itself as an authentic enormous success; and because Mr. Prohack did not care for it, because it bored him, because he found it vulgar and tedious and expensive, because it tasted in his mouth like a dust-and-ashes sandwich, the fellow actually felt sad; he felt even bitter. He hated to see the fashionable and splendid audience unwilling to leave the theatre, cheering one super-favourite, five arch-favourites and fifteen favourites, and cheering them again and again, and sending the curtain up and down and up and down time after time. He could not bear that what he detested should be deliriously admired. He went so far as to form views about the decadence of the theatre as an institution. Most of all he was disgusted because his beloved Eve was not disgusted. Eve said placidly that she did not think much of the affair, but that she had thoroughly enjoyed it and wouldn't mind coming on the next night to see it afresh. He said gloomily:

"And I've been bringing you up for nearly twenty-five years."

As for Sissie, she was quietly and sternly enthusiastic about a lot of the dancing. She announced her judgment as an expert, and Charlie agreed with her, and there was no appeal, and Mr. Prohack had the air of an ignorant outsider whose opinions were negligible. Further, he was absurd in that, though he assuredly had no desire whatever to go to the dance, he fretted at the delay in getting there. Even when they had all got out to the porch of the theatre he exhibited a controlled but intense impatience because Charlie did not produce the car instantly from amidst the confused hordes of cars that waited in the surrounding streets. Moreover, as regards the ball, he had foolishly put himself in a false position; for he was compelled to pretend that he had purchased the tickets because he personally wanted to go to the ball. Had he not been learning to dance? Now the fact was that he looked forward to the ball with terror. He had never performed publicly. He proceeded from one pretence to another. When Charlie stated curtly that he, Charlie, was going to no ball, he feigned disappointment, saying that Charlie ought to go for his sister's sake. Yet he was greatly relieved at Charlie's departure (even in Lady Massulam's car); he could not stomach the notion of Charlie cynically watching his infant steps on the polished, treacherous floor. In the matter of Charlie, Oswald Morfey also feigned disappointment, but for a different reason. Ozzie wanted to have Sissie as much as possible to himself.

Mr. Prohack yawned in the car.

"You're over-tired, Arthur. It's the Turkish bath," said Eve with commiseration. This was a bad enough mistake on her part, but she worsened it by adding: "Perhaps the wisest thing would be for us all to go home."

Mr. Prohack was extremely exhausted, and would have given his head to go home; but so odd, so contrary, so deceitful and so silly was his nature that he replied:

"Darling! Where on earth do you get these ideas from? There's nothing like a Turkish bath for stimulating you, and I'm not at all tired. I never felt better in my life. But the atmosphere of that theatre would make anybody yawn."

The ball was held in a picture-gallery where an exhibition of the International Portrait Society was in progress. The crush of cars at the portals was as keen as that at the portals of the Metropolitan. And all the persons who got out of the cars seemed as fresh as if they had just got out of bed. Mr. Prohack was astonished at the vast number of people who didn't care what time they went to bed because they didn't care what time they arose; he was in danger of being morbidly obsessed by the extraordinary prevalence of idleness. The rooms were full of brilliant idlers in all colours. Everybody except chorus girls had thought fit to appear at this ball in aid of the admirably charitable Chorus Girls' Aid Association. And as everybody was also on the walls, the dancers had to compete with their portraits—a competition in which many of them were well beaten.

After they had visited the supper-room, where both Sissie and her mother did wonderful feats of degustation and Mr. Prohack drank all that was good for him, Sissie ordered her father to dance with her. He refused. She went off with Ozzie, while her parents sat side by side on gold chairs like ancestors. Sissie repeated her command, and Mr. Prohack was about to disobey when Eliza Fiddle dawned upon the assemblage.

The supernatural creature had been rehearsing until 3 a. m., she had been trying on clothes from 9 a. m. until 5 p. m. She had borne the chief weight of *Smack Your Face,* on her unique shoulders for nearly three hours and a half. She had changed into an unforgettable black ball-dress, cut to demonstrate in the clearest fashion that her shoulders had suffered no harm; and here she was as fresh as Aphrodite from the foam. She immediately set herself to bear the chief weight of the ball on those same defenceless shoulders; for she was, in theory at any rate, the leading organiser of the affair, and according to the entire press it was "her" ball. As soon as he saw her Mr. Prohack had a most ridiculous fear lest she should pick him out for a dance, and to protect himself he said "All right" to his daughter.

A fox-trot announced itself. In his own drawing-room, with the door locked, Mr. Prohack could and did treat a fox-trot as child's play. But now he realised that he had utterly forgotten every movement of the infernal thing. Agony as he stood up and took his daughter's hand! An awful conviction that everybody (who was anybody) was staring to witness the Terror of the departments trying to jazz in public for the first time. A sick, sinking fear lest some of his old colleagues from the Treasury might be lurking in corners to guy him! Agony as he collected himself and swayed his body slightly to catch the rhythm of the tune! Where in heaven's name was the first beat in the bar?

"Walk first," said Sissie professionally. . . . He was in motion.

"Now!" said Sissie. "*One,* two. *One,* two." Miraculously he was dancing! It was as though the whole room was shouting: "They're off!" Sissie steered him.

"Don't look at your feet!" said she sharply, and like a schoolboy he chucked his chin obediently up. . . . Then he was steering her. Although her feet were the reverse of enormous he somehow could not keep off them; but that girl was made of hardy stuff and never winced. He was doing better. Pride was puffing him. Yet he desired the music to stop. The music did stop.

"Thanks," he breathed.

"Oh, no!" said she. "That's not all." The dancers clapped and the orchestra resumed. He started again. Couples surged around him, and sometimes he avoided them and sometimes he did not. Then he saw a head bobbing not far away, as if it were one cork and he another on a choppy sea. It resembled Eve's head. It was Eve's head. She was dancing with Oswald Morfey. He had never supposed that Eve could dance these new dances.

"Let's stop," said he.

"Certainly not," Sissie forbade. "We must finish it." He finished it, rather breathless and dizzy. He had lived through it.

"You're perfectly wonderful, Arthur," said Eve when they met.

"Oh, no! I'm no good."

"I was frightfully nervous about you at first," said Sissie.

He said briefly:

"You needn't have been. I wasn't."

A little later Eve said to him:

"Aren't you going to ask *me* to dance, Arthur?"

Dancing with Eve was not quite like dancing with Sissie, but they safely survived deadly perils. And Mr. Prohack perspired in a very healthy fashion.

"You dance really beautifully, dear," said Eve, benevolently smiling.

After that he cut himself free and roamed about. He wanted to ask Eliza Fiddle to dance, and also he didn't want to ask her to dance. However, he had apparently ceased to exist for her. Ozzie had introduced him to several radiant young creatures. He wanted to ask them to dance; but he dared not. And he was furious with himself. To dance with one's daughter and wife was well enough in its way, but it was not the real thing. It was without salt. One or two of the radiances glanced at him with inviting eyes, but no, he dared not face it. He grew gloomy, gloomier. He thought angrily: "All this is not for me. I'm a middle-aged fool, and I've known it all along." Life lost its savour and became repugnant. Fatigue punished him, and simultaneously reduced two hundred and fifty thousand pounds to the value of about fourpence. It was Eve who got him away.

"Home," he called to Carthew, after Eve and Sissie had said good-bye to Ozzie and stowed themselves into the car.

"Excuse me," said Sissie. "You have to deliver me at the Grand Babylon first."

He had forgotten! This détour was the acutest torture of the night. He could no longer bear not to be in bed. And when, after endless nocturnal miles, he did finally get home and into bed, he sighed as one taken off the rack. Ah! The delicious contact with the pillow!

VI

But there are certain persons who, although their minds are logical enough, have illogical bodies. Mr. Prohack was one of these. His ridiculous physical organism (as he had once informed Dr. Veiga) was least capable of going to sleep when it was most fatigued. If Mr. Prohack's body had retired to bed four hours earlier than in fact it did, Mr. Prohack would have slept instantly and with ease. Now, despite delicious contact with the pillow, he could not 'get off.' And his mind, influenced by his body, grew restless, then excited, then distressingly realistic. His mind began to ask fundamental questions, questions not a bit original but none the less very awkward.

"You've had your first idle day, Mr. Prohack," said his mind challengingly instead of composing itself to slumber. "It was organised on scientific lines. It was carried out with conscientiousness. And look at you! And look at me! You've had a few good moments, as for example at the Turkish bath, but do you want a succession of such days? Could you survive a succession of such days? Would you even care to acquire a hundred and fifty thousand pounds every day? You have eaten too much and drunk too much and run too hard after pleasure, and been too much bored, and met too many antipathetic people, and squandered too much money, and set a thoroughly bad example to your family. You have been happy only in spasms. Your health is good; you are cured of your malady. Does that render you any more contented? It does not. You have complicated your existence in the hope of improving it. But have you improved it? No. You ought to simplify your existence. But will you? You will not. All your strength of purpose will be needed to prevent still further complications being woven into your existence. To inherit a hundred thousand pounds was your misfortune. But deliberately to increase the sum to a quarter of a million was your fault. You were happier at the Treasury. You left the Treasury on account of illness. You are not ill any more. Will you go back to the Treasury? No. You will never go back, because your powerful commonsense tells you that to return to the Treasury with an income of twenty thousand a year would be grotesque. And rather than be grotesque you would suffer. Again, rightly. Nothing is worse than to be grotesque."

"Further," said his mind, "you have started your son on a sinister career of adventure that may end in calamity. You have ministered to your daughter's latent frivolity. You have put temptations in the way of your wife which she cannot withstand. You have developed yourself into a waster. What is the remedy? Obviously to dispose of your money. But your ladies would not permit you to do so and they are entitled to be heard on the point. Moreover, how could you dispose of it? Not in charity, because you are convinced of the grave social mischievousness of charity. And not in helping any great social movement, because you are not silly enough not to know that the lavishing of wealth never really aids, but most viciously hinders, the proper evolution of a society. And you cannot save your income and let it accumulate, because if you did you would once again be tumbling into the grotesque; and you would, further, be leaving to your successors a legacy of evil which no man is justified in leaving to his successors. No! Your case is in practice irremediable. Like the murderer on the scaffold, you are the victim of circumstances. And not one human being in a million will pity you. You are a living tragedy which only death can end."

During this disconcerting session Eve had been mysteriously engaged in the boudoir. She now came into the dark bedroom.

"What?" she softly murmured, hearing Mr. Prohack's restlessness. "Not asleep, darling?" She bent over him and kissed him and her kiss was even softer, more soporific, than her voice. "Now do go to sleep."

And Mr. Prohack went to sleep, and his last waking thought was, with the feel of the kiss on his nose (the poor woman had aimed badly in the dark): "Anyway this tragedy has one compensation, of which a hundred quarter of a millions can't deprive me."

CHAPTER XV

THE HEAVY FATHER

I

WITHIN a few moments of his final waking up the next morning, Mr. Prohack beheld Eve bending over him, the image of solicitude. She was dressed for outdoor business.

"How do you feel?" she asked, in a tender tone that demanded to know the worst at once.

"Why?" asked Mr. Prohack, thus with one word, and a smile to match, criticising her tone.

"You looked so dreadfully tired last night. I did feel sorry for you, darling. Don't you think you'd better stay in bed to-day?"

"Can you seriously suggest such a thing?" he cried. "What about my daily programme if I stay in bed? I have undertaken to be idle, and nobody can be scientifically idle in bed. I'm late already. Where's my breakfast? Where are my newspapers? I must begin the day without the loss of another moment. Please give me my dressing-gown."

"I very much wonder how your blood-pressure is," Eve complained.

"And you, I suppose, are perfectly well?"

"Oh, yes, I am. I'm absolutely cured. Dr. Veiga is really very marvellous. But I always told you he was."

"Well," said Mr. Prohack. "What's sauce for the goose has to be sauce for the gander. If you're perfectly well, so am I. You can't have the monopoly of good health in this marriage. What's that pamphlet you've got in your hand, my dove?"

"Oh! It's nothing. It's only about the League of all the Arts. Mr. Morfey gave it to me."

"I suppose it was that pamphlet you were reading last night in the boudoir instead of coming to bed. Eve, you're hiding something from me. Where are you going to in such a hurry?"

"I'm not hiding anything, you silly boy. . . . I thought I'd just run along and have a look at that house. You see, if it isn't at all the kind of thing to suit us, me going first will save you the trouble of going."

"What house?" exclaimed Mr. Prohack with terrible emphasis.

"But Charlie told me he'd told you all about it," Eve protested innocently.

"Charlie told you no such thing," Mr. Prohack contradicted her. "If he told you anything at all, he merely told you that he'd mentioned a house to me in the most casual manner."

Eve proceeded blandly:

"It's in Manchester Square, very handy for the Wallace Gallery, and you know how fond you are of pictures. It's on sale, furniture and all; but it can be rented for a year to see how it suits us. Of course it may not suit us a bit. I understand it has some lovely rooms. Charlie says it would be exactly the thing for big receptions."

"*Big receptions!* I shall have nothing to do with it. Now we've lost our children even this house is too big for us. And I know what the houses in Manchester Square are. You've said all your life you hate receptions."

"So I do. They're so much trouble. But one never knows what may happen . . . ! And with plenty of servants . . . !"

"You understand me. I shall have nothing to do with it. Nothing!"

"Darling, please, please don't excite yourself. The decision will rest entirely with you. You know I shouldn't dream of influencing you. As if I could! However, I've promised to meet Charlie there this morning. So I suppose I'd better go. Carthew is late with the car." She tapped her foot. "And yet I specially told him to be here prompt."

"Well, considering the hour he brought us home, he's scarcely had time to get into bed yet. He ought to have had the morning off."

"Why? A chauffeur's a chauffeur after all. They know what they have to do. Besides, Carthew would do anything for me."

"Yes, that's you all over. You deliberately bewitch him, and then you shamelessly exploit him. I shall compare notes with Carthew. I can give him a useful tip or two about you."

"Oh! Here he is!" said Eve, who had been watching out of the window. "Au revoir, my pet. Here's Machin with your breakfast and newspapers. I daresay I shall be back before you're up. But don't count on me."

As he raised himself against pillows for the meal, after both she and Machin had gone, Mr. Prohack remembered what his mind had said to him a few hours earlier about fighting against further complications of his existence, and he set his teeth and determined to fight hard.

Scarcely had he begun his breakfast when Eve returned, in a state of excitement.

"There's a young woman downstairs waiting for you in the dining-room. She wouldn't give her name to Machin, it seems, but she says she's your new secretary. Apparently she recognised my car on the way from the garage and stopped it and got into it; and then she found out she'd forgotten something and the car had to go back with her to where she lives, wherever that is, and that's why Carthew was late for *me*." Eve delivered these sentences with a tremendous air of ordinariness, as though they related quite usual events and disturbances, and as though no wife could possibly see in them any matter for astonishment or reproach. Such was one of her methods of making an effect.

Mr. Prohack collected himself. On several occasions during the previous afternoon and evening he had meditated somewhat uneasily upon the domestic difficulties which might inhere in this impulsive engagement of Miss Winstock as a private secretary, but since waking up the affair had not presented itself to his mind. He had indeed completely forgotten it.

"Who told you all this?" he asked warily.

"Well, she told Machin and Machin told me."

"Let me see now," said Mr. Prohack. "Yes. It's quite true. After ordering a pair of braces yesterday morning, I did order a secretary. She was recommended to me."

"You didn't say anything about it yesterday."

"My dove, had I a chance to do so? Had we a single moment together? And you know how I was when we reached home, don't you? . . . You see, I always had a secretary at the Treasury, and I feel sort of lost without one. So I—"

"But, darling, *of course!* I always believe in letting you do exactly as you like. It's the only way. . . . Au revoir, my pet. Charlie will be frightfully angry with me." And then, at the door: "If she hasn't got anything to do she can always see to the flowers for me. Perhaps when I come back you'll introduce us."

As soon as he had heard the bang of the front-door Mr. Prohack rang his bell.

"Machin, I understand that my secretary is waiting in the dining-room."

"Yes, sir."

"Ask her to take her things off and then bring her up here."

"Up here, sir?"

"That's right."

In seven movements of unimaginable stealthy swiftness Machin tidied the worst disorders of the room and departed. Mr. Prohack continued his breakfast.

Miss Winstock appeared with a small portable typewriter in her arms and a notebook lodged on the typewriter. She was wearing a smart black skirt and a smart white blouse with a high collar. In her unsullied freshness of attire she somewhat resembled a stage secretary on a first night; she might have been mistaken for a brilliant imitation of a real secretary.

II

"Good morning. So you've come," Mr. Prohack greeted her firmly.

"Good morning. Yes, Mr. Prohack."

"Well, put that thing down on a chair somewhere."

Machin also had entered the room. She handed a paper to Mr. Prohack.

"Mistress asked me to give you that, sir."

It was a lengthy description, typewritten, of a house in Manchester Square.

"Pass me those matches, please," said Mr. Prohack to Mimi when they were alone. "By the way, why wouldn't you give your name when you arrived?"

"Because I didn't know what it was."

"Didn't know what it was?"

"When I told you my Christian name yesterday you said it wouldn't do at all, and I was never to mention it again. In the absence of definite instructions about my surname I thought I had better pursue a cautious policy of waiting. I've told the chauffeur that he will know my name in due course and that until I tell him what it is he mustn't know it. I was not sure whether you would wish the members of your household to know that I'm the person who had a collision with your car. Mrs. Prohack and I were both in a state of collapse after the accident, and I was removed before she could see me. Therefore she did not recognise me this morning. But on the other hand she has no doubt heard my name often enough since the accident and would recognise *that*."

Mr. Prohack lit the first cigarette of the day.

"Why did you bring that typewriter?" he asked gravely.

"It's mine. I thought that if you didn't happen to have one

here it might be useful. It was the typewriter that the car had to go back for. I'd forgotten it. I can take it away again. But if you like you can either buy it or hire it from me."

The girl could not have guessed it from his countenance, but Mr. Prohack was thunderstruck. She was bringing forward considerations which positively had not presented themselves to him. That she had much initiative was clear from her conduct of the previous day. She now disclosed a startling capacity for intrigue. Mr. Prohack, however, was not intimidated. The experience of an official life had taught him the value of taciturnity, and moreover a comfortable feeling of satisfaction stole over him as he realised that once again he had a secretary under his thumb. He seemed to be delightfully resuming the habits which ill-health had so ruthlessly broken.

"Mary Warburton," said he at length.

"Certainly," said she. "I'll tell your chauffeur."

"The initials will correspond—in case—"

"Yes," said she. "I'd noticed that."

"We will see what your typewriting machine is capable of, and then I'll decide about it."

"Certainly."

"Please take down some letters."

"Mr. Carrel Quire always told me what he wanted said, and I wrote the letters myself."

"That is very interesting," said Mr. Prohack. "Perhaps you can manage to sit at the dressing-table. Mind that necklace there. It's supposed to be rather valuable. Put it in the case, and put the case in the middle drawer."

"Don't you keep it in a safe?" said Miss Warburton, obeying.

"All questions about necklaces should be addressed direct to Mrs. Prohack."

"I prefer to take down on my knee," said Miss Warburton, opening her notebook, "if I am to take down."

"You are. Now. 'Dear Madam. I am requested by my Lords of the Treasury to forward to you the enclosed cheque for one hundred pounds for your Privy Purse.' New line. 'I am also to state that no account of expenditure will be required.' New line. 'Be good enough to acknowledge receipt. Your obedient servant. To Miss Prohack, Grand Babylon Hotel.' Got it? 'Dear Sir. With reference to the action instituted by your company against Miss Mimi Winstock, and to my claim against your company under my accident policy. I have seen the defendant. She had evidently behaved in an extremely foolish not to say criminal way;

but as the result of a personal appeal from her I have decided to settle the matter privately. Please therefore accept this letter as a release from all your liabilities to me, and also as my personal undertaking to pay all the costs of the action on both sides. Yours faithfully. Secretary, World's Car Insurance Corporation.' Wipe your eyes, wipe your eyes, Miss Warburton. You're wetting the notebook."

"I was only crying because you're so kind. I know I *did* behave in a criminal way."

"Just so, Miss Warburton. But it will be more convenient for me and for you too if you can arrange to cry in your own time and not in mine." And he continued to address her, in his own mind: "Don't think I haven't noticed your aspiring nose and your ruthless little lips and your gift for conspiracy and your wonderful weakness for tears! And don't confuse me with Mr. Carrel Quire, because we're two quite different people! You've got to be useful to me." And in a more remote part of his mind, he continued still further: "You're quite a decent sort of child, only you've been spoilt. I'll unspoil you. You've taken your first medicine rather well. I like you, or I shall like you before I've done with you."

Miss Warburton wiped her eyes.

"You understand," Mr. Prohack proceeded aloud, "that you're engaged as my confidential secretary. And when I say 'confidential' I mean 'confidential' in the fullest sense."

"Oh, quite," Miss Warburton concurred almost passionately.

"And you aren't anybody else's secretary but mine. You may pretend to be everybody else's secretary, you may pretend as much as you please—it may even be advisable to do so—but the fact must always remain that you are mine alone. You have to protect my interests, and let me warn you that my interests are sometimes very strange, not to say peculiar. Get well into your head that there are not ten commandments in my service. There is only one: to watch over my interests, to protect them against everybody else in the whole world. In return for a living wage, you give me the most absolute loyalty, a loyalty which sticks at nothing, nothing, nothing."

"Oh, Mr. Prohack!" replied Mary Warburton, smiling simply. "You needn't tell me all that. I entirely understand. It's the usual thing for confidential secretaries, isn't it?"

"And now," Mr. Prohack went on, ignoring her. "This being made perfectly clear, go into the boudoir—that's the room through there—and bring me here all the parcels lying about. Our next task is to check the accuracy of several of the leading tradesmen in the West End."

"I think there are one or two more parcels that have been delivered this morning, in the hall," said Miss Warburton. "Perhaps I had better fetch them."

"Perhaps you had."

In a few minutes, Miss Warburton, by dint of opening parcels, had transformed the bedroom into a composite of the principal men's shops in Piccadilly and Bond Street. Mr. Prohack recoiled before the chromatic show and also before the prospect of Eve's views on the show.

"Take everything into the boudoir," said he, "and arrange them under the sofa. It's important that we should not lose our heads in this crisis. When you go out to lunch you will buy some foolscap paper and this afternoon you will make a schedule of the goods, divided according to the portions of the human frame which they are intended to conceal or adorn. What are you laughing at, Miss Warburton?"

"You are so amusing, Mr. Prohack."

"I may be amusing, but I am not susceptible to the flattery of giggling. Endeavour not to treat serious subjects lightly."

"I don't see any boots."

"Neither do I. You will telephone to the bootmaker's, and to my tailor's; also to Sir Paul Spinner and Messrs. Smathe and Smathe. But before that I will just dictate a few more letters."

"Certainly."

When he had finished dictating, Mr. Prohack said:

"I shall now get up. Go downstairs and ask Machin—that's the parlourmaid—to show you the breakfast-room. The breakfast-room is behind the dining-room, and is so called because it is never employed for breakfast. It exists in all truly London houses, and is perfectly useless in all of them except those occupied by dentists, who use it for their beneficent labours in taking things from, or adding things to, the bodies of their patients. The breakfast-room in this house will be the secretary's room—your room if you continue to give me satisfaction. Remove that typewriting machine from here, and arrange your room according to your desire. . . . And I say, Miss Warburton."

"Yes, Mr. Prohack," eagerly responded the secretary, pausing at the door.

"Yesterday I gave you a brief outline of your duties. But I omitted one exceedingly important item—almost as important as not falling in love with my son. You will have to keep on good terms with Machin. Machin is indispensable and irreplaceable. I could get forty absolutely loyal secretaries while my wife was unsuccessfully searching for another Machin."

"I have an infallible way with parlourmaids," said Miss Warburton.

"What is that?"

"I listen to their grievances and to their love-affairs."

Mr. Prohack, though fatigued, felt himself to be inordinately well, and he divined that this felicity was due to the exercise of dancing on the previous night, following upon the Turkish bath. He had not felt so well for many years. He laughed to himself at intervals as he performed his toilette, and knew not quite why. His secretary was just like a new toy to him, offering many of the advantages of official life and routine without any of the drawbacks. At half past eleven he descended, wearing one or two of the more discreet of his new possessions, and with the sensation of having already transacted a good day's work, into the breakfast-room and found Miss Warburton and Machin in converse. Machin feverishly poked the freshly-lit fire and then, pretending to have urgent business elsewhere, left the room.

"Here are some particulars of a house in Manchester Square," said Mr. Prohack. "Please read them."

Miss Warburton complied.

"It seems really very nice," said she. "Very nice indeed."

"Does it? Now listen to me. That house is apparently the most practical and the most beautiful house in London. Judging from the description, it deserves to be put under a glass-case in a museum and labelled 'the ideal house.' There is no fault to be found with that house, and I should probably take it at once but for one point. I don't want it. I do not want it. Do I make myself clear? I have no use for it whatever."

"Then you've inspected it."

"I have not. But I don't want it. Now a determined effort will shortly be made to induce me to take that house. I will not go into details or personalities. I say merely that a determined effort will shortly be made to force me to act against my will and my wishes. This effort must be circumvented. In a word, the present is a moment when I may need the unscrupulous services of an utterly devoted confidential secretary."

"What am I to do?"

"I haven't the slightest idea. All I know is that my existence must not on any account be complicated, and that the possession of that house would seriously complicate it."

"Will you leave the matter to me, Mr. Prohack?"

"What shall you do?"

"Wouldn't it be better for you not to know what I should do?" Miss Warburton glanced at him oddly. Her glance was agreeable, and yet disconcerting. The attractiveness of the young woman seemed to be accentuated. The institution of the confidential secretary was magnified, in the eyes of Mr. Prohack, into one of the greatest achievements of human society.

"Not at all," said he, in reply. "You are under-rating my capabilities, for I can know and not know simultaneously."

"Well," said Miss Warburton. "You can't take an old house without having the drains examined, obviously. Supposing the report on the drains was unfavourable?"

"Do you propose to tamper with the drains?"

"Certainly not. I shouldn't dream of doing anything so disgraceful. But I might tamper with the surveyor who made the report on the drains."

"Say no more," Mr. Prohack adjured her. "I'm going out."

And he went out, though he had by no means finished instructing Miss Warburton in the art of being his secretary. She did not even know where to find the essential tools of her calling, nor yet the names of tradesmen to whom she had to telephone. He ought to have stayed in if only to present his secretary to his wife. But he went out—to reflect in private upon her initiative, her ready resourcefulness, her great gift for conspiracy. He had to get away from her. The thought of her induced in him qualms of trepidation. Could he after all manage her? What a loss would she be to Mr. Carrel Quire! Nevertheless she was capable of being foolish. It was her foolishness that had transferred her from Mr. Carrel Quire to himself.

III

Mr. Prohack went out because he was drawn out, by the force of an attraction which he would scarcely avow even to himself,—a mysterious and horrible attraction which, if he had been a logical human being like the rest of us, ought to have been a repulsion for him.

And as he was walking abroad in the pleasant foggy sunshine of the West End streets, a plutocratic idler with nothing to do but yield to strange impulses, he saw on a motor-bus the placard of a financial daily paper bearing the line: "The Latest Oil Coup." He immediately wanted to buy that paper. As a London citizen he held the opinion that whenever he wanted a thing he ought to be able to buy it at the next corner. Yet now he looked in every direction but could see no symptom of a newspaper shop anywhere. The time was morning—for the West End it was early morning—and there were newsboys on the pavements, but by a curious anomaly they were selling evening and not morning newspapers. Daringly he asked one of these infants for the financial daily; the infant sniggered and did no more. Another directed him to a shop up an alley off the Edgware Road. The shopman doubted the existence of any such financial daily as Mr. Prohack indicated, apparently attaching no importance to the fact that it was advertised on every motor-bus travelling along the Edgware Road, but he suggested that if it did exist, it might just conceivably be purchased at the main bookstall at Paddington Station. Determined to obtain the paper at all costs, Mr. Prohack stopped a taxi-cab and drove to Paddington, squandering eighteenpence on the journey, and reflecting as he rolled forward upon the primitiveness of a so-called civilisation in which you could not buy a morning paper in the morning without spending the whole morning over the transaction—and reflecting also upon the disturbing fact that after one full day of its practice, his scheme of scientific idleness had gone all to bits. He got the paper, and read therein a very exciting account of Sir Paul Spinner's deal in oil-lands. The amount of Paul's profit was not specified, but readers were given to understand that it was enormous and that Paul had successfully bled the greatest Oil Combine in the world. The article, though discreet and vague in phraseology, was well worth a line on any placard. It had cost Mr. Prohack the price of a complete Shakespere, but he did not call it dear. He threw the paper away with a free optimistic gesture of delight. Yes, he had wisely put his trust in old Paul and he was veritably a rich man—one who could look down on mediocre fortunes of a hundred thousand pounds or so. Civilisation was not so bad after all.

Then the original attraction which had drawn him out of the house resumed its pull. . . . Why did his subconscious feet take him in the direction of Manchester Square? True, the Wallace Collection of pictures is to be found at Hertford House, Manchester Square, and Mr. Prohack had always been interested in pictures! Well, if he did happen to find himself in Manchester Square he might perhaps glance at the exterior of the dwelling which his son desired to plant upon him and his wife desired him to be planted with. . . . It was there right enough. It had not been spirited away in the night hours. He recognised the number. An enormous house; the largest in the Square after Hertford House. Over its monumental portico was an enormous sign, truthfully describing it as "this noble mansion." As no automobile stood at the front-door Mr. Prohack concluded that his wife's visit of inspection was over. Doubtless she was seeking him at home at that moment to the end of persuading him by her soft, unscrupulous arts to take the noble mansion.

The front-door was ajar. Astounding carelessness on the part of the caretaker! Mr. Prohack's subconscious legs carried him into the house. The interior was amazing. Mr. Prohack had always been interested, not only in pictures, but in furniture. Pictures and furniture might have been called the weakness to which his circumstances had hitherto compelled him to be too strong to yield. He knew a good picture, and he knew a good piece of furniture, when he saw them. The noble mansion was full of good pictures and good furniture. Evidently it had been the home of somebody who had both fine tastes and the means to gratify them. And the place was complete. Nothing had been removed, and nothing had been protected against the grimy dust of London. The occupiers might have walked out of it a few hours earlier. The effect of dark richness in the half-shuttered rooms almost overwhelmed Mr. Prohack. Nobody preventing, he climbed the beautiful Georgian staircase, which was carpeted with a series of wondrous Persian carpets laid end to end. A woman in a black apron appeared in the hall from the basement, gazed at Mr. Prohack's mounting legs, and said naught. On the first-floor was the drawing-room, a magnificent apartment exquisitely furnished in Louis Quinze. Mr. Prohack blenched. He had expected nothing half so marvellous. Was it possible that he could afford to take this noble mansion and live in it? It was more than possible; it was sure.

Mr. Prohack had a foreboding of a wild, transient impulse to take it. The impulse died ere it was born. No further complications of his existence were to be permitted; he would fight against them to the last drop of his blood. And the complications incident to residence in such an abode would be enormous. Still, he thought that he might as well see the whole house, and he proceeded upstairs, wondering how many people there were in London who possessed the taste to make, and the money to maintain, such a home. Even the stairs from the first to the second floor, were beautiful, having a lovely carpet, lovely engravings on the walls, and a delightful balustrade. On the second-floor landing were two tables covered with objects of art, any of which Mr. Pro-back might have pocketed and nobody the wiser; the carelessness that left the place unguarded was merely prodigious.

Mr. Prohack heard a sound; it might have been the creak of a floor-board or the displacement of a piece of furniture. Startled, he looked through a half-open door into a small room. He could see an old gilt mirror over a fire-place; and in the mirror the images of the upper portions of a young man and a young woman. The young woman was beyond question Sissie Prohack. The young man, he decided after a moment of hesitation—for he could distinguish only a male overcoated back in the glass—was Oswald Morfey. The images were very close together. They did not move. Then Mr. Prohack overheard a whisper, but did not catch its purport. Then the image of the girl's face began to blush; it went redder and redder, and the crimson seemed to flow downwards until the exposed neck blushed also. A marvellous and a disconcerting spectacle. Mr. Prohack felt that he himself was blushing. Then the two images blended, and the girl's head and hat seemed to be agitated as by a high wind. And then both images moved out of the field of the mirror.

The final expression on the girl's face as it vanished was one of the most exquisite things that Mr. Prohack had ever witnessed. It brought the tears to his eyes. Nevertheless he was shocked.

His mind ran:

"That fellow has kissed my daughter, and he has kissed her for the first time. It is monstrous that any girl, and especially my daughter, should be kissed for the first time. I have not been consulted, and I had not the slightest idea that matters had gone so far. Her mother has probably been here, with Charlie, and gone off leaving these doves together. Culpable carelessness on her part. Talk about mothers! No father would have been guilty of such negligence. The affair must be stopped. It amounts to an outrage."

A peculiar person, Mr. Prohack! No normal father could have had such thoughts. Mr. Prohack could of course have burst in upon the pair and smashed an idyll to fragments. But instead of doing so he turned away from the idyll and descended the stairs as stealthily as he could.

Nobody challenged his exit. In the street he breathed with relief as if he had escaped from a house of great peril; but he did not feel safe until he had lost himself in the populousness of Oxford Street.

"For social and family purposes," he reflected, "I have

not seen that kiss. I cannot possibly tell them, or tell anybody, that I spied upon their embrace. To put myself right I ought to have called out a greeting the very instant I spotted them. But I did not call out a greeting. By failing to do so I put myself in a false position. . . . How shall I get official news of that kiss? Shall I ever get news of it?"

He had important business to transact with tradesmen. He could not do it. On leaving home he had not decided whether he would lunch domestically or at the Grand Babylon. He now perceived that he could do neither. He would lunch at one of his clubs. No! He could not bring himself to lunch at either club. He could face nobody. He resembled a man who was secretly carrying a considerable parcel of high explosive. He wandered until he could wander no more, and then he entered a tea-shop that was nearly full of young girls. It was a new world to him. He saw "Mutton pie 8d" on the menu and ordered it haphazard. He discovered to his astonishment that he was hungry. Having eaten the mutton pie, he ordered a second one, and ate it. The second mutton pie seemed to endow the eater with the faculty of vision—a result which perhaps no other mutton pie had ever before in the whole annals of eating achieved. He felt much better. He was illuminated by a large, refreshing wisdom, which thus expressed itself in his excited brain:

"After all, I suppose it's not the first or the only instance of a girl being kissed by a man. Similar incidents must occur quite often in the history of the human race."

IV

When he returned home his house seemed to be pitiably small, cramped, and lacking in rich ornament; it seemed to be no sort of a house for a man with twenty thousand a year. But he was determined to love his house at all costs, and never to leave it. The philosopher within himself told him that happiness does not spring from large houses built with hands. And his own house was bright that afternoon; he felt as soon as he entered it that it was more bright than usual. The reason was immediately disclosed. Sissie was inside it. She had come for some belongings and to pay a visit to her mother.

"My word!" she greeted her father in the drawing-room, where she was strumming while Eve leaned lovingly on the piano. "My word! We are fine with our new private secretary!"

Not a sign on that girl's face, nor in her demeanour, that she had an amorous secret, that something absolutely unprecedented had happened to her only a few hours earlier! The duplicity of women astonished even the philosopher in Mr. Prohack.

"Will she mention it or won't she?" Mr. Prohack asked himself; and then began to equal Sissie in duplicity by demanding of his women in a tone of raillery what they thought of the new private secretary. He reflected that he might as well know the worst at once.

"She'll do," said Sissie gaily, and Eve said: "She seems very willing to oblige."

"Ah!" Mr. Prohack grew alert. "She's been obliging you already, has she?"

"Well," said Eve. "It was about the new house—"

"What new house?"

"But you know, darling. Charlie mentioned it to you last night, and I told you that I was going to look at it this morning."

"Oh! *That!*" Mr. Prohack ejaculated disdainfully.

"I've seen it. I've been all over it, and it's simply lovely. I never saw anything equal to it."

"Of course!"

"And so cheap!"

"Of course!"

"But it's ripping, dad, seriously."

"Seriously ripping, it is? Well, so far as I am concerned I shall let it rip."

"I rushed back here as soon as I'd seen it," Eve proceeded, quietly ignoring the last remark. "But you'd gone out without saying where. Nobody knew where you'd gone. It was very awkward, because if we want this house we've got to decide at once—at latest in three days, Charlie says. Miss Warburton—that's her name, isn't it?—Miss Warburton had a very bright idea. She seems to know quite a lot about property. She thought of the drains. She said the first thing would be to have the drains inspected, and that if there was any hurry the surveyors ought to be instructed instantly. She knew some surveyor people, and so she's gone out to see the agents and get permission from them for the surveyors to inspect, and she'll see the surveyors at the same time. She says we ought to have the report by to-morrow afternoon. She's very enterprising."

The enterprisingness of Miss Warburton frightened Mr. Prohack. She had acted exactly as he would have wished—only better; evidently she was working out his plot against the house in the most efficient manner. Yet he was frightened. So much so that he could find nothing to say except: "Indeed!"

"You never told me she used to be with Mr. Carrel Quire and is related to the Paulle family," observed Eve, mingling a mild reproach with joyous vivacity, as if saying: "Why did you keep this titbit from me?"

"I must now have a little repose," said Mr. Prohack.

"We'll leave you," Eve said, eager to be agreeable. "You must be tired, you poor dear. I'm just going out to shop with Sissie. I'm not sure if I shall be in for tea, but I will be if you think you'll be lonely."

"Did you do much entertaining at lunch, young woman?" Mr. Prohack asked.

"Charlie had several people—men—but I really don't know who they were. And Ozzie Morfey came. And permit me to inform you that Charlie was simply knocked flat by my qualities as a hostess. Do you know what he said to me afterwards? He said: 'That lunch was a bit of all right, kid.' Enormous from Charlie, wasn't it?"

Mother and daughter went out arm in arm like two young girls. Beyond question they were highly pleased with themselves and the world. Eve returned after a moment.

"Are you comfortable, dear? I've told Machin you mustn't on any account be disturbed. Charlie's borrowed the car. We shall get a taxi in the Bayswater Road." She bent down and seemed to bury her soft lips in his cheek. She was beginning to have other interests than himself. And since she had nothing now to worry about, in a maternal sense, she had become a child. She was fat—at any rate nobody could describe her as less than plump—and over forty, but a child, an exquisite child. He magnificently let her kiss him. However, he knew that she knew that she was his sole passion. She whispered most intimately and persuasively into his ear:

"Shall we have a look at that house to-morrow morning, just you and I? You'll love the furniture."

"Perhaps," he replied. What else could he reply? He very much desired to have a talk with her about Sissie and the fellow Morfey; but he could not broach the subject because he could not tell her in cold blood that he had seen Sissie in Morfey's arms. To do so would have an effect like setting fire to the home. Unless, of course, Sissie had already confided in her mother? Was it conceivable that Eve had a secret from him? It was certainly conceivable that he had a secret from Eve. Not only was he hiding from her his knowledge of the startling development in the relations between Sissie and Morfey,—he had not even told her that he had seen the house in Manchester Square. He was leading a double life,—consequence of riches! Was she?

As soon as she had softly closed the door he composed himself, for he was in fact considerably exhausted. Remembering a conversation at the club with a celebrated psycho-analyst about the possibilities of auto-suggestion, he strove to empty his mind and then to repeat to himself very rapidly in a low murmur: "You will sleep, you will sleep, you will sleep, you will sleep," innumerable times. But the incantation would not work, probably because he could not keep his mind empty. The mysterious receptacle filled faster than he could empty it. It filled till it flowed over with the flooding realisation of the awful complexity of existence. He longed to maintain its simplicity, well aware that his happiness would result from simplicity alone. But existence flatly refused to be simple. He desired love in a cottage with Eve. He could have bought a hundred cottages, all in ideal surroundings. The mere fact, however, that he was in a position to buy a hundred cottages somehow made it impossible for him to devote himself exclusively to loving Eve in one cottage. . . .

His imagination leaped over intervening events and he pictured the wedding of Sissie as a nightmare of complications—no matter whom she married. He loathed weddings. Of course a girl of Sissie's sense and modernity ought to insist on being married in a registry office. But would she? She would not. For a month previous to marriage all girls cast off modernity and became Victorian. Yes, she would demand real orange-blossom and everything that went with it. . . . He got as far as wishing that Sissie might grow into an old maid, solely that he might be spared the wearing complications incident to the ceremony of marriage as practised by intelligent persons in the twentieth century. His character was deteriorating, and he could not stop it from deteriorating. . . .

Then Sissie herself came very silently into the room.

"Sit down, my dear. I want to talk to you," he said in his most ingratiating and sympathetic tones. And in quite another tone he addressed her silently: "It's time I taught you a thing or two, my wench."

"Yes, father," she responded charmingly to his wily ingratiatingness, and sat down.

"If you were the ordinary girl," he began, "I shouldn't say a word. It would be no use. But you aren't. And I flatter myself

I'm not the ordinary father. You are in love. Or you think you are. Which is the same thing—for the present. It's a fine thing to be in love. I'm quite serious. I like you tremendously just for being in love. Yes, I do. Now I know something about being in love. You've got enough imagination to realise that, and I want you to realise it. I want you to realise that I know a bit more about love than you do. Stands to reason, doesn't it?"

"Yes, father," said Sissie, placidly respectful.

"Love has got one drawback. It very gravely impairs the critical faculty. You think you can judge our friend Oswald with perfect impartiality. You think you see him as he is. But if you will exercise your imagination you will admit that you can't. You perceive that, don't you?"

"Quite, dad," the adorable child concurred.

"Well, do you know anything about him, really?"

"Not much, father."

"Neither do I. I've nothing whatever against him. But I shouldn't be playing straight with you if I didn't tell you that at the club he's not greatly admired. And a club is a very good judge of a man, the best judge of a man. And then as regards his business. Supposing you were not in love with him, should you like his business? You wouldn't. Naturally. There are other things, but I won't discuss them now. All I suggest to you is that you should go a bit slow. Exercise caution. Control yourself. Test him a little. If you and I weren't the greatest pals I shouldn't be such an ass as to talk in this strain to you. But I know you won't misunderstand me. I know you know there's absolutely no conventional nonsense about me, just as I know there's absolutely no conventional nonsense about you. I'm perfectly aware that the old can't teach the young, and that oftener than not the young are right and the old wrong. But it's not a question of old and young between you and me. It's a question of two friends—that's all."

"Dad," said she, "you're the most wonderful dad that ever was. Oh! If everybody would talk like that!"

"Not at all! Not at all!" he deprecated, delighted with himself and her. "I'm simply telling you what you know already. I needn't say any more. You'll do exactly as you think best, and whatever you do will please me. I don't want you to be happy in my way—I want you to be happy in your own way. Possibly you'll decide to tell Mr. Morfey to wait for three months."

"I most decidedly shall, dad," Sissie interrupted him, "and I'm most frightfully obliged to you."

He had always held that she was a marvellous girl, and here was the proof. He had spoken with the perfection of tact and sympathy and wisdom, but his success astonished him. At this point he perceived that Sissie was not really sitting in the chair at all and that the chair was empty. So that the exhibition of sagacity had been entirely wasted.

"Anyhow I've had a sleep," said the philosopher in him.

The door opened. Machin appeared, defying her mistress's orders.

"I'm sorry to disturb you, sir, but a Mr. Morfey is on the telephone and asks whether it would be convenient for you to see him to-night. He says it's urgent." Mr. Prohack braced himself, but where his stomach had been there was a void.

V

"Had an accident to your eye-glass?" asked Mr. Prohack, shaking hands with Oswald Morfey, when the latter entered, by appointment, Mr. Prohack's breakfast-room after dinner. Miss Warburton having gone home, Mr. Prohack had determined to employ her official room for formal interviews. With her woman's touch she had given it an air of business which pleasantly reminded him of the Treasury.

Ozzie was not wearing an eye-glass, and the absence of the broad black ribbon that usually ran like a cable-connection between his eye and his supra-umbilical region produced the disturbing illusion that he had forgotten an essential article of attire.

"Yes," Ozzie replied, opening his eyes with that mien of surprise that was his response to all questions, even the simplest. "Miss Sissie has cracked it."

"I'm very sorry my daughter should be so clumsy."

"It was not exactly clumsiness. I offered her the eye-glass to do what she pleased with, and she pleased to break it."

"Surely an impertinence?"

"No. A favour. Miss Sissie did not care for my eye-glass."

"You must be considerably incommoded."

"No. The purpose of my eye-glass was decorative, not optical." Ozzie smiled agreeably, though nervously.

Mr. Prohack was conscious of a certain surprising sympathy for this chubby simpering young man with the peculiar vocation whom but lately he had scorned and whom on one occasion he had described as a perfect ass.

"Well, shall we sit down?" suggested the elder, whom the younger's nervousness had put into an excellent state of easy confidence.

"The fact is," said Ozzie, obeying, "the fact is that I've come to see you about Sissie. I'm very anxious to marry her, Mr. Prohack."

"Indeed! Then you must excuse this old velvet coat. If I'd had notice of the solemnity of your visit, my dear Morfey, I'd have met you in a dinner jacket. May I just put one question? Have you kissed Sissie already?"

"I—er—have."

"By force or by mutual agreement?"

"Neither."

"She made no protest?"

"No."

"The reverse rather?"

"Yes."

"Then why do you come here to me?"

"To get your consent."

"I suppose you arranged with Sissie that you should come here?"

"Yes, I did. We thought it would be best if I came alone."

"Well, all I can say is that you're a very old-fashioned pair. I'm afraid that you must have forgotten to alter your date calendar when the twentieth century started. Let me assure you that this is not by any means the nineteenth. I admit that I only altered my own date calendar this afternoon, and even then only as the result of an unusual dream."

"Yes?" said Ozzie politely, and he said nothing else, but i seemed to Mr. Prohack that Ozzie was thinking: "This quee old stick is taking advantage of his position to make a fool o himself in his queer old way."

"Let us examine the circumstances," Mr. Prohack proceeded "You want to marry Sissie. Therefore you respect her. Therefor you would not have invited her to marry unless you had bee reasonably sure that you possessed the brains and the materia means to provide for her physical and moral comfort not merel during the next year but till the end of her life. It would b useless, not to say impolite, for me to question you as to you situation and your abilities, because you are convinced about both and if you failed to convince me about both you would leav here perfectly sure that the fault was mine and not yours, an you would pursue your plans just the same. Moreover, you are man of the world—far more a man of the world than I am myself—and you are unquestionably the best judge of your powers to do your duty towards a wife. Of course some might argue that I, being appreciably older than you, am appreciably wiser than you and that my opinion on vital matters is worth more than yours. But you know, and perhaps I know too, that in growing old a man does not really become wiser; he simply acquires a different sort of wisdom—whether it is a better or a worse sort nobody can decide. All we know is that the extremely young and the extremely old are in practice generally foolish. Which leads you nowhere at all. But looking at history we perceive that the ideas of the moderately young have always triumphed against the ideas of the moderately old. And happily so, for otherwise there could be no progress. Hence the balance of probability is that, assuming you and I were to differ, you would be more right than I should be."

"But I hope that we do not differ, sir," said Ozzie. And Mr. Prohack found satisfaction in the naturalness, the freedom from pose, of Ozzie's diffident and disconcerted demeanour. His sympathy for the young man was increased by the young man's increasing consternation.

"Again," resumed Mr. Prohack, ignoring Ozzie's hope. "Take the case of Sissie herself. Sissie's education was designed and superintended by myself. The supreme aim of education should be to give sound judgment in the great affairs of life, and moral stamina to meet the crises which arrive when sound judgment is falsified by events. If I were to tell you that in my opinion Sissie's judgment of you as a future husband was unsound, it would be equivalent to admitting that my education of Sissie had been unsound. And I could not possibly admit such a thing. Moreover, just as you are a man of the world, so Sissie is a woman of the world. By heredity and by natural character she is sagacious, and she has acquainted herself with all manner of things as to which I am entirely ignorant. Nor can I remember any instance of her yielding, from genuine conviction, to my judgment when it was opposed to hers. From all which it follows, my dear Morfey, that your mission to me here this evening is a somewhat illogical, futile, and unnecessary mission, and that the missioner must be either singularly old-fashioned and conventional—or laughing in his sleeve at me. No!" Mr. Prohack with a nineteenth century wave of the hand deprecated Ozzie's interrupting protest. "No! There is a third alternative, and I accept it. You desired to show me a courtesy. I thank you."

"But have you no questions to ask me?" demanded Ozzie.

"Yes," said Mr. Prohack. "How did you first make the acquaintance of my daughter?"

"Do you mean to say you don't know? Hasn't Sissie ever told you?"

"Never. What is more, she has never mentioned your name in any conversation until somebody else had mentioned it. Such is the result of my educational system, and the influence of the time-spirit."

"Well, I'm dashed!" exclaimed Ozzzie sincerely.

"I hope not, Morfey. I hope not, if by dashed you mean 'damned.'"

"But it was the most wonderful meeting, Mr. Prohack," Ozzie burst out, and he was in such an enthusiasm that he almost forgot to lisp. "You knew I was in M. I. in the war, after my trench fever."

"M. I., that is to say, Secret Service."

"Yes. Secret Service if you like. Well, sir, I was doing some work in the East End, in a certain foreign community, and I had to get away quickly, and so I jumped into a motor-van that happened to be passing. That van was driven by Sissie!"

"An example of fact imitating fiction!" remarked Mr. Prohack, seeking, not with complete success, to keep out of his voice the emotion engendered in him by Ozzie's too brief recital. "Now that's one question, and you have answered it brilliantly. My second and last question is this: Are you in love with Sissie—"

"Please, Mr. Prohack!" Ozzie half rose out of his chair.

"Or do you love her? The two things are very different."

"I beg your pardon, sir. I hadn't quite grasped," said Ozzie apologetically, subsiding. "I quite see what you mean. I'm both."

"You are a wonder!" Mr. Prohack murmured.

"Anyway, sir, I'm glad you don't object to our engagement."

"My dear Oswald," said Mr. Prohack in a new tone. "Do you imagine that after my daughter had expressed her view of you by kissing you I could fail to share that view. You have a great opinion of Sissie, but I doubt whether your opinion of her is greater than mine. We will now have a little whiskey together."

Ozzie's chubby face shone as in his agreeable agitation he searched for the eye-glass ribbon that was not there.

"Well, sir," said he, beaming. "This interview has not been at all like what I expected."

"Nor like what I expected either," said Mr. Prohack. "But who can foresee the future?" And he added to himself: "Could

I foresee when I called this youth a perfect ass that in a very short time I should be receiving him, not unpleasantly, as a prospective son-in-law? Life is marvellous."

At the same moment Mrs. Prohack entered the room.

"Oh!" cried she, affecting to be surprised at the presence of Ozzie.

"Wife!" said Mr. Prohack, "Mr. Oswald Morfey has done you the honour to solicit the hand of your daughter in marriage. You are staggered!

"How ridiculous you are, Arthur!" said Mrs. Prohack, and impulsively kissed Ozzie.

VI

The wedding festivities really began the next evening with a family dinner to celebrate Sissie's betrothal. The girl arrived magnificent from the Grand Babylon, escorted by her lover, and found Mrs. Prohack equally magnificent—indeed more magnificent by reason of the pearl necklace. It seemed to Mr. Prohack that Eve had soon become quite used to that marvellous necklace; he had already had to chide her for leaving it about. Ozzie also was magnificent; even lacking his eye-glass and ribbon he was magnificent. Mr. Prohack, esteeming that a quiet domestic meal at home demanded no ceremony, had put on his old velvet, but Eve had sharply corrected his sense of values—so shrewishly indeed that nobody would have taken her for the recent recipient of a marvellous necklace at his hands—and he had yielded to the extent of a dinner-jacket. Charlie had not yet come. Since the previous afternoon he had been out of town on mighty enterprises, but Sissie had seen him return to the hotel before she left it, and he was momently expected. Mr. Prohack perceived that Eve was treating Ozzie in advance as her son, and Ozzie was responding heartily: a phenomenon which Mr. Prohack in spite of himself found agreeable. Sissie showed more reserve than her mother towards Ozzie; but then Sissie was a proud thing, which Eve never was. Mr. Prohack admitted privately that he was happy—yes, he was happy in the betrothal, and he had most solemnly announced and declared that he would have naught to do with the wedding beyond giving a marriage gift to his daughter and giving his daughter to Ozzie. And when Sissie said that as neither she nor Ozzie had much use for the state of being merely engaged the wedding would occur very soon, Mr. Prohack rejoiced at the prospect of the upset being so quickly over. After the emotions and complications of the wedding he would settle down to simplicity,—luxurious possibly, but still simplicity: the plain but perfect. And let his fortune persist in accumulating, well it must accumulate and be hanged to it!

"But what about getting a house?" he asked his daughter.

"Oh, we shall live in Ozzie's flat," said Sissie.

"Won't it be rather small?"

"The smaller the better," said Sissie. "It will match our income."

"Oh, my dear girl," Eve protested, with a glance at Mr. Prohack to indicate that for the asking Sissie could have all the income she wanted. "And I'll give you an idea," Eve brightly added. "You can have *this* house rent free."

Sissie shook her head.

"Don't make so sure that they can have this house," said Mr. Prohack.

"But, Arthur! You've agreed to go and look at Manchester Square! And it's all ready excepting the servants. I'm told that if you don't want less than seven servants, including one or two menservants, there's no difficulty about servants at all. I shall be very disappointed if we don't have the wedding from Manchester Square."

Mr. Prohack writhed, though he knew himself safe. Seven servants; two menservants? No! And again no! No complications!

"I shall only agree to Manchester Square," said he with firmness and solemnity, "subject to the drains being all right. Somebody in the place must show a little elementary sagacity and restraint."

"But the drains are bound to be all right!"

"I hope so," said the deceitful father. "And I believe they will be. But until we're sure—nothing can be done." And he laughed satanically to himself.

"Haven't you had the report yet?" Sissie complained. "Miss Warburton was to try to get hold of it to-night."

A moment later Machin, in a condition of high excitement due to the betrothal, brought in a large envelope, saying that Miss Warburton had just left it. The envelope contained the report of Messrs. Doy and Doy on the drains of the noble mansion. Mr. Prohack read it, frowned, and pursed his judicial lips.

"Read it, my dear," he said to Eve.

Eve read that Messrs. Doy and Doy found themselves unable, after a preliminary inspection, which owing to their instructions to be speedy had not been absolutely exhaustive, to certify the drains of the noble mansion. They feared the worst, but there was of course always a slight hope of the best, or rather the second best. (They phrased it differently but they meant that.) In the meantime they would await further instructions. Mr. Prohack reflected calmly: "My new secretary is an adept of the first conspiratorial order." Eve was shocked into silence. (Doy and Doy used very thick and convincing note-paper.) The entrance of Charlie loosed her tongue.

"Charlie!" she cried. "The drains are all wrong. Look at this. And didn't you say the option expired to-morrow?"

Charlie read the report.

"Infernal rascals!" he muttered. "Whose doing is this? Who's been worrying about drains?" He looked round accusingly.

"I have;" said Mr. Prohack bravely, but he could not squarely meet the boy's stern glance.

"Well, dad, what did you take me for? Did you suppose I should buy an option on a house without being sure of the drains? My first act was to have the drains surveyed by Flockers, the first firm in London, and I've got their certificate. As for Doy and Doy, they're notorious. They want to stop everybody else but themselves getting a commission on that house, and this—" he slapped the report—"this is how they're setting about it."

Eve adored her son.

"You see," she said victoriously to Mr. Prohack, who secretly trembled.

"I shall bring an action against Doy and Doy," Charlie continued. "I'll show the whole rascally thing up."

"I hope you'll do no such thing, my boy," said Mr. Prohack, foolishly attempting the grandiose.

"I most positively shall, dad."

Mr. Prohack realised desperately that all was lost except honour, and he was by no means sure about even honour.

CHAPTER XVI

TRANSFER OF MIMI

I

Mr. Prohack passed a very bad night—the worst for months, one of the outstanding bad nights of his whole existence.

"Why didn't I have it out with Charlie before he left?" he asked himself some scores of times while listening to the tranquil regular breathing of Eve, who of course was now sure of her house and probably had quite forgotten the meaning of care. "I'm bound to have it out with him sooner or later, and if I'd done it at once I should at any rate have slept. They're all sleeping but me."

He simply could not comprehend life; the confounded thing called life baffled him by its mysterious illogicalness. He was adored by his spouse, beloved by his children, respected by the world. He had heaps of money, together with the full control of it. His word, if he chose, was law. He had only to say: "I will not take the house in Manchester Square," and nobody could thwart him. He powerfully desired not to take it. There was no sensible reason why he should take it. And yet he would take it, under the inexplicable compulsion of circumstances. In those sombre hours he had a fellow-feeling for Oriental tyrants, who were absolute autocrats but also slaves of exactly the same sinister force that had gripped himself. He perceived that in practice there is no such thing as an autocrat. . . .

Not that his defeat in regard to the house really disturbed him. He could reconcile himself to the house, despite the hateful complications which it would engender. What disturbed him horribly was the drains business, the Doy and Doy business, the Mimi business; he could see no way out of that except through the valley of humiliation. He remembered, with terrible forebodings, the remark of his daughter after she heard of the heritage: "You'll never be as happy again."

When the household day began and the familiar comfortable distant noises of domestic activity announced that the solar system was behaving much as usual in infinite and inconceivable space, he decided that he was too tired to be scientifically idle that day—even though he had a trying-on appointment with Mr. Melchizidek. He decided, too, that he would not get up, would in fact take everything lying down, would refuse to descend a single step of the stairs to meet trouble. And he had a great wish to be irritated and angry. But the place seemed to be full of angels who turned the other cheek—and the other cheek was marvellously soft and bewitching.

Eve, Sissie (who had called), and Machin—they were all in a state of felicity, for the double reason that Sissie was engaged to be married, and that the household was to move into a noble mansion. Machin saw herself at the head of a troup of sub-parlourmaids and housemaids and tweenies, and foretold that she would stand no nonsense from butlers. They all treated Mr. Prohack as a formidable and worshipped tyrant, whose smile was the sun and whose frown death, and who was the fount of wisdom and authority. They knew that he wanted to be irritated, and they gave him no chance to be irritated. Their insight into his psychology was uncanny. They knew that he was beaten on the main point, and with their detestable feminine realism they exquisitely yielded on all the minor points. Eve, fresh as a rose, bent over him and bedewed him, and said that she was going out and that Sissie had gone again.

When he was alone he rang the bell for Machin as though the bell had done him an injury.

"What time is it?"

"Eleven o'clock, sir."

"Eleven o'clock! Good God! Why hasn't Miss Warburton come?"

As if Machin was responsible for Miss Warburton! . . . No! Mr. Prohack was not behaving nicely, and it cannot be hidden that he lacked the grandeur of mind which distinguishes most of us.

"Miss Warburton was here before ten o'clock, sir."

"Then why hasn't she come up?"

"She was waiting for orders, sir."

"Send her up immediately."

"Certainly, sir."

Miss Warburton was the fourth angel—an angel with another spick-and-span blouse, and the light of devotion in her eyes and the sound of it in her purling voice.

"Good morning," the gruff brute started. "Did I hear the telephone-bell just now?"

"Yes, sir. Doy and Doy have telephoned to say that Mr. Charles Prohack has just been in to see them, and they've referred him to you, and—and—"

"And what? And what? And what?" (A machine-gun.)

"They said he was extremely unpleasant."

Instinctively Mr. Prohack threw away shame. Mimi was his minion. He treated her as an Oriental tyrant might treat the mute guardian of the seraglio, and told her everything,—that Charlie had forestalled them in the matter of the drains of the noble mansion, that Charlie had determined to destroy Doy and Doy, that he, Mr. Prohack, was caught in a trap, that there was the devil to pay, and that the finest lies that ingenuity could invent would have to be uttered. He abandoned all pretence of honesty and uprightness.

Mimi showed no surprise whatever, nor was she apparently in the least shocked. She seemed to regard the affair as a quite ordinary part of the day's routine. Her insensitive calm frightened Mr. Prohack.

"Now we must think of something," said the iniquitous monster.

"I don't see that there need be any real difficulty," Mimi replied. "*You* didn't know anything about my plot with Doy and Doy. I got the notion—quite wrongly—that you preferred not to have the house, and I acted as I did through an excess of zeal. I must confess the plot. I alone am to blame, and I admit that what I did was quite inexcusable."

"What a girl! What a girl!" thought Mr. Prohack. But there were limits to his iniquity, and he said aloud, benevolently, grandiosely: "But I did know about it. You as good as told me exactly what you meant to do, and I let you do it. I approved, and I am responsible. Nothing will induce me to let you take the responsibility. Let that be clearly understood, please."

He looked squarely at the girl, and watched with apprehension her aspiring nose rise still further, her delicate ruthless mouth become still more ruthless.

"Excuse me," she said. "My plan is the best. It's the obvious plan. Mr. Carrel Quire often adopted it. I'm afraid you're hesitating to trust me as I expect to be trusted. Please don't forget that you sacrificed an empire for me—I shall always remember that. And what's more, you said you expected from me absolute loyalty to your interests. I can stand anything but not being trusted—*fully!*"

Mr. Prohack sank deeper into the bed, and laughed loudly, immoderately, titanically. His ill-humour vanished as a fog will vanish. Nevertheless he was appalled by the revelation of the possibilities of the girl's character.

The strange scene was interrupted by the arrival of Charlie, who, thanks to his hypnotic influence over Machin, came masterfully straight upstairs, entered the bedroom without asking permission to do so, and, in perfect indifference to the alleged frailty of his father's health, proceeded to business.

II

"Dad," said he, after Mimi had gone through her self-ordained martyrdom and left the room. "I wonder whether you quite realise what a top-hole creature that Warburton girl is. She's perfectly astounding."

"She is," Mr. Prohack admitted.

"She's got ideas."

"She has."

"And she isn't afraid of carrying them out."

"She is not."

"She's much too good for you, dad."

"She is."

"I mean, you can't really make full use of her, can you? She's got no scope here."

"She makes her own scope," said Mr. Prohack.

"Now I honestly do need a good secretary," Charlie at last unmasked his attack. "I've got a temporary idiot, and I want a first-rater, preferably a woman. I wish you'd be decent and turn Miss Warburton over to me. She'd be invaluable to me, and with me she really *would* have scope for her talents." Charlie laughed.

"What are you laughing at?"

"I was only thinking of her having the notion of queering the drains like that because she wanted to please you. It was simply great. It's the best thing I ever heard." He laughed again. "Now, dad, will you turn her over to me?"

"You appear to think she's a slave to be bought and sold and this room the slave-market," said Mr. Prohack. "It hasn't occurred to you that *she* might object to the transfer."

"Oh! I can soon persuade *her*." said Charlie, lightly.

"But you couldn't easily persuade me. And I may as well inform you at once, my poor ingenuous boy, that I won't agree. I will never agree. Miss Warburton is necessary to my existence."

"All in two or three days, is she?" Charlie observed sarcastically.

"Yes."

"Well, father, as we're talking straight, let's talk straight. I'm going to take her from you. It's a very little help I'm asking you for, and that you should refuse is a bit thick. I shall speak to the mater."

"And what shall you say?"

"I shall tell her all about the plot against the new house. It was really a plot against her, because she wants the house—the house is nothing to me. I may believe that you knew nothing about the plot yourself, but I'll lay you any odds the mater won't."

"Speaking as man to man, my boy, I lay you any odds you can't put your mother against me."

"Oh!" cried Charlie, "she won't *say* she believes you're guilty, but she'll believe it all the same. And it's what people think that matters, not what they say they think."

"That's wisdom," Mr. Prohack agreed. "I see that I brought you up not so badly after all. But doesn't it strike you that you're trying to blackmail your father? I hope I taught you sagacity, but I never encouraged you in blackmail—unless my memory fails me."

"You can call it by any name you please," said Charlie.

"Very well, then, I will. I'll call it blackmail. Give me a cigarette." He lit the offered cigarette. "Anything else this morning?"

Father and son smiled warily at one another. Both were amused and even affectionate, but serious in the battle.

"Come along, dad. Be a sport. Anyhow, let's ask the girl."

"Do you know what my answer to blackmail is?" Mr. Prohack blandly enquired.

"No."

"My answer is the door. Drop the subject entirely. Or sling your adventurous hook."

Mr. Prohack was somewhat startled to see Charlie walk straight out of the bedroom. A disturbing suspicion that there might be something incalculable in his son was rudely confirmed.

He said to himself: "But this is absurd."

III

That morning the Prohack bedroom seemed to be transformed into a sort of public square. No sooner had Charlie so startlingly left than Machin entered again.

"Dr. Veiga, sir."

And Dr. Veiga came in. The friendship between Mr. Prohack and his picturesque quack had progressed—so much so that Eve herself had begun to twit her husband with having lost his head about the doctor. Nevertheless Eve was privately very pleased with the situation, because it proved that she had been right and Mr. Prohack wrong concerning the qualities of the fat, untidy, ironic Portuguese. Mr. Prohack was delighted to see him, for an interview with Dr. Veiga always meant an unusual indulgence in the sweets of candour and realism.

"This is my wife's doing, no doubt," said Mr. Prohack, limply shaking hands.

"She called to see me, ostensibly about herself, but of course in fact about you. However, I thought she needed a tonic, and I'll write out the prescription while I'm here. Now what's the matter with you?"

"No!" Mr. Prohack burst out, "I'm hanged if I'll tell you. I'm not going to do your work for you. Find out."

Dr. Veiga examined, physically and orally, and then said: "There's nothing at all the matter with you, my friend."

"That's just where you're mistaken," Mr. Prohack retorted. "There's something rather serious the matter with me. I'm suffering from grave complications. Only you can't help me. My trouble is spiritual. Neither pills nor tonics can touch it. But that doesn't make it any better."

"Try me," said Dr. Veiga. "I'm admirable on the common physical ailments, and by this time I should have been universally recognised as a great man if common ailments were uncommon; because you know in my profession you never get any honour unless you make a study of diseases so rare that nobody has them. Discover a new disease, and save the life of some solitary nigger who brought it to Liverpool, and you'll be a baronet in a fortnight and a member of all the European academies in a month. But study colds, indigestion and insomnia, and change a thousand lives a year from despair to felicity, and no authority will take the slightest notice of you. . . . As with physical, so with mental diseases—or spiritual, if you like to call them so. You don't suspect that in the common mental diseases I'm a regular benefactor of mankind; but I am. I don't blame you for not knowing it, because you're about the last person I should have thought susceptible to any mental disease, and so you've had no chance of finding out. Now, what is it?"

"Don't I tell you I'm suffering from horrible complications?" cried Mr. Prohack.

"What kind of complications?"

"Every kind. My aim has always been to keep my life simple, and I succeeded very well—perhaps too well—until I inherited money. I don't mind money, but I do mind complications. I don't want a large house—because it means complications. I desire Sissie's happiness, but I hate weddings. I desire to be looked after, but I hate strange servants. I can find pleasure in a motor-car, but I hate even the risk of accidents. I have no objection to an income, but I hate investments. And so on. All I ask is to live simply and sensibly, but instead of that my existence is transformed into a quadratic equation. And I can't stop it. My happiness is not increasing—it's decreasing. I spend more and more time in wondering whither I am going, what I am after, and where precisely is the point of being alive at all. That's a fact, and now you know it."

Dr. Veiga rose from his chair and deliberately sat down on the side of his patient's bed. The gesture in itself was sufficiently unprofessional, but he capped it with another of which probably no doctor had ever been guilty in a British sick-room before; he pulled out a pocket-knife and became his own manicure, surveying his somewhat neglected hands with a benevolently critical gaze, smiling at them as if to say: "What funny hands you are!"

And Mr. Prohack felt that the doctor was saying: "What a funny Prohack you are!"

"My friend," said Dr. Veiga at length (with his voice), "my friend, I will not conceal from you that your alarm was justified. You are suffering from one of the commonest and one of the gravest mental derangements. I'm surprised, but there it is. You haven't yet discovered that it's the earth you're living on. You fancy it may be Sirius, Uranus, Aldebaran or Jupiter—let us say Jupiter. Perhaps in one of these worlds matters are ordered differently, and their truth is not our truth; but let me assure you that the name of your planet is the Earth and that on the earth one great unalterable truth prevails. Namely:—You can't do this"—here Dr. Veiga held up a pared and finished finger and wagged it to and fro with solemnity—"you can't do this without moving your finger. . . . You were aware of this great truth? Then why are you upset because you can't wag your finger without moving it? . . . Perhaps I'm being too subtle for you. Let me put the affair in another way. You've lost sight of the supreme earthly fact that everything has not merely a consequence, but innumerable consequences. You knew when you married that you were creating endless consequences, and now you want to limit the consequences. You knew when you accepted a fortune that you were creating endless consequences, and now you want to limit them too. You want to alter the rules after the game has started. You set in motion circumstances which were bound to influence the development of the members of your family, and when the inevitable new developments begin, you object, simply because you hadn't foreseen them. You knew that money doesn't effectively exist until it's spent and that you can't spend money without causing consequences, and when your family causes consequences by bringing the money to life you complain that you're a martyr to the consequences and that you hadn't bargained for complications. My poor friend, you have made one crucial mistake in your career,—the mistake of being born. Happily the mistake is curable. I can give you several prescriptions. The first is prussic acid. If you don't care for that you can donate the whole of your fortune to the Sinking Fund for extinguishing the National Debt and you can return to the Treasury. If you don't care for that you can leave your family mysteriously and go and live in Timbuctoo by yourself. If you don't care for that you can buy a whip and forbid your wife and daughter to grow older or change in any way on pain of a hundred lashes. And if you don't like that you can acquaint yourself with the axioms that neither you nor anybody else are the centre of the universe and that what you call complications are simply another name for life itself. Worry is life, and life is worry. And the absence of worry is death. I won't say to you that you're rich and beloved and therefore you've nothing to worry about. I'll say to you, you've got a lot to worry about because you're rich and beloved. . . . I'll leave the other hand for to-morrow." Dr. Veiga snapped down the blade of the pocket-knife.

"Platitudes!" ejaculated Mr. Prohack.

"Certainly," agreed the quack. "But I've told you before that it's by telling everybody what everybody knows that I earn my living."

"I'll get up," said Mr. Prohack.

"And not too soon," said the quack. "Get up by all means and deal with your worries. All worries can be dealt with."

"It doesn't make life any better," said Mr. Prohack.

"Nothing makes life any better, except death—and there's a

disgusting rumour that there is no death. Where shall I find a pencil, my dear fellow? I've forgotten mine, and I want to prescribe Mrs. Prohack's tonic."

"In the boudoir there," said Mr. Prohack. "What the deuce are you smiling at?"

"I'm smiling because I'm so glad to find you aren't so wise as you look." And Dr. Veiga disappeared blithely into the boudoir.

Almost at the same moment Mimi knocked and entered. She entered, stared harshly at Mr. Prohack, and then the corners of her ruthless mouth twitched and loosened and she began to cry.

"Doctor," called Mr. Prohack, "come here at once." The doctor came. "You say all worries can be dealt with? How should you deal with this one?"

The doctor dropped a slip of paper on to the bed and walked silently out of the room, precisely as Charlie had done.

IV

In regard to the effect of the sermon of Dr. Veiga on Mr. Prohack, it was as if Mr. Prohack had been a desk with many drawers and one drawer open, and the sermon had been dropped into the drawer and the drawer slammed to and nonchalantly locked. The drawer being locked, Mr. Prohack turned to the weeping figure in front of him, which suddenly ceased to weep and became quite collected and normal.

"Now, my child," said Mr. Prohack, "I have just been informed that everything has a consequence. I've seen the consequence. What is the thing?"

He was rather annoyed by Mimi's tears, but in his dangerous characteristic desire to please, he could not keep kindness out of his tone, and Mimi, reassured and comforted, began feebly to smile, and also Mr. Prohack remarked that her mouth was acquiring firmness again.

"I ought to tell you in explanation of anything of a personal nature that I may have said to him in your presence, that the gentleman just gone is my medical adviser, and I have no secrets from him; in that respect he stands equal with you and above everybody else in the world without exception. So you must excuse my freedom in directing his attention to you."

"It's I who ought to apologise," said Miss Warburton, positively. "But the fact is I hadn't the slightest idea that you weren't alone. I was just a little bit upset because I understand that you want to get rid of me."

"Ah!" murmured Mr. Prohack, "who put that notion into your absurd head?"

He knew he was exercising his charm, but he could not help it.

"Mr. Charles. He's just been down to my room and told me."

"I hope you remembered what I said to you about your duty so far as he is concerned."

"Of course, Mr. Prohack." She smiled anew; and her smile, so clever, so self-reliant, so enigmatic, a little disturbed Mr. Prohack.

"What did my son say to you?"

"He said that he was urgently in need of a thoroughly competent secretary at once—confidential—and that he was sure I was the very woman to suit him, and that he would give me double the salary I was getting."

"Did you tell him how much you're getting?"

"No."

"Well, neither did I! And then?"

"Then he told me all about his business, how big it was, and growing quickly, too, and how he was after a young woman who had tact and resource and could talk to any one from a bank director to a mechanic or a clergyman, and that tens of thousands of pounds might often depend on my tact, and that you wouldn't mind my being transferred from you to him."

"And I suppose he asked you to go off with him immediately?"

"No, at the beginning of next week."

"And what did you say?" demanded Mr. Prohack, amazed and frightened at the manœuvres of his unscrupulous son.

"Naturally I said that I couldn't possibly leave you—unless you told me to go, and that I owed everything to you. Then he asked me what I did for you, and I said I was particularly busy at present making a schedule of all your new purchases and checking the outfitters' accounts, and so on. That reminds me, I haven't been able to get the neckties right yet."

"Good heavens!" exclaimed Mr. Prohack. "Not been able to get the neckties right! But this is very serious. The neckties are most important. Most important!"

"Oh!" said Mimi. "If necessary I shall run round to Bond Street in my lunch-hour."

At this point the drawer in the desk started to unlock itself and open of its own accord, and Mr. Prohack's eye caught a glimpse of a page of the sermon.

Mimi continued:

"We mustn't forget there'll be hundreds of things to see to about the new house."

"Will there?"

"Well, Mrs. Prohack told Machin, and Machin has just told me, that it's all settled about taking the house. And I know what taking a house is. Mr. Carrel Quire was always taking new houses."

"But perhaps you could keep an eye on the house even if you went over to Mr. Charles?"

"Then it's true," said Mimi. "You do want me to go." But she showed no sign of weeping afresh.

"You must understand," Mr. Prohack said with much benevolence, "that my son is my son. Of course my clothes are also my clothes. But Charles is in a difficult position. He's at the beginning of his career, whereas I'm at the end of mine. He needs all the help he can get, and he can afford to pay more than I can. And even at the cost of having to check my own neckties I shouldn't like to stand in his way. That's how I look at it. Mind you, I have certainly not told Charlie that I'll set you free."

"I quite see," said Mimi. "And naturally if you put it like that—"

"You'll still be in the family."

"I shall be very sorry to leave you, Mr. Prohack."

"Doubtless. But you'll be even gladder to go over to Charles, though with him you'll be more like a kettle tied to the tail of a mad dog than a confidential secretary."

Mimi raised the tip of her nose.

"Excuse me, Mr. Prohack, I shall *not* be gladder to go over to Mr. Charles. Any girl will tell you that she prefers to work for a man of your age than for a boy. Boys are not interesting."

"Yes," murmured Mr. Prohack. "A comfortable enough theory. And I've already heard it more than once from girls. But I've never seen any confirmation of it in practice. And I don't believe it. I'll tell you something about yourself you don't know. You're delighted to go over to my son. And if I'd refused to let you go I should have had a martyr instead of a secretary. You want adventure. You want a field for your remarkable talent for conspiracy and chicane. You know by experience there's little scope for it here. But under my son your days will be breathless. . . . No, no! I don't wish to hear anything. Run away and get on with your work. And you can telephone my decision to Charles. I'm now going to get up and wear all my new neckties at once."

Miss Warburton departed in a state of emotion.

As, with all leisureliness, Mr. Prohack made himself beautiful to behold, he reflected: "I'm very impulsive. I've simply thrown that girl into the arms of that boy. Eve will have something to say about it. Still, there's one complication off my chest."

Eve returned home as he was descending the stairs, and she blew him upstairs again and shut the door of the bedroom and pushed him into the privacy of the boudoir.

"It's all settled," said she. "I've signed the tenancy agreement for a year. Charlie said I could, and it would save you trouble. It doesn't matter the cheque for the first half-year's rent being signed by you, only of course the house will be in my name. How handsome you are, darling!" And she kissed him and re-tied one of the new cravats. "But that's not what I wanted to tell you, darling." Her face grew grave. "Do you know I'm rather troubled about Charlie—and your friend Lady Massulam. They're off again this morning."

"My friend?"

"Well, you know she adores you. It would be perfectly awful if—if—well, you understand what I mean. I hear she really is a widow, so that—well, you understand what I mean! I'm convinced she's at least thirty years older than Charlie. But you see she's French, and French women are so clever. . . . You can never be sure with them."

"Fluttering heart," said Mr. Prohack, suddenly inspired. "Don't get excited. I've thought of all that already, and I've taken measures to guard against it. I'm going to give Charlie my secretary. She'll see that Lady Massulam doesn't make any more headway, trust her!"

"Arthur, how clever you are! Nobody but you would have thought of that. But isn't it a bit dangerous, too? You see—don't you?"

Mr. Prohack shook his head.

"I gather you've been reading the love-story in *The Daily Picture*," said he. "In *The Daily Picture* the typist always marries the millionaire. But outside *The Daily Picture* I doubt whether these romantic things really happen. There are sixty-five thousand girls typists in the City alone, besides about a million in Whitehall. The opportunities for espousing millionaires and ministers of state are countless. But no girl-typist has been married at St. George's, Hanover Square, since typewriters were invented."

CHAPTER XVII

ROMANCE

I

The very next day Mr. Prohack had a plutocratic mood of overbearingness, which led to a sudden change in his location—the same being transferred to Frinton-on-Sea. The mood was brought about by a visit to the City, at the summons of Paul Spinner; and the visit included conversations not only with Paul, but with Smathe and Smathe, the solicitors, and with a firm of stockbrokers. Paul handed over to his crony saleable securities, chiefly in the shape of scrip of the greatest oil-combine and its subsidiaries, for a vast amount, and advised Mr. Prohack to hold on to them, as, owing to the present depression due to the imminence of a great strike, they were likely to be "marked higher" before Mr. Prohack was much older. Mr. Prohack declined the advice, and he also declined the advice of solicitors and stockbrokers, who were both full of wisdom and of devices for increasing capital values. What these firms knew about the future, and about the consequences of causes and about "the psychology of the markets" astounded the simple Terror of the departments; and it was probably unanswerable. But, being full of riches, Mr. Prohack did not trouble to answer it; he merely swept it away with a tyrannical and impatient gesture, which gesture somehow mysteriously established him at once as a great authority on the art of investment.

"Now listen to me," said he imperiously, and the manipulators of shares listened, recalling to themselves that Mr. Prohack had been a Treasury official for over twenty years and must therefore be worth hearing—although the manipulators commonly spent many hours a week in asserting, in the press and elsewhere, that Treasury officials comprehended naught of finance. "Now listen to me. I don't care a hang about my capital. It may decrease or increase, and I shan't care. All I care for is my interest. I want to be absolutely sure that my interest will tumble automatically into my bank on fixed dates. No other consideration touches me. I'm not a gambler. I'm not a usurer. Industrial development leaves me cold, and if I should ever feel any desire to knit the Empire closer together I'll try to do it without making a profit out of it. At the moment all I'm after is certain, sure, fixed interest. Hence—Government securities, British Government or Colonial! Britain is of course rotten to the core, always was, always will be. Still, I'll take my chances. I'm infernally insular where investment is concerned. There's one thing to be said about the British Empire—you do know where you are in it. And I don't mind some municipal stocks. I even want some. I can conceive the smash-up of the British Empire, but I cannot conceive Manchester defaulting in its interest payments. Can you?" And he looked round and paused for a reply, and no reply came. Nobody dared to boast himself capable of conceiving Manchester's default.

Towards the end of the arduous day Mr. Prohack departed from the City, leaving behind him an immense reputation for financial sagacity, and a scheme of investment under which he could utterly count upon a modest regular income of £17,000 per annum. He was sacrificing over £5,000 per annum in order to be free from an investor's anxieties, and he reckoned that his peace of mind was cheap at a hundred pounds a week. This detail alone shows to what an extent the man's taste for costly luxuries had grown.

Naturally he arrived home swollen. Now it happened that Eve also, by reason of her triumph in regard to the house in Manchester Square, had swelled head. A conflict of individualities occurred. A trifle, even a quite pleasant trifle! Nothing that the servants might not hear with advantage. But before you could say 'knife' Mr. Prohack had said that he would go away for a holiday and abandon Eve to manage the removal to Manchester Square how she chose, and Eve had leapt on to the challenge and it was settled that Mr. Prohack should go to Frinton-on-Sea.

Eve selected Frinton-on-Sea for him because Dr. Veiga had recommended it for herself. She had a broad notion of marriage as a commonwealth. She loved to take Mr. Prohack's medicines, and she was now insisting on his taking her watering-places. Mr. Prohack said that the threatened great strike might prevent his journey. Pooh! She laughed at such fears. She drove him herself to Liverpool Street.

"You may see your friend Lady Massulam," said she, as the car entered the precincts of the station. (Once again he was struck by the words 'your friend' prefixed to Lady Massulam; but he offered no comment on them.)

"Why Lady Massulam?" he asked.

"Didn't you know she's got a house at Frinton?" replied Mrs. Prohack. "Everybody has in these days. It's the thing."

She didn't see him into the train, because she was in a hurry about butlers. Mr. Prohack was cast loose in the booking-hall and had a fine novel sensation of freedom.

II

Never since marriage had he taken a holiday alone—never desired to do so. He felt himself to be on the edge of romance. Frinton, for example, presented itself as a city of romance. He knew it not, knew scarcely any English seaside, having always managed to spend his holidays abroad; but Frinton must, he was convinced, be strangely romantic. The train thither had an aspect which strengthened this conviction. It consisted largely of first-class coaches, and in the window of nearly every first-class compartment and saloon was exhibited a notice: "This compartment (or saloon) is reserved for members of the North Essex Season-Ticket-Holders Association." Mr. Prohack, being still somewhat swollen, decided that he was a member of the North Essex Season-Ticket-Holders Association and acted accordingly. Otherwise he might never have reached Frinton.

He found himself in a sort of club, about sixty feet by six, where everybody knew everybody except Mr. Prohack, and where cards and other games, tea and other drinks, tobacco and other weeds, were being played and consumed in an atmosphere of the utmost conviviality. Mr. Prohack was ignored, but he was not objected to. His fellow-travellers regarded him cautiously, as a new chum. The head attendant and dispenser was very affable, as to a promising neophyte. Only the ticket-inspector singled him out from all the rest by stopping in front of him.

"My last hour has come," thought Mr. Prohack as he produced his miserable white return-ticket.

All stared; the inspector stared; but nothing happened. Mr. Prohack had a sense of reprieve, and also of having been baptised or inducted into a secret society. He listened heartily to forty conversations about physical diversions and luxuries and about the malignant and fatuous wrong-headedness of men who went on strike, and about the approaching catastrophic end of all things.

Meanwhile, at any rate in the coach, the fabric of society seemed to be holding together fairly well. Before the train was half-way to Frinton Mr. Prohack judged—and rightly—that he was already there. The fact was that he had been there ever since entering the saloon. After two hours the train, greatly diminished in length, came to rest in the midst of a dark flatness, and the entire population of the coach vanished out of it in the twinkling of an eye, and Mr. Prohack saw the name 'Frinton' on a flickering oil-lamp, and realised that he was at the gates of the most fashionable resort in England, a spot where even the ozone was exclusive. The station staff marvelled at him because he didn't know where the Majestic Hotel was and because he asked without notice for a taxi, fly, omnibus or anything on wheels. All the other passengers had disappeared. The exclusive ozone was heavy with exciting romance for Mr. Prohack as the station staff considered his unique and incomprehensible case. Then a tiny omnibus materialised out of the night.

"Is this the Majestic bus?" Mr. Prohack enquired of the driver.

"Well, it is if you like, sir," the driver answered.

Mr. Prohack did like. . . .

The Majestic was large and prim, resembling a Swiss hotel in its furniture, the language and composition of the menu, the dialect of the waiters; but it was about fifteen degrees colder than the highest hotel in Switzerland. The dining-room was shaded with rose-shaded lamps and it susurrated with the polite whisperings of elegant couples and trios, and the entremet was cabinet pudding: a fine display considering the depth of winter and of the off-season.

Mr. Prohack went off after dinner for a sharp walk in the east wind. Solitude! Blackness! Night! East wind in the bushes of gardens that shielded the façades of large houses! Not a soul! Not a policeman! He descended precariously to the vast, smooth beach. The sound of the sea! Romance! Mr. Prohack seemed to walk for miles, like Ozymandias, on the lone and level sands. Then he fancied he descried a moving object. He was not mistaken. It approached him. It became a man and a woman. It became a man and a young woman arm-in-arm and soul-in-soul. And there was nothing but the locked couple, and the sound of the invisible, immeasurable sea, and the east wind, and Mr. Prohack. Romance thrilled through Mr. Prohack's spine.

"So I said to him," the man was saying to the young woman as the pair passed Mr. Prohack, "I said to him 'I could do with a pint o' that,' I said."

III

The next morning Mr. Prohack rose with alacrity from a hard bed, and was greeted in the hall by the manager of the hotel, an enormous, middle-aged, sun-burnt, jolly person in flannels and an incandescent blazer, who asked him about his interests in golf and hard-court tennis. Mr. Prohack, steeped as he felt himself to be in strange romance, was prepared to be interested in these games, but the self-protective instinct warned him that since these games could not be played alone they would, if he indulged in them, bring him into contact with people who might prove tedious. He therefore changed the conversation and asked whether he could have strawberry jam to his breakfast. The manager's face instantly changed, hardening to severity. Was Mr. Prohack eccentric? Did he desire to disturb the serene habits of the hotel? The manager promised to see. He did see, and announced that he was 'afraid' that Mr. Prohack could not have strawberry jam to his breakfast. And Mr. Prohack said to himself: "What would my son Charles have done?" During a solitary breakfast (with blackberry jam) in the huge dining-room, Mr. Prohack decided that Charles would have approached the manager differently.

After breakfast he saw the manager again, and he did not enquire from the manager whether there was any chance of hiring a motor-car. He said briefly:

"I want to hire a car, please. It must be round here in half an hour, sharp."

"I will attend to the matter myself," said the manager humbly.

The car kept the rendezvous, and Mr. Prohack inspected Frinton from the car. He admired the magnificent reserve of Frinton, which was the most English place he had ever seen. The houses gave nothing away; the shivering shopping ladies in the streets gave nothing away; and certainly the shops gave nothing away. The newspaper placards announced what seemed to be equivalent to the end of the existing social order; but Frinton apparently did not blench nor tremble; it went calmly and powerfully forward into the day (which was Saturday), relying upon the great British axiom: "To ignore is to destroy." It ignored the end of the existing social order, and lo! there was no end. Up and down various long and infinitely correct avenues of sheltered homes drove Mr. Prohack, and was everywhere baffled in his human desire to meet Frinton half-way. He stopped the car at the Post Office and telegraphed to his wife: "No strawberry jam in this city.

HARRIS PUBLIC LIBRARY PRESTON

Love. Arthur." The girl behind the counter said: "One and a penny, please," and looked hard at him. Five minutes later he returned to the Post Office and telegraphed to his wife: "Omitted to say in previous telegram that Frinton is the greatest expression of Anglo-Saxon character I have ever encountered. Love. Arthur." The girl behind the counter said: "Two and three, please," stared harder at him, and blushed. Perceiving the blush, Mr. Prohack at once despatched a third telegram to his wife: "But it has charming weaknesses. Love. Arthur." Extraordinarily happy and gay, he drove out of Frinton to see the remainder of North East Essex in the enheartening east wind.

In the evening he fell asleep in the lounge while waiting for dinner, having dressed a great deal too soon and being a great deal too full of east wind. When he woke up he noticed a different atmosphere in the hotel. Youth and brightness had entered it. The lounge had vivacity and expectation; and Mr. Prohack learned that Saturday night was gala, with a dance and special bridge. Not even the news that the star-guest of the hotel, Lord Partick, was suddenly indisposed and confined to his room could dash the new optimism of the place.

At dinner the manager walked around the little tables and gorgeously babbled with diners about the sportive feats of the day. And Mr. Prohack, seeing that his own turn was coming, began to feel as if he was on board a ship. He feared the worst and the worst came.

"Perhaps you'd like to make a fourth at bridge. If so—" said the manager jollily. "Or perhaps you dance. If so—"

Mr. Prohack shut his eyes and gave forth vague affirmatives.

And as soon as the manager had left him he gazed around the room at the too-blonde women young and old and wondered fearfully which would be his portion for bridge or dance. In the lounge after dinner he ignited a cigar and watched the lighting up of the ball-room (ordinarily the drawing-room) and the entry of the musicians therein. Then he observed the manager chatting with two haughty beldames and an aged gentleman, and they all three cast assaying glances upon Mr. Prohack, and Mr. Prohack knew that he had been destined for bridge, not dancing, and the manager moved towards him, and Mr. Prohack breathed his last sigh but one. . . .

But the revolving doors at the entrance revolved, and out of the Frintonian night appeared Lady Massulam, magnificently enveloped. Seldom had Mr. Prohack's breast received a deeper draught of mingled astonishment and solace. Hitherto he had not greatly cared for Lady Massulam, and could not see what Charlie saw in her. Now he saw what Charlie saw and perhaps more also. She had more than dignity,—she had style. And she femininely challenged. She was like a breeze off the French shore to a British barque cruising dully in the Channel. She welcomed the sight of Mr. Prohack, and her greeting of him made a considerable change in the managerial attitude towards the unassuming Terror of the departments. The manager respectfully informed Lady Massulam that Lord Partick was indisposed, and respectfully took himself off. Lady Massulam and Mr. Prohack then proceeded to treat each other like new toys. Mr. Prohack had to explain why he was at Frinton, and Lady Massulam explained that whenever she was in Frinton at the week-end she always came to the Majestic to play bridge with old Lord Partick. It flattered him; she liked him, though he had bought his peerage; he was a fine player—so was she; and lastly they had had business relations, and financially Lord Partick watched over her as over a young girl.

Mr. Prohack was relieved thus to learn that Lady Massulam had not strolled into the Majestic Hotel, Frinton, to play bridge with nobody in particular. Still, she was evidently well known to the habitués, several of whom approached to greet her. She temporised with them in her calm Latin manner, neither encouraging nor discouraging their advances, and turning back to Mr. Prohack by her side at every surcease.

"We shall be compelled to play bridge if we do not take care," she murmured in his ear, as a dowager larger than herself loomed up.

"Yes," murmured Mr. Prohack, "I've been feeling the danger ever since dinner. Will you dance with me,—not of course as a pleasure—I won't flatter myself—but as a means of salvation?"

The dowager bore down with a most definite suggestion for bridge in the card-room. Lady Massulam definitely stated that she was engaged to dance. . . .

Well, of course Lady Massulam was something of a galleon herself; but she was a beautiful dancer; that is to say, she responded perfectly to the male volition; she needed no pushing and no pulling; she moved under his will as lightly as a young girl. Her elaborately dressed hair had an agreeable scent; her complexion was a highly successful achievement; everything about her had a quiet and yet a dazzling elegance which had been obtained regardless of expense. As for her figure, it was on a considerable scale, but its important contours had a soft and delicate charm. And all that was nothing in the estimation of Mr. Prohack compared with her glance. At intervals in the fox-trot he caught the glance. It was arch, flirtatious, eternally youthful, challenging; and it expressed pleasure in the fox-trot. Mr. Prohack was dancing better than ever before in his career as a dancer. She made him dance better. She was not the same woman whom he had first met at lunch at the Grand Babylon Hotel. She was a new revelation, packed with possibilities. Mr. Prohack recalled his wife's phrase: "You know she adores you." He hadn't known. Honestly such an idea had not occurred to him. But did she adore him? Not "adore"—naturally—but had she a bit of a fancy for him?

Mr. Prohack became the youngest man in the room,—an extraordinary case of rejuvenescence. He surveyed the room with triumph. He sniffed up the brassy and clicking music into his vibrating nostrils. He felt no envy of any man in the room. When the band paused he clapped like a child for another dose of fox-trot. At the end of the third dose they were both a little breathless and they had ices. After a waltz they both realised that excess would be imprudent, and returned to the lounge.

"I wish you'd tell me something about my son," said Mr. Prohack. "I think you must be the greatest living authority on him."

"Here?" exclaimed Lady Massulam.

"Anywhere. Any time."

"It would be safer at my house," said Lady Massulam. "But before I go I must just write a little note to Lord Partick. He will expect it."

That was how she invited him to The Lone Cedar, the same being her famous bungalow on the Front.

IV

"Your son," said Lady Massulam, in a familiar tone, but most reassuringly like an aunt of Charlie's, after she had explained how they had met in Glasgow through being distantly connected by the same business deal, and how she had been impressed by Charlie's youthful capacity, "your son has very great talent for big affairs, but he is now playing a dangerous game—far more dangerous than he imagines, and he will not be warned. He is selling something he hasn't got before he knows what price he will have to pay for it."

"Ah!" breathed Mr. Prohack.

They were sitting together in the richly ornamented bungalow drawing-room, by the fire. Lady Massulam sat up straight in her sober and yet daring evening frock. Mr. Prohack lounged with formless grace in a vast easy-chair neighbouring a whiskey-and-soda. She had not asked him to smoke; he did not smoke, and he had no wish to smoke. She was a gorgeously mature specimen of a woman. He imagined her young, and he decided that he preferred the autumn to the spring. She went on talking of finance.

"She is moving in regions that Eve can never know," he thought. "But how did Eve perceive that she had taken a fancy to me?"

The alleged danger to Charlie scarcely disturbed him. Her appreciation or depreciation of Charlie interested him only in so far as it was a vehicle for the expression of her personality. He had never met such a woman. He responded to her with a vivacity that surprised himself. He looked surreptitiously round the room, brilliantly lighted here, and there obscure, and he comprehended how every detail of its varied sumptuosity aptly illustrated her mind and heart. His own heart was full of quite new sensations.

"Of course," she was saying, "if Charles is to become the really great figure that he might be, he will have to cure his greatest fault, and perhaps it is incurable."

"I know what that is," said Mr. Prohack, softly but positively.

"What is it?" Her glance met his.

"His confounded reserve, lack of elasticity, lack of adaptability. The old British illusion that everything will come to him who won't budge. Why, it's a ten-horse-power effort for him even to smile!"

Lady Massulam seemed to leap from her chair, and she broke swiftly into French:

"Oh! You comprehend then, you? If you knew what I have suffered in your terrible England! But you do not suspect what I have suffered! I advance myself. They retire before me. I advance myself again. They retire again. I open. They close. Do they begin? Never! It is always I who must begin! Do I make a natural gesture—they say to themselves, 'What a strange woman! How indiscreet! But she is foreign.' They lift their shoulders. Am I frank—they pity me. They give themselves never! They are shut like their lips over their long teeth. Ah, but they have taught me. In twenty years have I not learnt the lesson? There is nobody among you who can be more shut-tight than me. I flatter myself that I can be more terrible than any English woman or man. You do not catch me now! But what a martyrdom? . . . I might return to France? No! I am become too English. In Paris I should resemble an *émigrée.* And people would say: 'What is that? It is like nothing at all. It has no name.' Besides, I like you English. You are terrible, but one can count on you. . . . *Vous y êtes?*"

"J'y suis," replied Mr. Prohack, ravished.

Lady Massulam in her agitation picked up the tumbler and sipped.

"Pardon!" she cried, aghast. "It is yours," and planked the tumbler down again on the lacquered table.

Mr. Prohack had the wit to drink also. They went on talking. . . . A silver tongue vibrated from the hall with solemn British deliberation—One! Two! The air throbbed to the sound for many seconds.

"Good heavens!" exclaimed Mr. Prohack, rising in alarm. "And this is Frinton!" She let him out herself, with all soft precautions against shocking the Frintonian world. His manner of regaining the Majestic Hotel can only be described by saying that he 'effected an entrance' into it. He went to bed but not to sleep.

"What the deuce has happened to me?" he asked himself amazed. "Is it anything serious? Or am I merely English after all?"

V

Late the next morning, when he was dreaming, a servant awoke him with the information that a chauffeur was demanding him. But he was sleepy and slept again. Between noon and one o'clock he encountered the chauffeur. It was Carthew, who stated that his mistress had sent him with the car. She felt that he would need the car to go about in. As for her, she would manage without it.

Mr. Prohack remained silent for a few moments and then said: "Be ready to start in a quarter of an hour."

"Before lunch, sir?"

"Before lunch."

Mr. Prohack paid his bill and packed.

"Which way, sir?" Carthew asked, as the Eagle moved from under the portico of the hotel.

"There is only one road out of Frinton," said Mr. Prohack. "It's the road you came in by. Take it. I want to get off as quickly as possible. The climate of this place is the most dangerous and deceptive I was ever in."

"Really, sir!" responded Carthew, polite but indifferent. "The east wind I suppose, sir?"

"Not at all. The south wind."

CHAPTER XVIII

A HOMELESS NIGHT

I

How exhilarating (Mr. Prohack found it) to be on the road without a destination! It was Sunday morning, and the morning was marvellous for the time of year. Mr. Prohack had had a very fine night, and he now felt a curious desire to defy something or somebody, to defend himself, and to point out, if any one accused him of cowardice, that he had not retreated from danger until after he had fairly affronted it. More curious still was the double, self-contradictory sensation of feeling both righteous and sinful. He would have spurned a charge of wickedness, and yet the feeling of being wicked was really very jolly. He seemed to have begun a new page of life, and then to have ripped the page away—and possibly spoilt the whole book. Deference to Eve, of course! Respect for Eve! Or was it merely that he must always be able to look Eve in the face? In sending the car for his idle use, Eve had performed a master-stroke which laid him low by its kindliness, its wifeliness, its touches of perverse self-sacrifice and of vague, delicate malice. Lady Massulam hung in the vast hollow of his mind, a brilliant and intensely seductive figure; but Eve hung there too, and Mr. Prohack was obliged to admit that the simple Eve was holding her own.

"My sagacity is famous," said Mr. Prohack to himself. "And I never showed more of it than in leaving Frinton instantly. Few men would have had the sense and the resolution to do it." And he went on praising himself to himself. Such was the mood of this singular man.

Hunger—Mr. Prohack's hunger—drew them up at Frating, a village a few miles short of Colchester. The inn at Frating had been constructed ages earlier entirely without reference to the fact that it is improper for certain different types of humanity to eat or drink in each other's presence. In brief, there was obviously only one dining-room, and not a series of dining-rooms classified according to castes. Mr. Prohack, free, devil-may-care and original, said to his chauffeur:

"You'd better eat with me, Carthew."

"You're very kind, sir," said Carthew, and at once sat down and ceased to be a chauffeur.

"Well, I haven't been seeing much of you lately," Mr. Prohack edged forward into the fringes of intimacy when three glasses of beer and three slices of Derby Round had been unequally divided between them, "have I?"

"No, sir."

Mr. Prohack had in truth been seeing Carthew almost daily; but on this occasion he used the word "see" in a special sense.

"That boy of yours getting on all right?"

"Pretty fair, considering he's got no mother, if you understand what I mean, sir," replied Carthew, pushing back his chair, stretching out his legs, and picking his teeth with a fork.

"Ah! yes!" said Mr. Prohack commiseratingly. "Very awkward situation for you, that is."

"It isn't awkward for me, sir. It's my boy it's awkward for. I'm as right as rain."

"No chance of the lady coming back, I suppose?"

"Well, she'd better not try," said Carthew grimly.

"But does this mean you've done with the sex, at your age?" cried Mr. Prohack.

"I don't say as I've *done* with the sex, sir. Male and female created He them, as the good old Book says; and I'm not going behind that. No, not me! All I say is, I'm as right as rain—*for* the present—and she'd better not try."

"I bet you anything you won't keep it up," said Mr. Prohack, impetuously exceeding the limits of inter-caste decorum.

"Keep what up?"

"This attitude of yours."

"I won't bet, sir," said Carthew. "Because nobody can see round a corner. But I promise you I'll never take a woman *seriously* again. That's the mistake we make, taking 'em seriously. You see, sir, being a chauffeur in the early days of motor-cars, I've had a tidy bit of experience, if you understand what I mean. Because in them days a chauffeur was like what an air-pilot is to-day. He didn't have to ask, he didn't. And what I say is this—I say we're mugs to take 'em seriously."

"You think we are!" bubbled Mr. Prohack emptily, perceiving that he had to do with an individual whom misfortune had rendered impervious to argument.

"I do, sir. And what's more, I say you never know where you are with any woman."

"That I agree with," said Mr. Prohack, with a polite show of eagerness. "But you're cutting yourself off from a great deal you know, Carthew," he added, thinking magnificently upon his adventure with Lady Massulam.

"There's a rare lot as would like to be in my place," murmured Carthew with bland superiority. "If it's all the same to you, sir, I'll just go and give her a look over before we start again." He scraped his chair cruelly over the wood floor, rose, and ceased to be an authority on women.

It was while exercising his privilege of demanding, awaiting, and paying the bill, that Mr. Prohack happened to see, at the other end of the long, empty dining-room table, a copy of *The Sunday Picture,* which was the Sabbath edition of *The Daily Picture.* He got up and seized it, expecting it to be at least a week old. It proved, however, to be as new and fresh as it could be. Mr. Prohack glanced with inimical tolerance at its pages, until his eye encountered the portraits of two ladies, both known to him, side by side. One was Miss Eliza Fiddle, the rage of the West End, and the other was Mrs. Arthur Prohack, wife of the well-known Treasury official. The portraits were juxtaposed, it seemed, because Miss Eliza Fiddle had just let her lovely home in Manchester Square to Mrs. Arthur Prohack.

The shock of meeting Eve in *The Sunday Picture* was terrible, but equally terrible to Mr. Prohack was the discovery of his ignorance in regard to the ownership of the noble mansion. He had understood—or more correctly he had been given to understand—that the house and its contents belonged to a certain peer, whose taste in the arts was as celebrated as that of his lordly forefathers had been. Assuredly neither Eliza Fiddle nor anybody like her could have been responsible for the exquisite decorations and furnishings of that house. On the other hand, it would have been very characteristic of Eliza Fiddle to leave the house as carelessly as it had been left, with valuable or invaluable bibelots lying about all over the place. Almost certainly Eliza Fiddle must have had some sort of effective ownership of the place. He knew that dazzling public favourites did sometimes enjoy astounding and mysterious luck in the matter of luxurious homes, and that some of them progressed through a series of such homes, each more inexplicable than the last. He would not pursue the enquiry, even in his own mind. He had of course no grudge against the efficient and strenuous Eliza, for he was perfectly at liberty not to pay money in order to see her. She must be an exceedingly clever woman; and it was not in him to cast stones. Yet, Pharisaical snob, he did most violently resent that she should be opposite his wife in *The Sunday Picture*. . . . Eve! Eve! A few short weeks ago, and you made a mock of women who let themselves get into *The Daily Picture*. And now you are there yourself! (But so, and often, was the siren Lady Massulam! A ticklish thing, criticism of life!)

And there was another point, as sharp as any. Ozzie Morfey must have known, Charlie must have known, Sissie must have known, Eve herself must have known, that the *de facto* owner of the noble mansion was Eliza Fiddle. And none had vouchsafed the truth to him.

"We'll struggle back to town I think," said Mr. Prohack to Carthew, with a pitiable affectation of brightness. And instead of sitting by Carthew's side, as previously, he sat behind, and reflected upon the wisdom of Carthew. He had held that Carthew's views were warped by a peculiar experience. He now saw that they were not warped at all, but shapely, sane and incontrovertible.

II

That evening, soon after dark, the Eagle, dusty and unkempt from a journey which had not been free from mishaps, rolled up to the front-door of Mr. Prohack's original modest residence behind Hyde Park; and Mr. Prohack jumped out; and Carthew came after him with two bags. The house was as dark as the owner's soul; not a gleam of light in any window. Mr. Prohack produced his familiar latch-key, scraped round the edge of the keyhole, savagely pushed in the key, and opened the door. There was still no light nor sign of life. Mr. Prohack paused on the threshold, and then his hand instinctively sought the electric switch and pulled it down. No responsive gleam!

"Machin!" called Mr. Prohack, as it were plaintively.

No sound.

"I am a fool," thought Mr. Prohack.

He struck a match and walked forward delicately, peering. He descried an empty portmanteau lying on the stairs. He shoved against the dining-room door, which was ajar, and lit another match, and started back. The dining-room was full of ghosts, furniture sheeted in dust-sheets; and a newspaper had been made into a cap over his favourite Chippendale clock. He retreated.

"Put those bags into the car again," he said to Carthew, who stood hesitant on the vague whiteness of the front-step.

How much did Carthew know? Mr. Prohack was too proud to ask. Carthew was no longer an authority on women lunching with an equal; he was a servitor engaged and paid on the clear understanding that he should not speak until spoken to.

"Drive to Claridge's Hotel," said Mr. Prohack.

"Yes, sir."

At the entrance to the hotel the party was received by gigantic uniformed guards with all the respect due to an Eagle. Ignoring the guards, Mr. Prohack passed imperially within to the reception office.

"I want a bedroom, a sitting-room and a bath-room, please."

"A private suite, sir?"

"A private suite."

"What—er—kind, sir? We have—"

"The best," said Mr. Prohack, with finality. He signed his name and received a ticket.

"Please have my luggage taken out of the car, and tell my chauffeur I shall want him at ten o'clock to-morrow morning, and that he should take the car to the hotel-garage, wherever it is, and sleep here. I will have some tea at once in my sitting-room."

The hotel-staff, like all hotel-staffs, loved a customer who knew his mind with precision and could speak it. Mr. Prohack was admirably served.

After tea he took a bath because he could think of nothing else to do. The bath, as baths will, inspired him with an idea. He set out on foot to Manchester Square, and having reached the Square cautiously followed the side opposite to the noble mansion. The noble mansion blazed with lights through the wintry trees. It resembled the set-piece of a pyrotechnic display. Mr. Prohack shivered in the dank evening. Then he observed that blinds and curtains were being drawn in the noble mansion, shutting out from its superb nobility the miserable, crude, poverty-stricken world. With the exception of the glow in the fan light over the majestic portals, the noble mansion was now as dark as Mr. Prohack's other house.

He shut his lips, steeled himself, and walked round the Square to the noble mansion and audaciously rang the bell. He had to wait. He shook guiltily, as though he, and no member of his family, had sinned. A little more, and his tongue would have cleaved to the gold of his upper denture. The double portals swung backwards. Mr. Prohack beheld the portly form of an intensely traditional butler, and behind the butler a vista of outer and inner halls and glimpses of the soaring staircase. He heard, somewhere in the distance of the interior, the ringing laugh of his daughter Sissie.

The butler looked carelessly down upon him, and, as Mr. Prohack uttered no word, challenged him.

"Yes, sir?"

"Is Mrs. Prohack at home?"

"No, sir." (Positively.)

"Is Miss Prohack at home?"

"No, sir." (More positively.)

"Oh!"

"Will you leave your name, sir?"

"No."

Abruptly Mr. Prohack turned away. He had had black moments in his life. This was the blackest.

Of course he might have walked right in, and said to the butler: "Here's a month's wages. Hook it." But he was a peculiar fellow, verging sometimes on silliness. He merely turned away. The vertiginous rapidity of his wife's developments, manœuvres and transformations had dazed him into a sort of numbed idiocy. In two days, in a day, with no warning to him of her extraordinary precipitancy, she had 'flitted'!

At Claridge's, through giving Monsieur Charles, the *maître d' hôtel,* carte blanche in the ordering of his dinner and then only half-eating his dinner, Mr. Prohack failed somewhat to maintain his prestige, though he regained ground towards the end by means of champagne and liqueurs. The black-and-gold restaurant was full of expensive persons who were apparently in ignorance of the fact that the foundations of the social fabric had been riven. They were all gay; the music was gay; everything was gay except Mr. Prohack—the sole living being in the place who conformed in face and heart to the historical conception of the British Sunday.

But Mr. Prohack was not now a man,—he was a grievance; he was the most deadly kind of grievance, the irrational kind. A superlatively fine cigar did a little—not much—to solace him. He smoked it with scientific slowness, and watched the restaurant empty itself. . . . He was the last survivor in the restaurant; and fifteen waiters and two hundred and fifty electric lamps were keeping him in countenance. Then his wandering, enfeebled attention heard music afar off, and he remembered some remark of Sissie's to the effect that Claridge's was the best place for dancing in London on Sunday nights. He would gaze Byronically upon the dance. He signed his bill and mooned towards the ball-room, which was full of radiant couples: a dazzling scene, fit to mark the end of an epoch and of a society.

The next thing was that he had an absurd delusion of seeing Sissie and Charlie locked together amid the couples. He might have conquered this delusion, but it was succeeded by another,—the illusion of seeing Ozzie Morfey and Eve locked together amid the couples. . . . Yes, they were there, all four of them. At first Mr. Prohack was amazed, as at an unprecedented coincidence. But he perceived that the coincidence was not after all so amazing. They had done what they had to do in the way of settling Eve into the noble mansion, and then they had betaken themselves to the nearest and the best dancing resort for the rest of the evening. Nothing could be more natural.

Mr. Prohack might have done all manner of feats. What he actually did do was to fly like a criminal to the lift and seek his couch.

III

The next morning at ten o'clock a strange thing happened. The hotel clocks showed the hour and Mr. Prohack's watch showed the hour, and Carthew was not there with the car. Mr. Prohack could not understand this unnatural failure to appear on the part of Carthew, for Carthew had never been known to be late (save when interfered with by Mimi), and therefore never could be late. Mr. Prohack fretted for a quarter of an hour, and then caused the hotel-garage to be telephoned to. The car had left the garage at nine-fifty. Mr. Prohack went out for a walk, not ostensibly, but really, to look for the car in the streets of London! (Such was his diseased mentality.) He returned at half past eleven, and at eleven thirty-two the car arrived. Immediately Mr. Prohack became calm; his exterior was apt to be very deceptive; and he said gently to Carthew, just as if nothing in the least unusual had occurred:

"A little late, aren't you?"

"Yes, sir," Carthew replied, with a calmness to match his employer's. "As I was coming here from the garage I met the mistress. She was looking for a taxi and she took me."

"But did you tell her that I asked you to be here at 10 o'clock?"

"No, sir."

"Did you tell her that I was in London?"

"No, sir."

Mr. Prohack hesitated a moment and then said:

"Drive into Hyde Park, please, and keep to the north side."

When the car had reached a quiet spot in the park, Mr. Prohack stopped it, and, tapping on the front window, summoned Carthew.

"Carthew," said he, through the side-window, which he let down without opening the door, "we're by ourselves. Will you kindly explain to me why you concealed from Mrs. Prohack that I was in London?"

"Well, sir," Carthew answered, very erect and slightly frowning, "I didn't know you were in London, if you understand what I mean."

"Didn't you bring me to London? Of course you knew I was in London."

"No, sir. Not if you understand what I mean."

"I emphatically do not understand what you mean," said Mr. Prohack, who, however, was not speaking the truth.

"May I put a question, sir?" Carthew suggested. "Having regard to all the circumstances—I say having regard as it were to all the circumstances, in a manner of speaking, what should you have done in my place, sir?"

"How do I know?" cried Mr. Prohack. "I'm not a chauffeur. What *did* you say to Mrs. Prohack?"

"I said that you had instructed me to return to London, as you didn't need the car, and that I was just going to the house for orders. And by the way, sir," Carthew added, glancing at the car-clock, "Madam told me to be back at twelve fifteen—I told her I ought to go to the garage to get something done to the carburetor—so that there is not much time."

Mr. Prohack jumped out of the car and said: "Go."

Wandering alone in the chilly Park he reflected upon the potentialities of human nature as exhibited in chauffeurs. The fellow Carthew had evidently come to the conclusion that there was something wrong in the more intimate relationships of the Prohack family, and, faced with a sudden contretemps, he had acted according to the best of his wisdom and according to his loyalty to his employer, but he had acted wrongly. But of course the original sinner was Mr. Prohack himself. Respectable State officials, even when on sick leave, do not call at empty houses and stay at hotels within a stone's throw of their own residences unknown to their families. No! Mr. Prohack saw that he had been steering a crooked course. Error existed and must be corrected. He decided to walk direct to Manchester Square. If Eve wanted the car at twelve fifteen she would be out of the house at twelve thirty, and probably out for lunch. So much the better. She should find him duly established on her return.

Reconnoitring later at Manchester Square he saw no car, and rang the bell of the noble mansion. On account of the interview of the previous evening he felt considerably nervous and foolish, and the butler suffered through no fault of the butler's.

"I'm Mr. Prohack," said he, with self-conscious fierceness. "What's your name? Brool, eh? Take my overcoat and send Machin to me at once." He lit a cigarette to cover himself. The situation, though transient, had been sufficiently difficult.

Machin came leaping and bounding down the stairs as if by magic. She had heard his voice, and her joy at his entry into his abode caused her to forget her parlour-maidenhood and to exhibit a humanity which pained Mr. Brool, who had been brought up in the strictest traditions of flunkeyism. Her joy pleased Mr. Prohack and he felt better.

"Good morning, Machin," said he, quite blithely. "I just want to see how things have been fixed up in my rooms." He had not the least notion where or what his rooms were in the vast pile.

"Yes, sir," Machin responded eagerly, delighted that Mr. Prohack was making to herself, as an old friend, an appeal which he ought to have made to the butler. Mr. Prohack, guided by the prancing Machin, discovered that, in addition to a study, he had a bedroom and a dressing-room and a share in Eve's bath-room. The dressing-room had a most agreeable aspect. Machin opened a huge and magnificent wardrobe, and in drawer after drawer displayed his new hosiery marvellously arranged, and in other portions of the wardrobe his new suits and hats and boots. The whole made a wondrous spectacle.

"And who did all this?" he demanded.

"Madam, sir. But Miss Warburton came to help her at nine this morning, and I helped too. Miss Warburton has put the lists in your study, sir."

"Thank you, Machin. It's all very nice." He was touched. The thought of all these women toiling in secret to please him was exceedingly sweet. It was not as though he had issued any requests. No! They did what they did from enthusiasm, unknown to him.

"Wait a second," he stopped Machin, who was leaving him. "Which floor did you say my study is on?"

She led him to his study. An enormous desk, and in the middle of it a little pile of papers crushed by a block of crystal! The papers were all bills. The amounts of them alarmed him momentarily, but that was only because he could not continuously and effectively remember that he had over three hundred pounds a week coming in. Still, the bills did somewhat dash him, and he left them without getting to the bottom of the pile. He thought he would voyage through the house, but he got no further than his wife's boudoir. The boudoir also had an enormous desk, and on it also was a pile of papers. He offended the marital code by picking up the first one, which read as follows:—"Madam. We beg to enclose as requested estimate for buffet refreshments for one hundred and fifty persons, and hire of one hundred gilt cane chairs and bringing and taking away same. Trusting to be honoured with your commands—" This document did more than alarm him; it shook him. Clearly Eve was planning a great reception. Even to attend a reception was torture to him, always had been; but to be the host at a reception . . . ! No, his mind refused to contemplate a prospect so appalling. Surely Eve ought to have consulted him before beginning to plan a reception. Why a reception? He glimpsed matters that might be even worse than a reception. And this was the same woman who had so touchingly arranged his clothes.

IV

He was idly regarding himself in an immense mirror that topped the fireplace, and thinking that despite the stylishness of his accoutrement he presented the appearance of a rather tousled and hairy person of unromantic middle-age, when, in the glass, he saw the gilded door open and a woman enter the room. He did not move,—only stared at the image. He knew the woman intimately, profoundly, exhaustively, almost totally. He knew her as one knows the countryside in which one has grown up, where every feature of the scene has become a habit of the perceptions. And yet he had also a strange sensation of seeing her newly, of seeing her for the first time in his life and estimating her afresh. In a flash he had compared her, in this boudoir, with Lady Massulam in Lady Massulam's bungalow. In a flash all the queer, frightening romance of 2 a. m. in Frinton had swept through his mind. Well, she had not the imposingness nor the mystery of Lady Massulam, nor perhaps the challenge of Lady Massulam; she was very much more prosaic to him. But still he admitted that she had an effect on him, that he reacted to her presence, that she was at any rate at least as incalculable as Lady Massulam, and that there might be bits of poetry gleaming in her prose, and that after a quarter of a century he had not arrived at a final judgment about her. Withal Lady Massulam had a quality which she lacked,—he did not know what the quality was, but he knew that it excited him in an unprecedented manner and that he wanted it and would renounce it with regret. "Is it conceivable," he thought, shocked at himself, "that all three of us are on the road to fifty years?"

Then he turned, and blushed, feeling exactly like an undergraduate.

"I knew you'd be bored up there in that hole." Eve greeted him.

"I wasn't bored for a single moment," said he.

"Don't tell me," said she.

She was very smart in her plumpness. The brim of her spreading hat bumped against his forehead as he bent to kiss her. The edge of the brown veil came half-way down her face, leaving her mouth unprotected from him, but obscuring her disturbing eyes. As he kissed her all his despondency and worry fell away from him, and he saw with extraordinary clearness that since the previous evening he had been an irrational ass. The creature had done nothing unusual, nothing that he had not explicitly left her free to do; and everything was all right.

"Did you see your friend Lady Massulam?" was her first question.

Marvellous the intuition—or the happy flukes—of women! Yet their duplicity was still more marvellous. The creature's expressed anxiety about the danger of Lady Massulam's society to Charlie must have been pure, wanton, gratuitous pretence.

He told her of his meeting with Lady Massulam.

"I left her at 2 a. m.," said he, with well-feigned levity.

"I knew she wouldn't leave you alone for long. But I've no doubt you enjoyed it. I hope you did. You need adventure, my poor boy. You were getting into a regular rut."

"Oh, was I!" he opposed. "And what are you doing here? Machin told me you were out for lunch."

"Oh! You've been having a chat with your friend Machin, have you? It seems she's shown you your beautiful dressing-room. Well, I was going out for lunch. But when I heard you'd returned I gave it up and came back. I knew so well you'd want looking after."

"And who told you I'd returned?"

"Carthew, of course! You're a very peculiar pair, you two. When I first saw him Carthew gave me to understand he'd left you at Frinton. But when I see him again I learn that you're in town and that you spent last night at Claridge's. You did quite right, my poor boy. Quite right. I want you to feel free. It must have been great fun stopping at Claridge's, with your own home close by. I'll tell you something. We were dancing at Claridge's last night, but I suppose you'd gone to bed."

"The dickens you were!" said he. "By the way, you might instruct one of your butlers to telephone to the hotel for my things and have the bill paid."

"So you'll sleep here to-night?" said she, archly.

"If there's room," said he. "Anyway you've arranged all my clothes with the most entrancing harmony and precision."

"Oh!" Eve exclaimed, in a tone suddenly changed. "That was Miss Warburton more than me. She took an hour off from Charlie this morning in order to do it."

Then Mr. Prohack observed his wife's face crumble to pieces, and she moved aside from him, sat down and began to cry.

"Now what next? What next?" he demanded with impatient amiability, for he was completely at a loss to keep pace with the twistings of her mind.

"Arthur, why did you deceive me about that girl? How could you do it? I hadn't the slightest idea it was M—miss W—instock. I can't make you out sometimes, Arthur—really I can't!"

The fellow had honestly forgotten that he had in fact grossly deceived his wife to the point of planting Mimi Winstock upon her as somebody else. He had been nourishing imaginary and absurd grievances against Eve for many hours, but her grievance against himself was genuine enough and large enough. No wonder she could not make him out. He could not make himself out. His conscience awoke within him and became exceedingly unpleasant. But being a bad man he laughed somewhat coarsely.

"Oh!" he said. "That was only a bit of a joke. But how did you find out, you silly child?"

"Ozzie saw her yesterday. He knew her. You can't imagine how awkward it was. Naturally I had to laugh it off. But I cried half the night."

"But why? What did it matter? Ozzie's one of the family. The girl's not at all a bad sort, and I did it for her sake."

Eve dried her eyes and looked up at him reproachfully with wet cheeks.

"When I think," said she, "that that girl might so easily have killed me in that accident! And it would have been all her fault. And then where would you have been without me? Where *would* you have been? You'd never have got over it. Never, never! You simply don't know what you'd be if you hadn't got me to look after you! And you bring her into the house under a false name, and you call it a joke! No, Arthur. Frankly I couldn't have believed it of you."

Mr. Prohack was affected. He was not merely dazzled by the new light which she was shedding on things,—he was emotionally moved. . . . Would Lady Massulam be capable of such an attitude as Eve's in such a situation? The woman was astounding. She was more romantic than any creature in any bungalow of romantic Frinton. She beat him. She rent his heart. So he said:

"Well, my beloved infant, if it's any use to you I'm prepared to admit once for all that I was an ass. We'll never have the wretched Mimi in the house again. I'll give the word to Charlie."

"Oh, not at all!" she murmured, smiling sadly. "I've got over it. And you must think of my dignity. How ridiculous it would be of me to make a fuss about her being here! Now, wouldn't it? But I'm glad I've told you. I didn't mean to, really. I meant never to say a word. But the fact is I can't keep anything from you."

She began to cry again, but differently. He soothed her, as none but he could, thinking exultantly: "What a power I have over this chit!" They were perfectly happy. They lunched alone together, talking exclusively for the benefit of Eve's majestic butler. And Mr. Prohack, with that many-sidedness that marked his strange regrettable mind, said to himself at intervals: "Nevertheless she's still hiding from me her disgusting scheme for a big reception. And she knows jolly well I shall hate it."

CHAPTER XIX

THE RECEPTION

I

THE reception pleased Mr. Prohack as a spectacle, and it cost him almost no trouble. He announced his decision that it must cost him no trouble, and everybody in the house, and a few people outside it, took him at his word—which did not wholly gratify him. Indeed the family and its connections seemed to be conspiring to give him a life of ease. Responsibilities were lifted from him. He did not even miss his secretary. Sissie, who returned home—by a curious coincidence—on the very day that Mimi Winstock was transferred to Charlie's service in the Grand Babylon, performed what she called 'secretarial stunts' for her father as and when required. On the afternoon of the reception, which was timed to begin at 9 p. m., he had an attack of fright, but, by a process well known to public executants, it passed off long before it could develop into stage-fright; and he was quite at ease at 9 p. m.

The first arrivals came at nine thirty. He stood by Eve and greeted them; and he had greeted about twenty individuals when he yawned (for a good reason) and Eve said to him:

"You needn't stay here, you know. Go and amuse yourself." (This suggestion followed the advent of Lady Massulam.)

He didn't stay. Ozzie Morfey and Sissie supplanted him. At a quarter to eleven he was in the glazed conservatory built over the monumental portico, with Sir Paul Spinner. He could see down into the Square, which was filled with the splendid and numerous automobiles incident to his wife's reception. Guests—and not the least important among them—were still arriving. Cars rolled up to the portico, gorgeous women and plain men jumped out on to the red cloth, of which he could just see the extremity near the kerb, and vanished under him, and the cars hid themselves away in the depths of the Square. Looking within his home he admired the vista of brilliantly illuminated rooms, full of gilt chairs, priceless furniture, and extremely courageous toilettes. For, as the reception was 'to meet the Committee of the League of all the Arts.' (Ozzie had placed many copies of the explanatory pamphlet on various tables), artists of all kinds and degrees abounded, and the bourgeois world (which chiefly owned the automobiles) thought proper to be sartorially as improper as fashion would allow; and fashion allowed quite a lot. The affair might have been described as a study in shoulder-blades. It was a very great show, and Mr. Prohack appreciated all of it, the women, the men, the lionesses, the lions, the kaleidoscope of them, the lights, the reflections in the mirrors and in the waxed floors, the discreetly hidden music, the grandiose buffet, the efficient valetry. He soon got used to not recognising, and not being recognised by, the visitors to his own house. True, he could not conceive that the affair would serve any purpose but one,—namely the purpose of affording innocent and expensive pleasure to his wife.

"You've hit on a pretty good sort of a place here," grunted Sir Paul Spinner, whose waistcoat buttons were surpassed in splendour only by his carbuncles.

"Well," said Mr. Prohack, "to me, living here is rather like being on the stage all the time. It's not real."

"What the deuce do you mean, it's not real? There aren't twenty houses in London with a finer collection of genuine bibelots than you have here."

"Yes, but they aren't mine, and I didn't choose them or arrange them."

"What does that matter? You can look at them and enjoy the sight of them. Nobody can do more."

"Paul, you're talking neo-conventional nonsense again. Have you ever in your career as a city man stood outside a money-changer's and looked at the fine collection of genuine banknotes in the window? Supposing I told you that you could look at them and enjoy the sight of them, and nobody could do more? . . . No, my boy, to enjoy a thing properly you've got to own it. And anybody who says the contrary is probably a member of the League of all the Arts." He gave another enormous yawn. "Excuse my yawning, Paul, but this house is a perfect Inferno for me. The church of St. Nicodemus is hard by, and the church of St. Nicodemus has a striking clock, and the clock strikes all the hours and all the quarters on a half cracked bell or two bells. If I am asleep every hour wakes me up, and most of the quarters. The clock strikes not only the hours and the quarters but me. I regulate my life by that clock. If I'm beginning to repose at ten minutes to the hour, I say to myself that I must wait till the hour before really beginning, and I do wait. It is killing me, and nobody can see that it is killing me. The clock annoys some individuals a little occasionally; they curse, and then go to sleep and stay asleep. For them the clock is a nuisance; but for me it's an assassination. However, I can't make too much fuss. Several thousands of people must live within sound of the St. Nicodemus clock; yet the rector has not been murdered nor the church razed to the ground. Hence the clock doesn't really upset many people. And there are hundreds of such infernal clocks in London, and they all survive. It follows therefore that I am peculiar. Nobody has a right to be peculiar. Hence I do not complain. I suffer. I've tried stuffing my ears with cotton-wool, and stuffing the windows of my bedroom with eiderdowns. No use. I've tried veronal. No use either. The only remedy would be for me to give the house up. Which would be absurd. My wife soothes me and says that of course I shall get used to the clock. I shall never get used to it. Lately she has ceased even to mention the clock. My daughter thinks I am becoming a grumbler in my latter years. My son smiles indifferently. I admit that my son's secretary is more sympathetic. Like most people who are both idle and short of sleep, I usually look very well, spry and wideawake. My friends remark on my healthy appearance. You did. The popular mind cannot conceive that I am merely helplessly waiting for death to put me out of my misery; but so it is. There must be quite a few others in the same fix as me in London, dying because rectors and other clergymen and officials insist on telling them the time all through the night. But they suffer in silence as I do. As I do, they see the uselessness of a fuss."

"You *will* get used to it, Arthur," said Sir Paul indulgently but not unironically, at the end of Mr. Prohack's disquisition. "You're in a nervous state and your judgment's warped. Now, I never even heard your famous clock strike ten."

"No, you wouldn't, Paul! And my judgment's warped, is it?" There was irritation in Mr. Prohack's voice. He took out his watch. "In sixty or seventy seconds you shall hear that clock strike eleven, and you shall give me your honest views about it. And you shall apologise to me."

Sir Paul obediently and sympathetically listened, while the murmur of the glowing reception and the low beat of music continued within.

"You tell me when it starts to strike," said he.

"You won't want any telling," said Mr. Prohack, who knew too well the riving, rending, smashing sound of the terrible bells.

"It's a pretty long seventy seconds," observed Sir Paul.

"My watch must be fast," said Mr. Prohack, perturbed.

But at eighteen minutes past eleven the clock had audibly struck neither the hour nor the quarter. Sir Paul was a man of tact. He said simply:

"I should like a drink, dear old boy."

"The clock's not striking," said Mr. Prohack, with solemn joy, as the wonderful truth presented itself to him. "Either it's stopped, or they've cut off the striking attachment." And to one of the maids on the landing he said as they passed towards the buffet: "Run out and see what time it is by the church clock, and come back and tell me, will you?" A few minutes later he was informed that the church clock showed half-past eleven. The clock therefore was still going but had ceased to strike. Mr. Prohack at once drank two glasses of champagne at the buffet, while Sir Paul had the customary whiskey.

"I say, old thing, I say!" Sir Paul protested.

"I shall sleep!" said Mr. Prohack in a loud, gay, triumphant voice. He was a new man.

II

The reception now seemed to him far more superb than ever. It was almost at its apogee. All the gilt chairs were occupied; all the couches and fauteuils of the room were occupied, and certain delicious toilettes were even spread on rugs or on the bare, reflecting floors. On every hand could be heard artistic discussions, serious and informed and yet lightsome in tone. If it was not the real originality of jazz music that was being discussed, it was the sureness of the natural untaught taste of the denizens of the East End and South London, and if not that then the greatness of male revue artistes, and if not that then the need of a national theatre and of a minister of fine arts, and if not that then the sculptural quality of the best novels and the fictional quality of the best sculpture, and if not that then the influence on British life of the fox-trot, and if not that then the prospects of bringing modern poets home to the largest public by means of the board schools, and if not that then the evil effects of the twin great London institutions for teaching music upon the individualities of the young geniuses entrusted to them, and if not that the part played by the most earnest amateurs in the destruction of opera, and if not that the total eclipse of Beethoven, Brahms and Wagner since the efflorescence of the Russian Ballet. And always there ran like a flame through the conversations the hot breath of a passionate intention to make Britain artistic in the eyes of the civilised world.

What especially pleased Mr. Prohack about the whole affair, as he moved to and fro seeking society now instead of avoiding it, was the perfect futility of the affair, save as it affected Eve's reputation. He perceived the beauty of costly futility, and he was struck again, when from afar he observed his wife's conquering mien, by the fact that the reception did not exist for the League, but the League for the reception. The reception was a real and a resplendent thing; nobody could deny it. The League was a fog of gush. The League would be dear at twopence halfpenny. The reception was cheap if it stood him in five hundred pounds. Eve was an infant; Eve was pleased with gewgaws; but Eve had found herself and he was well content to pay five hundred pounds for the look on her ingenuous face.

"And nothing of this would have happened," he thought, impressed by the wonders of life, "if in a foolish impulse of generosity I hadn't once lent a hundred quid to that chap Angmering."

He descried Lady Massulam in converse with a tall, stout and magnificently dressed gentleman, who bowed deeply and departed as Mr. Prohack approached.

"Who is your fat friend?" said Mr. Prohack.

"He's from *The Daily Picture*. . . . But isn't this rather a strange way of greeting a guest after so long a separation? Do you know that I'm in your house and you haven't shaken hands with me?"

There was a note of intimacy and of challenge in Lady Massulam's demeanour that pleased Mr. Prohack immensely, and caused him to see that the romance of Frinton was neither factitious nor at an end. He felt pleasantly, and even thrillingly, that they had something between them.

"Ah!" he returned, consciously exerting his charm. "I thought you detested our English formality and horrible restraint. Further, this isn't my house; it's my wife's."

"Your wife is wonderful!" said Lady Massulam, as though teaching him to appreciate his wife and indicating that she alone had the right thus to teach him,—the subtlest thing. "I've never seen an evening better done—*réussie.*"

"She is rather wonderful," Mr. Prohack admitted, his tone implying that while putting Lady Massulam in a class apart, he had wit enough to put his wife too in a class apart,—the subtlest thing.

"I quite expected to meet you again in Frinton," said Lady Massulam simply. "How abrupt you are in your methods!"

"Only when it's a case of self-preservation," Mr. Prohack responded, gazing at her with daring significance.

"I'm going to talk to Mrs. Prohack," said Lady Massulam, rising. But before she left him she murmured confidentially in his ear: "Where's your son?"

"Don't know. Why?"

"I don't think he's come yet. I'm afraid the poor boy's affairs are not very bright."

"I shall look after him," said Mr. Prohack, grandly. A qualm did pierce him at the sound of her words, but he would not be depressed. He smiled serenely, self-confidently, and said to himself: "I could look after forty Charleses."

He watched his wife and his friend chatting together as equals in *The Daily Picture.* Yes, Eve was wonderful, and but for sheer hazard he would never have known how wonderful she was capable of being.

"You've got a great show here to-night, old man," said a low, mysterious voice at his side. Mr. Softly Bishop was smiling down his nose and holding out his hand while looking at nothing but his nose.

"Hello, Bishop!" said Mr. Prohack, controlling a desire to add: "I'd no idea *you'd* been invited!"

"Samples of every world—except the next," said Mr. Softly Bishop. "And now the theatrical contingent is arriving after its night's work."

"Do you know who that fellow is?" Mr. Prohack demanded, indicating a little man with the aspect of a prize-fighter who was imperially conveying to Mrs. Prohack that Mrs. Prohack was lucky to get him to her reception.

"Why!" replied Mr. Bishop. "That's the Napoleon of the stage."

"Not Asprey Chown!"

"Asprey Chown."

"Great Scott!" And Mr. Prohack laughed.

"Why are you laughing?"

"Mere glee. This is the crown of my career as a man of the world." He saw Mr. Asprey Chown give a careless brusque nod to Ozzie Morfey, and he laughed again.

"It's rather comic, isn't it?" Mr. Softly Bishop acquiesced. "I wonder why Oswald Morfey has abandoned his famous stock for an ordinary necktie."

"Probably because he's going to be my son-in-law," said Mr. Prohack.

"Ah!" ejaculated Mr. Softly Bishop. "I congratulate him."

Mr. Prohack looked grim in order to conceal his joy in the assurance that he would sleep that night, and in the sensations produced by the clear fact that Lady Massulam was still interested in him. Somehow he wanted to dance, not with any woman, but by himself, a reel.

"By Jove!" exclaimed Mr. Softly Bishop. "You *are* shining to-night. Here's Eliza Fiddle, and that's her half-sister Miss Fancy behind her."

And it was Eliza Fiddle, and the ageing artiste with her ravaged complexion and her defiant extra-vivacious mien created instantly an impression such as none but herself could have created. The entire assemblage stared, murmuring its excitement, at the renowned creature. Eliza loved the stare and the murmur. She was like a fish dropped into water after a gasping spell in mere air.

"I admit I was in too much of a hurry when I spoke of having reached the zenith," said Mr. Prohack. "I'm only just getting there now. And who's the half-sister?"

"She's not precisely unknown on the American stage," answered Mr. Softly Bishop. "But before we go any further I'd perhaps better tell you a secret." His voice and his gaze dropped still lower. "She's a particularly fine girl, and it won't be my fault if I don't marry her. Not a word of course! Mum!" He turned away, while Mr. Prohack was devising a suitable response.

"Welcome to your old home. And do come with me to the buffet. You must be tired after your work," Mr. Prohack burst out in a bold, loud voice to Eliza, taking her away from his wife, whose nearly exhausted tact almost failed to hide her relief.

"I do hope you like the taste of my old home," Eliza answered. "My new house up the river is furnished throughout in real oriental red lacquer. You must come and see it."

"I should love to," said Mr. Prohack bravely.

"This is my little sister, Miss Fancy. Fan, Mr. Prohack."

Mr. Prohack expressed his enchantment.

At the buffet Eliza did not refuse champagne, but Miss Fancy refused. "Now don't put on airs, Fan," Eliza reproved her sister heartily and drank off her glass while Mr. Prohack sipped his somewhat cautiously. He liked Eliza's reproof. He was beginning even to like Eliza. To say that her style was coarse was to speak in moderation; but she was natural, and her individuality seemed to be sending out waves in all directions, by which all persons in the vicinity were affected whether they desired it or not. Mr. Prohack met Eliza's glance with satisfaction. She at any rate had nothing to learn about life that she was capable of learning. She knew everything—and was probably the only creature in the room who did. She had succeeded. She was adored—strangely enough. And she did not put on airs. Her original coarseness was apparently quite unobscured, whereas that of Miss Fancy had been not very skilfully painted over. Miss Fancy was a blonde, much younger than Eliza; also slimmer and more finickingly and luxuriously dressed and jewelled. But Mr. Prohack cared not for her. She was always keeping her restless inarticulate lips in order, buttoning them or sewing them up or caressing one with the other. Further, she looked down her nose; probably this trait was the secret lien between her and Mr. Softly Bishop. Mr. Prohack, despite a cloistral lifetime at the Treasury, recognised her type immediately. She was of the type that wheedles, but never permits itself to be wheedled. And she was so pretty, and so simpering, and her blue eyes were so steely. And Mr. Prohack, in his original sinfulness, was pleased that she was thus. He felt that "it would serve Softly Bishop out." Not that Mr. Softly Bishop had done him any harm! Indeed the contrary. But he had an antipathy to Mr. Softly Bishop, and the spectacle of Mr. Softly Bishop biting off more than he could chew, of Mr. Softly Bishop being drawn to his doom, afforded Mr. Prohack the most genuine pleasure. Unfortunately Mr. Prohack was one of the rare monsters who can contemplate with satisfaction the misfortunes of a fellow being.

Mr. Softly Bishop unostentatiously joined the sisters and Mr. Prohack.

"Better have just a sip," he said to Miss Fancy, when told by Eliza that the girl would not be sociable. His eyes glimmered at her through his artful spectacles. She listened obediently to his low-voiced wisdom and sipped. She was shooting a million fascinations at him. Mr. Prohack decided that the ultimate duel between the two might be a pretty even thing after all; but he would put his money on the lady. And he had thought Mr. Softly Bishop so wily!

A fearful thought suddenly entered his mind: supposing the failure of the church-clock's striking powers should be only temporary; supposing it should recover under some verger's treatment, and strike twelve!

"Let's go into the conservatory and look at the Square," said he. "I always look at the Square at midnight, and it's nearly twelve now."

"You're the most peculiar man I ever met," said Eliza Fiddle, eyeing him uneasily.

"Very true," Mr. Prohack agreed.

"I'm half afraid of you."

"Very wise," said Mr. Prohack absently.

They crossed the rooms together, arousing keen interest in all beholders. And as they crossed Charlie entered the assemblage. He certainly had an extremely perturbed—or was it merely self-conscious—face. And just in front of him was Mimi Winstock, who looked as if she was escaping from the scene of a crime. Was Lady Massulam's warning about Charlie about to be justified? Mr. Prohack's qualm was renewed. The very ground trembled for a second under his feet and then was solid and moveless again. No sooner had the quartette reached the conservatory than Eliza left it to go and discuss important affairs with Mr. Asprey Chown, who had summoned Ozzie to his elbow. They might not have seen one another for many years, and they might have been settling the fate of continents.

Mr. Prohack took out his watch, which showed a minute to twelve. He experienced a minute's agony. The clock did not strike.

"Well," said Mr. Softly Bishop, who during the minute had been whispering information about the historic Square to Miss Fancy, who hung with all her weight on his words, "Well, it's very interesting and even amusing, we three being alone here together isn't it? . . . The three heirs of the late Silas Angmering! How funny life is!" And he examined his nose with new curiosity.

All Mr. Prohack's skin tingled, and his face flushed, as he realised that Miss Fancy was the mysterious third beneficiary under Angmering's will. Yes, she was in fact jewelled like a woman who had recently been handling a hundred thousand pounds or so. And Mr. Softly Bishop might be less fascinated by the steely blue eyes than Mr. Prohack had imagined. Mr. Softly Bishop might in fact win the duel. The question, however, had no interest for Mr. Prohack, who was absorbed in a sense of gloomy humiliation. He rushed away from his co-heirs. He simply had to rush away right to bed.

CHAPTER XX

THE SILENT TOWER

I

THE fount of riches and the Terror of the departments, clothed in the latest pattern of sumptuous pyjamas, lay in the midst of his magnificent and spacious bed, and, with the shaded electric globe over his brow, gazed at the splendours of the vast bedroom which Eve had allotted to him. It was full, but not too full, of the finest Directoire furniture, and the walls were covered with all manner of engravings and watercolours. Evidently this apartment had been the lair of the real owner and creator of the great home. Mr. Prohack could appreciate the catholicity and sureness of taste which it displayed. He liked the cornice as well as the form of the dressing-table, and the Cumberland landscape by C. J. Holmes as well as the large Piranesi etching of an imaginary prison, which latter particularly interested him because it happened to be an impression between two "states"—a detail which none but a true amateur could savour. The prison depicted was a terrible place of torment, but it was beautiful, and the view of it made Mr. Prohack fancy, very absurdly, that he too was in prison, just as securely as if he had been bolted and locked therein. His eye ranged about the room and saw nothing that was not lovely and that he did not admire. Yet he derived little or no authentic pleasure from what he beheld, partly because it was the furnishing of a prison and partly because he did not own it. He had often preached against the mania for owning things, but now—and even more clearly than when he had sermonised Paul Spinner—he perceived, and hated to perceive, that ownership was probably an essential ingredient of most enjoyments. The man, foolishly priding himself on being a philosopher, was indeed a fleshly mass of strange inconsistencies.

More important, he was losing the assurance that he would sleep soundly that night. He could not drag his mind off his co-heiress and his co-heir. The sense of humiliation at being intimately connected and classed with them would not leave him. He felt himself—absurdly once again—to be mysteriously associated with them in a piece of sharp practice or even of knavery. They constituted another complication of his existence. He wanted to disown them and never to speak to them again, but he knew that he could not disown them. He was living in gorgeousness for the sole reason that he and they were in the same boat.

Eve came in, opening the door cautiously at first and then rushing forward as soon as she saw that the room was not in darkness. He feared for an instant that she might upbraid him for deserting her. But no! Triumphant happiness sat on her forehead, and affectionate concern for him was in her eyes. She plumped down, in her expensive radiance, on the bed by his side.

"Well?" said he.

"I'm so glad you decided to go to bed," said she. "You must be tired, and late nights don't suit you. I just slipped away for a minute to see if you were all right. Are you?" She puckered her shining brow exactly as of old, and bent and kissed him as of old. One of her best kisses.

But the queer fellow, though touched by her attention, did not like her being so glad that he had gone to bed. The alleged philosopher would have preferred her to express some dependence upon his manly support in what was for her a tremendous event.

"I feel I shall sleep," he lied.

"I'm sure you will, darling," she agreed. "Don't you think it's all been a terrific success?" she asked naïvely.

He answered, smiling:

"I'm dying to see *The Daily Picture* to-morrow. I think I shall tell the newsagent in future only to deliver it on the days when you're in it."

"Don't be silly," she said, too pleased with herself, however, to resent his irony. She was clothed in mail that night against all his shafts.

He admitted, what he had always secretly known, that she was an elementary creature; she would have been just as at home in the Stone Age as in the twentieth century—and perhaps more at home. (Was Lady Massulam equally elementary? No? Yes?) Still, Eve was necessary to him.

Only, up to a short while ago, she had been his complement; whereas now he appeared to be her complement. He, the philosopher and the source of domestic wisdom, was fully aware, in a superior and lofty manner, that she was the eternal child deceived by toys, gewgaws, and illusions; nevertheless he was only her complement,—the indispensable husband and payer-out. She was succeeding without any brain-work from him. He noticed that she was not wearing the pearls he had given her. No doubt she had merely forgotten at the last moment to put them on. She was continually forgetting them and leaving them about. But this negligent woman was the organiser in chief of the great soirée! Well, if it had succeeded, she was lucky.

"I must run off," said she, starting up, busy, proud, falsely calm, the general of a victorious army as the battle draws to a close. She embraced him again, and he actually felt comforted. . . . She was gone.

"As I grow older," he reflected, "I'm hanged if I don't understand life less and less."

II

He was listening to the distant rhythm of the music when he mistily comprehended that there was no music and that the sounds in his ear were not musical. He could not believe that he had been asleep and had awakened, but the facts were soon too much for his delusion and he said with the air of a discoverer: "I've been asleep," and turned on the light.

There were voices and footsteps in the corridors or on the landing,—whispers, loud and yet indistinct talking, tones indicating that the speakers were excited, if not frightened, and that their thoughts had been violently wrenched away from the pursuit of pleasure. His watch showed two o'clock. The party was over, the last automobile had departed, and probably even the tireless Eliza Fiddle was asleep in her new home. Next Mr. Prohack noticed that the door of his room was ajar.

He had no anxiety. Rather he felt quite gay and careless,—the more so as he had wakened up with the false sensation of complete refreshment produced by short, heavy slumber. He thought:

"Whatever has happened, I have had and shall have nothing to do with it, and they must deal with the consequences themselves as best they can." And as a measure of precaution against being compromised, he switched off the light. He heard Eve's voice, surprisingly near his door:

"I simply daren't tell him! No, I daren't!"

The voice was considerably agitated, but he smiled maliciously to himself, thinking:

"It can't be anything very awful, because she only talks in that strain when it's nothing at all. She loves to pretend she's afraid of me. And moreover I don't believe there's anything on earth she daren't tell me."

He heard another voice, reasoning in reply, that resembled Mimi's. Hadn't that girl gone home yet? And he heard Sissie's voice and Charlie's. But for him all these were inarticulate.

Then his room was filled with swift blinding light. Somebody had put a hand through the doorway and turned the light on. It must be Eve. . . . It was Eve, scared and distressed, but still in complete war-paint.

"I'm so relieved you're awake, Arthur," she said, approaching the bed as though she anticipated the bed would bite her.

"I'm not awake. I'm asleep, officially. My poor girl, you've ruined the finest night I was ever going to have in all my life."

She ignored his complaint, absolutely.

"Arthur," she said, her face twitching in every direction, and all her triumph fallen from her, "Arthur, I've lost my pearls. They're gone! Some one must have taken them!"

Mr. Prohack's reaction to this piece of more-than-midnight news was to break into hearty and healthy laughter; he appeared to be genuinely diverted; and when Eve protested against such an attitude he said:

"My child, anything that strikes you as funny after being wakened up at two o'clock in the morning *is* very funny, very funny indeed. How can I help laughing?" Eve thereupon began to cry, weakly.

"Come here, please," said he.

And she came and sat on the bed, but how differently from the previous visit! She was now beaten by circumstances, and she turned for aid to his alleged more powerful mind and deeper wisdom. In addition to being amused, the man was positively happy, because he was no longer a mere complement! So he comforted her, and put his hands on her shoulders.

"Don't worry," said he, gently. "And after all I'm not surprised the necklace has been pinched."

"Not surprised? Arthur!"

"No. You collect here half the notorious smart people in London. Fifty per cent of them go through one or other of the Courts; five per cent end by being detected criminals, and goodness knows what per cent end by being undetected criminals. Possibly two per cent treat marriage seriously, and possibly one per cent is not in debt. That's the atmosphere you created, and it's an atmosphere in which pearls are apt to melt away. Hence I am not surprised, and you mustn't be. Still, it would be interesting to know *how* the things melted away. Were you wearing them?"

"Of course I was wearing them. There was nothing finer here to-night—that *I* saw."

"You hadn't got them on when you came in here before."

"Hadn't I?" said Eve, thoughtful.

"No, you hadn't."

"Then why didn't you tell me?" Eve demanded suddenly, almost fiercely, through her tears, withdrawing her shoulders from his hands.

"Well," said Mr. Prohack. "I thought you'd know what you'd got on, or what you hadn't got on."

"I think you might have told me. If you had perhaps the—"

Mr. Prohack put his hand over her mouth.

"Stop," said he. "My sweet child, I can save you a lot of trouble. It's all my fault. If I hadn't been a miracle of stupidity the necklace would never have disappeared. This point being agreed to, let us go on to the next. When did you find out your sad loss?"

"It was Miss Winstock who asked me what I'd done with my necklace. I put my hand to my throat, and it was gone. It must have come undone."

"Didn't you say to me a fortnight or so ago that the little safety-chain had gone wrong?"

"Did I?" said Eve, innocently.

"Did you have the safety-chain repaired?"

"I was going to have it done to-morrow. You see, if I'd sent it to be done to-day, then I couldn't have worn the necklace to-night, could I?"

"Very true," Mr. Prohack concurred.

"But who could have taken it?"

"Ah! Are you sure that it isn't lying on the floor somewhere?"

"Every place where I've been has been searched—thoroughly. It's quite certain that it must have been picked up and pocketed."

"Then by a man, seeing that women have no pockets—except their husbands'. I'm beginning to feel quite like a detective already. By the way, lady, the notion of giving a reception in a house like this without a detective disguised as a guest was rather grotesque."

"But of course I had detectives!" Eve burst out. "I had two private ones. I thought one ought to be enough, but as soon as the agents saw the inventory of knicknacks and things, they advised me to have two men. One of them's here still. In fact he's waiting to see you. The Scotland Yard people are very annoying. They've refused to do anything until morning."

That Eve should have engaged detectives was something of a

blow to the masculine superiority of Mr. Prohack. However, he kept himself in countenance by convincing himself in secret that she had not thought of the idea; the idea must have been given to her by another person—probably Mimi, who nevertheless was also a woman.

"And do you seriously expect me to interview a detective in the middle of the night?" demanded Mr. Prohack.

"He said he should like to see you. But of course if you don't feel equal to it, my poor boy, I'll tell him so."

"What does he want to see *me* for? I've nothing to do with it, and I know nothing."

"He says that as you bought the necklace he must see you—and the sooner the better."

This new aspect of the matter seemed to make Mr. Prohack rather thoughtful.

III

Eve brought in to her husband, who had improved his moral stamina and his physical charm by means of the finest of his dressing-gowns, a dark, thin young man, clothed to marvellous perfection, with a much-loved moustache, and looking as fresh as if he was just going to a party. Mr. Prohack of course recognised him as one of the guests.

"Good morning," said Mr. Prohack. "So *you* are the detective."

"Yes, sir," answered the detective, formally.

"Do you know, all the evening I was under the impression that you were First Secretary to the Czecho-Slovakian Legation."

"No, sir," answered the detective, formally.

"Well! Well! I think there is a proverb to the effect that appearances are deceptive."

"Is there indeed, sir?" said the detective, with unshaken gravity. "In our business we think that appearances ought to be deceptive."

"Now talking of your business," Mr. Prohack remarked with one of his efforts to be very persuasive. "What about this unfortunate affair?"

"Yes, sir, what about it?" The detective looked askance at Eve.

"I suppose there's no doubt the thing's been stolen— By the way, sit on the end of the bed, will you? Then you'll be near me."

"Yes, sir," said the detective, sitting down. "There is no doubt the necklace has been removed by some one, either for a nefarious purpose or for a joke."

"Ah! A joke?" meditated Mr. Prohack, aloud.

"It certainly hasn't been taken for a joke," said Eve warmly. "Nobody that I know well enough for them to play such a trick would dream of playing it."

"Then," said Mr. Prohack, "we are left all alone with the nefarious purpose. I had a sort of a notion that I should meet the nefarious purpose, and here it is! I suppose there's little hope?"

"Well, sir. You know what happens to a stolen pearl necklace. The pearls are separated. They can be sold at once, one at a time, or they can be kept for years and then sold. Pearls, except the very finest, leave no trace when they get a fair start."

"What I can't understand," Eve exclaimed, "is how it could have dropped off without me noticing it."

"Oh! I can easily understand that," said Mr. Prohack, with a peculiar intonation.

"I've known ladies lose even their hair without noticing anything," said the detective firmly. "Not to mention other items."

"But without anybody else noticing it either?" Eve pursued her own train of thought.

"Somebody did notice it," said the detective, writing on a small piece of paper.

"Who?"

"The person who took the necklace."

"Well, of course I know that," Eve spoke impatiently. "But who can it be? I feel sure it's one of the new servants or one of the hired waiters."

"In our business, madam, we usually suspect servants and waiters last." Then turning round very suddenly he demanded: "Who's that at the door?"

Eve, startled, moved towards the door, and in the same instant the detective put a small piece of paper into Mr. Prohack's lap, and Mr. Prohack read on the paper:

"Should like see you alone." The detective picked up the paper again. Mr. Prohack laughed joyously within himself.

"There's nobody at the door," said Eve. "How you frightened me!"

"Marian," said Mr. Prohack, fully inspired. "Take my keys off there, will you, and go to my study and unlock the top right-hand drawer of the big desk. You'll find a blue paper at the top at the back. Bring it to me. I don't know which is the right key, but you'll soon see."

And when Eve, eager with her important mission, had departed, Mr. Prohack continued to the detective:

"Pretty good that, eh, for an improvisation? The key of that drawer isn't on that ring at all. And even if she does manage to open the drawer there's no blue paper in there at all. She'll be quite some time."

The detective stared at Mr. Prohack in a way to reduce his facile self-satisfaction.

"What I wish to know from you, sir, personally, is whether you want this affair to be hushed up, or not."

"Hushed up?" repeated Mr. Prohack, to whom the singular suggestion opened out new and sinister avenues of speculation. "Why hushed up?"

"Most of the cases we deal with have to be hushed up sooner or later," answered the detective. "I only wanted to know where I was."

"How interesting your work must be," observed Mr. Prohack, with quick sympathetic enthusiasm. "I expect you love it. How did you get into it? Did you serve an apprenticeship? I've often wondered about you private detectives. It's a marvellous life."

"I got into it through meeting a man in the Piccadilly Tube. As for liking it, I shouldn't like any work."

"But some people love their work."

"So I've heard," said the detective sceptically. "Then I take it you do want the matter smothered?"

"But you've telephoned to Scotland Yard about it," said Mr. Prohack. "We can't hush it up after that."

"I told *them,*" replied the detective grimly, indicating with his head the whole world of the house. "I told *them* I was telephoning to Scotland Yard; but I wasn't. I was telephoning to our head-office. Then am I to take it you want to find out all you can, but you want it smothered?"

"Not at all. I have no reason for hushing anything up."

The detective gazed at him in a harsh, lower-middle-class way, and Mr. Prohack quailed a little before that glance.

"Will you please tell me where you bought the necklace?"

"I really forget. Somewhere in Bond Street."

"Oh! I see," said the detective. "A necklace of forty-nine pearls, over half of them stated to be as big as peas, and it's slipped your memory where you bought it." The detective yawned.

"And I'm afraid I haven't kept the receipt either," said Mr. Prohack. "I have an idea the firm went out of business soon after I bought the necklace. At least I seem to remember noticing the shop shut up and then opening again as something else."

"No jeweller ever goes out of business in Bond Street," said the detective, and yawned once more. "Well, Mr. Prohack, I don't think I need trouble you any more to-night. If you or Mrs. Prohack will call at our head-office during the course of to-morrow you shall have our official report, and if anything really fresh should turn up I'll telephone you immediately. Good night, Mr. Prohack" The man bowed rather awkwardly as he rose from the bed, and departed.

"That chap thinks there's something fishy between Eve and me," reflected Mr. Prohack. "I wonder whether there is!" But he was still in high spirits when Eve came back into the room.

"The sleuth-hound has fled," said he. "I must have given him something to think about."

"I've tried all the keys and none of them will fit," Eve complained. "And yet you're always grumbling at me for not keeping my keys in order. If you wanted to show him the blue paper why have you let him go?"

"My dear," said Mr. Prohack, "I didn't let him go. He did not consult me, but merely and totally went."

"And what is the blue paper?" Eve demanded.

"Well, supposing it was the receipt for what I paid for the pearls?"

"Oh! I see. But how would that help?"

"It wouldn't help," Mr. Prohack replied. "My broken butterfly, you may as well know the worst. The sleuth-hound doesn't hold out much hope."

"Yes," said Eve. "And you seem delighted that I've lost my pearls! I know what it is. You think it will be a lesson for me, and you love people to have lessons. Why! Anybody might lose a necklace."

"True. Ships are wrecked, and necklaces are lost, and Nelson even lost his eye."

"And I'm sure it *was* one of the servants."

"My child, you can be just as happy without a pearl necklace as with one. You really aren't a woman who cares for vulgar display. Moreover, in times like these, when society seems to be toppling over, what is a valuable necklace, except a source of worry? Felicity is not to be attained by the—"

Eve screamed.

"Arthur! If you go on like that I shall run straight out of the house and take cold in the Square."

"I will give you another necklace," Mr. Prohack answered this threat, and as her face did not immediately clear, he added: "And a better one."

"I don't want another one," said Eve. "I'd sooner be without one. I know it was all my own fault. But you're horrid, and I can't make you out, and I never could make you out. I never did know where I am with you. And I believe you're hiding something from me. I believe you picked up the necklace, and that's why you sent the detective away."

Mr. Prohack had to assume his serious voice which always carried conviction to Eve, and which he had never misused. "I haven't picked your necklace up. I haven't seen it. And I know nothing about it." Then he changed again. "And if you'll kindly step forward and kiss me good morning I'll try to snatch a few moments' unconsciousness."

IV

Mr. Prohack's life at this wonderful period of his career as a practising philosopher at grips with the great world seemed to be a series of violent awakenings. He was awakened, with even increased violence, at about eight o'clock the next—or rather the same—morning, and he would have been awakened earlier if the servants had got up earlier. The characteristic desire of the servants to rise early had, however, been enfeebled by the jolly vigils of the previous night. It was, of course, Eve who rushed in to him—nobody else would have dared. She had hastily cast about her plumpness the transformed Chinese gown, which had the curious appearance of a survival from some former incarnation.

"Arthur!" she called, and positively shook the victim. "Arthur!"

Mr. Prohack looked at her, dazed by the electric light which she had ruthlessly turned on over his head.

"There's a woman been caught in the area. She's a fat woman, and she must have been there all night. The cook locked the area gate and the woman was too fat to climb over. Brool's put her in the servants' hall and fastened the door, and what do you think we ought to do first? Send for the police or telephone to Mr. Crewd—he's the detective you saw last night?"

"If she's been in the area all night you'd better put her to bed, and give her some hot brandy and water," said Mr. Prohack.

"Arthur, please, please, be serious!" Eve supplicated.

"I'm being as serious as a man can who has been disturbed in this pleasant fashion by a pretty woman," said Mr. Prohack attentively examining the ceiling. "You go and look after the fat lady. Supposing she died from exposure. There'd have to be an inquest.

Do you wish to be mixed up in an inquest? What does she want? Whatever it is, give it her, and let her go, and wake me up next week. I feel I can sleep a bit."

"Arthur! You'll drive me mad. Can't you see that she must be connected with the necklace business. She *must* be. It's as clear as day-light!"

"Ah!" breathed Mr. Prohack, thoughtfully interested. "I'd forgotten the necklace business."

"Yes, well, I hadn't!" said Eve, rather shrewishly. "I had not."

"Quite possibly she may be mixed up in the necklace business," Mr. Prohack admitted. "She may be a clue. Look here, don't let's tell anybody outside—not even Mr. Crewd. Let's detect for ourselves. It will be the greatest fun. What does she say for herself?"

"She said she was waiting outside the house to catch a young lady with a snub-nose going away from my reception—Mimi Winstock, of course."

"Why Mimi Winstock?"

"Well, hasn't she got a turned-up nose? And she didn't go away from my reception. She's sleeping here," Eve rejoined triumphantly.

"And what else does the fat woman say?"

"She says she won't say anything else—except to Mimi Winstock."

"Well, then, wake up Mimi as you wakened me, and send her to the servants' hall—wherever that is—I've never seen it myself!"

Eve shook her somewhat tousled head vigorously.

"Certainly not. I don't trust Miss Mimi Winstock—not one bit—and I'm not going to let those two meet until you've had a talk with the burglar."

"Me!" Mr. Prohack protested.

"Yes, you. Seeing that you don't want me to send for the police. Something has to be done, and somebody has to do it. And I never did trust that Mimi Winstock, and I'm very sorry she's gone to Charlie. That was a great mistake. However, it's got nothing to do with me." She shrugged her agreeable shoulders. "But my necklace has got something to do with me."

Mr. Prohack thought "What would Lady Massulam do in such a crisis? And how would Lady Massulam look in a dressing-gown and her hair down? I shall never know." Meanwhile he liked Eve's demeanour—its vivacity and simplicity. "I'm afraid I'm still in love with her," the strange fellow reflected, and said aloud: "You'd better kiss me. I shall have an awful headache if you don't." And Eve reluctantly kissed him, with the look of a martyr on her face.

Within a few minutes Mr. Prohack had dismissed his wife, and was descending the stairs in a dressing-gown which rivalled hers. The sight of him in the unknown world of the basement floor, as he searched unaided for the servants' hall, created an immense sensation,—far greater than he had anticipated. A nice young girl, whom he had never seen before and as to whom he knew nothing except that she was probably one of his menials, was so moved that she nearly had an accident with a tea-tray which she was carrying.

"What is your name?" Mr. Prohack benignly asked.

"Selina, sir."

"Where are you going with that tea-tray and newspaper?"

"I was just taking it upstairs to Machin, sir. She's not feeling well enough to get up yet, sir."

Mr. Prohack comprehended the greatness of the height to which Machin had ascended. Machin, a parlourmaid, drinking tea in bed, and being served by a lesser creature, who evidently regarded Machin as a person of high power and importance on earth! Mr. Prohack saw that he was unacquainted with the fundamental realities of life in Manchester Square.

"Well," said he. "You can get some more tea for Machin. Give me that." And he took the tray. "No, you can keep the newspaper."

The paper was *The Daily Picture.* As he held the tray with one hand and gave the paper back to Selina with the other, his eye caught the headlines: "West End Sensation. Mrs. Prohack's Pearls Pinched." He paled; but he was too proud a man to withdraw the paper again. No doubt *The Daily Picture* would reach him through the customary channels after Machin had done with it, accompanied by the usual justifications about the newsboy being late; he could wait.

"Which is the servants' hall," said he. Selina's manner changed to positive alarm as she indicated, in the dark subterranean corridor, the door that was locked on the prisoner. Not merely the presence of Mr. Prohack had thrilled the basement floor; there was a thrill greater even than that, and Mr. Prohack, by demanding the door of the servants' hall was intensifying the thrill to the last degree. The key was on the outside of the door, which he unlocked. Within the electric light was still burning in the obscure dawn.

The prisoner, who sprang up from a chair and curtsied fearsomely at the astonishing spectacle of Mr. Prohack, was fat in a superlative degree, and her obesity gave her a middle-aged air to which she probably had no right by the almanac. She looked quite forty, and might well have been not more than thirty. She made a typical London figure of the nondescript industrial class. It is inadequate to say that her shabby black-trimmed bonnet, her shabby sham-fur coat half hiding a large dubious apron, her shabby frayed black skirt, and her shabby, immense, amorphous boots,—it is inadequate to say that these things seemed to have come immediately out of a tenth-rate pawnshop; the woman herself seemed to have come, all of a piece with her garments, out of a tenth-rate pawnshop; the entity of her was at any rate homogeneous; it sounded no discord.

She did nothing so active as to weep, but tears, obeying the law of gravity, oozed out of her small eyes, and ran in zigzags, unsummoned and unchecked, down her dark-red cheeks.

"Oh, sir!" she mumbled in a wee, scarcely articulate voice. "I'm a respectable woman, so help me God!"

"You shall be respected," said Mr. Prohack. "Sit down and drink some of this tea and eat the bread-and-butter. . . . No! I don't want you to say anything just yet. No, nothing at all."

When she had got the tea into the cup, she poured it into the saucer and blew on it and began to drink loudly. After two sips she plucked at a piece of bread-and-butter, conveyed it into her mouth, and before doing anything further to it, sirruped up some more tea. And in this way she went on. Her table manners convinced Mr. Prohack that her claim to respectability was authentic.

"And now," said Mr. Prohack, gazing through the curtained window at the blank wall that ended above him at the edge of the pavement, so as not to embarrass her, "will you tell me why you spent the night in my area?"

"Because some one locked the gate on me, sir, while I was hiding under the shed where the dustbins are."

"I quite see," said Mr. Prohack, "I quite see. But why did you go down into the area? Were you begging, or what?"

"Me begging, sir!" she exclaimed, and ceased to cry, fortified by the tonic of aroused pride.

"No, of course you weren't begging," said Mr. Prohack. "You may have given to beggars—"

"That I have, sir." She cried again.

"But you don't beg. I quite see. Then what?"

"It's no use me a-trying to tell you, sir. You won't believe me."

Her voice was extraordinarily thin and weak, and seldom achieved anything that could fairly be called pronunciation.

"I shall," said Mr. Prohack. "I'm a great believer. You try me. You'll see."

"It's like this. I was converted last night, and that's where the trouble began, if it's the last word I ever speak."

"Theology?" murmured Mr. Prohack, turning to look at her and marvelling at the romantic quality of basements.

"There was a mission on at the Methodists' in Paddington Street, and in I went. Seems strange to me to be going into a Methodists', seeing as I'm so friendly with Mr. Milcher."

"Who is Mr. Milcher?"

"Milcher's the sexton at St. Nicodemus, sir. Or I should say sacristan. They call him sacristan instead of sexton because St. Nicodemus is High, as I daresay *you* know, sir, living so close."

Mr. Prohack was conscious of a slight internal shiver, which he could not explain, unless it might be due to a subconscious premonition of unpleasantness to come.

"I know that I live close to St. Nicodemus," he replied. "Very close. Too close. But I did not know how High St. Nicodemus was. However, I'm interrupting you." He perceived with satisfaction that his gift of inspiring people with confidence was not failing him on this occasion.

"Well, sir, as I was saying, it might, as you might say, seem strange me popping like that into the Methodists', seeing what Milcher's views are; but my mother was a Methodist in Canonbury,—a great place for dissenters, sir, North London, you know, sir, and they do say blood's thicker than water. So there I was, and the Mission a-going on, and as soon as ever I got inside that chapel I knew I was done in. I never felt so all-overish in all my days, and before I knew where I was I had found salvation. And I was so happy, you wouldn't believe. I come out of that Methodists' as free like as if I was coming out of a hospital, and God knows I've been in a hospital often enough for my varicose veins, in the legs, sir. You might almost have guessed I had 'em, sir, from the kind way you told me to sit down, sir. And I was just wondering how I should break it to Milcher, sir, because me passing St. Nicodemus made me think of him—not as I'm not always thinking of him—and I looked up at the clock—you know it's the only 'luminated church clock in the district, sir, and the clock was just on eleven, sir, and I waited for it to strike, sir, and it didn't strike. My feet was rooted to the spot, sir, but no, that clock didn't strike, and then all of a sudden it rushed over me

about that young woman asking me all about the to
clock and telling me as her young man was so intereste
towers and he wanted to go up, and would I lend her
the tower-door because Milcher always gives me th
church-keys to keep for him while he goes into the
Groom public-house, sir, him not caring to take church keys into a public-house. He's rather particular, sir. They are, especially when they're sacristans. It rushed over me, and I says to myself, 'Bolsheviks,' and I thought I should have swounded, but I didn't."

Mr. Prohack had to make an effort in order to maintain his self-control, for the mumblings of the fat lady were producing in him the most singular and the most disturbing sensations.

"If there's any tea left in the pot," said he, "I think I'll have it."

"*And* welcome, sir," replied the fat lady. "But there's only one cup. But I have but hardly drunk out of it, sir."

Mr. Prohack first of all went to the door, transferred the key from the outside to the inside, and locked the door. Then he drank the dregs of the tea out of the sole cup; and seeing a packet of Mr. Brool's Gold Flake cigarettes on the mahogany sideboard, he ventured to help himself to one.

"Yes, sir," resumed the fat lady. "I nearly swounded, and I couldn't feel happy no more until I'd made a clean breast of it all to Milcher. And I was setting off for Milcher when it struck me all of a heap as I'd promised the young lady with the turned-up nose as I wouldn't say nothing about the keys to nobody. It was very awkward for me, sir, me being converted and anxious to do right, and not knowing which was right and which was wrong. But a promise is a promise whether you're converted or not—that I do hold. Anyhow I says to myself I must see Milcher and tell him the clock hadn't struck eleven, and I prayed as hard as I could for heavenly guidance, and I was just coming down the Square on my way to Milcher's when who should I see get out of a taxi and run into this house but that young lady and her young man. I said in my haste that was an answer to prayer, sir, but I'm not so sure now as I wasn't presuming too much. I could see there was something swanky a-going on here and I said to myself, 'That young lady's gone in. She'll come out again; she's one of the gues's, she is,' I said, 'and him too, and I'll wait till she does come out and then I'll catch her and have it out with her even if it means policemen.' And the area-gate being unfastened, I slipped down the area-steps, sir, with my eye on the front-door. And that was what did me. I had to sit down on the stone steps, sir, because of my varicose veins and then one of the servants comes in *from* the street, sir, and I more like dropped down the area-steps, sir, than walked, sir, and hid between two dustbins, and when the coast was clear I went up again and found gate locked and nothing doing. And it's as true as I'm standing here—sitting, I should say."

Mr. Prohack paused, collecting himself, determined to keep his nerve through everything. Then he said:

"When did the mysterious young lady borrow the keys from you?"

"Last night, sir, I mean the night before last."

"And where are the keys now?"

"Milcher's got 'em, sir. I lay he's up in the tower by this time, a-worrying over that clock. It'll be in the papers—you see if it isn't, sir."

"And he's got no idea that you ever lent the keys?"

"That he has not, sir. And the question is: must I tell him?"

"What exactly are the relations between you and Mr. Milcher?"

"Well, sir, he's a bit dotty about me, as you might say. And he's going to marry me. So he says, and I believe him."

And Mr. Prohack reflected, impressed by the wonder of existence:

"This woman too has charm for somebody, who looks on her as the most appetising morsel on earth."

"Now," he said aloud, "you are good enough to ask my opinion whether you ought to tell Mr. Milcher. My advice to you is: Don't. I applaud your conversion. But as you say, a promise is a promise—even if it's a naughty promise. You did wrong to promise. You will suffer for that, and don't think your conversion will save you from suffering, because it won't. Don't run away with the idea that conversion is a patent-medicine. It isn't. It's rather a queer thing, very handy in some ways and very awkward in others, and you must use it with commonsense or you'll get both yourself and other people into trouble. As for the clock, it's stopping striking is only a coincidence, obviously. Abandon the word 'Bolshevik.' It's a very overworked word, and wants a long repose. If the clock had been stopped from striking by your young friends it would have stopped the evening before last, when they went up the tower. And don't imagine there's any snub-nosed young lady living here. There isn't. She must have left while you were down among the dustbins, Mrs. Milcher—that is to be. She paid you something for your trouble, quite possibly. If so, give the money to the poor. That will be the best way to be converted."

"So I will, sir."

"Yes. And now you must go." He unlocked the door and opened it. "Quick. Quietly. Into the area, and up the area-steps. And stop a moment. Don't you be seen in the Square for at least a year. A big robbery was committed in this very house last night. You'll see it in to-day's papers. My butler connected your presence in the area—and quite justifiably connected it—with the robbery. Without knowing it you've been in the most dreadful danger. I'm saving you. If you don't use your conversion with discretion it may land you in prison. Take my advice, and be silent first and converted afterwards. Good morning. Tut-tut!" He stopped the outflow of her alarmed gratitude. "Didn't I advise you to be silent? Creep, Mrs. Milcher. Creep!"

V

"Well, what have you said to her? What does she say? What have you done with her?" questioned Eve excitedly, who had almost finished dressing when Mr. Prohack, gorgeously, but by no means without misgivings, entered her bedroom.

"I've talked to her very seriously and let her go," answered Mr. Prohack.

Eve sat down as if stabbed on the chair in front of her dressing-table, and stared at Mr. Prohack.

"You've let her go!" cried she, with an outraged gasp, implying that she had always suspected that she was married to a nincompoop, but not to such a nincompoop. "Where's she gone to?"

"I don't know."

"What's her name? Who is she?"

"I don't know that either. I only know that she's engaged to be married, and that a certain sacristan is madly but I hope honourably in love with her, and that she's had nothing whatever to do with the disappearance of your necklace."

"I suppose she told you so herself!" said Eve, with an irony that might have shrivelled up a husband less philosophic.

"She did not. She didn't say a word about the necklace. But she did make a full confession. She's mixed up in the clock-striking business."

"The what business?"

"The striking of the church-clock. You know it's stopped striking since last night, under the wise dispensation of heaven."

As he made this perfectly simple announcement, Mr. Prohack observed a sudden change in his wife's countenance. Her brow puckered: a sad, protesting, worried look came into her eyes.

"Please don't begin on the clock again, my poor Arthur! You ought to forget it. You know how bad it is for you to dwell on it. It gets on your nerves and you start imagining all sorts of things, until, of course, there's no chance of you sleeping. If you keep on like this you'll make me feel a perfect criminal for taking the house. You don't suspect it, but I've several times wished we never had taken it—I've been so upset about your nervous condition."

"I was merely saying," Mr. Prohack insisted, "that our fat visitor, who apparently has enormous seductive power over sacristans, had noticed about the clock just as I had, and she thought—"

Eve interrupted him by approaching swiftly and putting her hands on his shoulders, as he had put his hands on her shoulders a little while earlier, and gazing with supplication at him.

"Please, please!" she besought him. "To oblige me. Do drop the church-clock. I know what it means for you."

Mr. Prohack turned away, broke into uproarious and somewhat hysterical laughter, and left the bedroom, having perceived to his amazement that she thought the church-clock was undermining his sanity.

Going to his study, he rang the bell there, and Brool, with features pale and drawn, obeyed the summons. The fact that his sanity was suspect, however absurdly, somehow caused Mr. Prohack to assume a pontifical manner of unusual dignity.

"Is Miss Warburton up yet?"

"No, sir. One of the servants knocked at her door some little time ago, but received no answer."

"She must be wakened, and I'll write a note that must be given to her immediately."

Mr. Prohack wrote: "Please dress at once and come to my study. I want to see you about the church-clock. A. P." Then he waited, alternately feeling the radiator and warming his legs at the newly-lit wood fire. He was staggered by the incredible turn of events, and he had a sensation that nothing was or ever would be secure in the structure of his environment.

"Well, I'm hanged! Well, I'm hanged!" he kept saying to himself, and indeed several times asserted that an even more serious fate had befallen him.

"Here I am!" Mimi exclaimed brazenly, entering the room.

The statement was not exaggerated. She emphatically was there, aspiring nose and all—in full evening dress, the costume of the night before.

"Have you slept in your clothes?" Mr. Prohack demanded.

Her manner altered at his formidable tone.

"No, sir," she replied meekly. "But I've nothing else here. I shall put a cloak on and drive off in a taxi to change for the day. May I sit down?"

Mr. Prohack nodded. Indubitably she made a wonderful sight in her daring splendour.

"So you've found out all about it already!" said she, still meekly, while Mr. Prohack was seeking the right gambit. "Please do tell me how," she added, disposing the folds of her short skirt about the chair.

"I'm not here to answer questions," said Mr. Prohack. "I'm here to ask them. How did you do it? And was it you or Charlie or both of you? Whose idea was it?"

"It was my idea," Mimi purred. "But Mr. Charles seemed to like it. It was really very simple. We first of all found out about the sexton."

"And how did you do that?"

"Private enquiry agents, of course. Same people who were in charge here last night. I knew of them when I was with Mr. Carrel Quire, and it was I who introduced them to Mrs. Prohack."

"It would be!" Mr. Prohack commented. "And then?"

"And then when we'd discovered Mrs. Slipstone—or Miss Slipstone—"

"Who's she?"

"She's a rather stout charwoman who has a fascination for the sexton of St. Nicodemus. When I'd got her it was all plain sailing. She lent me the church keys and Mr. Charles and I went up the tower to reconnoitre."

"But that was more than twenty-four hours before the clock ceased to strike, and you returned the keys to her."

"Oh! So you know that too, do you?" said Mimi blandly. "Mr. Prohack, I hope you'll forgive me for saying that you're most frightfully clever. I *did* give the keys back to Mrs. Slipstone a long time before the clock stopped striking, but you see, Mr. Charles had taken an impression of the tower key in clay, so that last night we were able to go up with an electric torch and our own key. The clock is a very old one, and Mr. Charles removed a swivel or something—I forget what he called it, but he seems to understand everything about every kind of machinery. He says it would take a tremendous long time to get another swivel, or whatever it is, cast, even if it ever could be cast without a pattern, and that you'll be safe for at least six months, even if we don't rely on the natural slowness of the Established Church to do anything really active. You see it isn't as if the clock wasn't going. It's showing the time all right, and that will be sufficient to keep the rector and the church-wardens quiet. It keeps up appearances. Of course if the clock had stopped entirely they would have had to do something. . . . You don't seem very pleased, dear Mr. Prohack. We thought you'd be delighted. We did it all for you."

"Did you indeed!" said Mr. Prohack ruthlessly. "And did you think of the riskiness of what you were doing? There'll be a most appalling scandal, certainly police-court proceedings. and I shall be involved, if it comes to light."

"But it can't come to light!" Mimi exploded.

"And yet it came to my light."

"Yes, I expect Mr. Charles was so proud that he couldn't help telling you some bits about it. But nobody else can know. Even if Mrs. Slipstone lets on to the sexton, the sexton will never let on because if he did he'd lose his place. The sexton will always have to deny that he parted with the keys even for a moment. It will be the loveliest mystery that ever was, and all the police in the world won't solve it. Of course, if you aren't pleased, I'm very sorry."

"It isn't a question of not being pleased. The breath is simply knocked out of me—that's what it is! Whatever possessed you to do it?"

"But something had to be done, Mr. Prohack. Everybody in the house was terribly upset about you. You couldn't sleep because of the clock, and you said you never would sleep. Mrs. Prohack was at her wit's end."

"Everybody in the house was terribly upset about me! This is the first I've heard of anybody being terribly upset about me. I thought that everybody except me had forgotten all about the infernal clock."

"Naturally!" said Mimi, with soothing calmness. "Mrs. Prohack quite rightly forbade any mention of the clock in your presence. She said the best thing to do was to help you to forget it by never referring to it, and we all agreed with her. But it weighed on us dreadfully. And something really had to be done."

Mr. Prohack was not unimpressed by this revelation of the

existence of a social atmosphere which he had never suspected. But he was in no mood for compromise.

"Now just listen to me," said he. "You are without exception the most dangerous woman that I have ever met. All women are dangerous, but you are an acute peril."

"Yes," Mimi admitted, "Mr. Carrel Quire used to talk like that. I got quite used to it."

"Did he really? Well, I think all the better of him, then. The mischief with you is that your motives are good. But a good motive is no excuse for a criminal act, and still less excuse for an idiotic act. I don't suppose I shall do any good by warning you, yet I do hereby most solemnly warn you to mend your ways. And I wish you to understand clearly that I am not a bit grateful to you. In fact the reverse."

Mimi stiffened herself.

"Perhaps you would prefer us to restore the missing part and start the clock striking again. It would be perfectly easy. We still have our own key to the tower and we could do it to-night. I am sure it will be at least a week before the church-wardens send an expert clock-maker up the tower."

In that moment Mr. Prohack had a distressing glimpse into the illogical peculiarities of the human conscience, especially his own. He knew that he ought to accept Mimi's offer, since it would definitely obviate the possible consequences of a criminal act and close a discreditable incident. But he thought of his bad nights instead of thinking of Mimi's morals and the higher welfare of society.

"No," he said. "Let sleeping clocks lie." And he saw that Mimi read the meanness of his soul and was silently greeting him as a fellow-sinner.

She surprised him by saying:

"I assure you, Mr. Prohack, tha my sole idea—that our sole idea—was to make the house more possible for you." And as she uttered these words she gazed at him with a sort of delicious pouting, challenging reproach.

What a singular remark, he thought! It implied a comprehension of the fact, which he had considerately never disclosed, that he objected to the house *in toto* and would have been happier in his former abode. And, curiously, it implied further that she comprehended and sympathised with his objections. She knew she had not done everything necessary to reconcile him to the noble mansion, but she had done what she could—and it was not negligible.

"Nothing of the kind," said he. "You simply had no 'sole idea.' When I admitted just now that your motives were good I was exaggerating. Your motives were only half good, and if you think otherwise you are deceiving yourself; you are not being realistic. In that respect you are no better than anybody else."

"What was my other motive, then?" she enquired submissively, as if appealing for information to the greatest living authority on the enigmas of her own heart.

"Your other motive was to satisfy your damnable instinct for dubious and picturesque adventure," said Mr. Prohack. "You were pandering to the evil in you. If you could have stopped the clock from striking by walking down Bond Street in Mrs. Slipstone's clothes and especially her boots, would you have done it? Certainly not. Of course you wouldn't. Don't try to come the self-sacrificing saint over me, because you can't do it."

These words, even if amounting to a just estimate of the situation, were ruthless and terrible. They might have accomplished some genuine and lasting good if Mr. Prohack had spoken them in a tone corresponding to their import. But he did not. His damnable instinct for pleasing people once more got the better of him, and he spoke them in a benevolent and paternal tone, his voice vibrating with compassion and with appreciation of her damnable instinct for dubious and picturesque adventure. The tone destroyed the significance of the words.

Moreover, not content with the falsifying tone, he rose up from his chair as he spoke, approached the charming and naughty girl, and patted her on the shoulder. The rebuke, indeed, ended by being more agreeable to the sinner than praise might have been from a man less corroded with duplicity than Mr. Prohack.

Mimi surprised him a second time.

"You're perfectly right," she said. "You always are." And she seized his limp hand in hers and kissed it,—and ran away, leaving him looking at the kissed hand.

Well, he was flattered, and he was pleased; or at any rate something in him, some fragmentary part of him, was flattered and pleased. Mimi's gesture was a triumph for a man nearing fifty; but it was an alarming triumph. . . . Odd that in that moment he should think of Lady Massulam! His fatal charm was as a razor. Had he been playing with it as a baby might play with a razor? . . . Popinjay? Coxcomb? Perhaps. Nevertheless, the wench had artistically kissed his hand, and his hand felt self-complacent, even if he didn't.

Brool, towards whom Mr. Prohack felt no impulse of good-will, came largely in with a salver on which were the morning letters and the morning papers, including the paper perused by Machin with her early bedside tea and doubtless carefully folded again in its original creases to look virginal.

The reappearance of that sheet had somewhat the quality of a sinister miracle to Mr. Prohack. He asked no questions about it so that he might be told no lies, but he searched it in vain for a trace of the suffering Machin. It was, however, full of typographical traces of himself and his family. The description of the reception was disturbingly journalistic, which adjective, for Mr. Prohack, unfortunately connoted the adjective vulgar. All the wrong people were in the list of guests, and all the decent quiet people were omitted, A value of twenty thousand pounds was put upon the necklace, contradicting another part of the report which stated the pearls to be "priceless." Mr. Prohack's fortune was referred to; also his Treasury past; the implication being that the fortune had caused him to leave the Treasury. His daughter's engagement to Mr. Morfey was glanced at; and it was remarked that Mr. Morfey—"known to all his friends and half London as 'Ozzie' Morfey"—was intimately connected with the greatest stage Napoleon in history, Mr. Asprey Chown. Finally a few words were given to Charlie; who was dubbed "a budding financier already responsible for one highly successful *coup* and likely to be responsible for several others before much more water has run under the bridges of the Thames."

Mr. Prohack knew, then, in his limbs the meaning of the word "writhe," and he was glad that he had not had his bath, because even if he had had his bath he would have needed another one. His attitude towards his fellow men had a touch of embittered and cynical scorn unworthy of a philosopher. He turned, in another paper, to the financial column, for, though all his money was safe in fixed-interest-bearing securities, the fluctuations of whose capital value could not affect his safety, yet he somehow could not remain quite indifferent to the fluctuations of their capital value; and in the financial column he saw a reference to a "young operator," who, he was convinced, could be no other than Charlie; in the reference there was a note of sarcasm which hurt Mr. Prohack and aroused anew his apprehensions.

And among his correspondence was a letter which had been delivered by hand. He thought he knew the handwriting on the envelope, and he did: it was from Mr. Softly Bishop. Mr. Softly Bishop begged, in a very familiar style, that Mr. Prohack and wife would join himself and Miss Fancy on an early day at a little luncheon party, and he announced that the 'highly desirable event to the possibility of which he had alluded' on the previous evening, had duly occurred. Strange, the fellow's eagerness to publish his engagement to a person of more notoriety than distinction! The fellow must have "popped the question" while escorting Miss Fancy home in the middle of the night, and he must have written the note before breakfast and despatched it by special messenger. What a mentality!

Mr. Prohack desired now a whole series of baths. And he was very harassed indeed. If he, by a fluke, had discovered the escapade of the church-tower and the church-clock, why should not others discover it by other flukes? Was it conceivable that such a matter should forever remain a secret? The thing, to Mr. Prohack's sick imagination, was like a bomb with a fuse attached and the fuse lighted. When the bomb did go off, what trouble for an entirely innocent Mr. Prohack! And he loathed the notion of his proud, strong daughter being affianced to a man who, however excellent intrinsically, was the myrmidon of that sublime showman, Mr. Asprey Chown. And he hated his connection with Mr. Softly Bishop and with Miss Fancy. Could he refuse the invitation to the little luncheon party? He knew that he could not refuse it. His connection with these persons was indisputable and the social consequences of it could not be fairly avoided. As for the matter of the necklace, he held that he could deal with that,—but could he? He lacked confidence in himself. Even his fixed interest-bearing securities might, by some inconceivable world-catastrophe, cease to bear interest, and then where would he be?

Philosophy! Philosophy was absurdly unpractical. Philosophy could not cope with real situations. Where had he sinned? Nowhere. He had taken Dr. Veiga's advice and given up trying to fit his environment to himself instead of vice versa. He had let things rip and shown no egotistic concern in the business of others. But was he any better off in his secret soul? Not a whit. He ought to have been happy; he was miserable. On every hand the horizon was dark, and the glitter of seventeen thousand pounds per annum did not lighten it by the illuminative power of a single candle. . . . But his feverish hand gratefully remembered Mimi's kiss.

VI

Nevertheless, as the day waxed and began to wane, it was obvious even to Mr. Prohack that the domestic climate grew sunnier and more bracing. A weight seemed to have been lifted from the hearts of all Mr. Prohack's entourage. The theft of the twenty thousand pound necklace was a grave event, but it could not impair the beauty of the great fact that the church-clock had ceased to strike, and that therefore the master would be able to sleep. The shadow of a menacing calamity had passed, and everybody's spirits, except Mr. Prohack's, reacted to the news; Machin, restored to duty, was gaiety itself; but Mr. Prohack, unresponsive, kept on absurdly questioning his soul and the universe: "What am I getting out of life? Can it be true that I am incapable of arranging my existence in such a manner that the worm shall not feed so gluttonously on my damask cheek?"

Eve's attitude to him altered. In view of the persistent silence of the clock she had to admit to herself that her husband was still a long way off insanity, and she was ashamed of her suspicion and did all that she could to make compensation to him, while imitating his discreet example and not referring even distantly to the clock. When she mentioned the necklace, suggesting a direct appeal to Scotland Yard, and he discountenanced the scheme, she at once in the most charming way accepted his verdict and praised his superior wisdom. When he placed before her the invitation from Mr. Softly Bishop, she beautifully offered to disentangle him from it if he should so desire. When she told him that she had been asked to preside over the Social Amenities Committee of the League of all the Arts, and he advised her not to bind herself by taking any official position, and especially one which would force her into contact with a pack of self-seeking snobbish women, she beamed acquiescence and heartily concurred with him about the pack of women. In fact the afternoon became one of those afternoons on which every caprice was permitted to Mr. Prohack and he could do no wrong. But the worm still fed on his cheek.

Before tea he enjoyed a sleep, without having to time his repose so as to avoid being wakened by the clock. And then tea for one was served with full pomp in his study. This meant either that his tireless women were out, or that Eve had judged it prudent to indulge him in a solitary tea; and, after the hurried thick-cupped teas at the Treasury, he certainly did not dislike a leisurely tea replete with every luxury proper to the repast. He ate, drank, and read odd things in odd corners of *The Times,* and at last he smoked.

He was on the edge of felicity in his miserableness when his indefatigable women entered, all smiles. They had indeed been out, and they were still arrayed for the street. On by one they removed or cast aside such things as gloves, hats, coats, bags, until the study began to bear some resemblance to a boudoir. Mr. Prohack, though cheerfully grumbling at this, really liked it, for he was of those who think that nothing furnishes a room so well as a woman's hat, provided it be not permanently established.

Sissie even took off one shoe, on the plea that it hurt her, and there the trifling article lay, fragile, gleaming and absurd. Mr. Prohack appreciated it even more than the hats. He understood, perhaps better than ever before, that though he had a vast passion for his wife, there was enough emotion left in him to nourish an affection almost equally vast for his daughter. She was a proud piece, was that girl, and he was intensely proud of her. Nor did a realistic estimate of her faults of character seem in the least to diminish his pride in her. She had distinction; she had race. Mimi might possibly be able to make rings round her in the pursuit of any practical enterprise, but her mere manner of existing from moment to moment was superior to Mimi's. The simple-minded parent was indeed convinced at heart that the world held no finer young woman than Sissie Prohack. He reflected with satisfaction: "She knows I'm old, but there's something young in me that forces her to treat me as young; and moreover she adores me." He also reflected: "Of course they're after something, these two. I can see a put-up job in their eyes." Ah! He was ready for them, and the sensation of being ready for them was like a tonic to him, raising him momentarily above misery.

"You look much better, Arthur," said Eve, artfully preparing.

"I am," said he. "I've had a bath."

"Had you given up baths, dad?" asked Sissie, with a curl of the lips.

"No! But I mean I've had two baths. One in water and the other in resignation."

"How dull!"

"I've been thinking about the arrangements for the wedding," Eve started in a new, falsely careless tone, ignoring the badinage between her husband and daughter, which she always privately regarded as tedious.

There it was! They had come to worry him about the wedding. He had not recovered from one social martyrdom before they were plotting to push him into another. They were implacable, insatiable, were his women. He got up and walked about.

"Now, dad," Sissie addressed him. "Don't pretend you aren't interested." And then she burst into the most extraordinary laughter—laughter that bordered on the hysterical—and twirled herself round on the shod foot. Her behaviour offended Eve.

"Of course if you're going on like that, Sissie, I warn you I shall give it all up. After all, it won't be my wedding."

Sissie clasped her mother's neck.

"Don't be foolish, you silly old mater. It's a wedding, not a funeral."

"Well, what about it?" asked Mr. Prohack, sniffing with pleasure the new atmosphere created in his magnificent study by these feminine contacts.

"Do you think we'd better have the wedding at St. George's, Hanover Square, or at St. Nicodemus's?"

At the name of Nicodemus, Mr. Prohack started, as it were guiltily.

"Because," Eve continued, "we can have it at either place. You see Ozzie lives in one parish and Sissie in the other. St. Nicodemus has been getting rather fashionable lately, I'm told."

"What saith the bride?"

"Oh, don't ask me!" answered Sissie lightly. "I'm prepared for anything. It's mother's affair, not mine, in spite of what she says. And nobody shall be able to say after I'm married that I wasn't a dutiful daughter. I should love St. George's and I should love St. Nicodemus's too." And then she exploded again into disconcerting laughter, and the fit lasted longer than the first one.

Eve protested again and Sissie made peace again.

"St. Nicodemus would be more original," said Eve.

"Not so original as you," said Mr. Prohack.

Sissie choked on a lace handkerchief. St. Nicodemus was selected for the august rite. Similar phenomena occurred when Eve introduced the point whether the reception should be at Manchester Square or at Claridge's Hotel. And when Eve suggested that it might be well to enliven the mournfulness of a wedding with an orchestra and dancing, Sissie leaped up and seizing her father's hand whizzed him dangerously round the room to a tune of her own singing. The girl's mere physical force amazed him. The dance was brought to a conclusion by the overturning of an occasional table and a Tanagra figure. Whereupon Sissie laughed more loudly and hysterically than ever.

Mr. Prohack deemed that masculine tact should be applied. He soothed the outraged mother and tranquillised the ecstatic daughter, and then in a matter-of-fact voice asked: "And what about the date? Do let's get it over."

"We must consult Ozzie," said the pacified mamma.

Off went Sissie again into shrieks.

"You needn't," she spluttered. "It's not Ozzie's wedding. It's mine. You fix your own date, dearest, and leave Ozzie to me. Ozzie's only function at my wedding is to be indispensable." And still laughing in the most crude and shocking way she ran on her uneven feet out of the room, leaving the shoe behind on the hearth-rug to prove that she really existed and was not a hallucination.

"I can't make out what's the matter with that girl," said Eve.

"The sooner she's married the better," said Mr. Prohack, thoroughly reconciled now to the tedium of the ceremonies.

"I daresay you're right. But upon my word I don't know what girls are coming to," said Eve.

"Nobody ever did know that," said Mr. Prohack easily, though he also was far from easy in his mind about the bridal symptoms.

VII

"Can Charlie speak to you for a minute?" The voice was Eve's, diplomatic, apologetic. Her smiling and yet serious face, peeping in through the bedroom door, seemed to say: "I know we're asking a great favour and that your life is hard."

"All right," said Mr. Prohack, as a gracious, long-suffering autocrat, without moving his eyes from the book he was reading.

He had gone to bed. He had of late got into the habit of going to bed. He would go to bed on the slightest excuse, and would justify himself by pointing out that Voltaire used to do the same. He was capable of going to bed several times a day. It was early evening. The bed, though hired for a year only, was of extreme comfortableness. The light over his head was in exactly the right place. The room was warm. The book, by a Roman Emperor popularly known as Marcus Aurelius, counted among the world's masterpieces. It was designed to suit the case of Mr. Prohack, for its message was to the effect that happiness and content are commodities which can be manufactured only in the mind, from the mind's own ingredients, and that if the mind works properly no external phenomena can prevent the manufacture of the said commodities. In short, everything was calculated to secure Mr. Prohack's felicity in that moment. But he would not have it. He said to himself: "This book is all very fine, immortal, supreme, and so on. Only it simply isn't true. Human nature won't work the way this book says it ought to work; and what's more the author was obviously afraid of life, he was never really alive and he was never happy. Finally the tendency of the book is mischievously anti-social." Thus did Mr. Prohack seek to destroy a reputation of many centuries and to deny opinions which he himself had been expressing for many years.

"I don't want to live wholly in myself," said Mr. Prohack. "I want to live a great deal in other people. If you do that you may be infernally miserable but at least you aren't dull. Marcus Aurelius was more like a potato than I should care to be."

And he shoved the book under the pillow, turned half-over from his side to the flat of his back, and prepared with gusto for the evil which Charlie would surely bring. And indeed one glance at Charlie's preoccupied features confirmed his prevision.

"You're in trouble, my lad," said he.

"I am," said Charlie.

"And the hour has struck when you want your effete father's help," Mr. Prohack smiled benevolently.

"Put it like that," said Charlie amiably, taking a chair and smoothing out his trousers.

"I suppose you've seen the references to yourself in the papers?"

"Yes."

"Rather sarcastic, aren't they?"

"Yes. But that rather flatters me, you know, dad. Shows I'm being taken notice of."

"Still, you *have* been playing a dangerous game, haven't you?"

"Admitted," said Charlie, brightly and modestly. "But I was reading in one of my new books that it is not a bad scheme to live dangerously, and I quite agree. Anyhow it suits me. And it's quite on the cards that I may pull through."

"You mean if I help you. Now listen to me, Charlie. I'm your father, and if you're on earth it's my fault, and everything that happens to you is my fault. Hence I'm ready to help you as far as I can, which is a long way, but I'm not ready to throw my money into a pit unless you can prove to my hard Treasury mind that the pit is not too deep and has a firm unbreakable bottom. Rather than have anything to do with a pit that has all attractive qualities except a bottom, I would prefer to see you in the Bankruptcy Court and make you an allowance for life."

"That's absolutely sound," Charlie concurred with beautiful acquiescence. "And it's awfully decent of you to talk like this. I expect I could soon prove to you that my pit is the sort of pit you wouldn't mind throwing things into, and possibly one day I might ask you to do some throwing. But I'm getting along pretty well so far as money is concerned. I've come to ask you for something else."

"Oh!" Mr. Prohack was a little dashed. But Charlie's demeanour was so ingratiating that he did not feel in the least hurt.

"Yes. There's been some trouble between Mimi and me this afternoon, and I'm hoping that you'll straighten it out for me."

"Ah!" Mr. Prohack's interest became suddenly intense and pleasurable.

"The silly girl's given me notice. She's fearfully hurt because you told her that I told you about the church-clock affair, after it had been agreed between her and me that we wouldn't let on to anybody at all. She says that she can't possibly stay with anybody who isn't loyal, and that I'm not the man she thought I was, and she's given notice! . . . And I can't do without that girl! I knew she'd be perfectly invaluable to me, and she is."

Mr. Prohack was staggered at this revelation concerning Mimi. It seemed to make her heroic and even more incalculable.

"But *I* never told her you'd told me anything about the clock-striking business!" he exclaimed.

"I felt sure you hadn't," said Charlie, blandly. "I wonder how she got the idea into her head."

"Now I come to think of it," said Mr. Prohack, "she did assume this morning that you must have told me about the clock, and I didn't contradict her. Why should I!"

"Just so," Charlie smiled faintly. "But I'd be awfully obliged if you'd contradict her now. One word from you will put it all right."

"I'll ask her to come and see me first thing in the morning," said Mr. Prohack. "But would you believe it, my lad, that she never gave me the slightest sign this morning that your telling me anything about the clock would upset her. Not the slightest sign!"

"Oh! She wouldn't!" said Charlie. "She's like that. She's the strangest mixture of reserve and rashness you ever saw."

"No, she isn't. Because they're all the strangest mixture—except of course your esteemed mother, who we all agree is perfect. Anything else I can do for you to-night?"

"You might tell me how you *did* find out about the church-clock."

"With pleasure. The explanation will surprise you. I found out because in my old-world way I'm jolly clever. And that's all there is to it."

"Good night, dad. Thanks very much."

After Charlie had gone, Mr. Prohack said to himself: "That boy's getting on. I can remember the time when he would have come snorting in here full of his grievance, and been very sarcastic when I offered him money he didn't want. What a change! Oh, yes, he's getting on all right. He'll come through."

And Mr. Prohack was suddenly much fonder of the boy and more inclined to see in him the possibility of genius. But he was aware of apprehension as to the relations forming between his son and Mimi. That girl appeared to be establishing an empire over the great youthful prodigy of finance. Was this desirable? . . . No, that was not the question. The question was: Would Eve regard it as desirable? He could never explain to his wife how deeply he had been touched by Mimi's mad solicitude for the slumber of Charlie's father. And even if he could have explained Eve would never have consented to understand.

CHAPTER XXI

EVE'S MARTYRDOM

I

After a magnificent night's sleep, so magnificent indeed that he felt as if he had never until that moment really grasped the full significance of the word "sleep," Mr. Prohack rang the bell for his morning tea. Of late he had given orders that he must not under any circumstances be called, for it had been vouchsafed to him that in spite of a multitude of trained servants there were still things that he could do for himself better than anybody else could do for him, and among them was the act of waking up Mr. Prohack. He knew that he was in a very good humour, capable of miracles, and he therefore determined that he would seize the opportunity to find the human side of Mr. Brool and make a friend of him. But the tea-tray was brought in by Mrs. Prohack, who was completely and severely dressed. She put down the tray and kissed her husband not as usual, but rather in the manner of a Roman matron, and Mr. Prohack divined that something had happened.

"I hope Brool hasn't dropped down dead," said he, realising the foolishness of his facetiousness as he spoke.

Eve seemed to be pained.

"Have you slept better?" she asked, solicitous.

"I have slept so well that there's probably something wrong with me," said he. "Heavy sleep is a symptom of several dangerous diseases."

"I'm glad you've had a good night," she began, again ignoring his maladroit flippancy, "because I want to talk to you."

"Darling," he responded. "Pour out my tea for me, will you? Then I shall be equal to any strain. I trust that you also passed a fair night, madam. You look tremendously fit."

Visions of Lady Massulam flitted through his mind, but he decided that Eve, seriously pouring out tea for him under the lamp in the morning twilight of the pale bedroom, could not be matched by either Lady Massulam or anybody else. No, he could not conceive a Lady Massulam pouring out early tea; the Lady

Massulams could only pour out afternoon tea—a job easier to do with grace and satisfaction.

"I have not slept a wink all night," said Eve primly. "But I was determined that nothing should induce me to disturb you."

"Yes?" Mr. Prohack encouraged her, sipping the first glorious sip.

"Well, will you believe me that Sissie slipped out last night after dinner without saying a word to me or any one, and that she didn't come back and hasn't come back? I sat up for her till three o'clock—I telephoned to Charlie, but no! he'd seen nothing of her."

"Did you telephone to Ozzie?"

"Telephone to Ozzie, my poor boy! Of course I didn't. I wouldn't have Ozzie know for anything. Besides, he isn't on the telephone at his flat."

"That's a good reason for not telephoning, anyway," said Mr. Prohack.

"But did you ever hear of such a thing? The truth is, you've spoilt that child."

"I may have spoilt the child," Mr. Prohack admitted. "But I *have* heard of such a thing. I seem to remember that in the dear dead days of dancing studios, something similar occurred to your daughter."

"Yes, but we did know where she was."

"You didn't. I did," Mr. Prohack corrected her.

"Do you want me to cry?" Eve demanded suddenly.

"Yes," said Mr. Prohack. "I love to see you cry."

Eve pursed her lips and wrinkled her brows and gazed at the window, performing great feats of self-control under extreme provocation to lose her temper.

"What do you propose to do?" she asked with formality.

"Wait till the girl comes back," said Mr. Prohack.

"Arthur! I really cannot understand how you can take a thing like this so casually! No, I really can't!"

"Neither can I!" Mr. Prohack admitted, quite truthfully.

He saw that he ought to have been gravely upset by Sissie's prank and he was merely amused. "Effect of too much sleep, no doubt," he added.

Eve walked about the room.

"I pretended to Machin this morning that Sissie had told me that she was sleeping out, and that I had forgotten to tell Machin. It's a good thing we haven't engaged lady's maids yet. I can trust Machin. I know she didn't believe me this morning, but I can trust her. You see, after Sissie's strange behaviour these last few days. . . . One doesn't know what to think. And there's something else. Every morning for the last three or four weeks Sissie's gone out somewhere, for an hour or two, quite regularly. And where she went I've never been able to find out. Of course with a girl like her it doesn't do to ask too direct questions. . . . Ah! I should like to have seen my mother in my place. I know what she'd have done!"

"What would your mother have done? She always seemed to me to be a fairly harmless creature."

"Yes, to you! . . . Do you think we ought to inform the police!"

"No!"

"I'm so glad. The necklace and Sissie coming on top of each other! No. it would be too much!"

"It never rains but it pours, does it?" observed Mr. Prohack.

"But what *are* we to do?"

"Just what your mother would have done. Your mother would have argued like this: Either Sissie is staying away against her will or she is staying away of her own accord. If the former, it means an accident, and we are bound to hear shortly from one of the hospitals. If the latter, we can only sit tight. Your mother had a vigorous mind and that is how she would have looked at things."

"I never know how to take you, Arthur," said Mrs. Prohack, and went on: "And what makes it all the more incomprehensible is that yesterday afternoon Sissie went with me to Jay's to see about the wedding-dress."

"But why should that make it all the more incomprehensible?"

"Don't you think it does, somehow? I do."

"Did she giggle at Jay's?"

"Oh, no! Except once. Yes, I think she giggled once. That was when the fitter said she hoped we should give them plenty of time, because most customers rushed them so. I remember thinking how queer it was that Sissie should laugh so much at a perfectly simple remark like that. Oh! Arthur!"

"Now, my child," said Mr. Prohack firmly. "Don't get into your head that Sissie has gone off hers. Yesterday you thought for quite half an hour that I was suffering from incipient lunacy. Let that suffice you for the present. Be philosophical. The source of tranquillity is within. Remember that, and remind me of it too, because I'm apt to forget it. . . . We can do nothing at the moment. I will now get up, and I warn you that I shall want a large breakfast and you to pour out my coffee and read the interesting bits out of *The Daily Picture* to me."

II

At eleven o'clock of the morning the *status quo* was still maintaining itself within the noble mansion at Manchester Square. Mr. Prohack, washed, dressed, and amply fed, was pretending to be very busy with correspondence in his study, but he was in fact much more busy with Eve than with the correspondence. She came in to him every few minutes, and each time needed more delicate handling. After one visit Mr. Prohack had an idea. He transferred the key from the inside to the outside of the door. At the next visit Eve presented an ultimatum. She said that Mr. Prohack must positively do something about his daughter. Mr. Prohack replied that he would telephone to his solicitors: a project which happily commended itself to Eve, though what his solicitors could do except charge a fee Mr. Prohack could not imagine.

"You wait here," said he persuasively.

He then left the room and silently locked the door on Eve. It was a monstrous act, but Mr. Prohack had slept too well and was too fully inspired by the instinct of initiative. He hurried downstairs, ignoring Brool, who was contemplating the grandeur of the entrance hall, snatched his overcoat, hat, and umbrella from the seventeenth-century panelled cupboard in which these articles were kept, and slipped away into the Square, before Brool could even open the door for him. As he fled he glanced up at the windows of his study, fearful lest Eve might have divined his purpose to abandon her and, catching sight of him in flight, might begin making noises on the locked door. But Eve had not divined his purpose.

Mr. Prohack walked straight to Bruton Street, where Oswald Morfey's Japanese flat was situated. Mr. Prohack had never seen this flat, though his wife and daughter had been invited to it for tea—and had returned therefrom with excited accounts of its exquisite uniqueness. He had decided that his duty was to inform Ozzie of the mysterious disappearance of Sissie as quickly as possible; and, as Ozzie's theatrical day was not supposed to begin until noon, he hoped to catch him before his departure to the beck and call of the mighty Asprey Chown.

The number in Bruton Street indicated a tall, thin house with four bell-pushes and four narrow brass-plates on its door-jamb. The deceitful edifice looked at a distance just like its neighbours, but, as the array on the door-jamb showed, it had ceased to be what it seemed, the home of a respectable Victorian family in easy circumstances, and had become a Georgian warren for people who could reconcile themselves to a common staircase provided only they might engrave a sound West End address on their notepaper. The front-door was open, disclosing the reassuring fact that the hall and staircase were at any rate carpeted. Mr. Prohack rang the bell attached to Ozzie's name, waited, rang again, waited, and then marched upstairs. Perhaps Ozzie was shaving. Not being accustomed to the organisation of tenements in fashionable quarters, Mr. Prohack was unaware that during certain hours of the day he was entitled to ring the housekeeper's bell, on the opposite door-jamb, and to summon help from the basement.

As he mounted it the staircase grew stuffier and stuffier, but the condition of the staircarpet improved. Mr. Prohack hated the place, and at once determined to fight powerfully against Sissie's declared intention of starting married life in her husband's bachelor-flat, for the sake of economy. He would force the pair, if necessary, to accept from him a flat rent-free, or he would even purchase for them one of those bijou residences of which he had heard tell. He little dreamed that this very house had once been described as a bijou residence. The third floor landing was terribly small and dark, and Mr. Prohack could scarcely decipher the name of his future son-in-law on the shabby name-plate.

"This den would be dear at elevenpence three farthings a year," said he to himself, and was annoyed because for months he had been picturing the elegant Oswald as the inhabitant of something orientally and impeccably luxurious, and he wondered that his women, as a rule so critical, had breathed no word of the flat's deplorable approaches.

He rang the bell, and the bell made a violent and horrid sound, which could scarcely fail to be heard throughout the remainder of the house. No answer! Ozzie had gone. He descended the stairs, and on the second-floor landing saw an old lady putting down a mat in front of an open door. The old lady's hair was in curl-papers.

"I suppose," he ventured, raising his hat. "I suppose you don't happen to know whether Mr. Morfey has gone out?"

The old lady scanned him before replying.

"He can't be gone out," she answered. "He's just been sweeping his floor enough to wake the dead."

"Sweeping his floor!" exclaimed Mr. Prohack, shocked, thunderstruck. "I understood these were service flats."

"So they are—in a way, but the housekeeper never gets up to this floor before half past twelve; so it can't be the housekeeper. Besides, she's gone out for me."

"Thank you," said Mr. Prohack, and remounted the staircase. His blood was up. He would know the worst about the elegant Oswald, even if he had to beat the door down. He was, however, saved from this extreme measure, for when he aimlessly pushed against Oswald's door it opened.

He beheld a narrow passage, which in the matter of its decoration certainly did present a Japanese aspect to Mr. Prohack, who, however, had never been to Japan. Two doors gave off the obscure corridor. One of these doors was open, and in the doorway could be seen the latter half of a woman and the forward half of a carpet-brush. She was evidently brushing the carpet of a room and gradually coming out of the room and into the passage. She wore a large blue pinafore apron, and she was so absorbed in her business that the advent of Mr. Prohack passed quite unnoticed by her. Mr. Prohack waited. More of the woman appeared, and at last the whole of her. She felt, rather than saw, the presence of a man at the entrance, and she looked up, transfixed. A deep blush travelled over all her features.

"How clever of you!" she said, with a fairly successful effort to be calm.

"Good morning, my child," said Mr. Prohack, with a similar and equally successful effort. "So you're cleaning Mr. Morfey's flat for him."

"Yes. And not before it needed it. Do come in and shut the door." Mr. Prohack obeyed, and Sissie shed her pinafore apron. "Now we're quite private. I think you'd better kiss me. I may as well tell you that I'm fearfully happy—much more so than I expected to be at first."

Mr. Prohack again obeyed, and when he kissed his daughter he had an almost entirely new sensation. The girl was far more interesting to him than she had ever been. Her blush thrilled him.

"You might care to glance at that," said Sissie, with an affectation of carelessness, indicating a longish, narrowish piece of paper covered with characters in red and black, which had been affixed to the wall of the passage with two pins. "We put it there—at least I did—to save trouble."

Mr. Prohack scanned the document. It began: "This is to

certify—" and it was signed by a "Registrar of births, deaths, and marriages."

"Yesterday, eh?" he ejaculated.

"Yes. Yesterday, at two o'clock. *Not* at St George's and *not* at St Nicodemus's. . . . Well, you can say what you like, dad—"

"I'm not aware of having said anything yet," Mr. Prohack put in.

"You can say what you like, but what *did* you expect me to do? It was necessary to bring home to some people that this is the twentieth century, not the nineteenth, and I think I've done it. And anyway what are you going to do about it? Did you seriously suppose that I—*I*—was going through all the orange-blossom rigmarole, voice that breathed o'er Eden, fully choral, red carpet on the pavement, flowers, photographers, vicar, vestry, *Daily Picture,* reception, congratulations, rice, old shoes, going-away dress, 'Be kind to her, Ozzie.' Not much! And I don't think. They say that girls love it and insist on it. Well, I don't, and I know some others who don't, too. I think it's simply barbaric, worse than a public funeral. Why, to my mind it's Central African; and that's all there is to it. So there!" She laughed.

"Well," said Mr. Prohack, holding his hat in his hand. "I'm a tolerably two-faced person myself, but for sheer heartless duplicity I give you the palm. You can beat me. Has it occurred to you that this dodge of yours will cost you about fifty per cent of the wedding presents you might otherwise have had?"

"It has," said Sissie. "That was one reason why we tried the dodge. Nothing is more horrible than about fifty per cent of the wedding presents that brides get in these days. And we've had the two finest presents anybody could wish for."

"Oh?"

"Yes, Ozzie gave me Ozzie, and I gave him me."

"I suppose the idea was yours?"

"Of course. Didn't I tell you yesterday that Ozzie's only function at my wedding was to be indispensable. He was very much afraid at first when I started on the scheme, but he soon warmed up to it. I'll give him credit for seeing that secrecy was the only thing. If we'd announced it beforehand, we should have been bound to be beaten. You see that yourself, don't you, dearest? And after all, it's our affair and nobody else's."

"That's just where you're wrong," said Mr. Prohack grandly. "A marriage, even yours, is an affair of the State's. It concerns society. It is full of reactions on society. And society has been very wise to invest it with solemnity—and a certain grotesque quality. All solemnities are a bit grotesque, and so they ought to be. All solemnities ought to produce self-consciousness in the performers. As things are, you'll be ten years in convincing yourself that you're really a married woman, and till the day of your death, and afterwards, society will have an instinctive feeling that there's something fishy about you, or about Ozzie. And it's your own fault."

"Oh, dad! What a fraud you are!" And the girl smiled. "You know perfectly well that if you'd been in my place, and had had the pluck—which you wouldn't have had—you'd have done the same."

"I should," Mr. Prohack immediately admitted. "Because I always want to be smarter than other people. It's a cheap ambition. But I should have been wrong. And I'm exceedingly angry with you and I'm suffering from a sense of outrage, and I should not be at all surprised if all is over between us. The thing amounts to a scandal, and the worst of it is that no satisfactory explanation of it can ever be given to the world. If your Ozzie is up, produce him, and I'll talk to him as e's never been talked to before. He's the elder, he's a man, and he's the most to blame."

"Take your overcoat off," said Sissie laughing and kissing him again. "And don't you dare to say a word to Ozzie. Besides, he isn't in. He's gone off to business. He always goes at eleven-thirty punctually."

There was a pause.

"Well," said Mr. Prohack. "All I wish to state is that if you had a feather handy, you could knock me down with it."

"I can see all over your face," Sissie retorted, "that you're so pleased and relieved you don't know what to do with yourself."

Mr. Prohack perfunctorily denied this, but it was true. His relief that the wedding lay behind instead of in front of him was immense, and his spirits rose even higher than they had been when he first woke up. He loathed all ceremonies, and the prospect of having to escort an orange-blossom-laden young woman in an automobile to a fashionable church, and up the aisle thereof, and raise his voice therein, and make a present of her to some one else, and breathe sugary nothings to a thousand gapers at a starchy reception,—this prospect had increasingly become a nightmare to him. Often had he dwelt on it in a condition resembling panic. And now he felt genuinely grateful to his inexcusable daughter for her shameless effrontery. He desired greatly to do something very handsome indeed for her and her excellent tame husband.

"Step in and see my home," she said.

The home consisted of two rooms, one of them a bedroom and the other a sitting-room, together with a small bathroom that was as dark and dank as a cell of the Spanish Inquisition, and another apartment which he took for a cupboard, but which Sissie authoritatively informed him was a kitchen. The two principal rooms were beyond question beautifully Japanese in the matter of pictures, prints and cabinets—not otherwise. They showed much taste; they were unusual and stimulating and jolly and refined; but Mr. Prohack did not fancy that he personally could have lived in them with any striking success. The lack of space, of light, and of air outweighed all considerations of charm and originality; the upper staircase alone would have ruined any flat for Mr. Prohack.

"Isn't it lovely!" Sissie encouraged him.

"Yes, it is," he said feebly. "Got any servants yet?"

"Oh! We can't have servants. No room for them to sleep, and I couldn't stand charwomen. You see, it's a service flat, so there's really nothing to do."

"So I noticed when I came in," said Mr. Prohack. "And I suppose you intend to eat at restaurants. Or do they send up meals from the cellar?"

"We shan't go to restaurants," Sissie replied. "You may be sure of that. Too expensive for us. And I don't count much on the cookery downstairs. No! I shall do the cooking in a chafing-dish—here it is, you see. I've been taking lessons in chafing-dish cookery every day for weeks, and it's awfully amusing, it is really. And it's much better than ordinary cooking, and cheaper too. Ozzie loves it."

Mr. Prohack was touched, and more than ever determined to be generous in the grand manner and start the simple-minded couple in married life on a scale befitting the general situation.

"You'll soon be clearing out of this place, I expect," he began cautionsly.

"Clearing out!" Sissie repeated. "Why should we? We've got all we need. We haven't the slightest intention of trying to live as you live. Ozzie's very prudent, I'm glad to say, and so am I. We're going to save hard for a few years, and then we shall see how things are."

"But you can't possibly stay on living in a place like this!" Mr. Prohack protested, smiling diplomatically to soften the effect of his words.

"Who can't?"

"You can't."

"But when you say me, do you mean your daughter or Ozzie's wife? Ozzie's lived here for years, and he's given lots of parties here—tea-parties, of course."

Mr. Prohack paused, perceiving that he had put himself in the wrong.

"This place is perfectly respectable," Sissie continued, "and supposing you hadn't got all that money from America or somewhere," she persisted, "would you have said that I couldn't 'possibly go on living in a place like this?'" She actually imitated his superior fatherly tone. "You'd have been only too pleased to see me living in a place like this."

Mr. Prohack raised both arms on high.

"All right," said the young spouse, absurdly proud of her position. "I'll let you off with your life this time, and you can drop your arms again. But if anybody had told me that you would come here and make a noise like a plutocrat I wouldn't have believed it. Still, I'm frightfully fond of you and I know you'd do anything for me, and you're nearly as much of a darling as Ozzie, but you mustn't be a rich man when you call on me here. I couldn't bear it twice."

"I retire in disorder, closely pursued by the victorious enemy," said Mr. Prohack. And in so saying he accurately described the situation. He had been more than defeated—he had been exquisitely snubbed. And yet the singular creature was quite pleased. He looked at the young girl, no longer his and no longer a girl either, set in the midst of a japanned and lacquered room that so resembled Ozzie in its daintiness; he saw the decision on her brow, the charm in her eyes, and the elegance in her figure and dress, and he came near to bursting with pride. "She's got character enough to beat even me," he reflected contentedly, thus exhibiting an ingenuousness happily rare among fathers of brilliant daughters. And even the glimpse of the cupboard kitchen, where the washing-up after a chafing-dish breakfast for two had obviously not yet been accomplished—even this touch seemed only to intensify the moral and physical splendour of his child in her bridal setting.

"At the same time," he added to the admission of defeat, "I seem to have a sort of idea that lately you've been carrying on rather like a plutocrat's daughter."

"That was only my last fling," she replied, quite unperturbed.

"I see," said Mr. Prohack musingly. "Now as regards my wedding present to you. Am I permitted to offer any gift, or is it forbidden? Of course with all my millions I couldn't hope to rival the gift which Ozzie gave you, but I might come in a pretty fair second, mightn't I?"

"Dad," said she. "I must leave all that to your good taste. I'm sure that it won't let you make any attack on our independence."

"Supposing that I were to find some capital for Ozzie to start in business for himself as a theatrical manager? He must know a good deal about the job by this time."

Sissie shook her delicious head.

"No, that would be plutocratic. And you see I've only just married Ozzie. I don't know anything about him yet. When I do, I shall come and talk to you. While you're waiting I wish you'd give me some crockery. One breakfast cup isn't quite enough for two people, after the first day. I saw a set of things in a shop in Oxford Street for £1. 19. 6 which I should love to have. . . . What's happened to the mater? Is she in a great state about me? Hadn't you better run off and put her out of her misery?"

He went, thoughtful.

III

He was considerably dashed on his return home, to find the door of his study still locked on the outside. The gesture which on his leaving the room seemed so natural, brilliant and excusable, now presented itself to him as the act of a coarse-minded idiot. He hesitated to unlock the door, but of course he had to unlock it. Eve sat as if at the stake, sublime.

"Arthur, why do you play these tricks on me—and especially when we are in such trouble?"

Why did he, indeed?

"I merely didn't want you to run after me," said he. "I made sure of course that you'd ring the bell at once and have the door opened."

"Did you imagine for a moment that I would let any of the servants know that you'd locked me in a room? No! You couldn't have imagined that. I've too much respect for your reputation in this house to do such a thing, and you ought to know it."

"My child," said Mr. Prohack, once again amazed at Eve's extraordinary gift for putting him in the wrong, and for making him still more wrong when he was wrong. "This is the second time this morning that I've had to surrender to overwhelming force. Name your own terms of peace. But let me tell you in extenuation that I've discovered your offspring. The fact is, I got her in one."

"Where is she?" Eve asked, not eagerly, rather negligently, for she was now more distressed about her husband's behaviour than about Sissie.

"At Ozzie's." As soon as he had uttered the words Mr. Prohack saw his wife's interest fly back from himself to their daughter.

"What's she doing at Ozzie's?"

"Well, she's living with him. They were married yesterday. They thought they'd save you and me and themselves a lot of trouble. . . . But, look here, my child, it's not a tragedy. What's the matter with you?"

Eve's face was a mask of catastrophe. She did not cry. The affair went too deep for tears.

"I suppose I shall have to forgive Sissie—some day; but I've never been so insulted in my life. Never! And never shall I forget it! And I've no doubt that you and Sissie treated it all as a great piece of fun. You would!"

The poor lady had gone as pale as ivory. Mr. Prohack was astonished—he even felt hurt—that he had not seen the thing from Eve's point of view earlier. Emphatically it did amount to an insult for Eve, to say naught of the immense desolating disappointment to her. And yet Sissie, princess among daughters, had not shown by a single inflection of her voice that she had any sympathy with her mother, or any genuine appreciation of what the secret marriage would mean to her. Youth was incredibly cruel; and age too, in the shape of Mr. Prohack himself, had not been much less cruel.

"Something's happened about that necklace since you left," said Eve, in a dull, even voice.

"Oh! What?"

"I don't know. But I saw Mr. Crewd the detective drive up to the house at a great pace. Then Brool came and knocked here, and as I didn't care to have to tell him that the door was locked, I kept quiet and he went away again. Mr. Crewd went away too. I saw him drive away."

Mr. Prohack said nothing audible, but to himself he said: "She actually choked off her curiosity about the necklace so as not to give me away! There could never have been another woman like her in the whole history of human self-control! She's prodigious!"

And then he wondered what could have happened in regard to the necklace. He foresaw more trouble there. And the splendour of the morning had faded. An appalling silence descended upon the whole house. To escape from its sinister spell Mr. Prohack departed and sought the seclusion of his secondary club, which he had not entered for a very long time. (He dared not face the lively amenities of his principal club.) He pretended, at the secondary club, that he had never ceased to frequent the place regularly, and to that end he put on a nonchalant air; but he was somewhat disconcerted to find, from the demeanour of his acquaintances there, that he positively had not been missed to any appreciable extent. He decided that the club was a dreary haunt, and could not understand why he had never before perceived its dreariness. The members seemed to be scarcely alive; and in particular they seemed to have conspired together to behave and talk as though humanity consisted of only one sex,—their own. Mr. Prohack, worried though he was by a too acute realisation of the fact that humanity did indeed consist of two sexes, despised the lot of them. And yet simultaneously the weaker part of him envied them, and he fully admitted, in the abstract, that something might convincingly be said in favour of monasteries. It was a most strange experience.

After a desolating lunch of excellent dishes, perfect coffee which left a taste in his mouth, and a fine cigar which he threw away before it was half finished, he abandoned the club and strolled in the direction of Manchester Square. But he lacked the courage to go into the noble mansion, and feebly and aimlessly proceeded northward until he arrived at Marylebone Road and saw the great historic crimson building of Madame Tussaud's Waxworks. His mood was such that he actually, in a wild and melancholy caprice, paid money to enter this building and enquired at once for the room known as the Chamber of Horrors. . . . When he emerged his gloom had reached the fantastic, hysteric, or giggling stage, and his conception of the all-embracingness of London was immensely enlarged.

"Miss Sissie and Mr. Morfey are with Mrs. Prohack, sir," said Brool, in a quite ordinary tone, taking the hat and coat of his returned master in the hall of the noble mansion.

Mr. Prohack started.

"Give me back my hat and coat," said he. "Tell your mistress that I may not be in for dinner." And he fled.

He could not have assisted at the terrible interview between Eve and the erring daughter who had inveigled her own betrothed into a premature marriage. Sissie at any rate had pluck, and she must also have had an enormous moral domination over Ozzie to have succeeded in forcing him to join her in a tragic scene. What a honeymoon! To what a pass had society come! Mr. Prohack drove straight to the Monument, and paid more money for the privilege of climbing it. He next visited the Tower. The day seemed to consist of twenty-four thousand hours. He dined at the Trocadero Restaurant, solitary at a table under the shadow of the bass fiddle of the orchestra; and finally he patronised Maskelyne and Cook's entertainment, and witnessed the dissipation of solid young women into air. He reached home, as it was humorously called, at ten thirty.

"Mrs. Prohack has retired for the night, sir," said Brool, who never permitted his employers merely to go to bed, "and wishes not to be disturbed."

"Thank God!" breathed Mr. Prohack.

"Yes, sir," said Brool, dutifully acquiescent.

IV

The next morning Eve behaved to her husband exactly as if nothing untoward had happened. She kissed and was kissed. She exhibited sweetness without gaiety, and a general curiosity without interest. She said not a word concerning the visit of Sissie and Ozzie. She expressed the hope that Mr. Prohack had had a pleasant evening and slept well. Her anxiety to be agreeable to Mr. Prohack was touching,—it was angelic. To the physical eye all was as usual, but Mr. Prohack was aware that in a single night she had built a high and unscalable wall between him and her; a wall which he could see through and which he could kiss through, but which debarred him utterly from her. And yet what sin had he committed against her, save the peccadillo of locking her for an hour or two in a comfortable room? It was Sissie, not he, who had committed the sin. He wanted to point this out to Eve, but he appreciated the entire futility of doing so and therefore refrained. About eleven o'clock Eve knocked at and opened his study door.

"May I come in—or am I disturbing you?" she asked brightly.

"Don't be a silly goose," said Mr. Prohack, whose rising temper —he hated angels—was drowning his tact. Smiling as though he had thrown her a compliment, Eve came in, and shut the door.

"I've just received this," she said. "It came by messenger." And she handed him a letter signed with the name of Crewd, the private detective. The letter ran: "Madam, I beg to inform you that I have just ascertained that the driver of taxi No. 5437 has left at New Scotland Yard a pearl necklace which he found in his vehicle. He states that he drove a lady and gentleman from your house to Waterloo Station on the evening of your reception, but can give no description of them. I mention the matter *pro forma,* but do not anticipate that it can interest you as the police authorities at New Scotland Yard declare the pearls to be false. Yours obediently. . . . P. S. I called upon you in order to communicate the above facts yesterday, but you were not at home."

Mr. Prohack turned a little pale, and his voice trembled as he said, looking up from the letter:

"I wonder who the thief was. Anyhow, women are staggering. Here some woman—I'm sure it was the woman and not the man—picks up a necklace from the floor of one of your drawing-rooms, well knowing it not to be her own, hides it, makes off with it, and then is careless enough to leave it in a taxi! Did you ever hear of such a thing?"

"But that wasn't my necklace, Arthur!" said Eve.

"Of course it was your necklace," said Mr. Prohack.

"Do you mean to tell me—" Eve began, and it was a new Eve.

"Of course I do!" said Mr. Prohack, who had now thoroughly subdued his temper in the determination to bring to a head that trouble about the necklace and end it for ever. He was continuing his remarks when the wall suddenly fell down with an unimaginable crash. Eve said nothing, but the soundless crash deafened Mr. Prohack. Nevertheless the mere fact that Sissie's wedding lay behind and not before him, helped him somewhat to keep his spirits and his nerve.

"I will never forgive you, Arthur!" said Eve with the most solemn and terrible candour. She no longer played a part; she was her formidable self, utterly unmasked and savagely expressive without any regard to consequences. Mr. Prohack saw that he was engaged in a mortal duel, with the buttons off the deadly foils.

"Of course you won't," said he, gathering himself heroically together, and superbly assuming a calm which he did not in the least feel. "Of course you won't, because there is nothing to forgive. On the contrary, you owe me your thanks. I never deceived you. I never told you the pearls were genuine. Indeed I beg to remind you that I once told you positively that I would never buy you a *pearl* necklace,—don't you remember? You thought they were genuine, and you have had just as much pleasure out of them as if they had been genuine. You were always careless with your jewellery. Think how I should have suffered if I had watched you every day being careless with a rope of genuine pearls! I should have had no peace of mind. I should have been obliged to reproach you, and as you can't bear to be reproached you would have picked quarrels with me. Further, you have lost nothing in prestige, for the reason that all our friends and acquaintances have naturally assumed that the pearls were genuine because they were your pearls and you were the wife of a rich man. A woman whose husband's financial position is not high and secure is bound to wear real pearls because people will *assume* that her pearls are false. But a woman like yourself can wear any pinchbeak pearls with impunity because people *assume* that her pearls are genuine. In your case there could be no advantage whatever in genuine pearls. To buy them would be equivalent to throwing money in the street. Now, as it is, I have saved money over the pearls, and therefore interest on money, though I did buy you the very finest procurable imitations! And think, my child, how relieved you are now,—oh, yes! you are, so don't pretend the contrary: I can deceive you, but you can't deceive me. You have no grievance whatever. You have had many hours of innocent satisfaction in your false jewels, and nobody is any the worse. Indeed my surpassing wisdom in the choice of a necklace has saved you from all further worry about the loss of the necklace, because it simply doesn't matter either one way or the other, and I say I defy you to stand there and tell me to my face that you have any grievance at all."

Mr. Prohack paused for a reply, and he got it.

"I will never forgive you as long as I live," said Eve. "Let us say no more about it. What time is that awful lunch that you've arranged with that dreadful Bishop man? And what would you like me to wear, please?" In an instant she had rebuilt the wall, higher than ever.

Mr. Prohack, always through the wall, took her in his arms and kissed her. But he might as well have kissed a woman in a trance. All that could be said was that Eve submitted to his embrace, and her attitude was another brilliant illustration of the fact that the most powerful oriental tyrants can be defied by their weakest slaves, provided that the weakest slaves know how to do it.

"You are splendid!" said Mr. Prohack, admiringly, conscious anew of his passion for her and full of trust in the virtue of his passion to knock down the wall sooner or later. "But you are a very naughty and ungrateful creature, and you must be punished. I will now proceed to punish you. We have much to do before the lunch. Go and get ready, and simply put on all the clothes that have cost the most money They are the clothes fittest for your punishment."

Three-quarters of an hour later, when Mr. Prohack had telephoned and sent a confirmatory note by hand to his bank, Carthew drove them away southwards, and the car stopped in front of the establishment of a very celebrated firm of jewellers near Piccadilly.

"Come along," said Mr. Prohack, descending to the pavement, and drew after him a moving marble statue, richly attired. They entered the glittering shop, and were immediately encountered by an expectant salesman who had the gifts of wearing a frock-coat as though he had been born in it, and of reading the hearts of men. That salesman saw in a flash that big business was afoot.

"First of all," said Mr. Prohack. "Here is my card, so that we may know where we stand."

The salesman read the card and was suitably impressed, but his conviction that big business was afoot seemed now to be a little shaken.

"May I venture to hope that the missing necklace has been found, sir?" said the salesman smoothly. "We've all been greatly interested in the newspaper story."

"That is beside the point," said Mr. Prohack. "I've come simply to buy a pearl necklace."

"I beg pardon, sir. Certainly. Will you have the goodness to step this way."

They were next in a private room off the shop; and the sole items of furniture were three elegant chairs, a table with a glass top, and a colossal safe. Another salesman entered the room with bows, and keys were produced, and the two salesmen between them swung back the majestic dark green doors of the safe. In another minute various pearl necklaces were lying on the table. The spectacle would have dazzled a connoisseur in pearls; but Mr. Prohack was not a connoisseur; he was not even interested in pearls, and saw on the table naught but a monotonous array of pleasing gewgaws, to his eye differing one from another only in size. He was, however, actuated by a high moral purpose, which uplifted him and enabled him to listen with dignity to the technical eulogies given by the experts. Eve of course behaved with impeccable correctness, hiding the existence of the wall from everybody except Mr. Prohack, but forcing Mr. Prohack to behold the wall all the time.

When he had reached a state of complete bewilderment regarding the respective merits of the necklaces, Mr. Prohack judged the moment ripe for proceeding to business. With his own hands he clasped a necklace round his wife's neck, and demanded:

"What is the price of this one?"

"Eight hundred and fifty pounds," answered the principal expert, who seemed to recognise every necklace at sight as a shepherd recognises every sheep in his flock.

"Do you think this would suit you, my dear?" asked Mr. Prohack.

"I think so," replied Eve politely.

"Well, I'm not so sure," said Mr. Prohack, reflectively. "What about this one?" And he picked up and tried upon Eve another and a larger necklace.

"That," said the original expert," is two thousand four hundred guineas."

"It seems cheap," said Mr. Prohack carelessly. "But there's something about the gradation that I don't quite like. What about this one?"

Eve opened her mouth, as if about to speak, but she did not speak. The wall, which had trembled for a few seconds, regained its monumental solidity.

"Five thousand guineas," said the expert of the third necklace.

"Hm!" commented Mr. Prohack, removing the gewgaw. "Yes. Not so bad. And yet—"

"That necklace," the expert announced with a mien from which all deference had vanished, "is one of the most perfect we have. The pearls have, if I may so express it, a homogeneity not often arrived at in any necklace. They are not very large of course—"

"Quite so," Mr. Prohack stopped him, selecting a fourth necklace.

"Yes," the expert admitted, his deference returning. "That one is undoubtedly superior. Let me see, we have not yet exactly valued it, but I think we could put it in at ten thousand guineas—perhaps pounds. I should have to consult one of the partners."

"It is scarcely," said Mr. Prohack, surveying the trinket judicially on his wife's neck, "scarcely the necklace of my dreams,—not that I would say a word against it. . . . Ah!" And he pounced suddenly, with an air of delighted surprise, upon a fifth necklace, the queen of necklaces.

"My dear, try this one. Try this one. I didn't notice it before. Somehow it takes my fancy, and as I shall obviously see much more of your necklace than you will, I should like my taste to be consulted."

As he fastened the catch of the thing upon Eve's delicious nape, he could feel that she was trembling. He surveyed the dazzling string. She also surveyed it, fascinated, spellbound. Even Mr. Prohack began to perceive that the reputation and value of fine pearls might perhaps be not entirely unmerited in the world.

"Sixteen thousand five hundred," said the expert.

"Pounds or guineas?" Mr. Prohack blandly enquired.

"Well, sir, shall we say pounds?"

"I think I will take it," said Mr. Prohack with undiminished blandness. "No, my dear, don't take it off. Don't take it off."

"Arthur!" Eve breathed, seeming to expire in a kind of agonised protest.

"May I have a few minutes' private conversation with my wife?" Mr. Prohack suggested. "Could you leave us?" One expert glanced at the other awkwardly.

"Pardon my lack of savoir vivre," said Mr. Prohack. "Of course you cannot possibly leave us alone with all these valuables. Never mind! We will call again."

The principal expert rose sublimely to the great height of the occasion. He had a courageous mind and was moreover well acquainted with the fantastic folly of allowing customers to call again. Within his experience of some thirty years he had not met half a dozen exceptions to the rule that customers who called again, if ever they did call, called in a mood of hard and miserly sanity which for the purposes of the jewellery business was sickeningly inferior to their original mood.

"Please, please, Mr. Prohack!" said he, with grand deprecation, and departed out of the room with his fellow.

No sooner had they gone than the wall sank. It did not tumble with a crash; it most gently subsided.

"Arthur!" Eve exclaimed, with a curious uncertainty of voice. "Are you mad?"

"Yes," said Mr. Prohack.

"Well," said she. "If you think I shall walk about London with sixteen thousand five hundred pounds round my neck you're mistaken."

"But I insist! You were a martyr and our marriage was ruined because I didn't give you real pearls. I intend you shall have real pearls."

"But not these," said Eve. "It's too much. It's a fortune."

"I am aware of that," Mr. Prohack agreed. "But what is sixteen thousand five hundred pounds to me?"

"Truly I couldn't, darling," Eve wheedled.

"I am not your darling," said Mr. Prohack. "How can I be

your darling when you're never going to forgive me? Look here. I'll let you choose another necklace, but only on the condition that you forgive all my alleged transgressions, past, present and to come."

She kissed him.

"You can have the one at five thousand guineas," said Mr. Prohack. "Nothing less. That is my ultimatum. Put it on. Put it on, quick! Or I may change my mind."

He recalled the experts who, when they heard the grave news, smiled bravely, and looked upon Eve as upon a woman whose like they might never see again.

"My wife will wear the necklace at once," said Mr. Prohack. "Pen and ink, please." He wrote a cheque. "My car is outside. Perhaps you will send some one up to my bank immediately and cash this. We will wait. I have warned the bank. There will be no delay. The case can be delivered at my house. You can make out the receipt and usual guarantee while we're waiting." And so it occurred as he had ordained.

"Would you care for us to arrange for the insurance? We undertake to do it as cheaply as anybody," the expert suggested, later.

Mr. Prohack was startled, for in his inexperience he had not thought of such complications.

"I was just going to suggest it," he answered placidly.

"I feel quite queer," said Eve, as she fingered the necklace, in the car, when all formalities were accomplished and they had left the cave of Aladdin.

"And well you may my child," said Mr. Prohack. "The interest on the price of that necklace would about pay the salary of a member of Parliament or even of a professional cricketer. And remember that whenever you wear the thing you are in danger of being waylaid, brutally attacked, and robbed."

"I wish you wouldn't be silly," Eve murmured. "I do hope I shan't seem self-conscious at the lunch."

"We haven't reached the lunch yet," Mr. Prohack replied. "We must go and buy a safe first. There's no safe worth twopence in the house, and a really safe safe is essential. And I want it to be clearly understood that I shall keep the key of that safe. We aren't playing at necklaces now. Life is earnest."

And when they had bought a safe and were once more in the car, he said, examining her impartially: "After all, at a distance of four feet it doesn't look nearly so grand as the one that's lying at Scotland Yard—I gave thirty pounds for that one."

CHAPTER XXII

MR. PROHACK'S TRIUMPH

I

"AND where is your charming daughter?" asked Mr. Softly Bishop so gently of Eve, when he had greeted her, and quite incidentally Mr. Prohack, in the entrance hall of the Grand Babylon Hotel. He was alone—no sign of Miss Fancy.

"Sissie?" said Eve calmly. "I haven't the slightest idea."

"But I included her in my invitations—and Mr. Morfey too."

Mr. Prohack was taken aback, foreseeing the most troublesome complications; and he glanced at Eve as if for guidance and support. He was nearly ready to wish that after all Sissie had not gone and got married secretly and prematurely. Eve, however, seemed quite undisturbed, though she offered him neither guidance nor support.

"Surely," said Mr. Prohack hesitatingly, "surely you didn't mention Sissie in your letter to me!"

"Naturally I didn't, my dear fellow," answered Mr. Bishop. "I wrote to her separately, knowing the position taken up by the modern young lady. And she telephoned me yesterday afternoon that she and Morfey would be delighted to come."

"Then if you know so much about the modern young lady," said Eve, with bright and perfect self-possession, "you wouldn't expect my daughter to arrive with her parents, would you?"

Mr. Softly Bishop laughed.

"You're only putting off the evil moment," said Mr. Prohack in the silence of his mind to Eve, and similarly he said to Mr. Softly Bishop:

"I do wish you wouldn't call me 'my dear fellow.' True, I come to your lunch, but I'm not your dear fellow and I never will be."

"I invited your son also, Prohack," continued Mr. Bishop. "Together with Miss Winstock or Warburton—she appears to have two names—to make a pair, to make a pair you understand. But unfortunately he's been suddenly called out of town on the most urgent business." As he uttered these last words Mr. Bishop glanced in a peculiar manner partly at his nose and partly at Mr.

Prohack; it was a singular feat of glancing, and Mr. Prohack uncomfortably wondered what it meant, for Charles lay continually on Mr. Prohack's chest, and at the slightest provocation Charles would lie more heavily than usual.

"Am I right in assuming that the necklace affair is satisfactorily settled?" Mr. Softly Bishop enquired, his spectacles gleaming and blinking at the adornment of Eve's neck.

"You are," said Eve. "But it wouldn't be advisable for you to be too curious about details."

Her aplomb, her sangfroid, astounded Mr. Prohack—and relieved him. With an admirable ease she went on to congratulate their host upon his engagement, covering him with petals of flattery and good wishes. Mr. Prohack could scarcely recognise his wife, and he was not sure that he liked her new worldiness quite as much as her old ingenuous and sometimes inarticulate simplicity. At any rate she was a changed woman. He steadied himself, however, by a pertinent reflection: she was always a changed woman.

Then Sissie and Ozzie appeared, looking as though they had been married for years. Mr. Prohack's heart began to beat. Ignoring Mr. Softly Bishop, Sissie embraced her mother with prim affectionateness, and Eve surveyed her daughter with affectionate solicitude. Mr. Prohack felt that he would never know what had passed between these two on the previous day, for they were a pair of sphinxes when they chose, and he was too proud to encourage confidences from Ozzie. Whatever it might have been it was now evidently buried deep, and the common life, after a terrible pause, had resumed.

"How do you do, Miss Prohack," said Mr. Softly Bishop, greeting. "So glad you could come."

Mr. Prohack suspected that his cheeks were turning pale, and was ashamed of himself. Even Sissie, for all her young, hard confidence, wavered.

But Eve stepped in.

"Don't you know, Mr. Bishop?—No. of course you don't. We ought to have told you. My daughter is now Mrs. Morfey. You see in our family we all have such a horror of the conventional wedding and reception and formal honeymoon and so on, that we decided the marriage should be strictly private, with no announcements of any kind. I really think you are the first to know. One thing I've always liked about actresses is that in the afternoon you can read of them getting married that day and then go and see them play the same evening. It seems to me so sensible. And as we were all of the same opinion at our house, especially Sissie and her father, there was no difficulty."

"Upon my word," said Mr. Softly Bishop shaking hands with Ozzie. "I believe I shall follow your example."

Mr. Prohack sank into a chair.

"I feel rather faint," he said. "Bishop, do you think we might have a cocktail or so?"

"My dear fellow, how thoughtless of me! Of course! Waiter! Waiter!" As Mr. Bishop swung round in the direction of waiters Eve turned in alarm to Mr. Prohack. Mr. Prohack with much deliberation winked at her, and she drew back. "Yes," he murmured. "You'll be the death of me one day, and then you'll be sorry."

"I don't think a cocktail is at all a good thing for you, dad," Sissie calmly observed.

The arrival of Miss Fancy provided a distraction more agreeable than Mr. Prohack thought possible; he positively welcomed the slim, angular blonde, for she put an end to a situation which, prolonged another moment, would have resulted in a severe general constraint.

"You're late, my dear," said Mr. Softly Bishop, firmly.

The girl's steely blue-eyed glance shot out at the greeting, but seemed to drop off flatly from Mr. Bishop's adamantine spectacles like a bullet from Bessemer armour.

"Am I?" she replied uncertainly, in her semi-American accent. "Where's the ladies' cloakroom of this place?"

"I'll show you," said Mr. Bishop, with no compromise.

The encounter was of the smallest, but it made Mr. Prohack suspect that perhaps Mr. Bishop was not after all going into the great warfare of matrimony blindly or without munitions.

"I've taken the opportunity to tell Miss Fancy that she will be the only unmarried woman at my lunch," said Mr. Bishop amusingly, when he returned from piloting his beloved. A neat fellow, beyond question!

Miss Fancy had apparently to re-dress herself, judging from the length of her absence. The cocktails, however, beguiled the suspense.

"Is this for me?" she asked, picking up a full glass when she came back.

"No, my dear," said Mr. Bishop. "It isn't. We will go in to lunch." And they went in to lunch, leaving unconsumed the cocktail which the abstemious and spartan Sissie had declined to drink.

II

"I suppose you've been to see the Twelve and Thirteen," said Eve, in her new grand, gracious manner to Miss Fancy, when the party was seated at a round, richly-flowered table specially reserved by Mr. Softly Bishop on the Embankment front of the restaurant, and the hors d'œuvre had begun to circulate on the white cloth, which was as crowded as the gold room.

"I'm afraid I haven't," muttered Miss Fancy weakly but with due refinement. The expression of fear was the right expression. Eve had put the generally brazen woman in a fright at the first effort. And the worst was that Miss Fancy did not even know what the Twelve and Thirteen was—or were. At the opening of her début at what she imagined to be the great, yet exclusive, fashionable world, Miss Fancy was failing. Of what use to be perfectly dressed and jewelled, to speak with a sometimes carefully-corrected accent, to sit at the best table in the London restaurant most famous in the United States, to be affianced to the cleverest fellow she had ever struck, if the wonderful and famous hostess, Mrs. Prohack, whose desirable presence was due only to Softly's powerful influence in high circles, could floor her at the very outset of the conversation? It is a fact that Miss Fancy would have given the emerald ring off her left first-finger to be able to answer back. All Miss Fancy could do was to smite Mr. Softly Bishop with a homicidal glance for that he had not in advance put her wise about something called the Twelve and Thirteen. It is also a fact that Miss Fancy would have perished sooner than say to Mrs. Prohack the simple words: "I haven't the slightest idea what the Twelve and Thirteen are." Eve did not disguise her impression that Miss Fancy's lapse was very strange and disturbing.

"I suppose you've seen the new version of the 'Sacre du Printemps,' Miss Fancy," said Mrs. Oswald Morfey, that exceedingly modern and self-possessed young married lady.

"Not yet," said Miss Fancy, and foolishly added: "We were thinking of going to-night."

"There won't be any more performances this season," said Ozzie, that prince of authorities on the universe of entertainment.

And in this way the affair continued between the four, while Mr. Softly Bishop, abandoning his beloved to her fate, chatted murmuringly with Mr. Prohack about the Oil Market, as to which of course Mr. Prohack was the prince of authorities. Mrs. Prohack and her daughter and son-in-law ranged at ease over all the arts without exception, save the one art—that of musical comedy—in which Miss Fancy was versed. Mr. Prohack was amazed at the skilled cruelty of his women. He wanted to say to Miss Fancy: "Don't you believe it! My wife is only a rather nice ordinary housekeeping sort of little woman, and as for my daughter, she cooks her husband's meals—and jolly badly, I bet." He ought to have been pleased at the discomfiture of Miss Fancy, whom he detested and despised; but he was not; he yearned to succour her; he even began to like her.

And not Eve and Sissie alone amazed him. Oswald amazed him. Oswald had changed. His black silk stock had gone the way of his ribboned eye-glass; his hair was arranged differently; he closely resembled an average plain man,—he, the unique Ozzie! With all his faults, he had previously been both good-natured and negligent, but his expression was now one of sternness and of resolute endeavour. Sissie had already metamorphosed him. Even now he was obediently following her lead and her mood. Mr. Prohack's women had evidently determined to revenge themselves for being asked to meet Miss Fancy at lunch, and Ozzie had been set on to assist them. Further, Mr. Prohack noticed that Sissie was eyeing her mother's necklace with a reprehending stare. The next instant he found himself the target of the same stare. The girl was accusing him of folly, while questioning Ozzie's definition of the difference between Georgian and neo-Georgian verse. The girl had apparently become the censor of society at large.

Mysterious cross-currents ran over the table in all directions. Mr. Prohack looked around the noisy restaurant packed with tables, and wondered whether cross-currents were running invisibly over all the tables, and what was the secret force of fashionable fleeting convention which enabled women with brains far inferior to his own to use it effectively for the fighting of sanguinary battles.

At last, when Miss Fancy had been beaten into silence and the other three were carrying on a brilliant high-browed conversation over the corpse of her up-to-dateness, Mr. Prohack's nerves reached the point at which he could tolerate the tragic spectacle no more, and he burst out vulgarly, in a man-in-the-street vein, chopping off the brilliant conversation as with a chopper:

"Now, Miss Fancy, tell us something about yourself."

The common-sounding phrase seemed to be a magic formula endowed with the power to break an awful spell. Miss Fancy gathered herself together, forgot that she had been defeated, and inaugurated a new battle. She began to tell the table not something, but almost everything, about herself, and it soon became apparent that she was no ordinary woman. She had never had a set-back; in innumerable conversational duels she had always given the neat and deadly retort, and she had never been worsted, save by base combinations deliberately engineered against her—generally by women, whom as a sex she despised even more than men. Her sincere belief that no biographical detail concerning Miss Fancy was too small to be uninteresting to the public amounted to a religious creed; and her memory for details was miraculous. She recalled the exact total of the takings at any given performance in which she was prominent in any city of the United States, and she could also give long extracts from the favourable criticisms of countless important American newspapers,—by a singular coincidence only unimportant newspapers had ever mingled blame with their praise of her achievements. She regarded herself with detachment as a remarkable phenomenon, and therefore she could impersonally describe her career without any of the ordinary restraints—just as a shopman might clothe or unclothe a model in his window. Thus she could display her heart and its history quite unreservedly,—did they not belong to the public?

The astounded table learnt that Miss Fancy was illustrious in the press of the United States as having been engaged to be married more often than any other actress. Yet she had never got as far as the altar, though once she had reached the church-door—only to be swept away from it by a cyclone which unhappily finished off the bridegroom. (What grey and tedious existences Eve and Sissie had led!) Her penultimate engagement had been to the late Silas Angmering.

"Something told me I should never be his wife," she said vivaciously. "You know the feeling we women have. And I wasn't much surprised to hear of his death. I'd refused Silas eight times; then in the end I promised to marry him by a certain date. He *wouldn't* take No, poor dear! Well, *he* was a gentleman anyway. Of course it was no more than right that he should put me down in his will, but not every man would have done. In fact it never happened to me before. Wasn't it strange I should have that feeling about never being his wife?"

She glanced eagerly at Mr. Prohack and Mr. Prohack's women, and there was a pause, in which Mr. Softly Bishop said, affectionately regarding his nose:

"Well, my dear, you'll be *my* wife, you'll find," and he uttered this observation in a sharp tone of conviction that made a quite disturbing impression on the whole company, and not least on Mr. Prohack, who kept asking himself more and more insistently:

"Why is Softly Bishop marrying Miss Fancy, and why is Miss Fancy marrying Softly Bishop?"

Mr. Prohack was interrupted in his private enquiry into this enigma by a very unconventional nudge from Sissie, who silently directed his attention to Eve, who seemingly wanted it.

"Your friend seems anxious to speak to you," murmured Eve, in a low, rather roguish voice.

'His friend' was Lady Massulam, who was just concluding a solitary lunch at a near table; he had not noticed her, being still sadly remiss in the business of existing fully in a fashionable restaurant. Lady Massulam's eyes confirmed Eve's statement.

"I'm sure Miss Fancy will excuse you for a moment," said Eve.

"Oh! Please!" implored Miss Fancy, grandly.

Mr. Prohack self-consciously carried his lankness and his big head across to Lady Massulam's table. She looked up at him with a composed but romantic smile. That is to say that Mr. Prohack deemed it romantic; and he leaned over the table and over Lady Massulam in a manner romantic to match.

"I'm just going off," said she.

Simple words, from a portly and mature lady—yet for Mr. Prohack they were charged with all sorts of delicious secondary significances.

"What *is* the difference between her and Eve?" he asked himself, and then replied to the question in a flash of inspiration: "I am romantic to her, and I am not romantic to Eve." He liked this ingenious explanation.

"I wanted to tell you," said she gravely, with beautiful melancholy, "Charles is *flambé*. He is done in. I cannot help him. He will not let me; but if I see him to-night when he returns to town I shall send him to you. He is very young, very difficult, but I shall insist that he goes to you."

"How kind you are!" said Mr. Prohack, touched.

Lady Massulam rose, shook hands, seemed to blush, and departed. An interview as brief as it had been strange! Mr. Prohack was thrilled, not at all by the announcement of Charlie's danger, perhaps humiliation, but by the attitude of Lady Massulam. He had his plans for Charlie. He had no plans affecting Lady Massulam.

Mr. Softly Bishop's luncheon had developed during the short absence of Mr. Prohack. It's splendour, great from the first, had increased; if tables ever do groan, which is perhaps doubtful, the table was certainly groaning; Mr. Softly Bishop was just dismissing, with bland and negligent approval, the major domo of the restaurant, with whom, like all truly important personages, he appeared to be on intimate terms. But the chief development of the luncheon disclosed itself in the conversation. Mr. Softly Bishop had now taken charge of the talk and was expatiating to a hushed and crushed audience his plans for a starring world-tour for his future wife, who listened to them with genuine admiration on her violet-tinted face.

"Eliza won't be in it with me when I come back," she exclaimed suddenly, with deep conviction, with anticipatory bliss, with a kind of rancorous ferocity.

Mr. Prohack understood. Miss Fancy was uncompromisingly jealous of her half-sister's renown. To outdo that renown was the main object of her life, and Mr. Softly Bishop's claim on her lay in the fact that he had shown her how to accomplish her end and was taking charge of the arrangements. Mr. Softly Bishop was her trainer and her manager; he had dazzled her by the variety and ingenuity of his resourceful schemes; and his power over her was based on a continual implied menace that if she did not strictly obey all his behests she would fail to realise her supreme desire.

And when Mr. Softly Bishop gradually drew Ozzie into a technical tête-à-tête, Mr. Prohack understood further why Ozzie had been invited to the feast. Upon certain branches of Mr. Bishop's theatrical schemes Ozzie was an acknowledged expert, and Mr. Bishop was obtaining, for the price of a luncheon, the fruity knowledge and wisdom acquired by Ozzie during long years of close attention to business.

For Mr. Prohack it was an enthralling scene. The luncheon closed gorgeously upon the finest cigars and cigarettes, the finest coffee, and the finest liqueurs that the unique establishment could provide. Sissie refused every allurement except coffee, and Miss Fancy was permitted nothing but coffee.

"Do not forget your throat, my dear," Mr. Softly Bishop authoritatively interjected into Miss Fancy's circumstantial recital of the expensiveness of the bouquets which had been hurled at her in the New National Theatre at Washington.

"And by the way," (looking at his watch), "do not forget the appointment with the elocutionist."

"But aren't you coming with me?" demanded Miss Fancy alarmed. Already she was learning the habit of helplessness—so attractive to men and so useful to them.

These remarks broke up the luncheon party, which all the guests assured the deprecating host had been perfectly delightful, with the implied addition that it had also constituted the crown and summit of their careers. Eve and Sissie were prodigious in superlatives to such an extent that Mr. Prohack began to fear for Mr. Softly Bishop's capacity to assimilate the cruder forms of flattery. His fear, however, was unnecessary. When the host and his beloved departed Miss Fancy was still recounting tit-bits of her biography.

"But I'll tell you the rest another time," she cried from the moving car.

She had emphatically won the second battle. From the first blow she had never even looked like losing. And she had shown no mercy, quite properly following the maxim that war is war. Eve and Sissie seemed to rise with difficulty to their knees, after the ruthless adversary, tired of standing on their prostrate form, had scornfully walked away.

III

"Well!" sighed Mrs. Prohack, with the maximum of expressiveness, glancing at her daughter as one woman of the world at another. They were lingering, as it were convalescent after the severe attack and defeat, in the foyer of the hotel.

"Well!" sighed Sissie, flattered by the glance, and firmly taking her place in the fabric of society. "Well, father, we always knew you had some queer friends, but really these were the limit! And the extravagance of the thing! That luncheon must have cost at least twenty pounds,—and I do believe he had special flowers, too. When I think of the waste of money and time that goes on daily in places like these, I wonder there's any England left. It ought to be stopped by law."

"My child," said Mr. Prohack. "I observe with approbation that you are beginning to sit up and take notice. Centuries already divide you from the innocent creature who used to devote her days and nights to the teaching of dancing to persons who had no conception of the seriousness of life. I agree with your general criticism, but let us remember that all this wickedness does not date from the day before yesterday. It's been flourishing for some thousands of years, and all prophecies about it being overtaken by Nemesis have proved false. Still, I'm glad you've turned over a new leaf."

Sissie discreetly but unmistakably tossed her young head.

"Oswald, dearest," said she. "It's time you were off."

"It is," Ozzie agreed, and off he went, to resume the serious struggle for existence,—he who until quite recently had followed the great theatrical convention that though space may be a reality, time is not.

"I don't mind the extravagance, because after all it's good for trade," said Eve. "What I—"

"Mother darling!" Sissie protested. "Where do you get these extraordinary ideas from about luxury being good for trade? Surely you ought to know—"

"I daresay I ought to know all sorts of things I don't know," said Eve with dignity. "But there's one thing I do know, and that is that the style of those two dreadful people was absolutely the worst I've ever met. The way that woman gabbled—and all about herself; and what an accent, and the way she held her fork!"

"Lady," said Mr. Prohack. "Don't be angry because she beat you."

"Beat me!"

"Yes. Beat you. Both of you. You talked her to a standstill at first; but you couldn't keep it up. Then she began and she talked you to a standstill, and she could keep it up. She left you for all practical purposes dead on the field, my tigresses. And I'm very sorry for her," he added.

"Dad," said Sissie sternly. "Why do you always try to be so clever with us? You know as well as we do that she's a *creature,* and that there's nothing to be said for her at all."

"Nothing to be said for her!" Mr. Prohack smiled tolerantly. "Why she was the star of the universe for Silas Angmering, the founder of our fortunes. She was the finest woman he'd ever met. And Angmering was a clever fellow, let me tell you. You call her a creature. Yes, the creature of destiny, like all of us, except of course you. I beg to inform you that Miss Fancy went out of this hotel a victim, an unconscious victim, but a victim. She is going to be exploited. Mr. Softly Bishop, my co-heir, will run her for all she is worth. He will make a lot of money out of her. He will make her work as she has never worked before. He will put a value on all her talents, for his own ends. And he will deprive her of most of her accustomed pleasures. In fifteen years there'll be nothing left of Miss Fancy except an exhausted wreck with a spurious reputation, but Mr. Softly Bishop will still be in his prime and in the full enjoyment of life, and he will spend on himself the riches that she has made for him and allow her about sixpence a week; and the most tragic and terrible thing of all is that she will think she owes everything to him! No! If I was capable of weeping, I should have wept at the pathos of the spectacle of Miss Fancy as she left us just now unconscious of her fate and revelling in the most absurd illusions. That poor defenceless woman, who has had the misfortune not to please you, is heading straight for a life-long martyrdom." Mr. Prohack ceased impressively.

"And serve her right!" said Eve. "I've met cats in my time, but—" And Eve also ceased.

"And I am not sure," added Mr. Prohack, still impressively, "And I am not sure that the ingenuous and excellent Oswald Morfey is not heading straight in the same direction." And he gazed at his adored daughter, who exhibited a faint flush, and then laughed lightly. "Yes," said Mr. Prohack, "you are very smart, my girl. If you had shown violence you would have made a sad mistake. That you should laugh with such a brilliant imitation of naturalness gives me hopes of you. Let us seek Carthew and the car. Mr. Bishop's luncheon, though I admit it was exceedingly painful, has, I trust, not been without its useful lessons to us, and I do not regret it. For myself I admit it has taught me that even the finest and most agreeable women, such as those with whom I have been careful to sourround myself in my domestic existence, are monsters of cruelty. Not that I care."

"I've arranged with mamma that you shall come to dinner to-night," said Sissie. "No formality, please."

"Mayn't your mother wear her pearls?" asked Mr. Prohack.

"I hope you noticed, Arthur," said Eve with triumphant satisfaction, "how your Miss Fancy was careful to keep off the subject of jewels."

"Mother's pearls," said Sissie primly, "are mother's affair."

Mr. Prohack did not feel at all happy.

"And yet," he asked himself. "What have I done? I am perfectly innocent."

IV

"I never in all my life," said Sissie, "saw you eat so much, dad. And I think it's a great compliment to my cooking. In fact I'm bursting with modest pride."

"Well," replied Mr. Prohack, who had undoubtedly eaten rather too much, "take it how you like. I do believe I could do with a bit more of this stuff that imitates an omelette but obviously isn't one."

"Oh! But there isn't any more!" said Sissie, somewhat dashed.

"No more! Good heavens! Then have you got some cheese, or anything of that sort?"

"No. I don't keep cheese in the place. You see, the smell of it in these little flats—"

"Any bread? Anything at all?"

"I'm afraid we've finished up pretty nearly all there was, except Ozzie's egg for breakfast to-morrow morning."

"This is serious," observed Mr. Prohack, tapping enquiringly the superficies of his digestive apparatus.

"Arthur!" cried Eve. "Why are you such a tease to-night? You're only trying to make the child feel awkward. You know you've had quite enough. And I'm sure it was all very cleverly cooked—considering. You'll be ill in the middle of the night if you keep on, and then I shall have to get up and look after you, as usual." Eve had the air of defending her daughter, but something, some reserve in her voice, showed that she was defending, not her daughter, but merely and generally the whole race of housewives against the whole race of consuming and hypercritical males; she was even defending the Eve who had provided much-criticised meals in the distant past. Such was her skill that she could do this while implying, so subtly yet so effectively, that Sissie, the wicked, shameless, mamma-scorning bride, was by no means forgiven in the secret heart of the mother.

"You are doubtless right, lady," Mr. Prohack agreed. "You always could judge better than I could myself when I had had enough, and what would be the ultimate consequences of my eating. And as for your lessons in manners, what an ill-bred lout I was before I met you, and what an impossible person I should have been had you not taken me in hand night and day for all these years! It isn't that I'm worse than the average husband; it is merely that wives are the sole repositories of the civilising influence. Were it not for them we should still be tearing steaks to pieces with our fingers. I daresay I have eaten enough—anyhow I've had far more than anybody else—and even if I hadn't, it would not be at all nice of me not to pretend that I hadn't. And after all, if the worst comes to the worst, I can always have a slice of cold beef and a glass of beer when I get home, can't I?"

Sissie, though blushing ever so little, maintained an excellent front. She certainly looked dainty and charming,—more specifically so than she had ever looked; indeed, utterly the young bride. She was in morning dress, to comply with her own edict against formality, and also to mark her new, enthusiastic disapproval of the modern craze for luxurious display; but it was a delightful, if inexpensive, dress. She had taken considerable trouble over the family dinner, devising, concocting, cooking, and presiding over it from beginning to end, and being consistently bright, wise, able, and resourceful throughout—an apostle of chafing-dish cookery determined to prove that chafing-dish cookery combined efficiency, toothsomeness and economy to a degree never before known. And she had neatly pointed out more than once that waste was impossible under her system and that, servants being dispensed with, the great originating cause of waste had indeed been radically removed. She had not informed her guests of the precise cost in money of the unprecedentedly cheap and nourishing meal, but she had come near to doing so; and she would surely have indicated that there had been neither too much nor too little, but just amply sufficient, had not her absurd and contrarious father displayed a not uncharacteristic lack of tact at the closing stage of the ingenious collation.

Moreover, she seemed, despite her generous build, to have somehow fitted herself to the small size of the flat. She did not dwarf it, as clumsier women are apt to dwarf their tiny homes in the centre of London. On the contrary she gave to it the illusion of spaciousness; and beyond question she had in a surprisingly short time transformed it from a bachelor's flat into a conjugal nest, cushiony, flowery, knicknacky, and perilously seductive to the eye without being too reassuring to the limbs.

Mr. Prohack was accepting a cigarette, having been told that Ozzie never smoked cigars, when there was a great ring which filled the entire flat as the last trump may be expected to fill the entire earth, and Mr. Prohack dropped the cigarette, muttering:

"I think I'll smoke that afterwards."

"Good gracious!" the flat mistress exclaimed. "I wonder who that can be. Just go and see, Ozzie, darling." And she looked at Ozzie as if to say: "I hope it isn't one of your indiscreet bachelor friends."

Ozzie hastened obediently out.

"It may be Charlie," ventured Eve. "Wouldn't it be nice if he called?"

"Yes, wouldn't it?" Sissie agreed. "I did 'phone him up to try to get him to dinner, but naturally he was away for the day. He's always as invisible as a millionaire nowadays. Besides I feel somehow this place would be too much, too humble, for the mighty Charles. Buckingham Palace would be more in his line. But we can't all be speculators and profiteers."

"Sissie!" protested their mother mildly.

After mysterious and intriguing noises at the front-door had finished, and the front-door had made the whole flat vibrate to its bang, Ozzie puffed into the room with three packages, the two smaller being piled upon the third.

"They're addressed to you," said Ozzie to his father-in-law.

"Did you give the man anything?" Sissie asked quickly.

"No, it was Carthew and the parlourmaid—Machin, is her name?"

"Oh!" said Sissie, apparently relieved.

"Now let us see," said Mr. Prohack, starting at once upon the packages.

"Don't waste that string, dad," Sissie enjoined him anxiously.

"Eh? What do you say?" murmured Mr. Prohack, carefully cutting string on all sides of all packages, and tearing first-rate brown paper into useless strips. He produced from the packages four bottles of champagne of four different brands, a quantity of pâté de foie gras, a jar of caviare, and several bunches of grapes that must have been grown under the most unnatural and costly conditions.

"What ever's this?" Sissie demanded, uneasily.

"Arthur!" said Eve. "Whatever's the meaning of this?"

"It has a deep significance," replied Mr. Prohack. "The only fault I have to find with it is that it has arrived rather late—and yet perhaps, like Blücher, not too late. You can call it a wedding present if you choose, daughter. Or if you choose you can call it simply caviare, pâté de foie gras, grapes and champagne. I really have not had the courage to give you a wedding present," he continued, "knowing how particular you are about ostentation. But I thought if I sent something along that we could all join in consuming instantly, I couldn't possibly do any harm."

"We haven't any champagne glasses," said Sissie coldly.

"Champagne glasses, child! You ought never to drink champagne out of champagne glasses. Tumblers are the only thing for champagne. Some tumblers, Ozzie. And a tin-opener. You must have a tin-opener. I feel convinced you have a tin-opener. Upon my soul, Eve, I was right after all. I *am* hungry, but my hunger is nothing to my thirst. I'm beginning to suspect that I must be the average sensual man."

"Arthur!" Eve warned him. "If you eat any of that caviare you're bound to be ill."

"Not if I mix it with pâté de foi gras, my pet. It is notorious that they are mutual antidotes, especially when followed by the grape cure. Now, ladies and Ozzie, don't exasperate me by being coy. Fall to! Ingurgitate. Ozzie, be a man for a change." Mr. Prohack seemed to intimidate everybody to such an extent that Sissie herself went off to secure tumblers.

"But why are you opening another bottle, father?" she asked in alarm on her return. "This one isn't half empty."

"We shall try all four brands," said Mr. Prohack.

"But what a waste!"

"Know, my child," said Mr. Prohack, with marked and solemn sententiousness. "Know that in an elaborately organised society, waste has its moral uses. Know further that nothing is more contrary to the truth than the proverb that enough is as good as a feast. Know still further that though the habit of wastefulness may have its dangers, it is not nearly so dangerous as the habit of self-righteousness, or as the habit of nearness, both of which contract the soul until it's more like a prune than a plum. Be a plum, my child, and let who will be a prune."

It was at this moment that Eve showed her true greatness.

"Come along, Sissie," said she, after an assaying glance at her husband and another at her daughter. "Let's humour him. It isn't often he's in such good spirits, is it?"

Sissie's face cleared, and with a wisdom really beyond her years she accepted the situation, the insult, the reproof, the lesson. As for Mr. Prohack, he felt happier, more gay, than he had felt all day,—not as the effect of champagne and caviare, but as the effect of the realisation of his prodigious sagacity in having foreseen that Sissie's hospitality would be what it had been. He was glad also that his daughter had displayed commonsense, and he began to admire her again, and in proportion as she perceived that he was admiring her, so she consciously increased her charm; for the fact was, she was very young, very impressionable, very anxious to do the right thing.

"Have another glass, Ozzie," urged Mr. Prohack.

Ozzie looked at his powerful bride for guidance.

"Do have another glass, you darling old silly," said the bride.

"There will be no need to open the other two bottles," said Mr. Prohack. "Indeed, I need only have opened one. . . . I shall probably call here again soon."

At this point there was another ring at the front-door.

"So you've condescended!" Sissie greeted Charles when Ozzie brought him into the room, and then, catching her father's eye and being anxious to rest secure in the paternal admiration, she added: "Anyway it was very decent of you to come. I know how busy you are."

Charles raised his eyebrows at this astonishing piece of sisterliness. His mother kissed him fondly, having received from Mr. Prohack during the day the delicatest, filmiest hint that perhaps Charlie was not at the moment fabulously prospering.

"Your father is very gay to-night," said she, gazing at Charlie as though she read into the recesses of his soul and could see a martyrdom there, though in fact she could not penetrate any further than the boy's eyeballs.

"I beg you to note," Mr. Prohack remarked. "That as the glasses have only been filled once, and three of them are at least a quarter full, only the equivalent of two and a half champagne glasses has actually been drunk by four people, which will not explain much gaiety. If the old gentleman is gay, and he does not assert that he is not, the true reason lies in either the caviare or the pâté de foie gras, or in his crystal conscience. Have a drink, Charles?"

"Finish mine, my pet," said Eve, holding forth her tumbler, and Charlie obeyed.

"A touching sight," observed Mr. Prohack. "Now as Charlie has managed to spare us a few minutes out of his thrilling existence, I want to have a few words with him in private about an affair of state. There's nothing that you oughtn't to hear," he addressed the company, "but a great deal that you probably wouldn't understand—and the last thing we desire is to humiliate you. That's so, isn't it, Carlos?"

"It is," Charles quickly agreed, without a sign of self-consciousness.

"Now then, hostess, can you lend us another room,—boudoir, morning-room, smoking-room, card-room, even ball-room; anything will do for us. Possibly Ozzie's study. . . . "

"Father! Father!" Sissie warned him against an excess of facetiousness. "You can either go into our bedroom or you can sit on the stairs, and talk."

As father and son disappeared together into the bedroom, which constituted a full half of the entire flat, Mr. Prohack noticed on his wife's features an expression of anxiety tempered by an assured confidence in his own wisdom and force. He knew indeed that he had made quite a favourable sensation by his handling of Sissie's tendency to a hard austerity.

Nevertheless, when Charles shut the door of the chamber and they were enclosed together, Mr. Prohack could feel his mighty heart beating in a manner worthy of a schoolgirl entering an examination room. The chamber had apparently been taken bodily out of a doll's house and furnished with furniture manufactured for pigmies. It was very full, presenting the aspect of a room in a warehouse. Everything in it was 'bijou,' in the trade sense, and everything harmonised in a charming Japanese manner with everything else, except an extra truckle-bed, showing crude iron feet under a blazing counterpane borrowed from a Russian ballet, which second bed had evidently just been added for the purposes of conjugal existence. The dressing-table alone was unmistakably symptomatic of a woman. Some of Ozzie's wondrous trousers hung from stretchers behind the door, and the inference was that these had been displaced from the wardrobe in favour of Sissie's frocks. It was all highly curious and somewhat pathetic; and Mr. Prohack, contemplating, became anew a philosopher as he realised that the tiny apartment was the true expression of his daughter's individuality and volition. She had imposed this crowded inconvenience upon her willing spouse,—and there was the grandiose Charles, for whom the best was never good enough, sitting down nonchalantly on the truckle-bed; and it appeared to Mr. Prohack only a few weeks ago that the two children had been playing side by side in the same nursery and giving never a sign that their desires and destinies would be so curious. Mr. Prohack felt absurdly helpless. True, he was the father, but he knew that he had nothing whatever to do, beyond trifling gifts of money and innumerable fairly witty sermons—divided about equally between the pair, with the evolution of those mysterious and fundamentally uncontrollable beings, his son and his daughter. The enigma of life pressed disturbingly upon him, as he took the other bed, facing Charles, and he wondered whether Sissie in her feminine passion for self-sacrifice insisted on sleeping in the truckle-contraption herself, or whether she permitted Ozzie to be uncomfortable.

V

"I just came along," Charlie opened simply, "because Lady M. was so positive that I ought to see you—she said that you very much wanted me to come. It isn't as if I wanted to bother you, or you could do any good."

He spoke in an extremely low tone, almost in a whisper, and Mr. Prohack comprehended that the youth was trying to achieve privacy in a domicile where all conversation and movements were necessarily more or less public to the whole flat. Charles's restraint, however, showed little or no depression, disappointment, or disgust, and no despair.

"But what's it all about? If I'm not being too curious," Mr. Prohack enquired cautiously.

"It's all about my being up the spout, dad. I've had a flutter, and it hasn't come off, and that's all there is to it. I needn't trouble you with the details. But you may believe me when I tell you that I shall bob up again. What's happened to me might have happened to anybody, and has happened to a pretty fair number of City swells."

"You mean bankruptcy?"

"Well, yes, bankruptcy's the word. I'd much better go right through with it. The chit thinks so, and I agree."

"The chit?"

"Mimi."

"Oh! So you call her that, do you?"

"No, I never call her that. But that's how I think of her. I call her Miss Winstock. I'm glad you let me have her. She's been very useful, and she's going to stick by me — not that there's any blooming sentimental nonsense about her! Oh, no! By the way, I know the mater and Sis think she's a bit harum-scarum, and you do, too. Nevertheless she was just as strong as Lady M. that I should stroll up and confess myself. She said it was *due* to you. Lady M. didn't put it quite like that."

The truckle-bed creaked as Charlie shifted uneasily. They caught a faint murmur of talk from the other room, and Sissie's laugh.

"Lady Massulam happened to tell me once that you'd been selling something before you knew how much it would cost you to buy it. Of course I don't pretend to understand finance myself—I'm only a civil servant on the shelf—but to my limited intelligence such a process of putting the cart before the horse seemed likely to lead to trouble," said Mr. Prohack, as it were ruminating.

"Oh! She told you that, did she?" Charlie smiled. "Well, the good lady was talking through her hat. *That* affair's all right. At least it would be if I could carry it through, but of course I can't now. It'll go into the general mess. If I was free, I wouldn't sell it at all; I'd keep it; there'd be no end of money in it, and I was selling it too cheap. It's a combine, or rather it would have been a combine, of two of the best paper mills in the country, and if I'd got it, and could find time to manage it,—my word, you'd see! No! What's done me in is a pure and simple Stock Exchange gamble, my dear father. Nothing but that! R. R. shares."

"R. R. What's that?"

"Dad! Where have you been living these years? Royal Rubber Corporation, of course. They dropped to eighteen shillings, and they oughtn't to have done. I bought a whole big packet on the understanding that I should have a fortnight to fork out. They were bound to go up again. Hadn't been so low for eleven years. How could I have foreseen that old Sampler would go and commit suicide and make a panic?"

"I never read the financial news, except the quotations of my own little savings, and I've never heard of old Sampler," said Mr. Prohack.

"Considering he was a front-page item for four days!" Charlie exclaimed, raising his voice, and then dropping it again. And he related in a few biting phrases the recent history of the R. R. "I wouldn't have minded so much," he went on. "If your particular friend, Mr. Softly Bishop, wasn't at the bottom of my purchase. His name only appears for some of the shares, but I've got a pretty good idea that it's he who's selling all of them to yours truly. He must have known something, and a rare fine thing he'd have made of the deal if I wasn't going bust, because I'm sure now he was selling to me what he hadn't got."

Mr. Prohack's whole demeanour changed at the mention of Mr. Bishop's name. His ridiculous snobbish pride reared itself up within him. He simply could not bear the idea of Softly Bishop having anything 'against' a member of his family. Sooner would the inconsistent fellow have allowed innocent widows and orphans to be ruined through Charlie's plunging than that Softly Bishop should fail to realise a monstrous profit through the same agency.

"I'll see you through, my lad," said he, briefly, in an ordinary casual tone.

"No thanks. You won't," Charlie replied. "I wouldn't let you, even if you could. But you can't. It's too big."

"Ah! How big is it?" Mr. Prohack challengingly raised his chin.

"Well, if you want to know the truth, it's between a hundred and forty and a hundred and fifty thousand pounds. I mean, that's what I should need to save the situation."

"You?" cried the Terror of the departments in amaze, accustomed though he was to dealing in millions. He had gravely miscalculated his son. Ten thousand he could have understood;

even twenty thousand. But a hundred and fifty . . . ! "You must have been mad!"

"Only because I've failed," said Charles. "Yes. It'll be a great affair. It'll really make my name. Everybody will expect me to bob up again, and I shan't disappoint them. Of course some people will say I oughtn't to have been extravagant. Grand Babylon Hotel and so on. What rot! A flea-bite! Why, my expenses haven't been seven hundred a month."

Mr. Prohack sat aghast; but admiration was not absent from his sentiments. The lad was incredible in the scale of his operations; he was unreal, wagging his elegant leg so calmly there in the midst of all that fragile Japanese lacquer—and the family, grotesquely unconscious of the vastness of the issues, chatting domestically only a few feet away. But Mr. Prohack was not going to be outdone by his son, however Napoleonic his son might be. He would maintain his prestige as a father.

"I'll see you through," he repeated, with studied quietness.

"But look here, dad. You only came into a hundred thousand. I can't have you ruining yourself. And even if you did ruin yourself—"

"I have no intention of ruining myself," said Mr. Prohack. "Nor shall I change in the slightest degree my mode of life. You don't know everything, my child. You aren't the only person on earth who can make money. Where do you imagine you get your gifts from? Your mother?"

"But—"

"Be silent. To-morrow morning gilt-edged, immediately saleable securities will be placed at your disposal for a hundred and fifty thousand pounds. I never indulge in wildcat stock myself. And let me tell you there can be no question of *your* permitting or not permitting. I'm your father, and please don't forget it. It doesn't happen to suit me that my infant prodigy of a son should make a mess of his career; and I won't have it. If there's any doubt in your mind as to whether you or I are the strongest, rule yourself out of the competition this instant,—it'll save you trouble in the end."

Mr. Prohack had never felt so happy in his life; and yet he had had moments of intense happiness in the past. He could feel the skin of his face burning.

"You'll get it all back, dad," said Charlie later. "No amount of suicides can destroy the assets of the R. R. It's only that the market lost its head and absolutely broke to pieces under me. In three months—"

"My poor boy," Mr. Prohack interrupted him. "Do try not to be an ass." And he had the pleasing illusion that Charles was just home from school. "And, mind, not one word, not one word, to anybody whatever."

VI

The other three were still modestly chatting in the living-room when the two great mysterious men of affairs returned to them, but Sissie had cleared the dining-room table and transformed the place into a drawing-room for the remainder of the evening. They were very feminine; even Ozzie had something of the feminine attitude of fatalistic attending upon events beyond feminine control; he had it, indeed, far more than the vigorous-minded Sissie had it. They were cheerful, with a cheerfulness that made up in tact what it lacked in sincerity. Mr. Prohack compared them to passengers on a ship which is in danger. With a word, with an inflection, he reassured everybody—and yet said naught—and the cheerfulness instantly became genuine.

Mr. Prohack was surprised at the intensity of his own feelings. He was thoroughly thrilled by what he himself had done. Perhaps he had gone too far in telling Charlie that the putting down of a hundred and fifty thousand pounds could be accomplished without necessitating any change in his manner of living; but he did not care what change might be involved. He had the sense of having performed a huge creative act, and of the reality of the power of riches,—for weeks he had not been imaginatively cognisant of the fact that he was rich.

He glanced secretly at the boy Charles, and said to himself: "To that boy I am like a god. He was dead, and I have resurrected him. He may achieve an enormous reputation after all. Anyhow he is an amazing devil of a fellow, and he's my son, and no one comprehends him as I do." And Mr. Prohack became jolly to the point of uproariousness—without touching a glass. He was intoxicated, not by the fermentation of grapes, but by the magnitude and magnificence of his own gesture. He was the monarch of the company, and getting a bit conceited about it.

The sole creature who withstood him in any degree was Sissie. She had firmness. "She has married the right man," said Mr. Prohack to himself. "The so-called feminine instinct is for the most part absurd, but occasionally it justifies its reputation. She has chosen her husband with unerring insight into her needs and

HARRIS PUBLIC LIBRARY PRESTON

his. He will be happy; she will have the anxieties of responsible power. But *I* am not her husband." And he spoke aloud, masterfully:

"Sissie!"

"Yes, dad? What now?"

"I've satisfactorily transacted affairs with my son. I will now try to do the same with my daughter. A few moments with you in the council-chamber, please. Oswald also, if you like."

Sissie smiled kindly at her awaiting spouse.

"Perhaps I'd better deal with my own father alone, darling."

Ozzie accepted the decision.

"Look here. I think I must be off," Charlie put in. "I've got a lot of work to do."

"I expect you have," Mr. Prohack concurred. "By the way, you might meet me at Smathe and Smathe's at ten fifteen in the morning."

Charlie nodded and slipped away.

"Infant," said Mr. Prohack to the defiantly smiling bride who awaited him in the council chamber. "Has your mother said anything to you about our wedding present?"

"No, dad."

"No, of course she hasn't. And do you know why? Because she daren't! With your infernal independence you've frightened the life out of the poor lady; that's what you've done. Your mother will doubtless have a talk with me to-night. And to-morrow she will tell you what she has decided to give you. Please let there be no nonsense. Whatever the gift is, I shall be obliged if you will accept it—and use it, without troubling us with any of your theories about the proper conduct of life. Wisdom and righteousness existed before you, and there's just a chance that they'll exist after you. Do you take me?"

"Quite, father."

"Good. You may become a great girl yet. We are now going home. Thanks for a very pleasant evening."

In the car, beautifully alone with Eve, who was in a restful mood, Mr. Prohack said:

"I shall be very ill in a few hours. Pâté de foi gras is the devil, but caviare is Beelzebub himself."

Eve merely gazed at him in gentle, hopeless reproach. He prophesied truly. He was very ill. And yet through the succeeding crises he kept smiling, sardonically.

"When I think," he murmured once with grimness, "that that

fellow Bishop had the impudence to ask us to lunch—and Charlie too! Charlie too!" Eve, attendant, enquired sadly what he was talking about.

"Nothing, nothing," said he. "My mind is wandering. Let it."

CHAPTER XXIII

THE YACHT

I

Mr. Prohack was lounging over his breakfast in the original old house in the Square behind Hyde Park. He came to be there because that same house had been his wedding present to Sissie, who now occupied it with her spouse, and because the noble mansion in Manchester Square was being re-decorated (under compulsion of some clause in the antique lease) and Eve had invited him to leave the affair entirely to her. In the few months since Charlie's great crisis, all things conspired together to prove once more to Mr. Prohack that calamities expected never arrive. Even the British Empire had continued to cohere, and revolution seemed to be further off than ever before. The greatest menace to his peace of mind, the League of all the Arts, had of course quietly ceased to exist; but it had established Eve as a hostess. And Eve as a hostess had gradually given up boring herself and her husband by large and stiff parties, and they had gone back to entertaining none but well-established and intimate friends with the maximum of informality as of old,—to such an extent that occasionally in the vast and gorgeous dining-room of the noble mansion Eve would have the roast planted on the table and would carve it herself, also as of old; Brool did not seem to mind.

Mr. Prohack had bought the lease of the noble mansion, with all the contents thereof, merely because this appeared to be the easiest thing to do. He had not been forced to change his manner of life; far from it. Owing to a happy vicissitude in the story of the R. R. Corporation Charlie had called upon his father for only a very small portion of the offered one hundred and fifty thousand pounds, and had even repaid that within a few weeks. Matters had thereafter come to such a pass with Charlie that he had reached the pages of *The Daily Picture,* and was reputed to be arousing the jealousy of youthful millionaires in the United States; also the figure which he paid weekly for rent of his offices in the Grand Babylon Hotel was an item of common knowledge in the best clubs and not to know it was to be behind the times in current information. No member of his family now ventured to offer advice to Charlie, who still, however, looked astonishingly like the old Charlie of motor-bicycle transactions.

The fact is, people do not easily change. Mr. Prohack had seemed to change for a space, but if indeed any change had occurred in him, he had changed back. Scientific idleness? Turkish baths? Dandyism? All vanished, contemned, forgotten. To think of them merely annoyed him. He did not care what necktie he wore. Even dancing had gone the same way. The dancing season was over until October, and he knew he would never begin again. He cared not to dance with the middle-aged, and if he danced with the young he felt that he was making a fool of himself.

It had been rather a lark to come and stay for a few days in his old home,—to pass the sacred door of the conjugal bedroom (closed for ever to him) and mount to Charlie's room, into which Sissie had put the bulk of the furniture from the Japanese flat—without overcrowding it. Decidedly amusing to sleep in Charlie's old little room! But the romantic sensation had given way to the sensation of the hardness of the bed.

Breakfast achieved, Mr. Prohack wondered what he should do next, for he had nothing to do; he had no worries, and almost no solicitudes; he had successfully adapted himself to his environment. Through the half-open door of the dining-room he heard Sissie and Ozzie. Ozzie was off to the day's business, and Sissie was seeing him out of the house, as Eve used to see Mr. Prohack out. Ozzie, by reason of a wedding present of ten thousand pounds given in defiance of Sissie's theories, and with the help of his own savings, was an important fellow now in the theatrical world, having attained a partnership with the Napoleon of the stage.

"You'd no business to send for the doctor without telling me," Sissie was saying in her harsh tone. "What do I want with a doctor?"

"I thought it would be for the best, dear," came Ozzie's lisping reply.

"Well, it won't, my boy."

The door banged.

"Eve never saw me off like that," Mr. Prohack reflected.

Sissie entered the room, some letters in her hand. She was exceedingly attractive, matron-like, interesting—but formidable.

Said Mr. Prohack, glancing up at her:

"It is the duty of the man to protect and the woman to charm—and I don't care who knows it."

"What on earth do you mean, dad?"

"I mean that it is the duty of the man to protect and the woman to *charm*."

Sissie flushed.

"Ozzie and I understand each other, but you don't," said she, and made a delicious rude face. "Carthew's brought these letters and he's waiting for orders about the car." She departed.

Among the few letters was one from Softly Bishop, dated Rangoon. It was full of the world-tour. "We had a success at Calcutta that really does baffle description," it said.

"'We!'" commented Mr. Prohack. There was a postcript: "By the way, I've only just learnt that it was your son who was buying those Royal Rubber shares. I do hope he was not inconvenienced. I need not say that if I had had the slightest idea who was standing the racket I should have waived—" And so on.

"Would you!" commented Mr. Prohack. "I see you doing it. And what's more I bet you only wrote the letter for the sake of the postcript. Your tour is not a striking success, and you'll be wanting to do business with me when you come back, but you won't do it. . . . And here I am lecturing Sissie about hardness!"

He rang the bell and told a servant who was a perfect stranger to him to tell Carthew that he should not want the car.

"May Carthew speak to you, sir?" said the servant returning.

"Carthew may," said he, and the servant thought what an odd gentleman Mr. Prohack was.

"Well, Carthew," said he, when the chauffeur, perturbed, entered the room. "This is quite like old times, isn't it? Sit down and have a cigarette. What's wrong?"

"Well, sir," replied Carthew, after he had lighted the cigarette and ejected a flake of tobacco into the hearth. "There may be something wrong or there mayn't, if you understand what I mean. But I'm thinking of getting married."

"Oh! But what about that wife of yours?"

"Oh! Her! She's dead, all right. I never said anything, feeling as it might be ashamed of her."

"But I thought you'd done with women?"

"So did I, sir. But the question always is, Have women done with you? I was helping her to lift pictures down yesterday, and she was standing on a chair. And something came over me. And there you are before you know where you are, sir, if you understand what I mean."

"Perfectly, Carthew. But who is it?"

"Machin, sir. To cut a long story short, sir, I'd been thinking about her for the better part of some time, because of the boy, sir, because of the boy. She likes him. If it hadn't been for the boy—"

"Careful, Carthew!"

"Well, perhaps you're right, sir. She'd have copped me anyway."

"I congratulate you, Carthew. You've been copped by the best parlourmaid in London."

"Thank you, sir. I think I'll be getting along, sir."

"Have you told Mrs. Prohack?"

"I thought I'd best leave that to Machin, sir."

Mr. Prohack waved a hand, thoughtful. He heard Carthew leave. He heard Dr. Veiga arrive, and then he heard Dr. Veiga leaving, and rushed to the dining-room door.

"Veiga! A moment. Come in. Everything all right?"

"Of course. Absolutely normal. But you know what these young husbands are. I can't stop unless you're really ill, my friend."

"I'm worse than really ill," said Mr. Prohack, shuttting the door. "I'm really bored. I'm surrounded by the most interesting phenomena and I'm really bored. I've taken to heart all your advice and I'm really bored. So there!"

The agreeable, untidy, unprofessional Portuguese quack twinkled at him, and then said in his thick, southern, highly un-English voice: "The remedy may be worse than the disease. You are bored because you have no worries, my friend. I will give you advice. Go back to your Treasury."

"I cannot," said Mr. Prohack. "I've resigned. I found out that my friend Hunter was expecting promotion in my place."

"Ah, well!" replied Dr. Veiga with strange sardonic indifference. "If you will sacrifice yourself to your frends you must take the consequences like a man. I will talk to you some other time, when I've got nothing better to do. I am very busy, telling people what they already know." And he went.

A minute later Charlie arrived in a car suitable to his grandeur.

"Look here, dad," said Charlie in a hurry. "If you're game for a day out I particularly want to show you something. And incidentally you'll see some driving, believe me!"

"My will is made! I am game," answered Mr. Prohack, delighted at the prospect of any diversion, however perilous.

II

When Charlie drew up at the Royal Pier, Southampton (having reached there in rather less time than the train journey and a taxi at each end would have required), he silently handed over the wheel to the chauffeur, and led his mystified but unenquiring father down the steps on the west side of the pier. A man in a blue suit with a peaked cap and a white cover on the cap was standing at the foot of the steps, just above the water and above a motor-launch containing two other men in blue jerseys with the name "Northwind" on their breasts and on their foreheads. A blue ensign was flying at the stern of the launch.

"How d'ye do, Snow?" Charlie greeted the first man, who raised his cap.

Father and son got into the launch and the man after them: the launch began to snort, and off it went at a racing speed from the pier towards midchannel. Mr. Prohack, who said not a word, perceived a string of vessels of various sizes which he judged to be private yachts, though he had no experience whatever of yachts. Some of them flew bunting and some of them didn't; but they all without exception appeared, as Mr. Prohack would have expected, to be the very symbols of complicated elegance and luxury, shining and glittering buoyantly there on the brilliant blue water under the summer sun. The launch was rushing headlong through its own white surge towards the largest of these majestic toys. As it approached the string Mr. Prohack saw that all the yachts were much larger than he imagined, and that the largest was enormous. The launch flicked itself round the stern of that yacht, upon which Mr. Prohack read the word "Northwind" in gold, and halted bobbing at a staircase whose rails were white ropes, slung against a dark blue wall; the wall was the side of the yacht. Mr. Prohack climbed out of the bobbing launch, and the staircase had the solidity under his feet of masonry on earth. High up, glancing over the wall, was a capped face.

"How d'ye do, skipper," called Charlie, and when he had got his parent on to the deck, he said: "Skipper, this is my father. Dad—Captain Crowley."

Mr. Prohack shook hands with a short, stoutish nervous man with an honest, grim, marine face.

"Everything all right?"

"Yes, sir. Glad you've come at last, sir."

"Good!"

Charlie turned away from the captain to his father. Mr. Prohack saw a man hauling a three-cornered flag up the chief of the three masts which the ship possessed, and another man hauling a large oblong flag up a pole at the stern.

"What is the significance of this flag-raising?" asked Mr. Prohack.

"The significance is that the owner has come aboard," Charlie replied, not wholly without self-consciousness. "Come on. Have a look at her. Come on, skipper. Do the honours. She used to be a Mediterranean trader. The former owner turned her into a yacht. He says she cost him a hundred thousand by the time she was finished. I can believe it."

Mr. Prohack also believed it, easily; he believed it more and more easily as he was trotted from deck to deck and from bedroom to bedroom, and sitting-room to sitting-room, and library to smoking-room, and music-room to lounge, and especially from bathroom to bathroom. In no land habitation had Mr. Prohack seen so many, or such marmoreal, or such luxurious bathrooms. What particularly astonished Mr. Prohack was the exceeding and minute finish of everything, and what astonished him even more than the finish was the cleanliness of everything.

"Dirty place to be in, sir, Southampton," grinned the skipper. "We do the best we can."

They reached the dining-room, an apartment in glossy bird's-eye maple set in the midst of the virgin-white promenade deck.

"By the way, lunch, please," said Charlie.

"Yes, sir," responded eagerly the elder of two attendants in jackets striped blue and white.

"Have a wash, guv'nor? Thanks, skipper, that'll do for the present."

Mr. Prohack washed in amplitudinous marble, and wiped his paternal face upon diaper into which was woven the name "Northwind." He then, with his son, ate an enormous and intricate lunch and drank champagne out of crystal engraved with the name "Northwind," served to him by a ceremonious person in white gloves. Charlie was somewhat taciturn, but over the coffee he seemed to brighten up.

"Well, what do you think of the old hulk?"

"She must need an awful lot of men," said Mr. Prohack.

"Pretty fair. The wages bill is seven hundred a month."

"She's enormous," continued Mr. Prohack lamely.

"Oh, no! Seven hundred tons Thames measurement. You see those funnels over there," and Charlie pointed through the port windows to a row of four funnels rising over great sheds. "That's the *Mauretania.* She's a hundred times as big as this thing. She could almost sling this affair in her davits."

"Indeed! Still, I maintain that this antique wreck is enormous," Mr. Prohack insisted.

They walked out on deck.

"Hello! Here's the chit. You can always count on *her!*" said Charles.

The launch was again approaching the yacht, and a tiny figure with a despatch case on her lap sat smiling in the stern-sheets.

"She's come down by train," Charles explained.

Miss Winstock in her feminineness made a delicious spectacle on the spotless deck. She nearly laughed with delight as she acknowledged Mr. Prohack's grave salute and shook hands with him, but when Charlie said: "Anything urgent?" she grew grave and tense, becoming the faithful, urgent, confidential employé in an instant.

"Only this," she said, opening the despatch case and producing a telegram.

"Confound it!" remarked Charles, having read the telegram. "Here, you, Snow. Please see that Miss Winstock has something to eat at once. That'll do, Miss Winstock."

"Yes, Mr. Prohack," she said dutifully.

"And his mother thought he would be marrying her!" Mr. Prohack senior reflected. "He'll no more marry her than he'll marry Machin. Goodness knows whom he will marry. It might be a princess."

"You remember that paper concern—newsprint stuff—I've mentioned to you once or twice," said Charlie to his father, dropping into a basket-chair. "Sit down, will you, dad? I've had no luck with it yet." He flourished the telegram. "Here the new manager I appointed has gone and got rheumatic fever up in Aberdeen. No good for six months at least, if ever. It's a great thing if I could only really get it going. But no! The luck's wrong. And yet a sound fellow with brains could put that affair into such shape in a year that I could sell it at a profit of four hundred per cent to the Southern Combine. However—"

Soon afterwards he went below to talk to the chit, and the skipper took charge of Mr. Prohack and displayed to him the engine-room, the officers' quarters, the forecastle, the galley, and all manner of arcana that Charlie had grandiosely neglected.

"It's a world!" said Mr. Prohack, but the skipper did not quite comprehend the remark.

"Well," said Charlie, returning. "We'll have some tea and then we must be off again. I have to be in town to-night. Have you seen everything? What's the verdict? Some ship, eh?"

"Some ship," agreed Mr. Prohack. "But the most shockingly uneconomic thing I've ever met with in all my life. How often do you use the yacht?"

"Well, I haven't been able to use her yet. She's been lying here waiting for me for nearly a month. I hope to get a few days off soon."

"I understand there's a crew of thirty odd, all able-bodied and knowing their job, I suppose. And all waiting for a month to give you and me a lunch and a tea. Seven hundred pounds in wages alone for lunch and a tea for two, without counting the food and the washing!"

"And why not, dad?" Charlie retorted calmly. "I've got to spend a bit of money uneconomically, and there's nothing like a yacht for doing it. I've no use for racing, and moreover it's too difficult not to mix with rascals if you go in for racing, and I don't care for rascals. Also it's a mug's game, and I don't want to be a mug. As for young women, no! They only interest me at present as dancing partners, and they cost me nothing. A good yacht's the sole possible thing for my case, and a yacht brings you into contact with clean and decent people, not bookmakers. I bought this boat for thirty-three thousand, and she's a marvellous bargain, and that's something."

"But why spend money uneconomically at all?"

"Because I said and swore I would. Didn't I come back from the war and try all I knew to obtain the inestimable privilege of earning my living by doing something useful? Did I succeed in obtaining the privilege? Why, nobody would look at me! And there were tens of thousands like me. Well, I said I'd take it out of this noble country of mine, and I am doing; and I shall keep on doing until I'm tired. These thirty men or so here might be at some useful productive work, fishing or merchant-marining. They're otherwise engaged. They're spending a pleasant wasteful month over our lunch and tea. That's what I enjoy. It makes me smile to myself when I wake up in the middle of the night. . . . I'm showing my beloved country who's won the Peace."

"It's a scheme," murmured Mr. Prohack, rendered thoughtful as much by the quiet and intense manner, as by the matter, of his son's oration. "Boyish, of course, but not without charm."

"We were most of us boys," said Charlie.

Mr. Prohack marshalled, in his head, the perfectly plain, simple reasoning necessary to crush Charlie to powder, and, before crushing him, to expose to him the crudity of his conceptions of organised social existence. But he said nothing, having hit on another procedure for carrying out his parental duty to Charles. Shortly afterwards they departed from the yacht in the launch. Long ere they reached the waiting motor-car the bunting had been hauled down.

In the car Mr. Prohack said:

"Tell me something more about that paper-making business. It sounds interesting."

III

When Mr. Prohack reached his daughter's house again late in the night, it was his wife who opened the door to him.

"Good heavens, Arthur! Where have you been? Poor Sissie is in such a state—I was obliged to come over and stay with her. She needs the greatest care."

"We had a breakdown," said Mr. Prohack, rather guiltily.

"Who's we? Where? What breakdown? You went off without saying a word to any one. I really can't imagine what you were thinking about. You're just like a child sometimes."

"I went down to Southampton with Charlie," the culprit explained, giving a brief and imperfect history of the day, and adding that on the way home he had made a détour with Charles to look at a paper-manufactory.

"And you couldn't have telephoned!"

"Never thought of it!"

"I'll run and tap at Sissie's door and tell her. Ozzie's with her. You'd better go straight to bed."

"I'm hungry."

Eve made a deprecating and expostulatory noise with her tongue against her upper teeth.

"I'll bring you something to eat. At least I'll try to find something," said she.

"And are you sleeping here, too? Where?" Mr. Prohack demanded when Eve crept into Charlie's old bedroom with a tray in her hands.

"I had to stay. I couldn't leave the girl. I'm sleeping in her old room."

"The worst of these kids' rooms," said Mr. Prohack, with an affectation of calm, "is that there are no easy chairs in them. It never struck me before. Look here, you sit on the bed and put the tray down *there,* and I'll occupy this so-called chair. Now, I don't want any sermons. And what is more, I can't eat unless you do. But I tell you I'm very hungry. So would you be, if you'd had my day."

"You won't sleep if you eat much."

"I don't care if I don't. Is this whiskey? What—bread and cheese? The simple life! I'm not used to it. . . . Where are you off to?"

"There came a letter for you. I brought it along. It's in the other bedroom."

"Open it for me, my good child," said Mr. Prohack, his mouth full and his hands occupied, when she returned. She did so.

"It seems to me that you'd better read this yourself," she said, naughtily.

The letter was from Lady Massulam, signed only with her initials, announcing with a queer brevity that she had suddenly decided to go back at once to her native country to live.

"How strange!" exclaimed Mr. Prohack, trying to be airy. "Listen! What do you make of it. You're a woman, aren't you?"

"I make of it," said Eve, "that she's running away from you. She's afraid of herself, that's what she is! Didn't I always tell you? Oh! Arthur. How simple you are! But fancy! At her age! Oh, my poor boy! Shall you get over it?" Eve bent forward and kissed the poor boy, who was cursing himself for not succeeding in not being self-conscious.

"Rot!" he exploded at last. "I said you were a woman, and by all the gods you are! Give me some more food."

He was aware of a very peculiar and unprecedented thrill. He hated to credit Eve's absurd insinuation, but . . . ! And Eve looked at him superiorly, triumphant, sure of him, sure of her everlasting power over him! Yet she was not romantic, and her plump person did not in the least symbolise romance.

"I've a piece of news for you," he said, after a pause. "After to-night I've done with women and idleness. I'm going into business. I've bought half of that paper-making concern from your singular son, and I'm going to put it on its legs. I know nothing about paper-making, and I can only hope that the London office is not as dirty and untidy as the works. I'd no idea what works were. The whole thing will be a dreadful worry, and I shall probably make a horrid mess of it, but Charlie seems to think I shan't."

"But why—what's come over you, Arthur? Surely we've got

enough money. What *has* come over you? I never could make you out and I never shall."

"Nothing! Nothing!" said he. "Only I've got a sort of idea that some one ought to be economic and productive. It may kill me, but I'll die producing, anyhow."

He waited for her to begin upbraiding him for capricious folly and expatiating upon the fragility of his health. But you never know where you are with an Eve. Eves have the most disconcerting gleams of insight. She said:

"I'm rather glad. I was getting anxious about you."